The Biggest Game of Chance

Steve Trounday

PUBLISHED BY:
Duckingham Press

The Biggest Game of Chance
Copyright © 2018 Steve Trounday

Print ISBN: 978-0-578-41726-4

Formatted for print by StevieDeInk. StevieDeInk.com
Edited by Marian Kelly. RavensGateEditing.com

Cover design by StevieDeInk.
Photos used to make the cover obtained from fotolia.com.

To Gail and Roger, my mom and dad.

ONE

THE HOODED MAN moved to the back of the room. Bright florescent lights illuminated the stark white walls. A key fell to the floor before being retrieved and inserted into the lock of the metal mesh door. Tumblers clicked as the key turned. The opened cabinet exposed shelves lined with brown metal boxes. The man pulled one from the cabinet and placed it on a table in the center of the room. A half-turn of a second key revealed the box's contents—money. The currency was a jumble of bills of every denomination.

The man reached inside the box searching for hundred-dollar bills, took two, then locked the box and returned it to the cabinet. He repeated this process with each box in the cabinet. After harvesting from the last one, the thief locked the cabinet and hurried to the door. He glanced through the small window in its center. All clear. He exited the room. Near the ceiling, the tiny red light on the bottom of the surveillance camera blinked on and off.

THE CASINO WAS crowded for a Thursday afternoon in late October, and Brian Shepard was forced to wait for a group of tourists to pass. The ringing of the slot machines, the cheers of the winners, and the moans of the losers were so loud, it was difficult to hear the craps dealers as they called out the rolls of the dice.

"Seven out, line away," a stickman said with a nasal twang. A throng of senior citizens leaned over the craps table railing, placing bets on the green felt layout.

Brian loved a busy casino. He enjoyed the gamblers' laughter and shrieks of joy over a jackpot or winning hand. The determination of the patrons and sense of anticipation were electric. He was pleased to see the casino jam-packed with people having a good time. In addition, Brian was delighted with himself. In his early thirties, he was the Director of Marketing at the Charleston Casino Resort—the largest and most prestigious casino property in Lake Tahoe, Nevada.

Brian's recent promotion, after several years as the advertising manager, was the result of a lot of hard work. He had a new office with a view of the lake, a salary that he considered comfortable, and the perks of working for a successful hotel and casino company. Yes, Brian's career was on the upswing, and he couldn't help smiling while contemplating the bustling aisles of the gaming floor.

Meandering through the casino of the opulent resort, Brian spotted Jack Mancini sitting at an empty blackjack table. Jack was drinking coffee and reading a document clipped to a file folder. Deep in thought, he didn't notice Brian draw near. "Care for some company?" Brian asked.

Startled, Jack looked up and smiled. "Sure, have a seat."

Brian pulled out a stool and sat down. "What's the good news?"

"This report." Jack handed him the file showing the most recent shift results. "For once, we beat the lucky bastard."

Brian scanned the page. "Who?"

Jack's face showed satisfaction. "Yamamoto. The guy lost fifty grand last night. It's about time our luck changed."

The corners of Brian's mouth turned up. "But I love sending out winners. It's great for promotion."

"You marketing people are all the same. You exploit the misfortune of others, and me in particular."

Brian laughed. "One person's loss is another's gain."

"Maybe, but I'm tired of being the Santa Claus of the casino business."

Brian chuckled.

Jack was the casino manager at the resort. He was a tall, muscular man, and his size and intellect commanded respect. He received less deference from Brian, though. Theirs was a more competitive relationship. They'd been friends since childhood and had spent most of their lives trying to one-up each other. In high school and college, the contest was to hit the most homeruns or get the more attractive girl. In the last couple of years, it was over their careers, so as expected, Brian had been bragging nonstop about his recent promotion.

"Enough talk of business," Jack said. "I almost forgot. Hailey has a friend she wants you to meet." Their competition over women had ended when Jack married a pretty co-ed. Ever since, she'd been determined to end Brian's bachelor lifestyle.

Brian groaned. He hated blind dates. The prospect of an awkward evening of meaningless small talk with another of Hailey's girlfriends sent shivers down his spine. He preferred eternal bachelorhood to dating Hailey's idea of the perfect woman. "I'm busy," he said.

"Okay, smart ass," Jack said. "Be that way, but this time you're missing out on a great girl."

"Sure, four-foot-ten and two hundred pounds of personality. What prison does she work at?"

Jack brushed a hand through his dark-brown hair. "This one's hot."

"You know I'm the last person to need help attracting a date. I went out with four different women last week. Managed to bed two of them."

"Listen, Brian, Hailey's made it her personal crusade to marry you off."

"I'm having too much fun for that."

"That's Hailey's point. She figures she'd save the virtue of a few dozen women if she took you off the market."

"How noble of her. Find her a new cause. Tell her to fight hunger or save the whales."

"Don't blame me—I'm on your side. You know that."

"Oh yeah? Then get your wife off my back."

"Hey, I'll try." Jack grinned, showing a mouthful of teeth

Brian glared at his friend. They'd had this conversation before. "I better be going. Our budget presentation to Montgomery is this afternoon."

"What budget?" Jack said sarcastically. "If this casino doesn't start winning some serious money, there won't be anything to spend."

"Just my luck." Brian stood and walked away from the blackjack table, setting out across the casino.

Approaching the elevators, he heard Jack shout out, "Her name's Robbie Taylor. She's coming over Saturday night."

Brian shook his head. Jack was Hailey's eager accomplice.

THE ELEVATOR STOPPED on the third floor, and Brian stepped out. The executive offices of the Charleston Resort were lavish with thick Berber carpeting leading to deep-grained paneling. The walls were decorated with paintings of Emerald Bay and other famous Tahoe landmarks.

Brian's office was past a reception desk and down a long

hallway. Entering the outer office, he found his secretary on the telephone. He wasn't surprised. Beatrice Carter spent half her time conversing with the other resort employees. She knew everything happening at the Charleston—who was sleeping with whom, who was about to be fired, and who was getting a promotion. When Brian needed to find out the real facts, he asked Beatrice.

Brian didn't condone her gossiping but made a point of treading with care. Beatrice spread as much as she collected. One harsh word to her would set tongues wagging all over the resort. For the most part, he ignored her passion for tidbits, as she could type with the fastest fingers he'd ever seen, knew where all the files were kept, and countered his own quirky eccentricities with humor.

Beatrice paused long enough to hand him his messages, then continued typing on her computer as she spoke into the phone. "I don't like her either," she said. "Something about her bothers me."

Brian laughed to himself as he took a seat behind his large oak desk. He had a lot of work to do before his budget meeting with Tom Montgomery, the general manager of the Charleston. Brian disliked preparing budgets. He was a creative person, great at producing advertising copy and flashy commercials. He wasn't fond of numbers, and the budget presentation was all about them. Begging for money to fund his latest idea was no fun at all.

Brian knew he needed to be well prepared for his meeting with Montgomery. The general manager listened to the accountants, who thought most advertising was a waste of money. He picked up the phone and dialed 3669. "It's Brian," he said when Alice McKay, his marketing manager, answered. "You ready?" A talented woman in her fifties, Alice was always upbeat and had a salty disposition Brian found endearing.

"We'll impress the hell out of him," she said. "Everything's in place, and I think our presentation's fantastic."

"It better be. Jack Mancini says money's going to be tight."

"I hear that every year."

"This time it's different. The table games haven't been generating the revenue we expect. It's putting a squeeze on the casino's cash flow. I believe it's pretty serious."

Alice raised her voice. "Why aren't we making money? The casino's almost always packed."

"That's the big question and I don't have an answer."

"Well, I'm not worrying about it. No one can say no to this presentation, cash crunch or not."

"I'm holding you to that. I'll see you at one o'clock."

BRIAN COULD FEEL a slight tremor in his hands. He was nervous. This was his first budget presentation as Director of Marketing. He'd bluffed his way through the interview process, convincing the Charleston Resort's general manager he could do the job despite his background in just advertising. He figured he'd learn the intricacies of casino marketing soon enough…once he was past this first budget process.

Brian and Alice sat in the waiting room outside Montgomery's office. The secretary asked if they wanted a cup of coffee. Alice said yes, she'd like it black, but Brian declined—he was anxious enough without the caffeine.

After what seemed an eternity, the secretary ushered them into Montgomery's office. The room was massive, with floor-to-ceiling windows and a panoramic view of Lake Tahoe. The back walls were covered with pictures. Brian noticed one of Montgomery and the current governor of California, another with him standing on Capitol Hill next to Senator Cortez Masto, and one where he was grinning beside a former Republican U.S. president. They were the mementos of an influential man and his powerful acquaintances.

Montgomery sat behind an enormous cherry wood desk. He

was an imposing figure, standing six-foot-two, in a well-tailored Brooks Brothers suit. His hair was full and combed straight back. The gold ring on his left pinkie was huge and encrusted in diamonds, overwhelming the smaller wedding band on the next finger. The ring was a statement. Tom Montgomery had married the daughter of the chairman of the board of the Wyman Corporation, the Las Vegas-based owner of the Charleston Casino Resort. He was always trying to prove to himself and others that his position of power was due to his skill and leadership—not his wife's father.

Already seated in front of Montgomery's desk was Elliot Thomas, the Director of Surveillance and Security. Brian wasn't sure why he was there. It was his job to secure the casino's assets. His large staff monitored hundreds of surveillance cameras throughout the resort day and night, trying to identify cheaters and crooks. It wasn't uncommon for the Surveillance Department to catch someone putting counterfeit money in a slot machine or trying to slip an extra ace into a deck of cards. His department's job was to apprehend those people. Nothing Elliot Thomas did was related to advertising or promotions, let alone budgets, and Brian gave him a curious look.

"Come in, Brian, Alice," Montgomery said. He motioned them to two chairs in front of his desk. "Elliot and I were discussing the low table games' hold in the pit."

"Tell me about this low hold percentage," Alice said. She was never one to mince words. "Why's it causing us budget problems?"

Elliot Thomas said, "For the last nine months or so, the table games have held fourteen percent of the drop. We expect to be keeping seventeen."

She gazed at him with narrowed eyes. "Explain this to me. What's the drop? I don't, as a habit, pay much attention to the mechanics of the casino."

"I can tell you work in marketing," Thomas said with a superior inflection. "The drop—"

Brian interrupted, annoyed by Thomas's comment, saying, "The drop's the money going into the metal boxes when our customers buy chips at a gaming table."

"Correct," Montgomery said, "and statistically, we can expect to hold seventeen percent of the drop. Some days we win thirty percent and others five, but over time, it should average seventeen percent."

"Is someone cheating?" Alice asked.

Montgomery crossed his arms. "That's what I believe."

"I don't know how," Thomas said. "I have hundreds of cameras monitoring every game in the casino, and we haven't spotted anything wrong. The Nevada Gaming Control Board's reviewed our surveillance videos and couldn't detect anything inappropriate."

"Then why the low hold?" Brian asked.

"We need a change of management in the casino department. Jack Mancini's too lax with the dealers when it comes to enforcing the procedures."

That's crazy, Brian thought. *Thomas is just looking for a fall guy.*

"Brian," Montgomery said, "I know you and Alice were planning to give your budget presentation this afternoon, but this meeting with Elliot's put me in a nasty state of mind. It would be wise if we moved you to next week. Is that a problem?"

Brian stared at the general manager. "No, sir," he said, lying. Alice had a half-dozen staff members and reps from the advertising agency waiting in the adjoining conference room, ready to dazzle him with their marketing brilliance.

Montgomery said, "You shouldn't ask me for money in my current mood. I promise you my full attention next week."

Brian nodded and glanced at Alice. He knew she wasn't happy, she didn't like delays.

Alice leaned over and said to him in a gruff whisper, "He's an ass."

BEATRICE AMBLED INTO Brian's office. "The comedian in the showroom refuses to go on tonight," she said. "Says he has a headache."

Brian contemplated her words with uneven eyebrows. *Skip Sullivan doesn't know what a real headache is*, he thought, rubbing his temples. "Tell him his contract doesn't cover that."

"You know there's nothing wrong with him. Skip's demanding a suite with a lake view. The one he has now faces the mountains."

"Funny, a year ago, he'd work for free cocktails. It's crazy what a hit television series will do for a man's ego."

"What do you want me to do?"

"Call Dave Weston at the hotel desk. See if he can spare a suite that looks toward the lake for our prima donna. Find out if the Ponderosa Suite's available."

"You're easy." Beatrice smiled and returned to her desk in the outer office.

Brian examined the papers in front of him and pushed them aside. The pile of manila envelopes in his inbox didn't interest him much either. He knew what was in them—daily financial recaps. He'd expected to have a decent budget next year and questioned whether he should be concerned about the low hold of the table games. He was requesting a significant increase to cover expanded advertising in the Los Angeles area. Then, too, there were the ever-spiraling costs of bringing in the big name celebrities to the showroom. He was sure Montgomery agreed that stars like Skip Sullivan drew in the high-limit gamblers and attracted the middle-aged men and women who played the slot machines.

Maybe he was worried over nothing. It'd been a long day.

It was time to wind down. He picked up the phone and dialed Jack Mancini's office.

"One moment, Brian," his friend's secretary said. "I'll see if he's available. It's been a zoo around here today."

Brian listened to the muzak while waiting, pondering the low hold percentage again. He wondered what Jack was doing about it.

"What's up?" Jack asked with obvious tension in his voice.

Brian said, "I was hoping you could sneak away, lift some weights, and see who can swim the most laps."

"Sorry, pal. I was just summoned by Montgomery. A lecture, no doubt. Why don't you stop by the house tonight, and we can enjoy a few beers and shoot pool? I think Hailey's cooking linguini in clam sauce."

"Sounds good. I'll see you later." Brian hung up and stared out the window as the last rays of sunlight glimmered on the lake. He'd be doing his workout alone but was better off than Jack. He knew Mancini would be enduring a contentious conversation with a very agitated general manager.

BRIAN TIED HIS shoes and sprang out of the locker room. The indoor spa at the Charleston Resort was one of the finest in the country. The complex was built to resemble a secluded mountain retreat. Its Olympic-size pool was shaped like an alpine lake, with a large waterfall cascading from a rock formation into the deep end. The facility sold spa memberships to many of the wealthy Lake Tahoe residents, but it was used for the most part by hotel guests and to impress travel agents touring the property.

Membership in the spa was one of the perks Brian enjoyed as an executive of the Wyman Corporation. It was one of his favorite benefits. He took pleasure in an invigorating workout after a stressful day at the office. Those nerve-racking days seemed to be occurring more often.

Brian warmed up on a stair climber. After fifteen minutes, he grew bored and wandered over to the juice bar for a quick sports drink. He surveyed the area and sipped his beverage. An overweight couple was wallowing in a whirlpool, drinking margaritas and splashing water at each other. The weight room to his right was almost empty, except for a dark-haired body-builder flexing his muscles in a mirror. At the far end of the spa, a middle-aged man was perspiring buckets while pedaling a stationary bike.

As Brian made his way over to the free weights, he spotted a petite brunette in a pink leotard stretching near the leg press. She was a beauty. Her long dark hair was pulled up, revealing a soft face with high cheekbones and hazel eyes. She looked at him and smiled. He'd never seen her before. She must be a guest in the hotel, he speculated as he said *"Hi there"* in the suave way he did with every pretty woman. She smiled again but didn't speak, concentrating on her exercises.

Brian began his weight-lifting regimen and watched the woman as she glided with grace along the floor mat. He was attractive, knew it, and expected to impress her with his well-toned body and chiseled features, but she continued to work out as if she were the only person in the room. She had zero personality, he decided, trying to explain why she wasn't flirting with him.

About an hour into his workout, Brian noticed the woman was gone. He felt a tinge of regret that he hadn't engaged her in a conversation, but shrugged and returned to the bench press. A half-hour later, hot and sweaty, he placed the barbells back on the rack and trudged toward the locker room. He enjoyed a nice steam sauna, took a quick shower, and dressed in the casual clothes he kept in his locker. Passing the mirror, he shook his sandy mop of hair and sauntered into the lobby of the spa. He was planning on a quick visit to Jack and

Hailey's house, followed by drinks with a cute new teller he'd met at the bank.

Moving toward the exit, Brian saw the brunette beauty near the juice bar. What could it hurt to introduce himself? At the counter, he purchased an orange Gatorade and strolled up to her table with a confident gait. "Mind if I join you?" he asked, sure she'd welcome his company.

She stared at him and frowned, her eyes dark. "I'd rather be alone if you don't mind."

His eyes widened. Oh, she had a personality all right, he realized, fumbling an apology and fleeing for the door. A lousy one. Brian wasn't used to being rebuffed. He had a reputation as a player and never had to work too hard to attract the ladies. He made excuses to himself—perhaps she liked older men, or ones with tattoos, or thick dark hair. Regardless, it was one of those rare days when he hadn't made a good impression on an alluring woman.

BRIAN STEERED HIS truck into the driveway of the Mancinis' home. Jack and Hailey lived high atop Cave Rock in an exclusive area overlooking the lake. Walking up to the house, Brian reviewed the day's events and concluded it hadn't been a good one at all. Nothing had gone right from beginning to end.

He wasn't able to get the budget problems out of his mind. Maybe he could find out more about the low table game hold from Sarah Calder, the cashier and credit manager at the Charleston. For all his bluffing during the meeting with Montgomery and Thomas, he didn't know much more than Alice about the actual inner workings of the casino. Sarah had thirty years of experience and had once offered to give him a tour of her operation. He made a mental note to call her in the morning.

Brian's mind flashed back to the woman at the spa, and he wondered why she'd upset him so. Sure, he wasn't accustomed to being turned down, but it wasn't the first time he'd been spurned by a female and he guessed it wouldn't be the last. Yes, it hadn't been a great day at all. He needed a beer. Brian rang the doorbell and heard Joker's crazed barking. When the door opened, the dog bolted toward him, his tail wagging with gusto.

"That dog loves you more than he does us," Hailey said.

Brian tried to calm the excited Golden Retriever. "That's my boy, Joker." He scratched him behind the ears. "Have you missed me?"

Hailey ran her fingers through her long blond hair. "I don't know how he could, Brian—you come over so often, you might as well live here."

He grinned, petting the pooch. "And what's wrong with that?"

"Nothing and you know it."

Brian stood.

She pecked him on the cheek. With her short stature, it was quite a reach. "Hold on a minute." The teasing tone in her voice was gone. "I need to speak with you about Jack." Her expression was solemn. The sparkle in her eyes had vanished, and tiny wrinkles stretched across her forehead.

"What's wrong?"

"I don't know. Jack hasn't been himself. He's so quiet, and that's not like him. He comes home from work, grabs a beer, and watches TV. He doesn't say a word to me, and I'm concerned."

Brian waved a hand. "It's nothing, I'm certain. Don't worry."

"He's worse than ever tonight. He yelled at me when I asked him what was wrong. He told me to leave him alone. What kind of talk's that?"

Brian cocked his head to the side. "Where is he?"

"Downstairs, shooting pool and pounding down one beer after another."

"I'll see what I can find out."

"Please tell him I can't live with this stress." She sniffled. "He won't listen to me."

Brian put an arm around her and gave her a hug. She wiped a tear from her eye.

Bounding down the stairs, he entered the rec room as Jack was hitting the cue ball. The eight ball ricocheted into a corner pocket. "Nice shot," Brian said.

Jack turned around. "Thanks. Maybe I should take up pool for a living. It can't be much worse than what I'm doing now."

"Mind if I cop a beer?"

Jack pointed to the bar.

Brian slipped behind the counter and pulled a Coors Light from the small refrigerator. "Where's the linguini dinner?"

"Not sure—why don't you ask Hailey?" Jack took a deep pull on his beer.

"Bad day, huh?"

Jack bunched up his lips. "The worst."

"Would you like to talk about it?"

"It's the low hold, Brian. Montgomery's coming down on me hard. He just about called me a thief."

"Aren't you exaggerating a little bit? Even he wouldn't go that far."

"The low hold percentage is costing the company a fortune. Millions of dollars. It's my department, and Montgomery says I'm responsible." He studied his beer label and took another drink. "I guess he's right."

Brian stared at Jack, unsure what to say to his friend, and offered him a glib response. "Your luck will change. The cards will turn."

"Ha, ha. By the time they do, I'll be long gone. So will this house, the cars, Hailey..." He stopped. His gaze met Brian's.

"Hey, you stupid son of a bitch, Hailey loves you. That I know for certain. No matter what happens, I'm confident she's the one thing you can always count on."

Jack exhaled a rush of air and closed his eyes.

Brian sat on a bar-stool. "I have my own selfish interests in mind, you know. If you two ever split up, I'd starve to death. *You* can't cook. So remember, she's there for you. She wants to help."

"Yeah, I haven't been pleasant to live with."

"You've been an asshole."

Jack bowed his head. "A big one."

"So, what are you doing about the low hold? Do you think it's a streak of bad luck, or is something wrong?"

Jack placed his beer on a nearby table. "I don't know, but I can guarantee if something funny's going on, I'll get to the bottom of it." He paused, grimacing. "If I'm not fired first."

They eyed each other for a moment.

Then Jack smiled and said, "Let's see if Hailey has the linguini ready."

Brian rubbed his stomach. "Sounds delicious—I'm hungry."

"You always are."

The two men barreled up the stairs, racing to the top. Hailey was pleased to see her husband in a happier frame of mind and waltzed to the kitchen to finish preparing dinner. When the linguini was cooked to perfection, the three of them sat in the dining room and discussed the troubles at the Charleston as they ate. Brian devoured three helpings while assuring Jack that everything would turn out fine. After dinner, the three of them walked to Brian's truck, and Hailey pulled him aside. She said in a whisper, "Thank you."

Brian hugged her.

Hailey had a wide grin on her face. "Don't forget to come Saturday night about seven. We're having some friends over for drinks and a barbecue."

Brian flashed her an accusing look. "What friends?"

"Michael and Cathy Albright and Cory and Susan."

"Can I bring a date?" He opened the truck door.

Hailey hesitated. Jack laughed.

She said, "Well, sure, if you want to, but I've also invited someone I know you'll like."

Brian glowered at her, his lips pressed tight. "Robbie Taylor?"

"Yes, Robbie Taylor." Hailey put her hands on her hips. "She's a great girl. Pretty, just your type. I know you'll hit it off. I've been hoping to get you two together ever since she moved back to Lake Tahoe."

"I've told you before, Hailey—I hate blind dates. I don't need them. I have a date with a knockout blonde in twenty minutes. You know full well that plenty of women are interested in me. If I say so myself, my sex life's pretty damn good."

"It's not a blind date, and it's different this time."

"Some of the women you've tried to hook me up with would've made good prison wardens. It's clear you don't know the kind of girl I prefer."

"Trust me on this one. Think of it as a few friends gathering for dinner and good conversation, and we'll see what happens. Robbie has no expectations."

Brian arched an eyebrow and hopped into his truck. "I'll consider it, but I bet I'll have other plans."

Hailey shook her head.

He started the engine and drove away.

THE HOODED MAN took the last hundred-dollar bill from the metal box and placed it with the others in a thin, soft leather bag. His hands trembled as he fumbled with the key and locked the box.

He glanced at the video camera in the corner of the room. The red light near its bottom blinked on and off. His breathing was heavy. The hood concealing his face made the heat almost unbearable. He knew, though, that he needed to take the precaution.

He returned the box to the cabinet and shut the metal mesh door. The late-night ritual was complete. He tucked the leather bag under his blazer and dashed out of the room, over to the open elevator. He darted into the empty car and the doors closed behind him.

TWO

THE ALARM BLARED, and Brian fought the urge to throw the clock across the room. He wasn't a morning person but was trying to get up earlier each day to eat a healthy breakfast. As the alarm continued to shriek, he wasn't so sure about his mental health. *At least it was Friday,* he thought, slamming the off button.

Brian lived in a rustic cabin on the Nevada side of Lake Tahoe, right on the beach. The place was a typical mountain cottage, with cedar-paneled walls and an open-beamed ceiling.

Buying a lakefront home like this would have cost a fortune—money Brian didn't have—but he rented the place from a widow whose husband had built it decades ago. She'd agreed to lease it to him for a reasonable amount if he'd fix it up. Although not a skilled craftsman, he'd done most of the work himself. He'd remodeled the bathrooms, put in a new kitchen, and was now constructing a redwood deck.

Still groggy, Brian pulled himself out of bed and traipsed over to the bathroom. He lingered in the shower, enjoying the warm spray of the water. Knowing he'd be late for work if he stayed any longer, he forced himself to turn off the water and grab a towel, then turned on the TV and shaved while listening to the morning newscast. He thought of the gorgeous woman at the Charleston Spa. "Her loss," he said to his image in the mirror. He posed and flexed his muscles.

Brian's breakfast was bland, but he'd vowed to try a healthier lifestyle. He was certain he couldn't keep up the pace he'd enjoyed in his twenties forever. He knew all the junk food, late nights, and alcohol would catch up with him sooner or later. *He was going to have at least one nutritious meal a day,* he thought as he choked down the dry wheat toast. Even if it killed him. He'd work on the late nights and alcohol later.

Watching the morning news and eating his breakfast, Brian contemplated his day. He had a busy schedule of meetings but hoped he could spare some time to visit with the cashier and credit manager. He wanted to see for himself how the huge sums of money generated at the Charleston Resort were handled.

When he finished getting ready for work—a process that seemed to take longer each day—Brian jumped into his truck and drove toward the Charleston. *Traffic was getting worse and worse,* he thought as his truck inched along with a pack of slow-moving cars. As he drove, he remembered Jack's words from the previous evening: *I don't know what the problem is, but I can guarantee you if something funny's going on, I'll get to the bottom of it.*

What could be the cause of the shortage? he wondered. How could anyone steal from the Charleston without being caught? There were hundreds of surveillance cameras in every corner and closet of the property. Security personnel were everywhere.

No, Brian decided, the casino had to be experiencing a period of bad luck.

AS EXPECTED, BEATRICE was on the telephone when Brian arrived at his office. "She must have some rich boyfriend," she said into the mouthpiece. "The rock has to be at least three carats. You're kidding! Well, I think she's hiding him because he's a married man."

Brian smiled and said good morning, but Beatrice was too intent on her conversation to respond. "If he's so wealthy," she said, "why's she working? Oh, sure, she's quitting after he asks her to marry him. If I were her, I wouldn't hold my breath."

Brian walked into his office and took a seat at the desk. He turned on the computer and read his email, deleting the majority of them, then rummaged through the inbox on his desk. After routing most of the papers to the garbage can and the rest back to Beatrice for filing and distribution, he picked up the phone and dialed the operator. When she answered, he asked for Sarah Calder.

"Okay, Brian," the operator said in a seductive voice. "I've been meaning to call you. How've you been?"

A frown crept over his face. "Busy."

"We'll have to get together again soon."

"Yes, if I can find the time." It was more than clear that the operator, Sheila, was infatuated with him. It was unfortunate, as the feeling wasn't mutual. She wasn't very bright and couldn't carry on a conversation for more than a minute or two. She was good in bed, but every time he slept with her, he felt a little guilty. He hadn't found a nice way of telling her to go away, so she was relentless in her pursuit. "What've you been up to?" he asked, trying to be engaging but not flirtatious.

"I just rented a new apartment," she said. "It's near Heavenly ski resort. You'll have to come visit."

"I'd like to." He was lying, of course.

"It has a hot tub."

"Great." Brian wondered how long he could keep up the faux enthusiasm.

"I'll connect you to Mrs. Calder's office. Let's have drinks soon."

"I'll call you." He wouldn't.

The phone rang an annoying seven times before it was answered. Brian asked for Sarah. "Hello, Brian," the cashier and credit manager said after a short wait." Her voice was flat.

"Did I catch you at a bad time?" he asked.

"It's budget season, you know."

"I recognize you're busy, but a few months ago, you offered to give me a tour of the main cashier. Do you have any free time this afternoon?"

"Hmm, let me see."

He could hear papers shuffling.

"I have a meeting with Montgomery at three, but I suppose I can spare a few minutes after lunch. How does that sound?"

"Perfect. I need to know how this casino works, and I can think of no better source than you."

Her tone was lighter now. "You flatter me, but I do oversee an impressive operation. I'll see you at one."

"Thanks, Sarah. I'm looking forward to it." Brian hung up the phone. *This should be interesting,* he thought, leaning back in the chair, tapping his fingers on the desk and pondering what the meeting might hold.

The morning breezed by. His marketing staff had rescheduled the budget presentation with Montgomery for the following Wednesday. Most of them seemed grateful for the extra week to prepare, but Alice was still annoyed at the delay. He ate lunch with Tony Connors from the Visitor's Authority. Against his better judgment, he had a double cheeseburger with fries. He thought of his healthy breakfast while ladling mayonnaise on the burger.

A little before one o'clock, Brian left his office for Sarah's. Business was picking up as the tourists from California arrived for a weekend of gambling, shows, and overindulgence. A woman screamed as the cherries lined up on her slot machine. She hugged her husband. "I won, I won!"

He shot her an expectant gaze. "How much?"

"Twenty dollars."

He frowned, unimpressed. "Let me know when you've won enough for me to retire."

Nearing the main cashier, Brian watched the men and women who were behind the metal bars hanging over the counter. As they peered through them, he knew why the place was referred to as *the cage*. He smiled at the security guard in a booth next to the cashier entrance. "I'm meeting with Sarah Calder," he said to the man.

The guard nodded. "Yes, Mr. Shepard, I saw your name on the access log."

Brian squinted. "Access log?"

"No one enters or leaves that door without signing this log." The guard handed it to him.

Brian gave it a quick once-over. "Any exceptions?"

"Never, not even Montgomery. Fill out the line next to your name."

Brian signed the log and returned it to the security guard.

"I'll buzz you in. Mrs. Calder's office is through the second door on the left."

"Thanks, Vince." A buzzer sounded, and Brian turned the knob and opened the thick, heavy door. He stepped into a wide hallway and saw another door at the far end. To his right was an alcove containing a metal cabinet divided into small compartments, each with a metal mesh door and a lock. Each cubical held a purse or carrying bag. Past the alcove was a long counter. On Brian's side, a beefy security guard with a crew cut was counting racks of casino chips while a pale female cashier on the other side placed them on a plastic tray.

"Yamamoto must be winning," the cashier said.

The guard signed his name on a slip of paper. "He is, big

time. This is the third fill in the last half-hour." He covered the chips with a clear plastic lid. "I'll be back in a few minutes."

"I hope not. I want to get paid this week."

The guard bobbed his head in agreement and exited the hallway, diving back into the crowded casino.

"May I help you?" the cashier asked, staring at Brian. She ran her fingers through her gray hair, her preening making it obvious she was attracted to him.

"Yes," he said. "I have an appointment with Sarah Calder."

"Sure. Her office is through that door and on the left." She gestured to her right.

"Thanks. By the way, out of curiosity, why are those purses locked up?" Brian aimed a finger toward the alcove around the corner.

"Those are ours. We're not allowed to bring them into the back corridors or the cashier's cage. We each have our own locker and put our belongings into it before we come to work."

"Makes sense." He tilted his head. "Sarah's office is the first one on the left?"

"Yes. You can't miss it." She fluttered her eyelashes at him.

The door at the end of the hallway buzzed, and Brian opened it, entering yet another passageway with a row of surveillance cameras perched above the entrance. He saw Sarah Calder and veered into her office.

Wearing a colorful patterned dress and blue sweater, Sarah was about sixty years old, with flaming red hair that she wore in an old-fashioned beehive. She looked up from her cluttered desk. "Brian, welcome to my world."

He smiled. "Thanks for taking the time to show me around."

"I thought I'd take you to see the main cage first."

Sarah rose from her chair and led him back into the hallway. She strutted to a door with a small window in it and pressed a button on the wall to its right. A woman's face appeared in the glass. A buzzer sounded, and Sarah opened the door, holding it for Brian.

"This is the heart of our operation," she said. Her pride was evident as she escorted Brian to the front of the cashier's cage. The room was a flurry of activity, with lines of customers waiting for service from the busy cashiers. Money moved back and forth across the counter, checks were written, and chips counted. Sarah crossed her arms. "I assume you're familiar with this part of the cage. This is where we service our players. We redeem chips, issue credit, and take care of their requests."

Brian watched as a stack of green chips was counted by a stoic male cashier and placed in a plastic rack. Sarah walked over to the man and verified the total before a woman on the other side of the counter was paid in currency.

Sarah said, "Each of our cashiers has a bank consisting of fifty thousand dollars in cash and chips. They're accountable for the money, and we expect them to balance at the end of their shift."

Brian looked at her. "Do they have much of a problem doing that?"

"We don't tolerate shortages," she said in an unyielding tone. "We conduct extensive training programs, so most of the cashiers are accurate. Those who aren't, don't stay employed for long."

"I have trouble balancing my checkbook."

"Then don't apply for a job with me." She gave him a wry smile.

Brian grinned.

Sarah pointed to a monitor. "The computers in front of each cashier window are used for casino credit and check cashing. There are over two hundred thousand names on file. Some of our customers have credit lines of a million dollars or more."

"I know we have a lot of players who lose that kind of money, but I still find it astounding. I guess it's because I was raised in a family that was pretty poor."

"Follow me." Sarah was like a general leading the troops, and he trailed after her without hesitation. She marched across the cashier's cage and led Brian through a doorway and into another room. She waved her hands around. "This is the main vault. All the casino cash transactions start here. Think of it as the casino's bank. We have about twenty million in currency, coin, and casino chips stored in this room." Rack after rack of gaming chips and metal tokens were stacked on the shelves along the walls, bags of coin on the floor.

"Do you worry about being robbed?" Brian asked.

Sarah shook her head. "No, look around. See the video cameras? Every move we make's being observed and recorded. Each workstation has a silent alarm switch. We have the security booth outside the cage and many guards roaming the casino floor. Joints this big don't get robbed often because the security's just too tight."

Brian inspected the room. "What work goes on here in the vault?"

"All the money in the casino goes through this place at one time or another—the table fills for the pit, slot jackpot payouts, and any other cash requests."

Brian was a little uncomfortable as he eyed the huge stacks of hundred-dollar bills in the open safe to his left. "Being close to all this cash makes me anxious."

"You become used to it." She was amused and her face showed it.

Brian glanced over at where a cashier and security guard were working and recognized the pale, gray-haired woman he'd spoken with earlier. She was once more counting chips with the security guard.

Sarah followed his gaze. "Lorraine's making pit fills," she said. "As our customers win or buy chips at a blackjack game and then leave it to cash out or play at a different table, we have to replenish the first game's inventory. The vault employees also count and distribute cash register banks for all the restaurants and bars, restock the money in the cashier's cage, and tally the currency as it comes in from the count room."

Brian bounced a forefinger over his lips. "This is impressive. I had no idea."

"Most people don't. We have a great deal of responsibility."

"Jeez, I've never seen so many keys." He motioned to a large glass-encased cabinet on one wall where hundreds, if not thousands, of keys hung on rows of hooks.

"Those are the security keys—the keys to the slot machines, drop boxes, and count rooms. Any important keys are kept in that cabinet. The people authorized to have certain ones are required to sign them in and out each day."

"The Charleston must have a lot of locksmiths."

She chuckled at his sarcasm, showing her dentures. "There quite a few."

The vault cashier was sneaking furtive glances at Brian as she counted her chips. Sarah saw her and said, "Lorraine, pay attention to what you're doing. This vault better balance at the end of the shift." She turned to Brian. "I need you out of here. You're distracting my cashiers. Come on back with me and I'll show you the count rooms."

They left the vault, walked to the rear of the cashier's cage, and returned to the hallway by her office. They navigated through a few more corridors and doorways until reaching an elevator. Sarah picked up a phone next to it. "Hi Pete," she said. "It's Sarah. I'm giving Brian Shepard from Marketing a tour of the place. I want him to see the count rooms." She listened for a second. "Okay, thanks."

The elevator doors glided open.

"Who were you talking with?" Brian asked.

"Surveillance," Sarah said. "The Surveillance Department controls this elevator. No one can get on or off without permission."

"It sounds like big brother."

"With this much money around, you can't be too careful."

They boarded the elevator, and the doors closed behind them. A tiny red light on the surveillance camera near the ceiling blinked at them as they descended one floor. The doors opened onto a hallway with large windows into the rooms on either side.

"To your left's the hard count," Sarah said. They stepped out of the elevator, and she gestured to the room. "Now that our slot machines no longer use coins, it's collecting dust most of the time. I miss the old days, when we counted all the coins using the wrapping machines. It was such a production and fun to watch."

Brian noted the rows of idle equipment. "I'm sorry I missed it. I guess technology changes every business."

"It sure has altered the casino industry. Who would've believed thirty years ago that most slots today would no longer accept coins?"

"I suppose the next innovation will be ATMs in the machines."

"I bet you're right. Look over here. That's the soft count." Sarah pointed to the large glass window across from the coin count room. "The soft count team's counting the currency."

Brian's eyes swept to the window. "Why call it that? Soft count."

"Well, it's the opposite of the hard count. The hard count team used to count the coins and metal tokens from the slot machines. The soft count team counts the paper money—

currency—from the table games and, nowadays, the slot bill accepters."

The room wasn't large, about twenty feet by ten. In the center, two men and four women were standing around a long table, sorting piles of money. At one end, another man was directing his attention to a computer screen. All the soft count team members were wearing white jumpsuits.

"When did they start the counting process?" Brian asked.

Sarah said, "The formal count began at six this morning. The supervisor arrived an hour earlier to get her paperwork ready."

"What are the procedures used for the count? Please walk me through the process."

Sarah seemed somewhat annoyed and peeked at her watch.

His eyes locked on hers. "Please, I'd appreciate it."

She sighed. "Oh, all right. As our customers buy-in with currency on a blackjack or craps game, the bills are put into the metal boxes attached to the tables. There's a small opening in each one that the dealer puts the money through. I'm sure you've seen a dealer drop bills before."

"Yes. I play blackjack on rare occasions."

"At the end of each shift, the boxes are brought down here to the count room where they're locked up in those cabinets." Sarah thrust a hand toward the cabinets against the back wall. Their shelves held row after row of numbered and lettered metal drop boxes. "Every morning, the soft count team comes and counts the currency. Nevada state law requires that at least three people count the money. The Charleston needs seven team members and two shifts to tally the huge volume of money this property generates."

Brian's forehead furrowed. "At least three soft count team members by law? Why's that?"

"For security reasons. Thousands of dollars are put into the drop box at each table, but the actual amount of money in the box is unknown. It's not until the drop boxes are opened here in the count room that the total in each box is determined. To protect the casino and ensure no one steals any of the currency before it's counted, three people are required to be in the room during the count. Each of the count team members observes the others, making certain they don't pilfer the uncounted cash."

"If you had a dishonest soft count team, what would keep them from stealing and sharing their profits after work?"

Sarah extended a finger toward a ceiling camera in the corner of the room. "With the video camera recording every move they make, it'd be impossible to do that without getting caught."

Brian turned his attention to the men and women in the soft count room. He could see they were very focused on their task. "You were telling me about the count procedures..."

"They count each of the three casino shifts separately. They start with graveyard, then day shift, and finish with swing. They open each drop box one at a time, dump the contents on the table, and prove that the box is empty by showing it to the video camera. It's then returned to the cabinet. They lay it on its side so they know it's been processed.

"The count team begins sorting the currency by denomination and places the money in the center of the table. The bills are put in the count machine, and the dollar amount in each box is posted to the computer. After all the pit drop cash is counted for the day, they proceed to the currency from the slot machines. Unlike the table games, the amount of slot currency is known in advance. The bill acceptor counts the money when it's inserted into the machine."

Brian watched as a jumble of bills was sorted into neat piles. "What are those white slips of paper in each box?"

"The pit fill slips. Remember the chips you saw our cashier give the security officer in the vault?"

He nodded. "Yes, in those plastic racks."

"The fill slips account for the money taken from the vault. The audit clerk uses them to determine how much money the table's won…or lost."

"How do they know how much the casino's won?"

"At the beginning of each shift, the pit supervisors count the chips on each table. They do it again at the end of the shift. They take the opening number, add to it the amount of money in the drop box, and subtract the fills and the chips on the table at the close of the shift. This calculation tells them what the table's won—or lost."

"And the amount of the win should be seventeen percent of the drop?"

"It should be. Sometimes we win more and others less, but in the long run we should hold about seventeen."

"How come we've been keeping just fourteen?"

Sarah shrugged. "It's a mystery to me. I hope the percentages average out by the end of the year. Maybe Jack Mancini has some crooked dealers. I don't know how they could steal from the casino, though. Like down here, the surveillance cameras are recording their every single move."

"This is a pretty cool process. Thanks a lot for showing me around."

Sarah led him back to the elevator, once again picking up the telephone on the wall, and speaking with a surveillance person. She hung up the phone, and the doors to the elevator parted. They entered the car, and she pushed the number one button on the panel.

Brian gestured to the "two" button. "What's on the second floor?" he asked.

"The Surveillance Department," Sarah said.

"Can I see it?"

"You'll have to ask Elliot Thomas. I'm not allowed up

there. They don't want anyone who works in the cashier's cage to view their monitors. They don't want us to know what they can see." Her tone was somewhat irritated. "They say it's for security reasons."

"I guess they have a point."

"You don't work in a department handling cash, so you might be able to arrange a visit. But Elliot doesn't like to give outsiders access. Don't be surprised if he says no."

"I'll call him and ask. I'd love to have a tour. Surveillance seems such an integral component of the casino."

"I suppose it is, but for me, they're a pain in the butt."

Brian rubbed his chin. "You've piqued my curiosity."

The elevator doors opened, and they set off down the hallway toward Sarah's office. "Have I answered all your questions?" she asked.

"Yes," Brian said. "It's been an education. So much is going on behind the scenes."

Sarah smiled and accompanied Brian through the maze of doors and passageways and onto the casino floor.

THREE

BACK AT HIS office, Brian found a stack of phone messages sitting on his desk. He returned most of the calls and spent the rest of the afternoon signing entertainment contracts and editing advertising copy. Alice stopped by to tell him the status of the slot tournament they were conducting that evening. It was full of high-limit gamblers, and she expected a busy weekend.

While working through the afternoon, Brian kept thinking about his trip to the cashier's cage, vault, and count rooms. The security was tight. It would be impossible for anyone to steal a significant amount of money without being caught. There had to be another explanation for the low hold percentage. He shook his head.

BEATRICE APPEARED IN Brian's doorway wearing a large plum-colored coat that didn't flatter her already plump figure. "I'm going now," she said. "I'll see you on Monday."

"Any exciting plans for the weekend?" Brian asked. He was making small talk but, in truth, wasn't much interested in what his secretary did in her personal life.

"Nothing special—I'm getting together with the girls from the Finance Department for a Tupperware party."

He rolled his eyes toward the ceiling. "It sounds like a rollicking time."

She had a wide grin on her face, making her cheeks puffy. "How else am I to catch up on the latest dirt?"

"What's the gossip of the day?"

Beatrice was eager to have someone to enlighten. In a whisper, she said, "Well, my friends tell me there's going to be some changes in the Table Games Department."

Brian gave her an inquiring expression. "What kind of changes?"

"I don't know yet. I'll find out at the Tupperware party."

"You do that."

"Good night." She turned and toddled out of the office.

Changes in the Table Games Department. Brian wondered how accurate Beatrice's information was. He thought for a moment—she'd never been wrong before.

Brian cleared his desk and exited the office. Most of the workspaces in the executive suites were vacant. The managers were on the casino floor, preparing for a busy weekend, and his own staff was readying for the slot tournament.

Brian hoofed it to the end of the hall and into the last outer office. He moved past the secretary's desk and could see a light in the back room. He peered through the doorway and saw Jack Mancini staring out of his huge window at the lake.

"Knock, knock," Brian said.

Jack swiveled his chair around and looked at him. His face was tense, and there were dark circles under his eyes.

Brian said in his best chipper voice, "I wanted to see if I could interest you in a beer."

"Whiskey's more like it," Jack said, "but sure." He led Brian out of the office and down to the casino floor. They crossed the gaming establishment, weaving in and out of the hundreds of tourists seeking their fortunes on the garish, flashing slot machines and the blackjack, roulette, and craps tables.

They ended up at the Edgewater Lounge and sat at a cocktail table in the back. An attractive young woman in a skimpy uniform strolled up to the table and asked them what they wanted to drink. They both ogled her with lustful eyes, and Brian ordered a light beer, Jack a scotch on the rocks.

Minutes later, the waitress delivered their beverages. Jack signed the comp slip and tipped her a couple of dollars. He sipped his whiskey, and instantly seemed more relaxed, saying, "What if I told you I may have found our black cat? The one who's been making us unlucky."

Brian raised his eyebrows. "I didn't know we had one. I'm not superstitious."

"I found something interesting while reviewing the casino win/loss records for the last nine months. We've been unlucky Wednesday through Sunday. On Mondays and Tuesdays, we're holding the expected win."

"What does that mean? I don't understand."

"It tells me two days a week, our thief takes some time off."

Brian scowled. "What thief?"

"I believe someone's taking money from the soft count room."

"Who? How can that be?"

Jack threw up his hands. "I don't know, but this Monday/Tuesday phenomenon confirms my suspicions that somebody's stealing from the casino."

Brian took a pull from his beer. "Whoever heard of a thief taking Mondays and Tuesdays off? It must be coincidence."

"I don't think so, Brian. Somebody's getting money from the drop boxes."

"I'd say that's impossible. There's no damn way. This afternoon, Sarah Calder showed me around the cashier's cage and the count rooms. The security's unbelievable."

"I know, but this is more than a fluke. Our thief may only have access to the money on the days he's working."

"Wednesday through Sunday?" Brian's expression was a question mark.

"That's right."

"Did you tell this to Montgomery and Thomas?"

"No, not yet. I need more evidence. I must have strong proof, or they might assume I'm making wild accusations to cover my own ass. I'm sure Montgomery believes my dealers are somehow taking the money."

"Sarah Calder thought so."

A look of irritation passed over Jack's face. "That old bitch. She wants to keep the focus of any investigation away from her own department. The dealers aren't stealing. When the low hold problem started earlier this year, I called Cory. He and his fellow agents at the Gaming Control Board spent hours watching the dealers and poring over the videos in the surveillance room. He tells me everything's fine on the gaming floor. My own people say the same thing. If there's something wrong, it's not in the pit."

"What's your next step?"

Jack took a swig of his whiskey. "I'm not certain. I'm going to think about this some more. In the meantime, pay attention to any rumors that may be floating around."

"I'll have to spend more time with my secretary."

Jack chuckled. "Good idea."

Brian's face turned serious. "Beatrice says the word on the street is there may be some changes in the games department. Any truth to that?"

Jack sighed, shaking his head. "Could be. Montgomery told me if the low hold problem isn't corrected soon, he'll be seeking new leadership. The pressure's starting to affect me."

"No worries, my friend. We'll find out what's going on."

"I hope so. Would you like another beer?"

Brian waved his almost empty bottle, and they hailed the cocktail waitress. She brought them a couple more drinks, and they continued to discuss the particulars of theft from the casino. Each time, though, they were stymied by the tight security and surveillance cameras.

Brian peeled off a corner of his beer label and said, "I intend to take a peek at the surveillance room. I have to know what they can see on their video monitors."

Jack's tone intensified. "They can view everything. Sometimes I wonder if Elliot Thomas records our visits to the restroom." He rattled the ice in his glass. "Good luck getting in, by the way. Thomas doesn't like to show off his little empire. He thinks he's the CIA. He loves the mystery. He enjoys it when people believe he observers their trips to the john. Too many visitors and his secrets will be exposed."

"I don't care—I'm checking out the place. I'm giving Thomas a call."

Jack put down his whiskey. "We have to be cautious—you know that. If someone is stealing from the casino, we're talking about a lot of money. I figure over two and a half million dollars could've been stolen. Whoever's involved won't appreciate our snooping around."

"I agree." Brian glanced at his watch. "I should check out the slot tournament. I need to make sure it's running okay. Care to join me?"

"Why not?" Jack grabbed his glass and downed the last few drops of scotch.

The two men left the lounge and walked through the casino. Jack stopped at a blackjack pit and spoke for a minute with the floor supervisor, and then they zigzagged through the slot machines. The number of gamblers had increased five-fold since they had their first drink. It was going to be a busy weekend.

They entered the Mount Tallac Ballroom to find it full of cheering customers. Along one wall was a row of fifty slot machines and in front of each one was a frantic person pushing the spin button. As the symbols lined up, the winning points were totaled on a meter above them. A banner hung from the ceiling: Welcome Slot Tournament Participants.

"You have a good crowd," Jack said.

Brian nodded. "The tournament's full. All players with high limits."

Jack studied the customers tapping the spin buttons on the machines. "I've never understood why anyone would want to play in a slot tournament. It takes no skill. You press a button and hope sevens materialize. Seems boring to me."

"The first-place prize is twenty-five thousand dollars. For that much money, I can take some monotony. Besides, the customers who play in the tournaments enjoy themselves. All of them have smiles on their faces."

Jack lifted his shoulders. He had to agree the room was full of people having a good time. Behind each of the slot tournament contestants were their family and friends, rooting them on. Everyone was laughing and appeared to be having fun. "Blue sevens, blue sevens," several of the boisterous players shouted, almost in unison.

Brian led Jack over to Alice MacKay, who was surveying the tournament like a proud mother.

"How's everything?" he asked.

Alice put the mug of coffee she was holding on a lectern. "It's going as planned."

"I had no doubt. When it comes to putting on a special event, no one's better than you."

"No question about that," Jack said.

Alice beamed at them, the wrinkles around her eyes turning up. "Thanks," she said. "All this goddamn effort better produce a good night in the casino."

"Let's hope so," Brian said. "We can sure use the revenue. I'm going to check on business in the showroom. I'll be there if you need me."

Alice picked up a megaphone and pranced in front of the tournament players. She led them in a rousing cheer, and they roared with delight.

"Do you want to see Skip Sullivan's show?" Brian asked, gazing at Jack.

"No," he said. "I'd better get home. Hailey's waiting for me, and I owe her some quality time. Besides, he doesn't do my kind of humor."

"Okay, I'll see you later."

"Don't forget to come over tomorrow night. I'm barbecuing some chicken and steaks."

"I'll think about it. If I'm hungry enough, I might stop by." Brian grinned.

They both laughed.

"Take it easy, buddy," Jack said.

Brian crossed the casino to the main showroom. The theater was full of expectant people, eating their entrees and waiting for Skip Sullivan's dinner show performance.

Sullivan had been an attractive but little known comic a year earlier. He'd performed in the Charleston's casino lounge as an opening act for a singer who was also obscure. Skip's fortunes took a dramatic change when he was cast as the lead in a television sitcom. The show became a surprise hit, and he was now the headliner in the Charleston's main showroom.

Brian meandered over to the short, stocky, tuxedoed maître d'. "It looks like we have a full house tonight," he said.

The man adjusted his bowtie. "Yes, but Sullivan's already a half-hour late for his performance. Everyone's getting restless."

Brian's face reflected his disapproval as the lights dimmed and the orchestra played.

The maître d' said in disgust, "Well, his majesty's decided to grace us with his presence."

Skip Sullivan jogged to center stage and began his routine of verbal abuse and political commentary, insulting a man in the front row of the audience while everyone howled with laughter. Brian watched half the show, then decided he'd seen enough. Sullivan's comedy hadn't changed that much from when he was a no-name lounge act.

There was a cute new waitress at the steakhouse at Harrah's Hotel, and Brian thought he'd go over there and find out what time she got off work. He was sure she'd be far more entertaining than the comedian.

FOUR

THE WOMAN SHIVERED in the cold. It was late October, and a dusting of snow was already on the peaks of the mountains. The first rays of morning sun hadn't yet had a chance to warm the air. Vanessa Daine was attractive in a simple, country-girl way and had deep-blue eyes and freckles on her nose. Her long brown hair was tousled and windblown and she was nervous and edgy, faint remnants of cocaine in her nostrils. Fidgeting with the large diamond ring on her finger, she wondered where he was. She'd been waiting in her car for over twenty minutes.

The location was the site of their daily rendezvous—a cheap motel on Highway 50 owned by the man who'd betrayed her. She didn't want to be there and had told him last night on the phone that it was over. He'd lied to her for the last time. A few weeks earlier, he'd promised to divorce his wife so they could get married and move to a small island in the Bahamas. She now knew there was little doubt it was all a sham.

Vanessa looked at the ring and shook her head. She didn't trust him anymore. How could he do this to her? After all, she'd helped him steal millions from the Charleston Resort.

When Vanessa found out he was seeing another woman, she couldn't believe it. She'd risked everything for this man. He didn't know she'd seen him hugging and kissing the red-haired bimbo and she saw them go into a hotel suite. A suite, she marveled. This sleazy dive was the place he took *her* for romance.

Vanessa questioned why she was there. She'd told him they were finished. He denied it all, but she knew better. She'd seen it all on a surveillance monitor. She shook her head again. He was smooth and had begged to see her, saying he couldn't bear to be without her. She'd speak with him, but their relationship was done. She'd made up her mind.

A gold Mercedes drove up next to her shiny new Honda. A distinguished, gray-haired gentleman slipped out of the car and walked around to the driver's side of her vehicle. Vanessa crept out of the Honda and stared at him. He was the type of man she'd dreamed about since she was a young girl— handsome, educated, and sophisticated. He was also a liar and a cheat.

"Darling," he said, his tone smooth, "let's go inside, where we can be more comfortable and talk."

Vanessa hugged herself as she trembled in the cold air.

He unlocked room eight. Room eight at the Lone Pine Motel had been their love nest. They'd shared their secrets, discussed plans for the future, and made passionate love. The memories flooded back as she sat on the bed.

The man took a seat next to her and leaned over to kiss her. She pushed him away, but he didn't give up. For a second, she considered accepting his advances. It was only a fleeting moment, and then she pulled back from him.

"I love you, Vanessa," he said. He caressed her shoulders.

Irate, she swatted his hands away and stood. "You don't know what that is." She turned to him. "You lied to me. I'm the one in jeopardy each night. I did it for you, and now you're cheating on me. I saw you with that woman on a video monitor. You were kissing her. You took her to the Tahoe Suite."

"It was nothing. I was drinking, and she caught me in a weak condition. You know I love you. It won't happen again."

Vanessa jabbed a finger in the air. "You're right about that. It's over. I'm tired of the risks. I don't sleep when I'm at home and now this. I can't take it anymore. I'm done."

He floated up from the bed and reached for her. "Please, Vanessa, honey, we almost have enough money. Another few years and we can leave the lake. We'll have what we require to live the rest of our lives in luxury."

Full of emotion, Vanessa felt tears seep to the corners of her eyes. "You're using me. You're just saying you love me to get the cash."

"You like it too, baby. In another year or two, you can quit your job and do anything you wish. No more working the graveyard shift."

Vanessa's inflection inched up. "I wanted you. You hatched this scheme. All I ever dreamed about was being with you."

"Yes, but you have to admit you were a willing partner. The idea of all that money appeals to you."

"We have plenty. If you love me, you'll take me away from here."

"Not yet. We need more."

Vanessa smashed her hands together. "No, I won't do it." She folded her arms over her chest. "If you keep pressuring me, I'm blowing the whistle on the whole goddamn thing." She peered at him with angry eyes, hoping the threat would scare him.

She was very wrong. He grabbed her left arm, his expression hostile, and with the back of his right hand, he slapped her hard across the face. "Never threaten me," he said. "Don't you ever think of opening your mouth or you'll regret it."

Vanessa sat down on the bed and wept. Her right cheek was swelling up.

"Baby," he said in a softer voice. He took a handkerchief from his pocket and bent over to wipe her tears. "Time will fly, and before long, we'll have enough money for a life of comfort."

"I told you," she said. "I'm finished."

He glared at her, seething, his demeanor changing in a flash. "It's not up to you. I expect you to be on the job tonight." He yanked her up off the bed and slammed her against a wall.

Vanessa squealed and shrieked in fear. "No."

He wrapped his hands around her throat. "Listen, sweetheart, be a good girl and do your part. Do you understand me?" He threw her on the bed and charged out of the motel room.

Vanessa quivered and sobbed uncontrollably.

BRIAN WOKE WITH Gina Allen in his arms. Her brunette hair was disheveled, and she was giving off a gentle snore. The steakhouse waitress had lived up to his expectations the night before. He rolled out of bed, making sure not to wake her, and looked out the window. The clear lake outside shimmered with the first streaks of sunlight, and he was in awe at the beauty of the place.

Brian glanced at the stack of redwood lumber in his yard. He needed to work on the deck but knew it wasn't happening today. He wasn't feeling ambitious enough. He hoped it wouldn't snow before he completed the project and checked the western mountains to see if any inclement weather was on the horizon. Puffy clouds hung over the peaks, though it didn't seem a storm was approaching.

October in Lake Tahoe was beautiful, but in his mind it wasn't the best time for outdoor recreation. It was too early to ski, too cold to go to the beach, and the same lack of ambition keeping him from toiling on his deck was preventing him from hiking or riding his mountain bike. He might as well go down to the Charleston and catch up on some paperwork. If he had a chance, he'd locate Elliot Thomas and see if he'd show him around the Surveillance Department.

Brian was in no hurry to get to the resort. Gina woke up, and they drove to a nice restaurant and had brunch. They engaged in light conversation, but he was preoccupied and knew the best way to quell his anxiety was by heading over to the casino.

THE MERCEDES SEDAN eased into the driveway of the little brown house. Giant Ponderosa pines dwarfed the structure, and the home was almost invisible from the street. Marcus Hatrix opened the front door and stepped onto the porch.

Hatrix was a large man, six-foot-four with a strong build. He had black hair and several tattoos on his arms. After he got out of the Navy, his physique had served him well as a bouncer, debt collector, and in his current occupation as a security guard at the Charleston Resort.

The security guard job had led to his stellar payday. No more petty thefts for him. He was in the big time now. He fancied himself a major player in his own form of organized crime. He loved watching gangster movies and fantasizing about their lives. With the money from the thefts at the Charleston, he was living the life he'd dreamed about as a small-time hood on the streets of Oakland.

The payoff was incredible. By the end of the year, he'd have collected his share of the close to three million dollars taken from the casino. That, plus the extra few hundred he managed to keep for himself each night, made life sweet for Marcus Hatrix. He had money to spend on women, drugs, the sleek little car in the garage, and his passion—betting on sports. Hatrix loved to gamble on any athletic event and spent most of his free time at the sports book. He hadn't won much but always knew that, at some point, his luck would change.

"We had a good night, boss," Hatrix said to the man who

got out of the Mercedes. "Business at the Charleston's excellent. That TV comedian's jamming the place. Come on in. Would you like a beer or something?"

The man grimaced. "No, it's a bit early for me."

The inside of Hatrix's house was a mess. Clothing and empty Budweiser cans were scattered across the floor. A football game was on the television. Hatrix motioned to the flat-screen. "I put a grand on the Steelers," he said. "The point spread's three and a half."

Deep creases lined the man's face. "Be careful how you throw money around. I've told you before, we can't afford for anyone to become suspicious."

"When someone asks, I tell them my rich grandmother died and left me a fortune."

"And you think they'll believe that?"

Hatrix grinned, his crooked teeth showing. "Why not?"

"Any problems last night?"

"None at all. This thing's slick as can be. I hope it goes on forever."

The other man's look was unsettled. "We may be running into problems with Vanessa."

"Oh, she's just high-strung."

"Damn video cameras—they're everywhere. Vanessa saw me with Judy. You remember the redhead I was telling you about? She watched me take her to the Tahoe Suite."

A quick burst of air spewed from Hatrix's mouth. "No wonder she's pissed off."

"I told her I loved her—the usual crap—and tried to calm her down, but she was upset. Says she wants out. She even threatened me. She said she'd expose us."

"She what?" Hatrix said in a voice of high-pitched disbelief. "The bitch better not even think about doing that. Why would she talk that way? We have a good thing going."

The man said with confidence, "She won't do anything. I scared her pretty good."

"Can we trust her anymore?"

"Yeah. She loves the cash, same as you and me. Keep an eye on her, though."

"I will. Let's take a look at last night's haul." Hatrix moved over to an oak cabinet and pulled out a soft leather bag. He carried it to the kitchen table and dumped the bag's contents. A massive flow of hundred-dollar bills poured out, and he smiled. "I told you we had a good night."

The two men sat at the table and sorted the bills, Benjamin Franklin's stare causing their hearts to beat faster. It took them almost half an hour to count the currency and stack it in neat rows.

"Thirty-one thousand seven hundred," Hatrix said with satisfaction. "It's like having a money factory."

The man jerked his head in the affirmative. "All tax free. And I'll need every cent of my portion to subsidize the damn *Sierra Queen*."

"You can't get that thing to make a dime, can you?"

He pounded a fist into his hand. "That frigging boat. It's been a loser since the day I bought it. Did I tell you I'm going to have to replace the engine? My mechanic says it's on its last legs."

Hatrix waved a fist full of bills. "You needn't worry about it if we keep having nights like this."

"Keep tabs on Vanessa, and it'll be flowing for a long time."

Hatrix followed his boss out of the house and onto the front porch. Before driving off, the man reprimanded him again for being too conspicuous with his share of the loot. Hatrix stood there grinning, without a care in the world, thinking about his profitable life of crime.

THE CASINO WAS hopping when Brian arrived at the Charleston Resort. Every slot machine was taken, and the table games were ringed with players. The bells and music of the slots were almost deafening. He paced up and down the aisles, observing the joy and anguish of the customers, who were staring, mesmerized, at the spinning reels.

Brian wondered what pleasure these people could get from playing these devices. For the same amount of money they were wagering, they could travel overseas or buy items for their homes. He knew he'd much rather take a hot blonde to Hawaii than gawk at a slot machine and watch the reels go around. He couldn't comprehend their desire to gamble but wasn't complaining. Their visits to the casino were paying his salary and the wages of a few thousand other Charleston employees.

At the office suites, Brian found the place deserted. Most of the executives didn't work on Saturday, and those who did were on the casino floor. He would often come in on weekends because it was quiet, the phone didn't ring, and he could get a lot done.

Sitting at his desk, Brian put his feet up and examined the previous day's financial summary. The report indicated business in the casino had been outstanding. The slot revenue was excellent, the table game volumes substantial. He noticed, however, that the table games held just twelve percent of the drop. He wondered how long a casino could be unlucky. Brian thought for a bit and decided he wanted more than ever to take a look at the surveillance room. He was certain it would reveal clues about this mysterious misfortune.

FIVE

ELLIOT THOMAS WAS sitting at a cocktail table in the Edgewater Lounge when Brian approached. Wearing an expensive blue suit, Thomas was an attractive man in his early fifties, tall, with full gray hair and piercing black eyes. When he gazed at you, it felt as if he could see right through to your soul. It made Brian uncomfortable.

"Elliot, can you spare a minute?" Brian asked.

With little emotion, Thomas said, "Sure, I guess so. It's a busy weekend. I can't talk long."

Brian sat down next to him. "Montgomery has to be pleased with the action."

Thomas turned up his nose. "He's never happy."

"I imagine it's difficult for the Surveillance Department to keep track of everything when business is this good. So much is going on."

"It is, but I manage a large staff and have plenty of surveillance cameras, so we can monitor most of it."

"What are the chances of getting a tour of your area? I'd love to see your operation."

Thomas eyed him with a wary look. "I don't know, Shepard. I like to keep our activities confidential for security reasons."

Brian nodded. "I appreciate that, but I have a marketing idea I can't pursue without your assistance."

Thomas squinted. "Oh, and what's that?"

"Well, I intend to put television and social media commercials together, showing some of our customers who've won big jackpots. I figured you'd have our previous winners on surveillance video. I could have the advertising agency edit a few of them and make a great promotional pitch."

In fact, Brian had never planned to make television spots with video of winners. The previous night, he'd decided that excuse would be the best way to gain entry into Thomas's department.

"Interesting concept," Thomas said. "Does Montgomery know about this?"

"No," Brian said. "I haven't had a chance to speak with him. As you know, he wasn't in a good mood this week. I've been avoiding him until he's in better spirits."

Thomas chewed on his lower lip for a moment. "I'll tell you what—I'll call him. If he says it's okay, you can come up and review some of our videos."

Brian smiled. "Great. I'll be in my office most of the afternoon. Give me a jingle after you've talked with Montgomery. I know he'll agree. It's a great advertising initiative."

"I'll let you know." Thomas stood up from the table and focused on Brian with eyes of steel. He wagged a finger at him. "No matter what Montgomery says, you must know that what goes on in the Surveillance Department's confidential. I don't let many outsiders up there. If I allow you into the surveillance room, I need your assurance you'll not discuss our operation with anyone. There are a lot of ongoing investigations, and I don't want them jeopardized."

"No problem, Elliot. I just want to make great television commercials. I have no intention of interfering with your business."

Thomas gave him a cold stare and stomped away without another word. Brian watched him cross the casino and disappear behind the door by the cashier's cage. He wondered if there was any possibility Elliot Thomas could be involved in a conspiracy to steal money.

BRIAN POPPED OVER to the coffee shop, ate a Caesar's salad with shrimp, and returned to his office. He tried to get some work done but couldn't get the Surveillance Department out of his mind.

Thomas said he had a large staff. If there was a scheme to steal from the count room, there would have to be several people involved. That scenario didn't seem reasonable, though. Convincing so many people to keep quiet would be risky, but then again, there was a lot of money at stake.

Brian kept reflecting on his trip to the count room and its tight security. His thoughts were interrupted when Jack stuck his head through the doorway. He took a seat, and Brian told him all about his discussion with the Director of Surveillance and Security.

"An okay from Montgomery?" Jack said. "Thomas doesn't require permission from Tom Montgomery. He wants an excuse not to let you see his operation."

"No, I don't believe so," Brian said. "I told him I hoped to acquire surveillance videos of our customers winning big jackpots and explained I plan to make television commercials with the recordings."

Jack gave him a questioning gaze. "And he bought that?"

"Of course. I have an honest face. Besides, it might not be a bad idea."

Jack grabbed a paperclip from Brian's desk and twisted it with nervous energy. "If you do go up there, I need you to find out something for me. See if the nice folks in Surveillance have access to the count room keys."

"They don't, Jack. Yesterday, when I toured the vault, I saw that all the high security keys were kept there. They sign each key in and out, and only certain authorized people can obtain them. Even the general manager can't sign out a key if he's not on the register."

Jack's forehead puckered. "Who sets up the list?"

"It's part of our internal controls, agreed to with the Nevada Gaming Control Board. I called and asked Cory. He told me the list of approved people's limited and must be endorsed by the state board. The Surveillance staff's not authorized to have count room keys."

"Even so, Brian, poke around. If thieves are getting into the drop boxes, somebody has to have a key."

The telephone rang. Brian picked up the receiver and, after a brief conversation of yeses and okays, hung up the phone. "Thomas is permitting me to go up to the surveillance room," he said. "I'm supposed to meet with a guy named Derrick Stagg at three."

Jack tossed the now-mangled paperclip onto Brian's desk. "Stagg's a good man. He's the day shift supervisor of the Surveillance Department. You may get a better idea of what goes on up there from him. He's not caught up in the cloak-and-dagger double-oh-seven mentality like Thomas."

"I was mulling this over earlier." Brian's voice was almost a whisper. "Do you suppose Elliot Thomas could be involved in the thefts?"

Jack stroked his chin with a finger. "Yes, I suppose everyone up there could be a suspect, Thomas included. Brian, I've been thinking—Thomas has a lot of employees, and during the day, there are many people around. We can assume if anyone's stealing from the soft count room, it's happening late at night, after the count crews have gone home and before the regulars come to work the next day.

"The swing shift drop boxes are brought in at two o'clock in the morning. That means our crooks could break into the count room between two and five. That's when the uncounted money from all three shifts is there. We have to find out who's working in the Surveillance Department at that time of night. Want to bet on whether some of them take Mondays and Tuesdays off?"

Brian narrowed his eyes. "Hell no."

"While you're up in the Surveillance Department, I'm going to visit a few of the local locksmiths, starting with the five here at the lake. The drop boxes use a special high security lock. Maybe I can learn how difficult it is to make or duplicate those keys." Jack ran a hand through his hair. "I'll tell you this, though—we need to find out what's happening soon. Montgomery believes my dealers are stealing, and it's tense in the department. It's not a great atmosphere."

The look Brian gave his friend was resolute. "We'll determine what's going on. You'll be a freaking hero, and Montgomery won't know how to thank us when we identify the thieves."

AT THREE O'CLOCK, Brian stood at the security booth outside the cashier's cage. Vince, the security guard, was at his post, monitoring the people who came in and out of the door. "You're becoming a regular around here," he said.

Brian grinned. "Yeah, I find this place fascinating."

"Wish I did. I can't wait until my shift's over. This is my seventh day. We're short a few officers, and I've had to work a lot of overtime."

"At least you get the time-and-a-half pay."

Vince nodded. "That's for sure. And I can use every cent. I have a family to feed, and nine bucks an hour doesn't go far."

This struck Brian as strange. The people responsible for the security of millions of dollars were making little more than minimum wage. His tone conveyed empathy. "It's difficult to make a living nowadays."

"You're right about that." Vince handed him the access log. "You know the routine. Fill out the information next to your name."

Brian signed the log, noting the time and the reason for his visit, and gave it back to Vince.

"Mr. Stagg's on his way down," the security guard said. "He should be here any minute."

While waiting for Stagg to arrive, Brian observed the cashiers in the cage deal with the customers on the other side of the bars. Handling the thousands of dollars going across the counter, they seemed almost oblivious to the fact they were dealing with large sums of money. Their behavior was professional and pleasant. Brian knew he couldn't be as composed. He admired them.

"Brian Shepard?" a male's voice behind him said. Brian turned to face the man exiting the doorway. He was a handsome guy in his mid-forties. His dark hair was wavy, and he was wearing a well-tailored black pin stripe suit. He looked like he'd walked out of a fashion magazine.

Brian held out his right hand. "That's me."

"Derrick Stagg." He clasped Brian's hand, his grip firm.

"I'm surprised we've never met."

Stagg unbuttoned his jacket. "Elliot Thomas keeps us surveillance types under wraps. We don't get out much."

"Well, it's nice to meet you. I've heard some good things about you."

"The same here. I like your idea of television commercials with video of our customers winning big jackpots. I hope we can assist you."

"I appreciate that."

The two men entered the hallway by the cashier's cage. Stagg led Brian through the many security doors and corridors until they arrived at the elevator. He picked up the receiver from the phone on the wall, stated his name, and the doors opened. The men boarded the car, and Stagg pushed the number two button on the panel. They rode in silence as the car ascended one floor, and when the doors parted, they stepped into a small, well-lit lobby. The area was plain, with white-painted walls and institutional linoleum on the floor.

"Let me give you a quick tour of the place," Stagg said. "I'm proud of this operation, and you don't work in a gaming area, so I see no harm. Don't tell Elliot, though." He winked.

Brian's smile was broad. He was pleased he wouldn't have to attempt to nose around in a covert way. "Thanks, I've always wondered what went on up here."

"It's all pretty simple. We're charged with watching the assets of the casino and keeping tabs on our customers—for their protection and ours." He lifted a ring of keys from his pocket, unlocked the door to their right, and directed Brian into a large room. "This is our training academy." The space was full of blackjack, craps, and roulette tables and slot machines of every theme imaginable.

"You have a mini casino in here," Brian said.

Stagg sat on a blackjack stool. "We require all our surveillance personnel to be well-versed in all aspects of the casino games, and we use this room for instruction. Our surveillance people are some of the best-trained dealers in the casino. By understanding the games they're observing, they can better spot a cheater."

Brian's eyes wandered the room. "Where's everybody now?" The area was deserted, the blinking lights on the slot machines the single sign of life.

"On the weekends, we don't use the training academy. We're too busy studying the video monitors and working out on the main casino floor. We utilize this place during the slower weekdays."

"Tell me, how can crooks cheat a slot machine?" Brian looked at the devices against the back wall. "I've always wondered how that's possible."

"It's not so easy anymore. On the mechanical slot machines, it was much simpler. The spinning of the reels determined the winners on the older machines. Experienced slot cheats used all kinds of methods to make those reels stop at a jackpot, halting the reels with wires and other outside devises. It's fortunate that we don't operate any of the vintage machines on our casino floor. All the slots at the Charleston have the latest technology, with a computer chip determining the outcome."

Brian pointed at the machines. "Are the new ones fool-proof?"

"No, but it's a lot more difficult to bilk the electronic slots. Their reels have nothing to do with the actual outcome of the spin. They're just there for show. A tiny computer determines the actual payout. A random generator decides what'll happen with each pull of the slot handle or press of the spin button. The computer tells the reels what symbols should be exposed on the pay-line, and they stop in the appropriate position. Anyway, it's challenging to cheat the computer. It's sealed deep inside the guts of the slot machine. However, some techno crooks have been caught with gadgets that can manipulate the new machines. We spend a lot of time searching for that type of theft."

There was a curious glint in Brian's eyes. "How do you catch them?"

"It's not easy, but we have a well-trained staff trying to detect those people we believe may have the necessary technology. Everything changes so fast, though. Most of the time, the cheaters are six months ahead of us. We've even hired a cheater or two. They are great at spotting crooks."

Brian chuckled.

"In the next few years, slot machines will become server-based. It's all going to be run through the internet."

"Do you often work with the Gaming Control Board?"

"We do. Their agents are a great help with our investigations. The state can't collect its gaming tax if the money's stolen, so they're motivated to help us find cheaters."

"Do you know Cory Wyatt? He's a gaming agent."

"Oh, sure. He's up here all the time."

"We were roommates and played baseball together for the University of Nevada. He's one of my best friends."

"He's a straight shooter. Knows some good jokes too." Stagg stood and turned toward the door. "Come on, I'll show you the main surveillance room."

They exited the training academy, and Stagg locked the door behind them. "It's through here," he said. He unlocked an unmarked door, and guided Brian into an area that was dark and illuminated, for the most part, by the flat-screen video monitors covering one entire wall. In front of the screens, a half-dozen or so people sat at workstations and stared intently at the monitors.

"This is the nucleus of our operation," Stagg said. "There are several hundred cameras throughout the resort, and most connect to these DVRs." He tilted his head toward another wall, with shelves full of digital video recorders. "Each one has a number and a corresponding monitor. We can observe almost every square inch of the property. It's all recorded digitally and saved onto memory cards."

Amazed, Brian examined the colorful video screens. Each of them showed different areas of the casino in vivid detail. He saw blackjack dealers pitching cards to gamblers and could read the faces as they were held in the customers' hands. He watched a man throw a pair of dice and could read their spots.

Other monitors displayed rows and rows of slot machines, with excited patrons pressing the spin buttons. He observed the reels on the machines rotate and the symbols line up. His eyes roved across the monitors featuring the cashier's cage, the vault, and the soft count room. Near the ceiling, screens showed the escalator going down to the sports book, numerous hallways in the hotel, and the interiors of several elevators.

"You can see everything from here," Brian said with a hint of dismay. He didn't know they could see so much.

Stagg said with authority, "We concentrate on any area containing cash or having a potential for liability. This protects us from frivolous lawsuits, like when a customer is falling-down drunk, trips over something, and sues the Charleston for negligence six months later. We scrutinize all the transactions on the casino floor and in the cashier areas, but we also search for purse thieves and people who may be in areas where they don't belong."

Brian motioned to a monitor. "What are you looking for on the blackjack tables?"

"Procedure errors the dealers might make. They're all trained to deal their cards the same way for every hand. If they don't follow these precise dealing techniques, we call the pit and inform the supervisor of the violation. Requiring them to deal the cards the exact same way every time makes it easier for us to spot a transaction that may not be legitimate."

"How often do you catch a dealer working with a gambler...you know, cheating?"

Stagg scratched his cheek. "It's rare. If we do, most the time, it's a dealer telling the player what their hole card is. They do this hoping the customer will give them a hefty tip. There have been cases of collusion—a dealer paying on a buddy's losing hand. It doesn't happen much, since they know we're recording every move they make. Most employees we catch cheating have drug habits or other personal problems. They need the money so bad, their judgment's clouded."

"How about marked cards? Do you see that a lot?"

"No. We change them on the tables on the hour and check for marks, and if we do find something, we eighty-six the player. The new deck is sealed in cellophane from the manufacturer, so we know it's clean."

Brian surveyed the people staring at the video screens. "Don't they get bored watching the monitors all shift long?"

"No, they have too much to do. They're always in contact with the cashier's cage and the pit. All transactions in the cage over a thousand dollars must first be approved by the Surveillance Department. This ensures a cashier doesn't pay out the wrong amount of money by accident. The pit calls us all the time, asking us to assess the play of individual players. They're always concerned about card counters."

"Is it illegal to do that?"

Stagg shook his head. "No, but it improves the counter's odds of winning. We use the old saying, *we reserve the right to refuse service to anyone*, and ask them to leave."

"I bet they get angry."

"Oh yeah, they do, but it's our prerogative as a business."

Brian pointed to the monitor showing the soft count team. "Sarah Calder gave me a tour of the count room area."

"That's the second shift. Except for the count, the only action in the room's when they bring in the full shift drop boxes and the slot money. We only pay attention to that place when the counts are in progress."

"What do you look for when they're counting?"

Stagg propped himself on the corner of a workstation. "Well, after each box is emptied of the money, a count team member's required to hold it up and aim it at the video camera. We verify it's currency-free. Other than that, we make certain they're following the count procedures and ensure no bills are stuck in their paperwork and retrieved later. The count teams all wear pocket-less jumpsuits so they can't hide any cash in their clothing without being conspicuous."

Brian gazed toward the men and women who seemed engrossed by the video monitors. "Do you maintain this large a staff all the time?"

"Our day and swing shift crews are sizeable—the swing shift in particular. We have a much smaller team on graveyard, since there's less business. But the video cameras are recording all the action in the resort twenty-four hours a day, seven days a week. As you know, the casino never closes."

"How long do you keep the recordings?"

"We preserve the video on the back-up memory cards for seven days. If there's nothing of interest to us after that, we record over them. The videos we do hold, for example, ones showing a cheater or some type of theft—are locked up in the evidence room and kept until we need them in court."

"You show the recordings at trial?"

Stagg's eyes flickered. "We sure do. The judges and juries have been good to us. Using the videos, we've never lost a case yet."

"Do you have any pending now?"

"We caught a guy trying to pinch his bet on a blackjack table last week. We'll be using our digital recordings in court next month."

"That's fascinating."

"We also store all the videos showing the big casino winners. That's what you're interested in for your television commercials."

"Why do you keep those?"

"In case the Gaming Control Board wants to review them later. They examine our recordings of significant money winners during an audit."

"Lucky for me. Now I can put them to an even better use as a sixty-second promotional spot."

Stagg gestured to his left. "Before we get your videos, let me show you our investigative offices." He led Brian across the video surveillance room and through another locked door. Inside were rows of desks, separated by partitions. Several men and women were at their workstations, absorbed with paperwork or on the telephone. "We run our undercover and casino investigations out of this room. We have people on the casino floor at all times— plain clothes agents searching for potential problems.

"We often set up purse-snatching stings. We'll place a purse between slot machines and wait. If there are any thieves in the casino, they'll try to take the purse. When they do, we detain them and call the sheriff. Last Fourth of July holiday, we caught nine purse snatchers in just one shift."

Brian said with great sarcasm, "I don't think I want to advertise that."

Stagg grinned. "In addition to the stings, we investigate potential problems occurring in the casino—embezzlements, bank shortages, that sort of thing."

"With all this going on, I can see why Jack Mancini doesn't believe the low hold's caused by the dealers stealing."

"I agree with him one hundred percent. I'm confident it's due to a stretch of bad luck. You'll see—it'll straighten out by the end of the year."

Brian's tone of voice was doubtful. "I'm not so sure Montgomery buys that. He's giving Mancini a hard time."

"Montgomery's getting heat from the corporate headquarters, so he's desperate to find a reason for the weak numbers. I'm certain he's focusing on the wrong place. We investigate any abnormality in the casino, from the low hold to shortages in the coffee shop cash register. Our investigators are thorough. They view hours of recordings, seeking the unusual. That's why I'm so convinced the low percentage is due to bad luck. We've considered all the possibilities and found nothing."

Brian appraised the room—taking in every detail. "After seeing this, I can understand why you'd feel that way. You seem to have this resort well protected."

"It's our job. The company has considerable money invested in the Surveillance Department, with a large staff and plenty of equipment. It's worth the outlay."

"Can we take a peek at some video of winners?"

"Sure, it's what you're here for. I know we have one of a Sacramento woman who won a million bucks on a progressive slot machine last August. I'm certain we can find a few others you can use as well."

Brian followed Stagg out of the investigation office and back into the main surveillance room. In the far corner was an area filled with shelves containing memory cards. A table in front of the shelves supported two DVRs with flat-panel video monitors.

Stagg pointed to a chair. "Have a seat," he said. "It'll just take me a minute to find the videos you need." He grabbed a large binder from one of the shelves and put it on the table. "There's a section in this for casino winners. We should be able to find some good footage."

Brian said, "You mentioned the lady who won the million dollar jackpot. If you can track down that recording, it'd be great."

Stagg checked the log and wrote a few numbers on a scratch pad. He turned and concentrated on the rows of memory cards, extracted three, then walked over to one of the DVRs next to Brian. He sat down, plugged a memory card in the machine, and pressed the play button. "These are powerful DVRs," he said. "Each memory card contains twenty-four hours of video. Of course, we don't want to watch the whole thing to locate what we're searching for. These machines have a quick scanning capability, and we can review an entire card in less than five minutes."

Stagg tapped the fast-forward button, and the images flashed by at a lightning pace. Brian could make out the casino floor and people playing the slots but couldn't see any more detail than that. Stagg hit another button, and the action on the monitor reverted to normal speed. "I think your jackpot winner will show up about now," he said.

Brian stared, engrossed, at the screen as the camera zoomed in on an older black woman who was jumping up and down and shaking the startled man next to her. The camera zoomed in closer and revealed the four sevens on her slot's third pay-line. The camera panned back and up to the meter above the machine that displayed the one million dollars the woman had won.

Brian was pleased, his eyes riveted on the screen. "This is the type of video I was hoping for," he said. "If I can acquire a few more recordings like this—add some jazzy music and catchy copy—I'll have great television ads."

The two men viewed videos until Brian had found several more he could use. He picked up the memory cards and said, "I want to take these to our advertising agency. They'll make copies and edit as necessary. I'll bring back the originals as soon as I can."

"Okay," Stagg said, "but I'll need you to sign the cards out." He took a file folder from a nearby shelf and itemized the memory cards on a form inside, then passed it to Brian. "Verify the numbers and sign at the bottom."

Brian did as instructed and gave the folder back to Stagg. "Derrick, I know you're busy, and I appreciate the extra time you've taken."

Stagg returned the folder to the shelf. "Think nothing of it. I enjoy letting people see the place and don't get to do it often. Elliot isn't a fan of visitors." He escorted Brian through the surveillance room and into the well-lit lobby. When he pushed the call button, the elevator doors slid open, and Brian noticed that from this floor, you didn't have to ask for permission to enter the elevator. After descending one floor, Stagg led Brian through the many doors and hallways and to the casino floor.

"Thanks again," Brian said. "This video will be awesome in my commercials."

"Anytime," Stagg said, then turned and vanished behind the security door.

Brian rocked on his heals for a moment. He was sure there was no way anyone could be stealing from the Charleston. Not without being seen.

SIX

BRIAN STOPPED AT the liquor store on his way to the Mancinis' house, where he purchased a bottle of Ferrari Carano cabernet sauvignon and a single red rose. As his truck approached the Mancinis' home, Joker ran up to it barking. Brian parked and climbed out of the vehicle. He petted the Golden Retriever, crossed the driveway to the front entrance, and rang the bell.

A short wait later, the door opened and Hailey, holding a mixing bowl, welcomed him. She was mashing something creamy in the dish. "Jack's on the deck, lighting the charcoal," she said. "Grab a beer and join him. He could use your company."

Brian handed Hailey the rose. She smiled and, on her tiptoes, kissed him on a cheek.

"What's for dinner?" he asked.

"Jack's barbecuing chicken and steaks," she said. "I'm making a casserole and a salad. The dessert's a surprise."

"Sounds scrumptious. I'm hungry." He gave her a peck on the forehead.

Brian and Hailey walked to the kitchen, and he set the cabernet next to a wooden chopping block, then took a light beer from the refrigerator and headed for the deck.

Jack was squirting starter fluid on the charcoal when Brian

stepped onto the deck through the sliding glass door. "Hey," Jack said. He lit a match, threw it on the gas-soaked briquettes, and moved back from the large flame that burst up.

"Don't burn the place down," Brian said.

Jack grinned. "I won't."

The two men watched in silence for a few minutes as the coals turned gray.

Jack took a spatula and poked at the glowing briquettes. He asked, "How was your visit to the surveillance empire?"

Brian took a drink of his beer and wiped foam from his lips. "They have one hell of an operation. Derrick Stagg gave me a complete tour, and I was impressed."

Jack said, "I bet Elliot Thomas didn't like you looking around."

"I lucked out—he wasn't there. Stagg showed me the entire place—their training academy, video surveillance room, and investigation area."

"Did you see anything that might shed some light on my low table games' hold?"

Brian shook his head. "No, the opposite. The Surveillance Department's well run. As you know, they have cameras covering almost every inch of the resort, and they monitor everything twenty-four seven. There's also a sophisticated investigation program. Their investigators examined the low hold, and it's their feeling the casino's having a bit of bad luck. Same old line."

"Did you mention to Stagg the differences in hold percentages on Mondays and Tuesdays?"

"No, I didn't. I don't know who to trust."

Jack put the grate on the grill. "Is it possible for everyone who works in the Surveillance Department on the graveyard shift to be in on a conspiracy to steal money?"

"There are four or five people up there late at night, but if the whole shift was in on it, we wouldn't have the Monday/Tuesday phenomenon. Besides, the DVRs are recording twenty-four hours a day, and the video's reviewed all the time. The Gaming Control Board's up there often as well. If someone's stealing, they're doing it out of sight of the surveillance people."

"But how?"

Brian's tone was frustrated. "I have no idea."

"I discovered that the keys used in the casino are custom designed and made by just a few key and lock companies. They're never duplicated. If the casino loses one, they replace every lock it fits rather than make a reproduction. They don't want to take the risk one's been stolen. The Charleston buys its keys from a locksmith in Reno, and I'm going down there on Monday. I need to understand the procedures for obtaining a key and learn who's authorized to order new ones."

Brian took a pull of his beer. "Let me know what you find out."

The doorbell rang. Jack said, "It sounds like some of our guests are arriving. I better go in and start preparing the drinks. By the way, you can relax—Robbie Taylor won't be able to make dinner. Hailey says she has some conflict."

A lopsided grin covered Brian's face. "What, a prison warden's convention?"

The doorbell rang again as the two good friends left the deck and trundled into the house. Inside, Hailey was greeting Cory Wyatt and his wife, Susan. Cory was tall, with a muscular build, and had black hair that was cut short. His wife was petite and had long brown hair and a pretty face. Hailey put their jackets in the hall closet and instructed them to go into the living room and get comfortable. Michael and Cathy Albright were already seated on the sofa when Cory and Susan entered the room. Michael, a chubby man, was an accountant for a bank. His very pregnant wife, Cathy, was just as heavy and practiced law with a prominent local firm.

Jack made certain everyone had a beverage and returned to the deck to finish cooking the chicken and steaks. Hailey played the doting hostess, running between the kitchen and living room, making sure they all had full cocktails and hors d'oeuvres. When the barbeque was ready, they sat down at the dining room table and enjoyed the feast.

The conversation was teasing and filled with humor. Cory told one joke after another. Everyone had gone to university together, and they were reciting old stories. As the wine flowed, the talk grew louder, and they laughed hysterically describing how Brian had dated just about every girl in the Delta, Theta, and Phi Pi sororities. He chuckled along with them—he didn't have much choice—but reminded Jack and Cory how jealous they were of his exploits.

Hailey was clearing the table when the doorbell chimed. "Oh, that must be Robbie," she said.

Brian frowned at her, unamused.

She glanced at him and smiled. "I told you dessert was a surprise."

He pursed his lips and glared at Jack, who shrugged wearing a *what am I supposed to do* expression.

Brian almost fell out of his chair when Hailey ushered Robbie into the room. It was her, the woman from the Charleston Spa— the one who might as well have told him to drop dead. *I'd rather be alone, if you don't mind.* In an instant, he flushed a pale crimson. He was being forced to confront one of the few women who'd ever spurned his advances.

Hailey introduced each of the people at the table. When she came to Brian, she paused, then told Robbie he was in charge of marketing for the Charleston Resort. By the look on her face, she didn't appear to be impressed. Hailey told her to sit down, and she did so on the single empty chair—the one next to Brian. He was so uncomfortable, he couldn't stand it and knew she was feeling the same. He saw it in her eyes and wished he could disappear. Even so, he couldn't help but admire how striking she was, with her long brown hair cascading over her shoulders.

Jack opened another bottle of wine, and the conversation bounced between politics, football, and the latest rumors around the lake. Robbie relaxed as the evening wore on. She laughed with ease, and that made Brian less self-conscious. He was somewhat tentative when speaking with her, but she seemed to show an interest in his opinions. He wondered if he was winning her over or if she was just being polite.

Around ten-thirty, the party broke up, and while walking to their cars, Robbie turned to Brian and said, "I'm sorry about the way I treated you the other day at the spa."

"I wasn't positive you recognized me," he said. His cheeks were tinged pink again with unexpected embarrassment.

"Yes, and I'm sorry. I'd had a tough day, and I wasn't in the mood to be hit on. It was nothing personal, and I hope you'll forgive me for being rude."

Brian was pleased that she didn't despise him after all. He was even more relieved he wasn't losing his touch with the ladies. "We all have bad days."

"I know, but I want to make it up to you. Would you be interested in taking a ride on one of the cruise boats over to Emerald Bay? I was thinking of going tomorrow morning."

He peered into her eyes, enchanted by her beauty. "I'd like that."

Robbie opened the door to her Toyota SUV and fished in her purse for keys. "The boat leaves the Ski Run Marina at eleven o'clock. Could you pick me up at ten?" She sank behind the wheel of the vehicle.

Brian nodded, still somewhat surprised at her invitation but more than willing. "Sure, it's a date."

"I live at thirteen sixty-five Elks Point Road. It's above the

Round Hill Mall about a half-mile from the Safeway on the right-hand side of the street."

"I'll be there. See you in the morning." He shut her car door, and she pulled away. Watching her taillights fade from view, he thought of Hailey Mancini and laughed.

SEVEN

VANESSA DAINE SAT down at her workstation. The thick makeup covering her bruised right cheek didn't hide the swelling. It was a little after eleven in the evening, and she wished she were anywhere but in the Charleston Resort's surveillance room. She noted the action on the video screens in front of her. The crowds were thinning, but it was still busy. Her phone rang, and she picked it up.

"It's me, pretty baby," a man said. "Send the elevator."

Vanessa hung up and pressed a button on the panel to her right. A few minutes later, there was a knock at the door. She rose from her chair, strode to the doorway, and peeked through the peephole. Standing in the elevator lobby was Marcus Hatrix, wearing his security guard uniform and appearing rather menacing. Light from the lobby flooded the surveillance room when she opened the door. The three other surveillance workers glanced toward Hatrix as he came inside. They each mumbled a hello and turned back to their work.

"I need to talk with you," Hatrix said, staring at Vanessa with a severe scowl on his face.

"Not here," she said in a whisper. Vanessa grabbed a ring of keys off a hook on a wall and said, looking at her co-workers,

"I'm going to the training room with Marcus. Will you guys watch my monitors for me? I'll just be a minute."

None of them stopped concentrating on the wall of video screens. "Sure," one of the men said over his shoulder.

Vanessa and Hatrix left the surveillance room and moved through the lobby. She unlocked the training academy and closed the door after Hatrix had followed her into the room. "What do you need with me?" she asked with venom in her tone.

"I hear you were thinking about sinking our little operation," he said, sounding threatening.

She bowed her head. "I want out. I'm always afraid. I can't take it anymore."

"And give up all this easy money? You have to be crazy."

"I was never in it for the cash—you know that. I did it for him."

"How romantic," he said with derision. "I don't suppose your little nose-candy habit had anything to do with it?"

Vanessa's eyes filled with hatred.

Hatrix seized her arms and pushed her against a wall. She struggled to break free, but he was much too strong for her to resist. "Vanessa, this is the best thing that's ever happened to me. No one, and I mean no one, is screwing this up. Do you understand?"

"Yes," she said in a meek voice. Tears ran down her cheeks.

"Thatta girl." Hatrix released her arms. "If it's loving you're after, I'm positive I can take good care of you." He caressed her shoulder.

Vanessa slapped him across the face. "Get your hands off me." She threw him a hostile glare.

"Okay." Hatrix massaged his jaw where she'd hit him. "But remember, pretty baby, this isn't a game, and I mean what I say. Keep your mouth shut and do your thing."

Vanessa wiped the tears from her eyes. "It's late. If you're going to the count room tonight, you better hurry."

Hatrix checked his wristwatch. "Time's flying."

"Give me a half-hour. I have some paperwork to do." She opened the training room door and held it.

He examined his watch again. "It's two-thirty. I'll be ready at three."

Vanessa agreed with a nod and walked into the lobby. She unlocked the door to the surveillance room, while Hatrix tapped the call button for the elevator.

Vanessa retreated to her workstation, sat down, and studied the video monitors.

"All's quiet," the man next to her said. "Wanda just went on her break."

She smiled at him. "Thanks for keeping an eye on things for me. Marcus wanted to tell me about a slot cheat they apprehended."

"No problem. I'll be taking my break when Wanda returns. Roger's going on his at four."

"I'll be working on reports and my special projects video."

At five minutes to three, Vanessa stood up from her workstation and stepped over to the video library. She pulled two memory cards from the middle shelf and went over to the bank of digital video recorders where she removed a memory card from one of the machines and replaced it with one she'd retrieved from the library. Instead of pressing record, she pushed the play button.

Vanessa looked to the video monitors and the one showing the elevator. It was empty. She extracted a memory card from another DVR and inserted the second one. Again, rather than hitting the record button, she selected play. She focused on another monitor—this time, the one of the soft count room which appeared unoccupied as it should be.

The wall of surveillance monitors displayed the action around the resort and her fellow workers were oblivious to the fact that two of them were showing prerecorded video. Vanessa circled back to her workstation and tried to relax as she observed the video screens in front of her. She flicked a switch on the console to her right. The picture of the hallway to the soft count room disappeared from one of the monitors and was replaced by one of the hotel front desk. She pressed another switch and the picture of the hallway to the elevator was substituted with one of valet parking. Her hands were trembling when she punched the button for the elevator, allowing it to descend to the basement.

TWO FLOORS BELOW the surveillance room, Marcus Hatrix exited the elevator. Entering the hallway, he laughed to himself. He eyed the camera near the ceiling and grinned, knowing Vanessa had switched it off.

He hurried to the door of the soft count room and, using a key, opened it and edged into the room. He sidled over to the drop box cabinet and unlocked the metal mesh door with another key, yanked the first box off the shelf, and laid it on the table. He opened it with a third key and removed some hundred-dollar bills from inside.

It was rare that Hatrix selected more than one or two, as it could raise red flags with the pit supervisors if he did so. He put the money on the table in neat piles and repeated this procedure with each of the boxes in the cabinet.

Hatrix procured the currency from the graveyard shift boxes first, followed by the day shift, then swing. He glanced at his watch. He'd started late, so he needed to pick up his pace. At three forty-five, he locked the cabinet and placed all the money into a leather bag. Before departing, he turned and surveyed the count room to verify that it looked the same as when he entered almost an hour earlier.

Hatrix shot out of the soft count room and over to the elevator. He lifted the phone receiver on the wall, and Vanessa answered. "Everything's fine, pretty baby," he said. "See you later." The elevator doors swooshed apart, and he lunged in and pushed the "one" button on the panel. He pulled off the hood, put it in the money bag, and tucked it in the back of his pants, his security guard blazer concealing the bulge in his clothing. He left the elevator on the first floor, cruised down the hallways, through several doors, and to the alcove where the purse storage cabinet was located. He placed the leather bag in one of the compartments and locked it. Vanessa would retrieve it later, at the end of her shift. Hatrix marched out of the hallway and into the casino with a satisfied smirk on his face.

VANESSA SAW HATRIX leave the hallway on one of the monitors. She crossed the room to the DVRs and removed the memory cards she'd put in earlier, replacing those cards with the ones she'd taken out before and pressing the record button on each of the machines. Her co-workers concentrated on the wall of surveillance screens, unconcerned by her actions. She took the prerecorded video cards and returned them to the library, then sat down at her workstation relieved another night of crime was almost finished without incident.

When Vanessa's shift ended, she briefed her relief on the activities she'd been observing and departed the surveillance room. She rode the elevator to the first floor and entered the passage leading to the casino. After making it to the alcove, she unlocked the compartment of her locker, and stuffed the leather bag in her large purse. She turned in her key, then strolled out the doorway and into the casino.

"Good morning," the security guard in the booth, handing her the access log.

"No, it's good night for me," Vanessa said. She signed her

name and gave the log back to him. "See you tomorrow, Harry." She made her way through the casino and went out the north entrance, bound for her parked car. Sitting in the passenger seat of her Honda was Hatrix. She opened the door, grabbed the money bag from her purse, and tossed it at him.

"You're in a good mood," he said. "You should be delighted. The drop boxes were full, and I bet we're taking home close to thirty-five grand."

"I don't care," Vanessa said in a wispy voice. "Take the money. I'm tired, and I want to go home and rest."

"As you wish. Are you sure you don't want some company?" He massaged her thigh.

She swatted his hand away. "Get out."

Hatrix raised his hands. "Okay, okay, take it easy. Jesus. I'll see you tonight—same time, same place." He sprang out of the vehicle and slammed the door.

Vanessa burst into tears.

BRIAN LAY IN bed as the first rays of sun streamed through the window. He looked at the time on the clock on the nightstand. It was too soon to be awake on a weekend. He closed his eyes and tried in vain to go back to sleep.

He thought about Robbie Taylor and had to admit he was intrigued. Brian supposed that, at some point, he'd like a serious relationship, but despite what could be described as serial dating, he hadn't found a woman he could see himself with for the rest of his life. Maybe he'd set his standards too high, or perhaps he knew too many people who lived in miserable marriages they couldn't wait to flee.

Brian reminded himself how happy he was being single, as he was never without female companionship. He was fortunate to be attractive and personable. The sex was good, and he didn't worry about commitment. He thought of Robbie again. She was so beautiful. He didn't know anything about her, but there was no question he intended to find out more.

Brian gave up on the effort to fall back to sleep and got out of bed. He put on a pair of pants and gazed out the window. Lake Tahoe sparkled like a giant blue sapphire. He turned to the clock on the wall and decided he might as well go to the Charleston Spa and sweat through a workout before showering and picking up Robbie later that morning.

ROBBIE SAT AT the kitchen table, perusing the morning newspaper and sipping a cup of coffee as the sun shone through the window and danced in her hair. She looked across the room when a car pulled into the driveway. A door slammed, and Robbie pushed up from her chair and peeked out a window, seeing her roommate approach their front door.

Robbie walked out of the kitchen and into the living room as Vanessa Daine stumbled into the house. Vanessa appeared haggard and tired. Her mascara was smeared and eyes puffy. Her makeup was all but gone, a nasty bruise showing through it on the right side of her face.

"Vanessa," Robbie said, "are you all right?"

Vanessa's hands quivered, and tears streamed down her cheeks.

Worried, Robbie rushed over to Vanessa and put her arms around her. "What's wrong?"

Vanessa sobbed and more tears gushed from her eyes. She wiped them. "I can't take it anymore."

"Did he hit you?"

"No, not tonight. I haven't seen him, and I don't plan to ever again. It's over between us, I swear."

Puzzled, Robbie's brow creased. "Then what is it?"

"Robbie, I'm in a lot of trouble. I'm caught up in something bad, and I'm scared. I don't know what I should do."

"Tell me what's going on."

"I can't. I won't tell anyone. I don't want anybody else involved. It's way too dangerous. I know that sounds crazy, but it's true."

Robbie gasped. "Dangerous? What are you talking about? Now you're frightening me."

Vanessa shuddered, clutching her arms. "I did it for him. I thought he loved me."

"That doesn't tell me what's happening, and if you're in trouble, I want to be there for you." Robbie led her over to the sofa. They sat, and she handed her a tissue.

Vanessa dabbed her eyes.

"Let me help you," Robbie said. "What did you do that's so bad?"

"I could go to jail," Vanessa said.

"Jail?" Robbie exclaimed, her voice raised. "My god! Why?"

"He made me."

"Vanessa, you're confusing me. Are you mixed up in something illegal?"

She nodded, more tears trickling down her cheeks.

"Look at me, okay? What have you been doing?"

"I can't say anything. You don't understand, they'll kill me."

"What? They? Who are they? I thought it was your boyfriend?"

Frantic, Vanessa wiped the tears from her face. "It's much bigger than that. I won't tell you any more. I'm not saying another word. If you get drawn in, you'll be in danger too."

Robbie grabbed her by both arms. "You can't expect me to ignore what you've said. You're my roommate, and I'm concerned about your welfare. Have you considered turning yourself in to the sheriff? They may be more lenient if you do, and at least you'll be protected."

Vanessa hesitated as she thought about what Robbie was saying. "No, I can't go to the authorities. They won't believe me."

Frustrated, Robbie swept hair over her shoulder. "You're not making any sense."

"I'm not saying anything further, so stop pressuring me. I'm not involving you in this. I shouldn't have mentioned it in the first place." Vanessa pulled away.

"So what do you intend to do?"

"I don't know. I need some time alone. I have to think. I must do something though. I can't live like this any longer."

Robbie stared at her roommate. The woman was confused and scared, and she wished she could help. It was also obvious Vanessa wouldn't let her. "Why don't you go to your room and relax?" she said. "Sleep on it. You'll feel better after you've had some rest. I'm here if you want to chat."

Vanessa rubbed her eyes. "Thanks, Robbie. I am tired." They stood up from the sofa, and Vanessa hugged Robbie. "You're a good friend. Don't worry, though, I'll be okay. I can take care of myself."

Robbie felt helpless as she watched Vanessa plod down the hall and enter her bedroom. She didn't know what to do and feared for her friend's safety.

Shaking her head, she glanced at the clock on the wall. Brian would be there soon. She'd have to hurry if she was going to be ready for their date. Before going to her room, she engaged the deadbolt on the front door. *What danger could Vanessa be in*, she wondered, tugging at the door to verify it was locked tight.

EIGHT

BRIAN ARRIVED AT Robbie's house at ten o'clock on the dot. All his life, he'd been punctual—pre-punctual, in fact. Many a time, he'd driven around the block, knowing he was way too early for an appointment.

Robbie's home was a modern, alpine-style structure with large windows and natural wood. The small house was perched high on a hill, and he was sure it had an exceptional view of Lake Tahoe.

Brian was somewhat nervous, which surprised him, as he couldn't remember the last time he felt that way before a date. He took a slow breath and rang the doorbell. A moment later, Robbie opened the door and invited him in. She was radiant, wearing a white sweater with faded blue jeans. Her hair was combed back, showing her strong cheekbones and magnificent, smooth skin. His heart skipped a beat. "It's a perfect day to be on the lake," he said.

Robbie smiled. "I haven't taken a cruise on Lake Tahoe in years. I'm looking forward to it. Brian, would you give me five minutes? I want to make sure my roommate's okay before we leave."

"You have a roommate?

"Yeah, the mortgage on this place is steep. With a roommate it's manageable. I can still travel, which I love to do."

"I can understand that."

"I want to check on Vanessa. She had a rough night."

He nodded. "Of course."

Robbie left him in the living room and moved down the hall. She knocked on Vanessa's door and opened it a crack, peering in. Vanessa was lying on her bed, staring at the ceiling.

"I'm leaving on my date now," Robbie said, swinging the door wider. "Are you sure you'll be okay?"

Vanessa clutched her pillow. "I'm fine. You go and enjoy yourself."

"Are you positive? I can cancel. I'm certain Brian would understand."

"Oh, no, go and have fun. I'll figure a way out of this mess. I need some time to think it through."

"You promise to be careful."

"Please don't be concerned about me. I know what I'm doing."

"I hope you're right." Robbie paused for a second, disconcerted. "Are you working tonight?"

Vanessa propped her head on her left hand. "Yes. I should be home at my usual time. I'll call if I'm going to be late. Now get out of here and have a great time. Is he cute?"

Robbie had a sparkle in her eyes. "Yes, he is. I'll see you later."

Vanessa said goodbye, and Robbie returned to the living room, where she found Brian sitting on the sofa, flipping through the pages of an *Architectural Digest* magazine. He glanced up as she came toward him. "Did you design this house?" he asked.

"No," she said, "but I did have my fingers in a lot of the construction."

"It's nice. I've done some remodeling of my own cabin. It's

not this grand, but I've put in a new kitchen and bathrooms. I've been working on a redwood deck, but as of late, I never seem to find the time or inclination to finish the job."

Robbie put on a jacket. "Shall we go? We don't want to miss the boat." She picked up her purse from the armoire.

"We should have smooth sailing. It's a glorious day."

Before they left the house, Brian watched as Robbie made sure all the doors were locked and secure. When she was satisfied they were, the two buckled into Brian's truck and drove toward the marina. During the ride, they exchanged a few words, but Robbie was a bit distant. Brian expected she'd relax when they were on the water.

The *Sierra Queen* was an old tour boat built to resemble a Mississippi paddle-wheeler. The *Queen* had at one time navigated the mighty river. Decades ago, the owners of the ship had taken it apart, transported it to Lake Tahoe, and reassembled it. In the last few years, it had changed hands several times and was showing its age. Brian would've preferred to cruise the lake in one of the newer ships, but they were all booked up. They both agreed the view of Lake Tahoe was spectacular despite the vessel, so they boarded the *Sierra Queen*.

The weather was warmer than usual for this time of the year, and Robbie and Brian selected seats on the top deck. The boat left the dock with the large white paddlewheel slapping against the clear blue water of the lake. They leaned back and enjoyed the panorama as the *Sierra Queen* began her twice-daily voyage across Lake Tahoe to Emerald Bay.

They sat in silence, for the most part, taking in the beauty of their surroundings. After a period devoid of conversation for so long it was awkward, he turned to her. "You've been quiet," he said. "I hope I'm not boring you."

Robbie's tone was apologetic. "Oh, Brian, I'm sorry. It's not you at all. I doubt you could ever be boring. I'm having a great time, but I've been preoccupied by thoughts of Vanessa, my roommate. She's in trouble, and I'm worried about her."

"If you don't mind my asking, what's the problem?"

"This is going to sound crazy, but believe it or not, she says she's caught up in something illegal. That's all she'll say, though. She won't give me any further explanation. Maybe you know her—she's employed at the Charleston Resort."

This piqued Brian's interest, and his eyes narrowed. "What's Vanessa's last name?"

"Daine. Vanessa Daine." She gave him an expectant look.

He shook his head. "No. Doesn't sound familiar, but we have thousands of employees. What does she do at the resort?"

"I'm not sure. She watches video screens in some type of security capacity."

Brian's eyebrows inched higher. "Surveillance?"

"Yeah, that's it—she works in the Surveillance Department."

His pulse quickened. "How long's she worked there?"

"Oh, about a year, I guess. She was a clerk in the accounting office at first, then transferred to the Surveillance Department. She doesn't like her hours, but I know the money's great. Anyway, the one thing I do know is whatever nefarious activity she's mixed up in, this guy she's been seeing's behind it."

"Tell me about him. Does he also have a job at the Charleston?"

"I don't know. She doesn't talk about him very often. I do know he's abusive. He's been hitting her, and I think she's had enough."

"Some strange things have been happening at the Charleston. I wonder if this could be connected."

Robbie's brow furrowed. "Strange? What kind?"

"It's complicated, and I don't want to bore you with all the details, but we believe there's a conspiracy to steal money from the table games. Jack Mancini and I have been making a quiet investigation into the possibility." It might not have been the smartest move, but Brian found himself telling her all he knew about the low hold percentage at the casino. He detailed his tour of the cashier's cage, the soft count room, and the Surveillance Department. He'd only just met her, but she was Hailey's friend and there was something about her. Something trustworthy. "The security in the casino's tight."

Robbie sounded troubled when she asked, "I know this is a stretch, but do you suppose Vanessa could be involved?"

He stroked his chin with a thumb and finger. "I guess it's possible. The only way someone could be stealing money from the count room is with the cooperation of someone in the Surveillance Department. What shift does she work?"

"The late one. She goes to work at eleven at night and is off at eight in the morning."

"It could be a coincidence, but I must talk with her."

"I'm concerned about her, and if you can find out what's going on, I'd be grateful."

"Maybe she can help us piece together this puzzle." Suddenly realizing they'd spent nearly the whole trip talking shop, he said, "Hey, enough of this. We're here to have a good time and get our minds off our problems. We're almost to Emerald Bay. Let's go up to the bow and see the Vikingsholm."

Brian took Robbie by the hand, and they wound their way to the front of the boat as the paddle-wheeler floated into Emerald Bay. It was one of the scenic wonders of the world. Carved by glaciers millions of years ago, it was surrounded by huge granite mountains, the water from Eagle Falls cascading down from high above the bay.

Over the loudspeaker, the captain of the *Sierra Queen* told the passengers about the history of the area and one of its unique features—the Vikingsholm. An irritating buzz periodically came from the amplifier while he spoke. "The Vikingsholm was built in the early nineteen-twenties by a wealthy woman named Lora Knight. She fell in love with the spot and decided it would be the perfect place for a summer home...*Bzzzz*. The location reminded her of the Scandinavian fjords, so she built a Viking manor. It took years for the workmen to handcraft the mansion. Shipping the building materials to the remote location was an arduous task...*Bzzzz*.

"For years after the home was completed, Mrs. Knight wined and dined the rich and powerful people of the day. After her death, it was sold by her heirs and passed from owner to owner until nineteen-fifty-three, when it was donated to the state of California...*Bzzzz*. The state transformed the magnificent estate and surrounding area into a park."

The *Sierra Queen* chugged around Fannette Island in the center of the bay. A tea house, used by the original owner to entertain visitors, sat high atop the tiny island.

The paddleboat made a loop through Emerald Bay and traveled back into the lake, en route to its dock in the city of South Lake Tahoe. It was turning cold, and Brian and Robbie purchased some hot beverages and found a cozy table inside the lounge. "We're so lucky to live here," Robbie said, sipping her steaming latte and staring out a window at the pristine lake as a cabin cruiser whizzed alongside the paddleboat, then sped away.

The excursion ended too soon for both of them, and they decided to eat a late lunch. After disembarking the *Sierra Queen*, they drove northwest to the town of Tahoma and the Chamber's Landing Restaurant. Their conversation was full of laughter as they got to know each other a bit better. Not once during their meal did they mention Vanessa Daine or the troubles at the Charleston. As the day progressed, Brian realized he wasn't just intrigued by Robbie Taylor, he was quite enamored. He was shocked at feeling this way after a few short hours. This date wasn't going as he'd expected.

The afternoon flew by, and Brian took her home a little before five o'clock. Robbie checked on her roommate and found Vanessa asleep. "I don't want to wake her," she said to Brian after coming back to the living room. "She needs the rest."

He was seated on the sofa. "Okay, but if you don't mind, I'll stop here on my way to work tomorrow morning. I'd still like to speak with her and see what she has to say."

"She gets home around eight-thirty."

Brian stood and walked toward the front door. "I had a great time today."

Robbie ran her fingers through her hair and followed him. "So did I. Don't take this wrong, but I wasn't sure I would."

His eyes glimmered. "In truth, me either, but I'm glad we went out and spent some time together. How about dinner tomorrow night? Let's see if we can tolerate each other's company two days in a row."

"That would be nice. I know of a great new restaurant in Incline Village."

"I'm always searching for good places to eat." Brian took Robbie into his arms and kissed her. She seemed to enjoy it, and he felt his heart miss a beat. He stepped back and looked at her. She blushed. Brian leaned over and gave her one more kiss. "I'll see you tomorrow," he said in a whisper.

She gave him a toothy smile.

Robbie accompanied him to the front porch. Half way to his truck, Brian turned around to see if she was still standing there. She was, and the grin on his face grew even bigger.

After Brian drove off, Robbie entered her house. Given the excitement of the day, she was tired and intended to turn in early.

NINE

VANESSA WEAVED THROUGH the casino to the booth next to the cashier's cage and looked at the guard. "Good evening, Gordon," she said. "I'm ready for another exciting night of staring at video screens."

The guard handed her the access log. He said with a laugh, "I bet you guys in the Surveillance Department are watching *I Love Lucy* reruns."

Vanessa chuckled. "Yeah, maybe tonight I can find some original programming." She gave him the completed log. A buzzer blared, and she opened the heavy door, secured her purse in her locker, and passed through the labyrinth of hallways.

Once in the surveillance room, Vanessa settled into her workstation and surveyed the video monitors as the action in the casino flickered back at her. She was mesmerized by the images moving in and out of the screens. Soon enough, though, she was no longer absorbed by the video. Instead, over and over in her mind, she rehearsed her plan for getting out of this dreadful ordeal.

The phone at her workstation rang, and she could feel her pulse accelerate. She trembled while picking it up. "Surveillance," she said.

"Vanessa, pretty baby," Hatrix said, "I'm glad to see you're at work and ready for another profitable night."

Vanessa said nothing and closed her eyes.

"I'm on schedule. I'll be ready to go at two-thirty."

"I'll be set."

"That's my girl. I have a feeling it'll be a great night. I'm certain the boss will be happy with the results."

Vanessa said through clenched teeth, "I don't want to talk about him." She hung up the phone, and her hands continued to shake.

"Are you all right?" Larry, the obese man sitting next to her, asked.

Vanessa faced him. "Yes, I'm just having man problems."

"You know the old cliché—you can't live with them and you can't live without."

"You have that right, but I'm going to try it alone."

He gave her a devilish grin, his eyes twinkling. "You can always stay with me."

She wagged a finger at the man she'd nicknamed *Larry the Lecher*. "You behave yourself."

At two o'clock, Vanessa stood up from her workstation and took a couple paces to the back of the surveillance room. She pulled coiled cables from her pocket, and with the confidence of a skilled technician, attached them to two of the DVRs, connecting the cables to two other DVRs on the adjoining shelf.

"Do you need any help?" Larry asked. He was standing right behind her.

Vanessa was so startled she jumped. "No, no, I'm fine," she said, trying to maintain her composure. "I'm making a double loop of the soft count room. I need to get two recordings of tomorrow morning's count."

"What for?" His tone was curious.

"The Gaming Control Board needs one for their annual

audit. The Finance Department left a note asking me to record two copies of the soft count for my special projects. One for us and the other for the GCB."

"You're sure I can't give you a hand?"

"No, I have it. Thanks anyway."

"You know I'm here if you need me." Larry waddled back to his workstation.

Watching him sit down in the chair, Vanessa wasn't sure her heart rate would ever return to normal. Regardless, she was proud of herself for making up a plausible response to his inquiries. She was lucky he wasn't really paying attention—it was only believable because he wasn't thinking it through. A copy of the digital recording could be made at any time with the click of a mouse.

Vanessa noted the time on one of the monitors. It was two-fifteen. Hatrix would be ready to take the elevator in fifteen minutes. She needed to hurry. She took the two prerecorded memory cards showing the empty elevator and the unoccupied soft count room and inserted them in the proper DVRs. She pressed the play buttons and glanced at the monitors. As expected, both of the areas now looked vacant.

Vanessa placed two new memory cards in the DVRs connected through the cable loop. Instead of pushing the play buttons, she hit record. The machines hummed, recording what was happening in the elevator and the soft count room. Because she'd put the double cable loop between the DVRs, only the prerecorded pictures appeared on the monitors while the other two DVRs recorded the real action in secret.

Vanessa returned to her workstation and again examined the monitors. She switched off the cameras in the hallways to the elevator and soft count room and sighed. The whir of the machines could be heard behind her, and she turned to look at the DVRs, knowing they would soon be capturing the criminal activities in the count room.

Her trap was now set. She hoped it would work. Her plan was to record the thefts in the soft count room and tell her cohorts about the videos. She'd inform them it was over—she was going back to Ohio. The videos were her insurance policy, guaranteeing they'd let her leave in peace. If they attempted to stop her or tried to make her continue as an accomplice, she'd call the authorities and blow the whole scheme wide open.

They could find a new girl if they wanted, but they'd leave her alone. Vanessa felt optimistic as she thought about her plan. She'd go to Ohio and start a new life.

At two-thirty sharp, her telephone rang, and she picked up the receiver.

"It's showtime, pretty baby," Hatrix said. "Send the elevator—I'm ready to go."

Vanessa engaged the elevator control and hung up the phone.

HATRIX ENTERED THE elevator and poked the basement button on the panel. The doors closed, and the car descended one floor. He pulled a hood over his head before entering the hallway. The hood might have been unnecessary, but he wore it in case something went wrong and someone in the Surveillance Department saw him. When the elevator doors glided open, he barreled down the hallway to the soft count door. After unlocking it, he ducked into the room and began his late-night ritual of undetected larceny.

Hatrix opened the drop boxes and extracted the hundred-dollar bills from inside, ignoring the lesser denominations and fill slips. He labored with ease as the small red light on the video camera in the corner of the room blinked.

VANESSA STARED AT the soft count room on the monitor. Her

fingers were crossed as she hoped the DVRs were functioning as they should and Hatrix was being recorded. A bead of perspiration trickled down her neck, but she smiled at Larry while he conversed on the phone with the pit supervisor in the casino.

HATRIX WORKED AS fast as he could, with the confidence he'd gained over the last nine months. The pit drop from the previous day was large and their take for the night would be substantial. "Thank you, TV star Skip Sullivan," he said aloud.

Almost an hour later, he locked up the last drop box, put it back on the shelf, and sealed the cabinet. He made his survey of the room, saw that everything was in its proper position, and slipped out the door. He hustled down the hallway and lifted the telephone from the wall.

"Surveillance," a man said.

"Vanessa Daine, please," Hatrix said, unhappy she hadn't answered. He tapped his foot while waiting. When she came on the line, he asked, "Damn it, Vanessa, why didn't you pick up the phone?"

"I couldn't," she said. "I was busy with another problem." There was sarcasm in her voice. "I do have a job to do."

Hatrix lightened his tone. "We had a good night. The drop was terrific."

"Great." She was clearly trying to sound enthusiastic. "Marcus, I need to see you after my shift. Why don't you meet me at the Lone Pine Motel at eight-thirty?"

"Sure, pretty baby. I've never received that invitation before. It's nice you're coming around to my way of thinking. Bring a sexy negligee."

"Just be there. I need to talk with you."

"Do you want me to bring the champagne?" The phone line

clicked off, and the doors to the elevator rumbled open. Hatrix shrugged, hung up the phone, and stepped into the car. After reaching the first floor, he deposited the money bag in Vanessa's locker and walked into the casino.

VANESSA HELD THE receiver of the telephone for a moment before hanging up. Her disgust of Hatrix was overpowering. She crossed to the back of the room. With haste, she shut down the DVRs and removed the connecting cables. She took the two prerecorded memory cards and put them into their appropriate place in the storage area.

Vanessa grabbed the cards she hoped would show Hatrix committing his crime and laid them on the table in the video library. She sat in front of a monitor, put one of the cards in a DVR, and pressed the play button. The machine emitted a whirring sound as the file was located, and she waited with anxious anticipation. The screen faced away from her co-workers, so she didn't worry about them seeing the video. The picture flickered in front of her, the time and date illuminated in the right-hand corner. The monitor showed the unoccupied soft count room. She hit the fast-forward button, and the images flashed by. When she saw a change in movement, she switched the video back to normal speed.

Vanessa could see Hatrix walk into the soft count room and begin to open the drop boxes. The hood concealed his face, but she could see how intent he was in harvesting the money. She watched in amazement as he seized the bills and lined them up in neat rows on the table. She tapped the stop button and ejected the memory card.

Inserting the second one in the DVR, Vanessa pushed the play button and saw Hatrix enter the elevator and pull the hood over his head. She watched him exit the car on the basement floor. Again, she halted the DVR and ejected the card. She hopped up from the table and took a *Special Projects* binder from the shelf. She flipped the pages to the last entry, which was number 3015, took a pen out of her pocket, and made two entries—3016 and 3017—with the description: *Thomas*. She wrote the location code on the labels of each of the memory cards and put them in the video library. She placed the binder back on the shelf and returned to her workstation. For the first time all night, she was able to relax. Vanessa was now confident her nightmare was coming to an end.

THE CLOCK SEEMED to tick backwards while Vanessa waited for her shift to finish. She wanted to leave this casino and her life at Lake Tahoe as soon as she could. Nothing would deter her. She thought of Robbie and realized she wouldn't have a chance to say goodbye to her roommate. She pulled out the keyboard on the computer to her left and logged on-to the internet, opened an email program, and typed:

> *Robbie,*
> *I regret I cannot say goodbye to you in person, but I must leave Tahoe as fast as possible. I'll call you with my new address when I know it. You've been my one true friend at the lake, and I'll miss you. The problems I've gotten myself into can only be remedied if I leave, so that's what I'm going to do. A month's rent and money for a moving company are on the armoire in the living room. I hope it's enough. I apologize for my messy room. There was no time to clean up.*
> *I believe I'm making the right decision. I've taken some steps to ensure they leave me alone, leaving a life insurance policy in the form of two video memory cards. They should keep me protected.*

Vanessa stopped for a second and contemplated what she was doing. Would they let her leave Lake Tahoe in peace? *Yes*, she thought, when she told them about the recordings. She started typing again:

I know this sounds paranoid, but you must understand how precarious my life's become.

Again, I'm sorry for leaving without saying goodbye. Please forgive me. Wish me luck.

Your friend, Vanessa.

Vanessa typed in Robbie's email address, clicked send, and watched the computer launch the message. She closed down the email program and waited for her shift to drag to a conclusion. At eight o'clock, she departed the surveillance room and boarded the elevator. On the first floor, she moved through the network of hallways to the alcove containing the purse cabinet. She opened her locker, stuffed the leather bag containing the night's thefts into her purse, and turned in the key. After entering the casino, she stopped at the security booth to sign out.

"How was your night?" the guard asked.

Vanessa smiled at him. "It was okay. Tomorrow will be even better. It's my day off."

"Enjoy yourself."

"I will, Harry. You take care." Handing him the access log, Vanessa realized she wouldn't see him again. By this time tomorrow morning, she'd be half-way to Ohio. She could feel the excitement, knowing the disaster that had become her world would be ending. *She'd start all over again,* she thought as she walked out of the casino to her Honda. She opened the door and slid in.

Vanessa unzipped the leather bag and grabbed a handful of currency. Hatrix would never know. After taking enough money for her trip, she started the car and drove down Highway 50.

VANESSA TURNED INTO the Lone Pine Motel's parking lot and spotted Hatrix's sports car. The motel was located about ten miles out of town and was a popular spot for couples seeking a place for a discreet afternoon rendezvous. She'd always looked forward to visiting the Lone Pine in the past, but not anymore. It reminded her of the love she'd lost.

Vanessa parked next to Hatrix's vehicle and raced to room eight. She knocked on the door, and a moment later, Hatrix opened it. He said, "It's my favorite pretty baby, bringing me gifts."

Vanessa threw the leather bag on the table without saying a word. Hatrix picked it up and emptied the bag's contents on the bed. He took a handful of the bills and flung them into the air, yelping with joy. "It's raining money, Vanessa," he said. "I can't believe how easy this is. We're making millions, and no one will ever know. It's the perfect crime."

Vanessa turned and stared at him, taking a full breath before speaking. "You'll have to find another girl for your little operation. Tonight was my last night. I'm not going back to the Charleston again."

Hatrix's face became pale, then red with fury. "It's over when we say it is. I thought I made my point the other night."

"Why don't you leave me alone? You can find someone to replace me."

"I don't know if we could ever get all the pieces in place again. I'm sorry to disappoint you, but we have you in the surveillance room and nothing's changing that." Hatrix stormed up to her and clamped a meaty hand around her left arm. "Do I need to make myself any clearer?"

Terrified by his harsh expression, Vanessa tried to compose her thoughts. "It's over, Marcus. I have a recording of you in action. If you don't leave me alone, I'll expose everything."

Hatrix raised his voice. "What recording?"

"A digital one. On a memory card. Last night, I recorded your activities in the soft count room. Let me go back to Ohio, and you'll never hear from me again. Otherwise, you're going to jail."

He snatched her purse and dumped out all the contents.

"I'm not stupid enough to bring the video with me. The memory card's in a nice safe place."

Hatrix didn't know what to do. He had to think but couldn't. "I...I don't believe you. You're m-m-making this up."

"Try me," she said, projecting as much confidence as she could.

"You won't say anything with a bullet in your head."

Vanessa's eyes widened. "I've told a friend about the memory card." It was an unfortunate lie. Her stomach tightened at the realization that she should've told Robbie the location of the videos before confronting Hatrix. Her overwhelming desire to flee Lake Tahoe had clouded her judgment. Now she had to bluff. "If I'm harmed in any way, she'll call the authorities."

Confused, Hatrix glared at her. "Damn you. We have a great thing going. Why do you want it to end?"

"He used me, and you know it. I'm tired of living in fear, and I want to get as far away from him as possible."

Hatrix dashed over to the nightstand and picked up the telephone. He glowered at her while dialing.

Vanessa stared back at him, wishing she hadn't confronted him in person. She wondered if she could bolt for the door and escape. She pursed her lips, knowing that he could easily block her exit.

"It's me," Hatrix said into the mouthpiece after the phone was answered. "We have a problem." Hatrix explained the situation to the man on the other end of the line. He listened. "We can't do that," Hatrix shouted. "Vanessa told a friend about the recording. She'll go to the sheriff if anything happens to her." Hatrix eyed her with disdain and concentrated on the phone. "Okay, I'll do it. I'll see you later this morning."

Hatrix hung up and looked at her, angrier than ever. "I'm sorry, pretty baby," he said, "but as you'd expect, he's not happy.

He's not letting you go to Ohio." He stuffed the money on the bed into the bag.

Vanessa glared at him. "It's not his decision."

"He wants to meet with you."

"He won't change my mind."

Hatrix finished tucking the bills into the bag, zipped it up, and stepped over to her. Again, he latched on-to an arm. "We need some time to work this out. We're going for a ride."

"No way. If you let me go, it'll be fine. I'll leave Tahoe, and you'll never see me again."

"We can't take the risk. How long until you decide to blackmail us?"

"I won't, Marcus." Tears formed in her eyes.

"It's not my decision." Hatrix grabbed the back of her neck and pushed her out of the motel room and to his car. He opened the passenger door and ordered her to get in. Tears poured down Vanessa's face, and she did what she was told.

TEN

BRIAN ARRIVED AT Robbie's home a little after eight-thirty in the morning. It was bitter cold and windy. It was remarkable how fast the weather had changed from the previous day. The forecasters were now predicting that the first winter storm of the year was blowing toward Lake Tahoe. Walking up to the front porch, he clasped his jacket close around his neck to shield himself from the frigid breeze. He rang the bell and waited a moment before Robbie opened the front door. She motioned for him to enter the house. A fire was blazing in the hearth, and he welcomed the warmth.

Robbie shut the door and clutched her shoulders with a shiver. "Oh, it's getting cold out," she said. She was wearing a dark-blue business dress, but the conservative cut of the outfit didn't diminish her femininity.

Brian reached out and pulled her close. He kissed her. *She had such soft lips*, he thought.

Robbie offered him a warm smile.

"Is your roommate here?" he asked.

Robbie wrinkled her nose. "No. She isn't home yet, and I don't know if I should be worried or not. She doesn't work tonight, so maybe she's out with a few of her co-workers for a drink or something. Are you in a hurry?"

"I have a few minutes." Brian checked the time on his watch.

"I'm sure she'll be home anytime. Come into the kitchen, I just made some coffee." Robbie led Brian through the living room and into the kitchen. The room was large with a high-beamed ceiling. Rows of picture windows lined the walls, and from each one, there was a breathtaking view of Lake Tahoe. In the center of the kitchen was an island with a stove, large copper pots hanging above it. She poured two cups of hot coffee and handed a mug to Brian. He inhaled the aroma and took a sip. "This is delicious," he said.

They lingered over a couple of cups until Brian knew he couldn't wait any longer. He had to get to work. "I wish I could stay," he said. "But I have a busy day ahead of me. When you hear from Vanessa, I'd appreciate it if you'd ask her if she'd be willing to speak with me. I can arrange my schedule at her convenience. It's important I talk with her. We need to know what's happening at the Charleston, and she may be able to provide some insight."

Robbie drank her coffee. "She did tell me she'd call if she was going to be late."

"How often does she have a drink after work?"

"Once in a while. I know she works graveyard, but it always strikes me as funny when she gets off-shift at eight in the morning and goes to a bar."

"I know, but graveyard workers are forced to live a different lifestyle. Robbie, I forgot to ask you yesterday—what are Vanessa's days off?"

"Monday and Tuesday. Does it make a difference?"

He nodded. "Those are the days the Charleston's holding the proper win percentage. It could be a link between Vanessa and our thefts at the casino."

"Oh, no, I can't believe that."

"Until I visit with her, it's something we should consider."

Robbie rubbed her chin, contemplating what he was saying.

Brian smiled. "I'm looking forward to our dinner tonight. What time do you want me to pick you up?"

Her eyes gleamed. "I'm getting off work at five. How about around six-thirty? That'll give me a chance to freshen up."

Brian stared at her with lust in his eyes. He couldn't imagine her ever needing to freshen up. She could be wearing overalls and cleaning a grease trap and still be stunning. He put his arms around her and kissed her, peering into her eyes. He wasn't sure he'd ever felt like this before and was surprised.

Robbie followed him to the front of the house. "You have a good day," she said.

Brian opened the door. "You too." He smiled at her one last time and headed for his truck.

Ten minutes later, briefcase in hand, Robbie left her home and drove to her job as the foreman for the largest construction company in Douglas County.

A TEAR STREAMED down Vanessa's face where she lay gagged and bound on the bed. The duct tape used to confine her hands and feet was too tight, and she could feel her extremities numbing. She tried to scream, but the gag stifled her attempts. She lay there in the dark, praying for help.

HATRIX WAS WATCHING a women's wrestling competition on a cable channel. He would've bet on the outcome if he'd had the chance. He took a hefty pull from his beer and looked over at the door of the room where Vanessa was. He didn't have any idea what they were going to do with her.

BEATRICE WAS, AS usual, on the telephone. "Have you met him yet?" she asked. "I can't believe he hit her. If I were her, I'd have been long gone. No man would ever beat me."

Brian waved to her as he walked into his office, but Beatrice didn't seem to notice. She was too engrossed with her phone call. He wondered if she knew Vanessa Daine and planned to ask when he had a chance.

Brian sat in his desk chair and reviewed the day's agenda. He had a busy schedule—meetings with the convention authority, a billboard company, and a conference call with the agent for last year's country music Grammy winner. The singer was spending Christmas at Lake Tahoe and was staying at the Charleston Resort. Brian wanted to see if he could persuade the superstar to do a few shows. He knew the high rollers would love a concert from the popular singer.

After a quick knock on the door, Alice MacKay swept into his office with a recap of the weekend's events. Business volumes created by the slot tournament were excellent, and she told him about the play of a few of the VIPs. They discussed the special events agenda for the week and conferred more about Wednesday's budget presentation with Montgomery. Brian told her about his idea of using the winners' surveillance videos in television commercials. Alice thought the concept was great and said she'd get the project rolling with the advertising agency. He gave her the memory cards he'd obtained from the Surveillance Department, and she returned to her office.

The morning sped by as Brian focused on being the Director of Marketing for the large hotel/casino. Soon after lunch, Beatrice poked her head into his office and informed him a Robbie Taylor was on the phone. She gave him the look she always did when a woman she didn't know was on his line. Brian shot the look right back and waited for her to leave the room before picking up the receiver. "Hi, Robbie," he said.

"Do you have a minute?" she asked.

"For you, of course. Did you speak with Vanessa?"

"No. I've been trying to reach her all morning, but there's no answer. Her smartphone goes to voicemail. I hope nothing's wrong."

"You said she doesn't work tonight. She could be out with friends."

"I guess that's true. She has one who's employed as a hotel operator, and they hang out frequently. They both enjoy shopping. Her name's Charlene, Shelly, something like that."

"How about Sheila? We have an operator named Sheila."

"She's about twenty-five with long black hair, slender."

"Yep, Sheila. I'll give her a ring and find out what she knows."

"I'll keep calling home and her iPhone. Vanessa has to show up sometime."

"If I don't hear from you before then, I'll see you tonight."

"Jonathan has a nice quiet table reserved for us."

His tone was quizzical. "Jonathan?"

"Yes, he's my friend who owns the restaurant."

"Oh, sure. Over in Incline. I can't wait to be with you." Brian couldn't believe he'd just said that with such vigor—or that he meant it for any other reason but sex.

"You have a good afternoon."

Brian hung up the phone. His heart was light, a feeling he realized he had every time he talked with Robbie.

BRIAN PICKED UP the telephone and hit zero.

"Operator," the woman said.

"May I speak with Sheila?" he asked.

"I'm sorry, Sheila's not working today."

"When will she be back?"

"She's taking an extra day off. She'll be here Thursday morning."

"Okay, thanks." Brian hung up and considered his situation. He didn't have Sheila's mobile number. That was hard to believe, considering how many times she'd given it to him.

Brian pressed the buzzer on his phone console and asked Beatrice to come into his office. Moments later, his secretary lumbered into the room carrying a notepad and pen. She wore a green print patterned dress that seemed to accentuate her girth. Her gray hair was up in a bun that wasn't becoming.

"The notepad's unnecessary," Brian said. "I want to visit."

She gave him a twisted grin. "Visit? Ha. You're planning to pump me for information, right?"

"I don't want to do that," he said in a tone of mock disbelief. "But everyone knows if they hope to find out what's happening at the Charleston, you're the one to ask."

Brian knew he had to be careful. While he intended to find out more about Vanessa Daine, he knew anything he said to Beatrice would be out on the casino grapevine ten minutes after she left his office.

"What do you need to know?" she asked, pulling up a chair.

Brian said, "I want the skinny on someone who's employed here. Vanessa Daine. She works in the Surveillance Department."

"Oh, I know her," Beatrice said in a tone of total contempt. "She used to be a clerk in the Finance Department. I don't like her much. Says she has this rich boyfriend. She's always bragging about how much money he has and how he's spending it on her."

"Do you know him?"

"No, I never met the guy. I find Vanessa snobbish, so I don't socialize with her. Mabel, down in the coffee shop, says she saw her with an attractive older man once, but what does she know? Mable can't see ten feet. She's blind without her glasses and too vain to wear them. She said he was distinguished, but Mabel has terrible taste. Have you ever seen her husband?"

Irritated, Brian frowned. "No, I don't believe so. Tell me more about Vanessa and her boyfriend."

Beatrice scooted forward in the chair. "I hear they had a huge argument. I saw her the other morning, and she had a bruise on her cheek. She tried to cover it with makeup, but I could see the swelling."

Brian patted his chin with his left hand. "Hmm, interesting."

"You know," Beatrice said, leaning toward him even more and speaking in a whisper, "the speculation in the secretarial pool is that her boyfriend's a married man. Why else would she keep him a secret? She never goes out with him in public. She's always telling everyone he's working or out of town, but I have my doubts."

Brian drummed fingers on the desk. "I need to talk with Vanessa. Would you see if you can track her down?"

"Sure, Brian, I'll try. It may take me a while, though. I hope you don't mind if I'm on the telephone a bit."

Brian wondered how she could spend any more time on the phone than she already did. "Not a problem. Thanks, Beatrice, I appreciate it. Let me know when you find her."

Beatrice rose from the chair and paraded back to her desk in the outer office. Minutes later, she was on the line, chatting away.

Brian sifted through the pile of papers on his desk. He had a lot of work to do and needed to be careful how he managed his time. He didn't want to be late for what was becoming a highly anticipated date with Robbie.

BRIAN WAS EDITING magazine advertising copy when Jack Mancini burst through the doorway. Mancini had a grin on his face and was humming.

Brian glanced up, laughed, and said, "This is a change. You're in a good mood. How come?"

"What the hell do you mean?" Jack asked. "I'm always in a fine spirits."

"As of late, I don't think anyone around here would agree."

"My visit to the locksmith in Reno was informative." Jack returned to the door and closed it. "As we discussed before, the security keys used here are all special-made." He sat in the chair in front of Brian's desk, adjusted his tie, and brushed some lint off his jacket. "Boy it sure is cold out today."

Brian hurled an eraser at him. "Get to the goddamned point. What did you find out from the locksmith?"

Jack smiled. "The one who did the keys for the Charleston wasn't talkative at first, but I ratcheted up my charm and promised him a few things. Then he chattered nonstop. It turns out all of the high security keys and locks are made in Reno and shipped up to the lake in an armored car."

"Who orders them?"

"The locksmith will only make and deliver a key and lock with the authorization of Montgomery."

"An obvious choice—he is the general manager."

"Key security is tight. The locksmith has special molds that are destroyed after they're used. Fabricating a replica's impossible. The design's unique, and special tools are required."

"So we're at a dead end. If a duplicate can't be made, how could anyone possess a copy and use it to enter the count room?"

"A copy wasn't necessary."

The lines on Brian's forehead glided up.

His cheeks ruddy, Jack rubbed his hands together. "In the past, the Charleston always ordered four keys at a time for each of the different high security locks. But in the last order for new locks, they requested five drop box, cabinet, and count room keys. Montgomery signed the P.O. for the new locks and extra keys last December. That's right before the low hold percentage problem began."

"Did the locksmith know why they wanted five sets of keys?"

"Yeah, he says it's not unusual for additional sets to be

requested by a casino. It's the norm. Most casinos keep spares on hand in case one of the keys breaks."

"Were all five sets delivered to the casino?"

"The locksmith shipped five sets of keys and the locks to the Charleston by armored car. He showed me the invoice from Brinks. I'm going to have to do more investigating to see where they landed once they were delivered."

Brian pounded his fist on the desk. "I've been thinking more about Elliot Thomas. Something about his demeanor bothers me, and it's not just that he's an asshole."

"I know, but I may be prejudiced. I've never liked the guy. How would he do it, though? How could he get the money out of the soft count room without being seen? He'd need accomplices. He couldn't just walk into the count room and take the cash. The people in the surveillance room would see him."

Brian let his satisfaction show as he leaned back in his chair. "Well, listen to this. I may know of someone who works in the Surveillance Department who could be in on this."

Jack's voice edged up. "Who?"

"Hailey's friend, Robbie Taylor? Her roommate's employed in the Surveillance Department on the graveyard shift. She has Mondays and Tuesdays off." Brian related everything Robbie had told him about Vanessa Daine. "With all this new information, do you think it's time we visited with Cory about this?"

"Let's wait a little longer. All we have is speculation and a few trails so far leading nowhere specific. Let's find out who took delivery of the drop box keys first, and then we'll speak with the Gaming Control Board. If Elliot Thomas is behind this, we have problems. It could get messy."

Brian's eyes drilled into Jack's. "I agree. Thomas is a powerful man in this company. He has Montgomery's ear. The wrong move could cost us both our jobs…or worse, I guess."

"It's the 'worse' that concerns me the most. We're talking

about a lot of money, Brian. Millions. If Thomas is involved, who knows what he'd do to protect himself. In the meantime, he's already setting the stage for my departure. That snake, Keith Wallace, has been transferred to my department. He's worked as a security supervisor in the past and is a protégé of Thomas.

"Thomas convinced Montgomery to put him in my department, and despite my protests, he agreed. Elliot Thomas would love to take control of the casino, and putting Wallace there gives him an information source. Wallace is a real rat, and he'll do whatever Thomas asks. The bottom line is, I'm screwed."

"More reason to be careful."

Jack bowed his head and fidgeted with his wedding ring. "By the way, I need to get a couple of people into Skip Sullivan's dressing room after the show Wednesday night. Autographs and pictures."

"Sullivan hasn't been too cooperative."

Jack looked up. "Come on, Brian, you have to get them to meet Sullivan. They're fans."

"I'll try. Are they staying in the hotel?"

"Yes, the Emerald Bay Suite."

"Must be big players."

"No, locksmiths." Jack smirked at him, stood, and ambled out of the room.

ELEVEN

THE GOLD MERCEDES turned into the driveway of Hatrix's home. The silver-haired man exited the car, advanced to the front entrance, and rang the bell. He was wearing a dark suit and a full-length leather coat with a fur trim.

After a short wait, Hatrix opened the door. "Boss, where've you been?" he asked. "I expected to hear from you hours ago."

The man waved a dismissive hand and entered the house. "I've had a hectic day."

"This isn't a social visit. We have big problems. Vanessa's tied up in my bedroom. She's threatened to go to the sheriff. What are we going to do?"

The man's face was taut. "Calm down. Let me talk some sense into her. I'm confident I can reason with her."

Worry wrinkles had formed around Hatrix's lips. "I don't think so, boss—she wants out. She hates you for sleeping with another chick."

"What did she expect? I'm a married man."

Hatrix snapped, his anger climbing, "It's not your wife she's upset about, and you know it." "Your little fling's cost us the whole operation. Millions of bucks."

"I don't need a lecture from you." The man thrust an index

finger against Hatrix's chest. "I've made you a great deal of money already. Don't you ever raise your voice to me again. Is that clear?"

"Yes, sir." Hatrix gave a submissive nod of his head.

"Where is she?"

"In the bedroom. The first door on the left." He pointed to the hallway.

"Stay here." The man trudged down the hall and into the bedroom. Vanessa lay on the bed, her arms behind her back. She eyed him with fear as he approached. He walked over to her, took the gag out of her mouth, and unwrapped the tape from her wrists. "I'm sorry, darling," he said with sugary inflection. "That ass, Hatrix, has no class. I'm very unhappy he did this to you. He wasn't supposed to tie you up. I just wanted a meeting."

Vanessa didn't speak and rubbed her sticky wrists.

"Now, what's this business about you going back to Ohio?"

With trembling hands, she wiped away tears and the mascara running down her cheeks.

He touched her shoulder. "Please, honey, speak to me. Don't give up everything we have."

Vanessa was incensed, and it showed on her face. "We have nothing. I'm going home to Ohio, and I have no desire to see you again."

"Vanessa, baby, what are you talking about? We have a great life. Remember our little house in the Bahamas?"

"Don't say that to me again, you son of a bitch. I know the truth. How stupid do you think I am? Do you believe I'm so dumb I'll let you string me along? It's over, and I have a video recording saying it is."

The man scowled at her, and his pleasant facade disappeared. "I don't like being threatened."

"It's not a threat. I'm leaving for Ohio, and you'll never hear from me again."

"Where's the recording?" His manner was cold, his upper lip curled.

"In a safe place. My friend's been instructed to call the sheriff if you lay a finger on me." Vanessa started to get up from the bed, but he slapped her face with the back of his left hand before she could. She cried out, the force of the blow knocking her down. He picked her up and pushed her against a wall, then wrapped his fingers around her throat and squeezed. She pounded her fists against his chest, trying to escape.

His expression was grim, his eyes thin slits. "Where's the recording?"

Vanessa shook her head. His hands compressed tighter around her neck, and she gasped for air.

"The memory card, Vanessa, where is it?" He squeezed with more force. She struggled for air. He pressed harder. She kneed him in the groin, and when he recoiled, she darted away from him. Vanessa scrambled over the bed toward the door. He leaped across the bed and grabbed her long hair. She screamed when he pulled her back.

"You're hurting me!"

"Shut up." He wrenched her up off the bed and reached around her neck with his left arm. "I want the video."

Vanessa tried without success to free herself, and he continued to tighten his forearm against her throat. "Stop it," she croaked. "I can't breathe." She kicked him in the shin.

"Goddamn it." Enraged, his face reddened. He jerked his arm up with immense power, the combination of pain and adrenaline giving him greater strength. Vanessa's skin turned blue, and her eyes rolled back. He didn't relax the pressure. She went limp, and when he released her from the chokehold, she slumped to the floor.

The man scrutinized her for a moment—his breathing heavy. She didn't move. He bent over and checked for a pulse.

Finding none, he stood. His hair was in disarray and clothes disheveled. He stepped to the dresser and gazed into the mirror, then retrieved a comb from his jacket and styled his hair. He straightened his tie and strolled out of the bedroom and down the hallway.

As the man strode into the living room, Hatrix jumped up from a chair and looked at him with anxious eyebrows. "What's going on?" he asked, biting his lower lip.

The man answered with eerie calm, "It'll be fine."

"Is she back with us? Will she keep working in the surveillance room?"

"She won't be causing us any more trouble. She's dead."

Hatrix's mouth flew open. He stared at the man in shock. "Dead? You killed her? Oh my god. Why the hell did you do that? You murdered her! How come?"

"I had to," he said with intensity. "Too much is at stake here. Vanessa threatened to expose me, and I'm not willing to accept the risk."

"But take her life? All she wanted to do was to go back to Ohio. Why didn't you let her do that?"

The man asked, indignant, "What would she do there? Work as a waitress? How long do you think it would have been before we received our first blackmail letter? No, it's better this way. Cleaner."

"What about the video? She said her friend will go to the cops if she's harmed."

The man flicked a wrist. "She had to be bluffing. How could she have recorded you in the soft count room without the entire Surveillance Department knowing? You sure as hell weren't seen by anyone or you'd be in jail right now."

"Boss, I'm scared. Maybe Vanessa wasn't lying. What if she did make a recording? Who's this woman who knows about the memory card? Vanessa must have lots of friends and family.

How are we going to explain her disappearance? Even if they don't know about the video they'll wonder about her. Someone will call the sheriff and file a missing person report."

"Let me think. Getting hysterical isn't solving anything. Get hold of yourself."

The man paced around the room, hands in pockets, jacket open, as Hatrix watched and waited in an exaggerated state of nervousness. Sweat trickled down his temples when he thought of the dead woman in the other room.

"We don't need to worry about Vanessa's family," the man said. "Her last remaining relatives were killed in a car accident a couple of years ago. And she didn't have as many friends as you imagine. To her friends and co-workers, we have to make it appear she's left town. I'll call the Charleston and tell the surveillance supervisor she's quitting her job and moving to Ohio."

"Did Vanessa live alone?" Hatrix asked.

"No, she has a roommate. As I recall, she was one of her few friends. If there's a video recording, she'd be the one to know about it."

"What do we tell her?"

The man peered at Hatrix with a somber face. "I'll require your help on that one. Call her and say you're her boyfriend. Explain to her that you and Vanessa are moving to Ohio. Then go over to their house and pick up Vanessa's belongings. See if the memory card she claimed to have is somewhere in her bedroom."

Hatrix's cheeks were turning scarlet. "She'd never believe me, and why do I have to do it? She was your woman."

The man glared at him with squinted eyes. "You know the answer to that."

"Oh, all right. You do understand her roommate will want to talk with Vanessa?"

"Make up some excuse."

"Where does...did Vanessa live?"

"Round Hill area—I'll give you the address. You must be careful. We don't want anyone to become suspicious."

"Her roommate. What if she knows about the video, the memory card? She might not believe me."

The man shook a finger at him. "You have to convince her you're telling the truth. Call her today, before she starts worrying about Vanessa." He lifted a pen and notepad from his jacket pocket. "Here's the telephone number and address." He wrote it out and handed it to Hatrix.

Hatrix examined it. "Okay. What about Vanessa? What do we do with her body?"

The silver-haired man smiled at Hatrix and put an arm around his shoulders. "My boy, there's a great big lake out there. Deep too. You get the picture."

Hatrix held up his hands. "What if she floats ashore?"

"Marcus, are you a total incompetent? Weight the goddamn body down. Make sure she sinks to the bottom. Do it now, before it gets dark. But be cautious—we don't need the Coast Guard poking around."

"I'll be careful—I can guarantee you that. What should I do with her car? It's parked at the Lone Pine Motel."

"Go retrieve it. Do you have room in your garage to store it?"

Hatrix shrugged. "I suppose so."

"Good, we can dispose of it later." The man grabbed his leather coat and took a few strides to the front door.

"How about our operation at the Charleston? When do we find someone to take Vanessa's place?"

The man turned to him. "Greedy bastard, aren't you? Vanessa's body isn't even cold, and you're already thinking about her replacement." He sneered, one corner of his mouth curving to the side. "It may take some time, but I'm certain we can get someone sooner or later."

A sliver of a grin crossed Hatrix's lips. "Great, boss, I'll take care of my end. You can count on me."

The man bounded to his Mercedes, opened the door, and dropped into the driver's seat. He started the engine and backed out of the driveway.

Hatrix stood at the doorway and watched the man speed away. He closed the door to the cold late autumn air, but the chill didn't leave his spine when he thought of the deceased woman in the bedroom.

TWELVE

BEATRICE GRIMACED. INTO the telephone, she said, "He shouldn't treat the dealers that way. It's not their fault when they lose. You're kidding! You know, I didn't like him when he worked in the Security Department." She bounced her chin up and down a few times. "Okay, well thanks. I'll talk with you later." She put down the receiver.

Brian was standing in front of her desk. "Any luck locating Vanessa Daine?" he asked.

"No," she said. "Sorry, Brian, no one knows where she is. Mabel has a friend who works in the cashier's cage, and she says Vanessa finished her shift and was seen getting into her car. Mabel's friend doesn't have any idea where she went after that."

He gestured to the phone. "I heard you talking about the dealers not winning. What was that all about?"

"You won't believe this, but Mabel's friend Carla—you know, she's a day-shift blackjack dealer—well anyway, Mabel said Carla said this new guy in the Table Games Department's giving the dealers a bad time. He stands behind them when they're dealing the cards and makes them nervous."

"Keith Wallace?"

"He has a terrible reputation with the employees. They call

him Comrade Wallace. If a dealer's losing, he yells at them when they leave the table. Right in front of the customers. All the dealers are upset."

"Well, I can't worry about that now. I have a meeting with our advertising agency in the conference room. We're going over the budget presentation one more time. Call there if you need me."

"I will, Brian." She began typing on her computer.

"Thanks, Beatrice." He walked out of the office.

WHEN BRIAN SLIPPED into the conference room, Rick Anderson, the account executive for the Hale, Sawyer, and Travis Advertising Agency, was reviewing the copy for the new television commercials. Anderson was a thin man with brown hair and horn-rimmed glasses.

At the conference table, in addition to Anderson, were Alice MacKay; Steve Webster, the advertising coordinator for the Charleston, and the agency's production coordinator, Bill Swanson. Webster was just out of college and wore a blue suit that didn't quite fit. Swanson was about thirty and had long blond hair. He was wearing a t-shirt with a rendering of Che Guevara on the front.

"Sorry I'm late," Brian said. He sat down at the table. "I've had one meeting after another, and I'm running behind."

"We understand," Anderson said. "We were reviewing the new television commercials. We want to add them to the budget presentation."

Brian's look was skeptical. "Can you get them done by Wednesday?"

"We have a production crew in town for a job with the convention authority. We should be able to put something together pretty fast. It'll be good enough to give Mr. Montgomery an idea of our direction."

"Describe the commercial layout," Alice said, gesturing to him.

Anderson held up the ad sketches and pointed to the first frame. "We want to start the spots with a panoramic view of Lake Tahoe. We'll take the shots from a helicopter. With the camera filming, we'll speed, low across the water to the edge of the lake, where the Charleston Casino Resort stands in all its glory.

"We selected some dramatic background music for great effect. Our voiceover will tell the viewers there's a luxurious property at beautiful Lake Tahoe. It'll go on to say visitors will enjoy a great view of the scenic alpine lake and can win big money in the casino as well. The narrative will boast that the Charleston has the loosest slot machines at Lake Tahoe."

"Is that true?" Alice asked.

"Sure is," Brian said. "Based on our total casino revenue and our payout percentages, we can make that claim without a worry."

"Should we get a letter from the GCB verifying that? In case we're challenged by one of our competitors."

Brian reached for his notebook. "Good idea. I'll have a letter emailed up tomorrow." He wrote down the suggestion.

Anderson said, "Anyway, we'll show a collage of winners extolling the virtues of the Charleston. We have some excellent recordings of happy customers claiming they always play here because they win more money. We'll fortify their claims with the surveillance videos you gave us."

Brian pushed a few wayward hairs out of his eyes. "How many versions of the commercial do you plan on making?"

Anderson raised an open palm. "Five."

"Do you have enough winners' videos?"

"I believe so. Can you get more if we need them?"

"Yes, but not by Wednesday."

"That's okay—there's a sufficient number to show Mr. Montgomery at the budget presentation."

Brian steepled his fingers. "What tagline are you using at the end of the spots?"

"After the video of the winners, we'll return to an image of the Charleston with the lake in the background. The graphic and the voiceover will say, 'The Charleston Casino Resort and Lake Tahoe. A winning combination.' We're trying to tie-in the numerous winners at the property with an already well-known and popular destination."

Brian tapped his fingertips against each other. "Sounds good, Rick. This will also complement our print and on-line campaign. The spots will be great on Facebook."

Anderson waved a hand at the sketches and looked at Brian. "If you're happy with this concept, we'll begin production at once. We've already started some of the preliminary work. The commercials we produce for the budget meeting won't be perfect, but I think Mr. Montgomery will approve."

"Yes, go ahead. Alice, what are your thoughts?"

She took off her reading glasses and said, "It'll be a refreshing change from what we've done in the past."

"Then it's settled," Anderson said. He put the commercial sketches in his briefcase. "I'll have a rough cut for you by late tomorrow afternoon."

Brian said, "Our timeframe's short. Call me if you run into any snags, so we can respond promptly. Our budget presentation has to impress Montgomery. I don't want any surprises."

"Don't you worry, Brian. Bill here can perform miracles. He's worked under tougher deadlines than this."

"There shouldn't be any problems," Swanson said. "It's all digital. I've already edited the winners' footage and completed the graphic overlays. The voiceover will be done this afternoon by KRLT disc jockey Parker Day."

"It sounds as if you have everything covered," Brian said. "I want to see the spots as soon as possible."

Anderson said, "The minute the production's completed."

"I'll be waiting with bated breath."

Anderson grinned. "Me too. I'll talk with you tomorrow." He stood. "Take care, Alice. Keep this boss of yours out of trouble."

Alice slapped a hand to her chest. "Hell no," she said. "That's not my job. I've tried in the past, and I can't keep him under control."

Everyone laughed. Swanson and Anderson left the room.

"I better get back to my office," Webster said. "I have a lot to do before the big meeting. I'm still lining up the costs of airing the TV commercials."

"Try to keep the expenditures reasonable," Brian said. "Money's going to be tight next year."

Webster nodded and exited the conference room, leaving Brian and Alice alone.

"Hey, Brian," Alice said, "you okay? You seem preoccupied. Are you all right?"

Brian smiled, a hint of red in his cheeks. "Yes. I'm fine. I've been on edge, waiting for the budget approval."

"Don't give me that crap. I know you. Something's bothering you, and it's not just the budget."

He leaned his head back. "It's nothing. Something I'm working on has taken me in some strange directions."

Alice gave him a confused look, but said, "Anything I can do to assist?"

"No, thanks. I'm convinced we'll get to the bottom of it sooner or later. You've helped enough by keeping the department running without a hitch."

"Okay, but you know I'm here if you need me."

"Alice, you're the first one I'd call."

THE SMALL BOAT navigated through the choppy waters of Lake Tahoe, the engine struggling to push the craft through the large waves crashing against the hull. Marcus Hatrix, dressed in a long, dark insulated jacket, tried to protect his face from the harsh wind. It was not a good afternoon for a "burial at sea."

Hatrix fought the wind, trying to maneuver the boat toward the center of the lake. He shifted his eyes over the cold water, where he could see the tall hotel/casinos on the south shore. The Charleston, Harrah's, Hard Rock, and Harvey's resorts loomed above the pine trees. He scanned the lake, searching for points of reference. He spotted Cave Rock, the prominent outcropping of stone that was a landmark on the east shore and turned to the California side of the lake and his eventual destination— Rubicon Point. The waters off Rubicon Point were some of Tahoe's deepest.

Far in the distance, Hatrix could see another watercraft and hoped it wasn't the Coast Guard. How would he explain a boat trip in this weather? He relaxed when it motored in the opposite direction.

Hatrix eased up on the throttle of the cruiser when it came upon what he thought was Rubicon Point. Once again, he looked for the familiar sites along the shore. He took a map out of a pocket and found his bearings. "This must be the place," he said aloud.

He slowed the boat to a crawl and put the engine in idle. A gust of wind struck it as it rolled over the large waves, and he was forced to grab the side rails to keep his balance, struggling against the wind as he worked his way to the stern.

The canvas-wrapped body of Vanessa Daine lay in the back, nylon rope stitched around her makeshift coffin. Attached to the rope were four fifty-pound weights Hatrix had purchased from a sporting goods store.

Hatrix tested the knots to ensure they were secure. Confident they wouldn't loosen, he lifted the canvas coffin and heaved it over the side of the boat. The splash couldn't be heard over the roar of the waves and the idling engine. He watched as the weights dragged the body below the surface.

A sense of relief, mixed with a slight feeling of guilt, rippled through his mind. He stared at the waves until he could no longer detect any air bubbles bursting up.

As the wind whipped by, he lifted the collar of his jacket and returned to the controls of the cruiser. He gunned the engine and turned the craft in the direction of the south shore, still fighting the waves.

Hatrix looked at the Charleston Resort—far in the distance and reflected on Vanessa and their perfect method of stealing money from the casino. He thought of all the cash they'd taken. A shiver ran up his backbone when his boss came to mind. It had nothing to do with the cold lake wind.

THIRTEEN

BRIAN AND ROBBIE arrived at the Incline Bistro a few minutes before seven. Robbie was wearing a tan jacket over a black knit dress that clung to her curvaceous body. Her hair was up off her shoulders, exposing the soft silky skin of her neck.

As they entered the restaurant, a bear of a man rushed over, picked Robbie up, and spun her around. "Robbie, sweetheart," he said in a booming voice, "it's so good to see you. Where've you been hiding?"

Robbie blushed at the scene he was making. "Jonathan, put me down."

He did as he was told but didn't release her from his clutches. "Robbie Taylor, I've missed you so much. Are you avoiding me?"

"Of course not. You know I've been busy." She pushed away from him. "Jonathan, I'd like you to meet Brian Shepard. Brian, this is Jonathan Reeves, a dear friend and the owner of this fine establishment."

Brian shook Reeves' hand but was uncomfortable with the situation. The way Reeves was eyeing Robbie, it was clear he had strong feelings for her. He was a tall, attractive man with thick blond hair and perfect teeth. His blue eyes shimmered as he gazed at her.

"It's good to meet you," Brian said, lying. "I can't wait to see your menu. Robbie says your cuisine's delicious."

"Ignore the menu," Reeves said with a flippant wave of his hand. "I've prepared a special feast for the two of you." He took Robbie by the arm. "This way, my love."

Robbie glanced at Brian, rolled her eyes, and moved with Reeves into the dining room. Brian trailed behind, looking at them with suspicion. Reeves took them to a table in the corner of the restaurant next to a large window facing Tahoe's south shore. A few stars blinked over the mountaintops on both the east and west sides of the lake.

"The best table in the house," Reeves said. He pulled out a chair and waited for Robbie to sit down. Brian also took a seat.

"I've ordered you a great little cabernet sauvignon," Reeves said. He snapped his fingers, and a tuxedoed waiter came over, holding a bottle of wine. He opened it and decanted a small amount of the vintage into a glass. Brian watched, bewildered, as Reeves sampled the wine.

"Delicious," Reeves said. "Jacque, please pour Robbie some wine...and you too—what was your name again?"

Brian's brow furrowed. "Brian. Brian Shepard."

"Oh, yes. Robbie was telling me about you. Well, enjoy your dinner." With that, he kissed Robbie's hand and headed for the kitchen.

An awkward silence fell between Robbie and Brian. Breaking it, she said, "I'm sorry about Jonathan's behavior. He can be such a boor."

Brian offered her a weak smile. "It's obvious he likes you."

"We dated a few times, but he's not my type."

"And what's that?" Brian winked at her and sipped his wine.

"Maybe someone not so dramatic."

He didn't want to spend all night talking about why another man was, or wasn't, right for her. "This is a nice restaurant, and the view's spectacular. I can't wait to try the food. I'm certain Hamlet in the kitchen has cooked up quite a spread."

"I'm sure he has. Despite (or perhaps because of) his ostentatious personality, he's a fabulous chef. He attended school in France and learned his technique from the gourmet masters."

"I look forward to tasting his fare. I love to eat."

"I've noticed that. Why don't you weigh three hundred pounds?"

"Exercise, exercise, exercise." He beamed at her. "I spend a lot of time in the weight room. Don't you remember?"

She peered at him out of the corner of one eye. "You haven't forgiven me for our first encounter at the spa."

"I have. You're so gorgeous, how could I carry a grudge?" His grin was wide.

"Thank you." Robbie reached across the table and took hold of his hand. As Brian squeezed it, a waiter carrying a covered silver tray interrupted them.

The waiter lifted the top, revealing two small appetizer plates. "Salmon ravioli in a lime cream sauce," he said with an accent difficult to describe. It could be European, or perhaps from South America. He placed the plates in front of them. "My name's Michelangelo. I'm at your service this evening. Enjoy."

Robbie picked up a fork and took a bite of the pasta. "Oh my god," she said. "This is delicious. The sauce is wonderful."

Brian sampled a ravioli and moaned his approval.

They ate and made small talk about their favorite foods for several minutes. Finally, Brian said, "Robbie, tell me about Vanessa. What's going on?"

"It's weird. I have some interesting news. When I arrived home from work, my phone was ringing. I answered it, and it was Vanessa's boyfriend. To say the least, I was shocked—after all he's put her through, I couldn't imagine what he wanted. He told me Vanessa had left Lake Tahoe for Columbus, Ohio. He said her aunt was ill."

"So she's gone?"

Robbie shrugged. "That's what he said."

"Why didn't Vanessa call you?"

"I asked him the same thing. He said she was so upset about her aunt, she caught the first bus to the airport in Reno."

"I thought she wanted nothing to do with him."

Robbie cut a ravioli with her fork. "I questioned him about that, too, and he told me it was all a misunderstanding. He said he loved her and they'd patched up their differences. He plans on joining her in Ohio as soon as he can. He said they intended to stay there for good."

Brian angled his head to the right. "It sounds to me like you don't believe him."

"I'm not certain, Brian. Vanessa was so bitter about their relationship. Yesterday morning, she was crying about the whole situation. I'm surprised at how this is working out. Anyway, the man told me he'd come by the house tomorrow and pick up her belongings."

"Can you get in touch with Vanessa?" He shoved the last ravioli into his mouth.

"I hope to, of course, as soon as I can. She's not answering her phone."

A busboy came over to the table, took their appetizer plates, and refreshed their waters. The waiter approached and put small tureens of cream soup in front of each of them. On top of the soup were sprinkles of melting cheddar cheese. "This is cream of broccoli," he said. "It's a special recipe created by Mr. Reeves. He receives requests for it often, but as you'd expect, keeps it a secret."

Brian and Robbie picked up their spoons and dipped them into their diminutive bowls of soup. Steam rose off the tureens as they took their first sips. Robbie closed her eyes in pleasure. "Oh my," she said. "It's so rich it's decadent."

Brian blew on another spoonful. "An extra half-hour on the treadmill tomorrow."

"We haven't even had the main course or dessert yet. I doubt that'll be enough."

They laughed.

"What time is this guy collecting Vanessa's stuff?" Brian asked.

Robbie took a sip of wine. "Tomorrow evening after I get off work."

Brian waved his soup spoon. "If you don't mind, I'd like to be there when he comes over. I want to talk with him. Besides, I don't think you should be alone when he's at your house. This whole situation makes me uncomfortable."

"I'd appreciate that. When I spoke with him on the phone, he gave me a creepy feeling."

"Robbie, what's his name?"

She paused, her eyes narrowing. "I don't know. He just said he was her boyfriend. He didn't mention his name. I was so startled by his call, I never thought to ask."

"I need to know. I want to see if he also works at the Charleston."

Robbie put her soup spoon down. "If he does, you'll recognize him when he comes over tomorrow night."

Brian nudged his soup tureen to the side. "Remember, I didn't know Vanessa. There are over two thousand employees at the resort. There are many of them I don't know. That's even more the case if they work on the graveyard shift."

Robbie nodded as Michelangelo sauntered up to the table. He removed their soup bowls and placed the main entree in front of them. The enormous platter contained scallops, short ribs, duck confit, and two lamb chops, all arranged and garnished with an artistic flair. In the center of the dish was a creamy risotto. The waiter said, "This is a sampling of Mr. Reeves's most popular dishes. We're serving it family style." He positioned a clean plate in front of each of them and, after ensuring everything was satisfactory, left them alone.

With a mouthful of the risotto, Brian said, "You're right, your friend may be a flake, but he knows how to cook."

Robbie grasped a knife and cut into a lamb chop. "He comes off as phony, but he's a sweet person."

Confusion lined Brian's forehead. "I thought you said he wasn't your type?"

"He's not, but sometimes I feel sorry for him. I understand that behind his gregarious facade's a lonesome person. You know, I should've introduced him to Vanessa. He would've been good for her." She took a bite of the lamb. "Yum."

"That's water under the bridge now. Vanessa's gone and will soon be joined by her abusive boyfriend."

Robbie pressed her lips together. "That still bothers me. When he hit her, she vowed it was over. She wasn't just afraid of him, she seemed to resent what he'd forced her to do. I'm surprised her attitude would change."

"He has some hold over her." Brian sipped his cabernet.

"I wonder what they've done. I find it difficult to believe they were stealing from the Charleston."

"We think somebody's been taking money from the count room, and that couldn't happen without the knowledge of someone in the Surveillance Department."

"Well, one thing's for certain, there aren't enough clues to this bizarre riddle." Robbie smiled at him. "I want to get my mind off the entire subject."

Brian agreed, and for the next hour or so, they enjoyed the good food, drink, and conversation. He was describing his job at the Charleston when he was interrupted in midsentence by

Jonathan Reeves. "Robbie, darling," Reeves said, "how was dinner? I trust you've enjoyed your meal." He pulled up a chair and sat next to them, his attention fixed on her.

An irritated glower crawled over Brian's face. "It was delicious," he said.

"Yes, Jonathan," Robbie said, "the food was exceptional. You've outdone yourself. The chops were beyond words."

Reeves said, "I'm pleased we were able to exceed your expectations. Would you like some champagne?"

She held a hand over her glass of wine. "Oh, no, I've had enough. I'm a bit tipsy from the cabernet."

"I'm okay," Brian said.

"Well, tonight's dinner's on me," Reeves said.

"No, Jonathan," Robbie said. "That's not necessary."

Reeves' tone was firm. "I insist, and I don't want to hear another word about it."

"That's generous of you," Brian said. "Thank you."

"Yes, thank you so much," Robbie said.

Reeves' expression was satisfied, his eyes still locked on hers. "It's my pleasure," he said. "I expect you'll visit my little restaurant more often?"

"Oh, yes," Brian said. "I'll tell all my friends about it as well."

"How's business been?" Robbie asked.

Reeves pushed up the sleeves of his jacket. "Excellent," he said. "The word of mouth's been tremendous, but I expect it'll slow until it snows and the skiers arrive."

"The weather report's favorable," Brian said. "A storm's supposed to be on the way."

"I know my waiters will love the ski crowd. They're good tippers."

Brian peeked at his watch. "We'd better be going." He'd had enough of Reeves. There was a limit to the amount of self-absorbed banter he could take. "We have to drive back to Round Hill."

"You're right," Robbie said, knowing he was uncomfortable.

They both stood up.

Reeves said in a mocking way, "I'm sure you two lovebirds want to get home soon. The bed's waiting."

Robbie said with a blush, "Mind your own business, Jonathan."

"I'm kidding, my dear. Please forgive me."

Exasperated, she frowned at him. "Thank you again for a delicious dinner."

"Yes," Brian said, "your hospitality's appreciated."

Reeves kissed Robbie on the cheek and hugged her. "Don't be a stranger," he said. "Call me once in a while."

She gave him a genuine smile. "You take care of yourself."

Leaving the restaurant, Brian asked, "Are you calling him?"

Robbie stopped, put her arms around his waist, and kissed him, deep and passionate.

Brian's face lit up. "Wow. I guess not."

She grinned and pointed. "Get in the truck."

As they drove down Highway 28 toward South Lake Tahoe, the sky was clear and full of stars. The lake was dark and ominous. Robbie said, "No sign of the storm on the other side of the lake."

"It's a slow-mover," Brian said. "It's supposed to pack quite a punch. I bet the folks at the ski resorts are excited."

They rode in silence for a while, staring into the dark. Brian reached over and took her left hand. Robbie gripped his palm tight and kissed his knuckles. "Thank you for tonight," she said. "I have fun when I'm with you."

Brian looked out across the water, adrenaline pumping. Should he do a gut check on his state of mind? Was he willing to forego his usual buffet of women for just one entrée? He took a deep breath. He wasn't quite sure why being with Robbie made him feel so good, but right now, he hoped it would last forever.

FOURTEEN

BRIAN WATCHED THE lake as the first glints of morning light pierced the mountaintops. The clear water was a window to the sandy bottom and granite boulders that led into the mysterious cold depths.

Outside the kitchen window, he could see the pilings of his unfinished redwood deck sticking up in the air like stilts. He knew he had to find the time to finish the project. He imagined the great parties and quiet romantic nights he'd enjoy once it was completed.

A knock at the door interrupted his thoughts. He walked through the living room, opened the front door, and was surprised to see Jack Mancini. Brian eyed the clock on the wall and said, "It's seven thirty. AM."

Jack entered the cabin. "I know. Seven-thirty should only come around once and after the sun's gone down—not up." Jack was even less of a morning person than Brian.

Brian laughed and closed the door. "I'll bite, what got you up at this time of the morning?"

"I'm meeting with Nelson Bates, the casino locksmith. He's showing me the procedures used for high security keys and locks."

"Do you want a cup of coffee?"

Jack yawned. "Yeah, maybe it'll help me wake up. I'm tired—didn't get much sleep last night."

They crossed the living room to the kitchen, and Brian poured two cups of coffee. He gave one to Jack and asked, "Why do you need to meet with this locksmith so early?"

Jack sipped from the mug. "He's working graveyard this week. We're replacing all the locks on the slot machines. We're doing it on the graveyard shift so we won't disturb too many customers. Nelson's an old friend of mine. We used to work together in Reno when I was an intern at the Eldorado. I called him yesterday and asked if I could see how the security keys are handled. He's more than happy to help me out."

"You know Montgomery ordered the drop box and soft count room keys."

"Right, he did." Jack blew on his coffee and took another sip. "The general manager's the sole person authorized to request high security keys. I don't know who received them once they reached the Charleston, though. That's why I need to talk with Nelson. I must determine if the keys can be traced and figure out who ended up with them when they were delivered to the casino and what they did with them. I have to find out if they passed through Elliot Thomas's fingers. I know I may be letting my imagination run away with me—it's improbable that the surveillance director of a large casino would be stealing—but I have to know for sure."

Brian nodded. "I keep wondering if that's too much of a stretch."

"Man, this coffee's strong. I'm awake now…and will be for days." Jack pivoted over to the counter and picked up a carton of milk. He poured a little into the mug. "How was your date with Robbie Taylor?"

Brian smiled. "I like her."

"I thought so. What did she say about her roommate?"

"Wait until you hear this—she's left Lake Tahoe." Brian told Jack what he knew about the departure of Vanessa Daine and her boyfriend's telephone call. "He's coming to get her things from Robbie's house tonight. I'm going to be there and ask him a few questions."

"Do you want me to join you?"

Brian shook his head. "No. That might scare the guy away. I just hope I can make a connection between him, Vanessa, and what's happening at the casino."

"I doubt he'll admit to a felony."

"I know, but I need to meet him and see what vibe I feel. Besides, I don't think Robbie should be alone with him. He has a history of violence with women. It wouldn't be right, leaving her to deal with this by herself."

Jack took a big gulp of his coffee. "Give me a yell if you need any help. I better get down to the Charleston. I can't risk missing Nelson. If I woke up this early in the morning for nothing, I'll be pissed."

"I'll stop by your office later today, and you can tell me what you found out."

Jack showed him a devious grin. "How was last evening's goodnight kiss?"

"None of your business."

"I have a twenty-dollar bet with Cory that you'll coax her into the sack within a week."

"She's not that kind of girl."

"But you're that type of guy, and I've seen you persuade more virgins into your bed than anyone I know. Well, since I've been off the market anyway."

"It won't be that way with Robbie."

"Hmm, something's up." He smiled wider. "Whoa...who'd ever believe it? You must be smitten. Wait until I tell Hailey."

"I'm not smitten, and keep your mouth shut. I don't feel like having that wife of yours gloating all over me, and I hate the thought of her saying anything to Robbie."

"If I can tell you're infatuated, I assure you, Hailey will know. The woman has radar when it comes to romance."

"It's none of her goddamn business."

"Okay, okay, have it your way. But I'll wager a steak dinner at Harrah's she figures it out."

Brian gestured to the door. "Get out of here. This early in the morning, I'm already tired of your ass."

Jack started whistling and danced off to his Jeep.

BRIAN STEPPED INTO the outer office and looked at his secretary. Beatrice pointed to his door. "You have a visitor," she said. "It's your favorite comedian, Skip Sullivan, and boy is he upset."

He glanced at the clock on the wall. "What's he doing here this early?"

"I don't think he's gone to bed yet, and he's drunker than my old Uncle Albert on a Saturday night."

"Oh great, just what I need to start the day. What does he want?"

"He babbled something about not having the other hotel rooms on his floor occupied by anyone else."

"What? Is he crazy?"

"You said it."

Brian sighed. "He's worse than a spoiled three-year-old."

She scrunched up her lips. "My grandson isn't that bad."

Brian edged through the doorway to his office and found Skip Sullivan sound asleep in the middle of the floor. He walked over to the dark-haired comedian and shook his shoulder. "Skip?" he said. "Skip, are you okay?"

Sullivan pushed Brian's hand away. "Don't touch me." His words were slurred. "Leave me alone."

"Please, Skip, get up. You'll be much more comfortable in your suite."

"I'm not going there. People are trying to hunt me down."

Brian attempted to sound sympathetic. "Who is?"

Sullivan curled himself into the fetal position. "They're after me. Trying to find me. Who do they think they are? I'm a star." He shuddered and closed his eyes.

Brian stared at the man, baffled. The comedian had fallen asleep again and was snoring. "Beatrice," Brian said, "I need some help in here. Would you call Security?"

She came to the doorway. "Is he all right?"

"I suppose so. He must want some Z's, and my office carpet was convenient. Contact Security, and let's see if we can help him up to his suite."

"Sure thing."

"Do we have any coffee made?"

"Do you want some for you or Sullivan?"

Brian spurted out a short laugh. "There's not enough caffeine in the entire resort for Skip right now. I'll take a cup—we'll let *him* sleep it off."

"I'll get hold of Security." Beatrice spun around and tramped to her desk.

Brian looked at Sullivan, then at his watch. He'd planned to phone the advertising agency and check on the progress of the new ad campaign. He thought about trying to work with the comedian snoring on the floor but, after a few minutes, decided he couldn't.

"I'm waiting out here," he said to Beatrice, exiting his office. "I can't do anything in there. It's impossible to concentrate."

Beatrice shuffled over to the coffee maker. "I've called Security. They'll be here in a moment. I had to explain the problem three times before the dispatch clerk understood what I was saying. He didn't believe me and thought I was a prank caller."

Mischief in his eyes, Brian said, "We should snap a few pictures and sell them to one of those celebrity gossip websites. We'll make a fortune."

Beatrice handed him a cup of coffee. "Don't tempt me. I could use the extra money."

They laughed as two uniformed security guards and Surveillance and Security Director Elliot Thomas flew into the room.

"I hear you're entertaining an unexpected guest," Thomas said in a dour tone. He marched into Brian's office, security guards tailing behind without a word. Brian and Beatrice hurried in after them.

"Take him to suite eighteen twenty-seven," Thomas said.

"Be gentle," Brian said. "He may be a drunk, but he's the headliner in our showroom. We need him to perform tonight."

"Perhaps you ought to be more careful about who you book."

Brian raised his voice. "Don't blame me for his behavior. I didn't make him a star. I arrange to get the most popular performers to fill the showroom."

Thomas adjusted his tie. "I hate big name personalities."

"Would you mind getting him out of my office and to his suite?"

The two security guards struggled to lift the comedian to his feet. In his drunken stupor, Sullivan attempted to free himself from their grasp. "Get away from me," he said with an angry growl.

"Don't worry, sir," one of the guards said. "We're helping you back to your suite."

"I want to go to a bar."

"I don't think so, Mr. Sullivan," the other guard said, trying to jockey the actor around.

"Take your hands off me," Sullivan squealed. "Do you know who I am? I'm a star. Whatever I desire, you must do."

Brian cut in and put a hand on his shoulders. "It's okay, Skip," he said. "Take the elevator up to your suite, and room service will deliver anything you request."

"That's better." Sullivan swayed, trying to focus on Brian and the others. "I'm a star. I expect to be pampered as one. You better treat me right, or I won't perform tonight."

"Skip, we'll take care of you like a king. Go with the security men here."

The two guards maneuvered the comedian out of the offices. Sullivan could be heard shouting obscenities as he staggered down the corridor.

"How can you grovel to that bastard?" Thomas asked.

"I'm keeping the talent happy," Brian said. "Like it or not, big names such as Skip Sullivan attract the high-limit gamblers. I tolerate his obnoxious conduct because he's a fantastic draw."

Thomas hissed. "I wouldn't do it. It's degrading. Jerks like Sullivan should be thrown out of the hotel for their behavior."

"What good would that do?"

"I don't care. Sullivan needs to be taken behind the casino and given a good beating."

"That's professional. I guess we see things in different ways."

Thomas flipped a hand. "Oh, don't give me that crap. This has nothing to do with professionalism. I'm a consummate professional."

"Thrashing entertainers is professional?"

"You marketing people don't understand the real world. You're all flash and no substance. You'd have a different view of the world if you ever had to work for a living."

Brian was taken aback by Thomas's words. "I work damn hard for this resort."

"Oh, forget it. Keep that comedian of yours out of trouble."

Brian shot him a fierce look. "I'll do my job—you do yours."

Thomas's face showed equal fury. "That's a strange comment,

coming from someone who spends more time snooping in other departments than he does his own. You've been hanging out in every area in the casino. I'm not certain I approve of that."

Brian folded his arms across his chest. "I can better market the property when I understand how it works. There's nothing wrong with that."

"I don't want you nosing around."

"Why, is there something you're hiding?"

Thomas gave him an icy stare. "I have work to do. We can talk about this some other time." He charged out of the office, and Brian watched him barrel toward the hallway.

"Elliot Thomas is a piece of work," Beatrice said. "He's not a pleasant man."

Brian was still glaring after Thomas. "You can say that again. I can't stand the guy."

"I heard he got into a shouting match with Mr. Montgomery last night. It takes a lot of guts to yell at the general manager and not worry about being fired."

Brian said under his breath, "Perhaps he has so much money, he doesn't need the job."

Beatrice gaped at him, perplexed. "What?"

"Never mind. Would you get the advertising agency on the phone? I'd like to find out how the new television commercials are coming."

She nodded. "Sure, Brian."

He thanked her and took a seat behind his desk, leaning back in the chair. He sat there for a moment, thinking about Elliot Thomas. Brian didn't appreciate what he'd said. More and more, he believed he and Jack were correct, and Thomas was involved with the casino thefts.

BRIAN SPENT THE better part of the morning and early afternoon preparing for the budget meeting. He spoke with Rick Anderson at the advertising agency and was told that production on the television commercials was taking longer than expected. They hoped to have them finished later that afternoon.

This made Brian uneasy, but he trusted the agency people and knew this account was important to them. They'd move mountains to complete the presentation.

After a late lunch, he decided to go over to the Human Resources Department and see what he could find out about Vanessa Daine. Swinging open the door to the HR office, he noticed the line of people waiting to fill out employment applications, their demeanors a mixture of anxiety and excitement.

"Hi, Brian," the young woman behind the counter said. Gail Franklin was a recent graduate of the local community college. While in school, she'd interned at the resort in the Marketing Department, working for Brian. After she graduated, he'd helped her get a job as an employee placement coordinator in the Human Resources office. Gail was a short woman and on the chunky side. Her face was milk-white, with rosy cheeks, and her blond hair was pulled up in a ponytail.

"Can you spare a minute?" Brian asked. "I need to check on one of our employees."

"You bet," she said. "Let's go back to one of the interview rooms."

Brian followed her down a hall and into a small space decorated with pictures of skiers on snow-covered mountains. "Are you ready for the slopes?" he asked, gesturing to one of the photos.

"I bought a new pair of Rossignols," she said. "I'm dying to try them out."

"It keeps threatening to snow. Let's hope we have a good winter."

Gail held up a hand and crossed two fingers. "Think snow. Who's the employee you want to know about?"

"Vanessa Daine. It's spelled D-A-I-N-E. She worked in the Surveillance Department."

"Worked as in past tense?"

"She quit yesterday. I was wondering if she might've left a forwarding address."

"I'll take a look." Gail sat in front of a computer and typed. "Daine, Vanessa…yes, here she is. She's been employed in the Surveillance Department for the last nine months. Before that, she was in the Finance Department. She quit yesterday afternoon."

"Any reason given?"

Gail gazed at the screen. "No, her termination hasn't been processed. It says here someone called and told us she was quitting for personal reasons. We can't complete the termination paperwork until we speak with her."

Brian gestured at her computer. "Any forwarding address?"

She hit a couple keys. "No, we have nothing."

"Is she owed any money?"

Gail pushed a few more buttons on the keyboard. "Just a second, I need to access the payroll accounts." She pressed additional keys and waited. "Let's see. Yes, we owe her two weeks' salary. I'm certain she'll be in soon to pick up her check. We can process her termination then."

Brian rubbed an index finger over his lower lip. "Was she a good employee?"

Gail poked at a couple more keys. "It says here she was a model worker. She's had several pay increases, and her reviews are above average. Why the interest in Vanessa Daine?"

"She was the roommate of a friend and left without saying goodbye. We were a little concerned."

Gail said with sincerity in her voice, "When she contacts us about her final check, I'll let you know."

"Thanks, Gail. That'd be great."

"No problem. I owe you one anyway. I do love this job."

Brian aimed a forefinger at her and wiggled it. "You earned this on your own merits. Never think otherwise."

Gail grinned, her red lips a striking contrast to her pale skin. "Oh, I know, but you helped grease the way, and I'm grateful."

Brian smiled back at her. "Hey, thanks for your time. Call me when you hear from Vanessa." Leaving the personnel office, he was pensive. All he'd gained by this visit were more questions.

FIFTEEN

BRIAN STROLLED INTO the room and asked Jack's pretty secretary, "Is your boss in?"

She looked up from her computer. "Yes, he is. Let me see if he's available. He hasn't had a great morning."

"The reason?"

She grimaced. "Keith Wallace. He's been causing a lot of issues. Poor Jack's spent most of the last two hours trying to talk some of our best dealers out of quitting." She picked up the handset and spoke with Jack. After a short conversation, she hung up and tilted her head toward the door. "Go on in," she said.

Brian thanked her and traipsed through the doorway of Jack's office. Jack didn't look good. Deep dark circles were under his eyes, he appeared to be exhausted. "Tough one?" Brian asked.

Jack rubbed his face. "A lot of trouble in the pit. It's not the best day I've ever had."

"So I've heard. Mine hasn't been the greatest either." He sat down and recounted his adventures with Skip Sullivan.

Jack tipped back in his chair. "I'd take all of your problems if you'd get rid of Keith Wallace. The man's crazy. The power's gone to his head. He walks through the casino thinking he's a god, leaving upset dealers and floor supervisors in his wake.

Two roulette dealers quit yesterday. Two of my best. Both worked here for many years. Worse yet, Wallace is trying to increase our hold percentage by adding six deck shoes and having the dealers shuffle the cards before they reach the end of the deck. It may increase the hold percentage a tad, but we'll no longer be competitive with the other casinos at the lake."

"Can't you stop him?"

Jack took a frustrated breath. "He has Montgomery's approval and is using it to the max. My hands are tied, and I don't know how long I can put up with his interference. I'd quit if I could afford to, but with the new house and all, I don't have much choice."

"Get to the bottom of the low hold problem. Then you'll regain control of your department. What did you find out from the casino locksmith?"

"Nelson showed me the key procedures for the casino. We reviewed the records, and they say four sets of soft count room, cabinet, and drop box keys were delivered to the vault."

Brian cocked his head. "I thought the locksmith in Reno said five sets of keys were ordered by Montgomery."

"You're right, but just four sets were transported to the main vault. The paperwork's clear."

"Who accepted the keys?"

Jack rocked his chair back. "All of them were brought to the security office. A guard signed for them, and four sets were delivered to the vault. Those keys were logged into the inventory using the proper procedures."

"Who was the security guard?"

"A man named Ben Genetti brought the keys to the vault. He's worked at the resort for over a decade."

"Did you see the receipt he signed when the keys were delivered?"

"I saw it, but the signature was illegible. It was a scribble."

"But you're certain the keys were given to Genetti?"

"No. I know he took four sets of keys to the vault. I'm not positive he signed for all five sets when they arrived from Reno. As I said, the signature on the receipt was unreadable. It could be anyone's."

"I guess we better talk with Genetti."

"We need to find out what he did with the fifth set."

Brian's jaw hardened. "I know what he did with them. He helped himself to the money in the drop boxes."

"Nelson says Genetti's a great guy with a nice family. Six children. He swears he's one of the most honest people you'll ever meet."

"It takes a lot of money to raise six kids. The security guards at the Charleston aren't paid much."

"Well, I'm going to confront him about the keys and see what he says."

"Are you ready to speak with Montgomery about this?"

"Not yet. I need to look around some more before we get the general manager involved."

"You still want to point the finger at Elliot Thomas?"

The creases on Jack's forehead were uneven. "Yeah, I think so."

"I had a run-in with him this morning. He's not happy I've been in the surveillance and count areas."

Jack slapped his hands on the desk. "Brian, he's concealing something. I'm sure of it."

"I flat out asked him if he had anything to hide, and he glared at me and changed the subject. He does control the Surveillance Department. Vanessa Daine worked for him."

"You understand I've never liked the man. But we need to speak with Daine. She may have our answers."

"I'm trying to locate her. She hasn't received her last paycheck yet. Personnel will call me when she gets in contact with them. I'll attempt to find out more from her boyfriend this evening." Brian stood and took a few paces toward the door. He turned to face Jack. "I'll call you later tonight and let you know what happens."

"I'm not certain what time I'll be home. I have to mend a lot of fences in the pit. Wallace never leaves this place. I believe he almost lives here. If I'm not home when you call, leave a message with Hailey. I'll get back to you as soon as I can."

ON THE WAY to his office, Brian found Rick Anderson waiting for him in the lobby.

"You have to see the commercials," Anderson said. "They're dynamite. You're going to love them." They proceeded down the hall, entered the outer office, and walked past Beatrice's desk.

Brian looked at his secretary, who was not on the phone for once, and said, "Would you call Alice and ask her to come over? I want her to see the new TV spots."

"Yes, Brian," Beatrice said and picked up the phone.

Brian led Anderson into his office and pulled three chairs up to the television located in one corner of the room. Anderson queued up the video in the DVR and explained that his crew had worked all night obtaining the right voiceover and perfect footage. "We've cut two versions of the commercials," he said. "We plan on having five but can't get them all ready by tomorrow."

Anderson outlined the timetable and a few minutes later, Alice joined them. They watched intently as the video rolled. After the first commercial ended, Anderson stared at Brian and Alice in anticipation. His eyes were gleaming, excitement on his face.

"What do you think?" Anderson asked. "Is it everything I said? Don't you love the way the camera races above the lake and into the Charleston? We had a computer generate some of the video. Did you notice we've eliminated the other hotels? It gives the impression the Charleston's the lone resort at Tahoe. It's digital magic."

Brian was pleased, and a quick smile flashed across his lips. "It's perfect. It makes even me want to take my vacation here. Tell your production people they did one hell of a job. Let's take a peek at the other one."

Anderson motioned to the television. "You'll love this. We took a different approach on the second spot. We highlighted the outdoor activities at Lake Tahoe and around the resort, focusing on skiing, sailing, the hotel pool, and the tennis courts. We then show the winning casino nightlife after the sun goes down."

Anderson changed the video and pressed the play button on the DVR. A surge of dramatic music paid tribute to the Charleston Casino Resort as the commercial flashed on the television. Anderson said, "Notice we used a different tagline at the end of this one. Our slogan's *Play all day, play all night*."

The spot ended, and Alice said, clapping her hands, "Damn, I like that."

Brian said, "We'll need to tie these new taglines into the budget presentation."

"I'm way ahead of you," Anderson said. "We're having them included in the packets we'll be giving to Mr. Montgomery. They'll be ready by tomorrow."

Brian rapped a pen on the table. "It sounds like we're ready. I wasn't happy about delaying the budget meeting at first, but it's working in our favor. These television commercials take our presentation to new creative heights."

Alice said, "The winners jumping up and down with excitement makes the spots fun. It's nice we can use them."

Brian turned to her. "Do you have the customers' release forms?"

She nodded. "Yes. I checked the file before I gave the videos to Rick. I'm guessing the guests will love having their good fortune shared with the world."

"I suspect you're correct, but as a courtesy, why don't we call and let them know they're becoming television stars?"

"I will. Even though we told them we'd use their pictures for publicity purposes, we ought to inform them they'll be seen five times a night during primetime television and on our social media sites. I'll have my secretary phone the winners as soon as this meeting's over. Do you want to call the cute ones yourself?"

Brian grinned at her. "No." He looked to Anderson. "Will it be easy to rotate more winners through these commercials?"

Anderson flicked his fingers. "A snap," he said. "That's the beauty of digital images. Every time you get a new big winner, we plan on editing the video into the spots as soon as we can. This will give us two benefits—you can promote the lucky winners, and it keeps the commercials fresh. It should increase the response from the viewers and let them know the Charleston Resort is always sending out a stream of happy customers."

"I know we have more videos in the surveillance library that we can use if necessary. New winner videos will come out of the casino each week as well."

Anderson tapped his chest with a knuckle. "Give me the recordings, and they'll be in the commercials within hours."

"This better impress that ass, Montgomery," Alice said. "I can't wait to see his reaction."

"You never know with him," Brian said. "If he's in a foul mood, he may kill the whole damn program. Television advertising's expensive, and with the cash problems the casino's been having, he may not be willing to spend the money."

"We have to appeal to his ego," Anderson said. "That's why we used video of Mr. Montgomery in the commercials. We expect he'll fancy being a television personality."

Brian pointed at Anderson. "Smart."

"We need to massage his ego by telling him how great he is."

"Yes, but we need to be subtle," Alice said. "We don't want to make our motives too obvious."

Brian said, "Let the spots speak for themselves and hope for the best. Are you ready for the rest of the budget presentation?"

"We're as prepared as we'll ever be," Anderson said. "The slides have been updated, and we threw in a few showgirls to spice up the financial portions. Nothing outrageous—just tasteful fun."

Brian blanched. "Showgirls? What does tasteful fun mean, and how does it fit into the financial overview?"

"Don't you worry, Brian. I promise Mr. Montgomery will love it. This is your first budget presentation as the Director of Marketing, and I guarantee it'll have flair and show everyone you're the best person for the job."

"Don't do anything to demonstrate I'm the wrong one. Montgomery doesn't have much of a sense of humor."

"Humor, no, but he enjoys the opposite sex—thus the showgirls. And, of course, he appreciates competence. He'll like the way we outline the budget. In all seriousness, Brian, Alice, we'll do everything appropriately and with maximum impact. Our work as your advertising agency's also at risk if it doesn't go well."

"Rick's right," Alice said. "They're professionals—one of the best advertising agencies on the West Coast."

Brian reached over and picked up his notebook. "We've worked hard," he said, "and have a great plan. Let's get together tomorrow morning at eleven and make one final run through before meeting with Montgomery."

Anderson asked with amused sarcasm, "Oh, the presentation's tomorrow?"

"Very funny," Alice said. "We better be in the conference room at one-thirty tomorrow afternoon ready to dazzle our vaunted general manager. Otherwise, we may all be out of a job."

SIXTEEN

BRIAN DROVE UP to Robbie's house as she was walking toward her mailbox. He grabbed a bottle of wine, jumped out of his truck, and waited for her, admiring her long silky hair.

Robbie opened the mail box and peered inside. "I thought about you all day," she said.

He gave her a hopeful look. "Why's that?"

"I imagine you know." She pulled out the mail and meandered over to him.

"I was thinking about you as well."

"I expect it was all good?"

Brian embraced her. "You know it." He had a smile in his eyes.

They laughed and strode arm in arm into her house as the first snow of the year began falling. Robbie put the mail on the kitchen counter, and Brian handed her the bottle of wine.

She examined the label. "What kind of wine do we have here?" she asked.

He took off his jacket and hung it on a chair. "Nothing fancy, a nice Bogle."

"Mmm, one of my favorites."

"Mine too. Bogle's not from Napa, did you know that? It's from the Sacramento Delta region."

"Will you open it?" She pointed to a cabinet. "Corkscrew's on the middle shelf."

Brian retrieved the corkscrew and removed the cork. Robbie placed two wine glasses on the counter and he poured some cabernet into each one. They both took a sip and admired its flavor.

Robbie opened the refrigerator and pulled out two covered dishes. She put them on the counter and turned on the oven. "How was your day?" she asked.

"Not bad," Brian said. "Except for a few exciting moments with Skip Sullivan. He's something else. Enjoys the sauce a tad too much."

"I don't think he's funny. I never watch his TV show."

Brian shrugged, slid out a chair, and sat down at the table. "He's a big draw. Fills the showroom every night."

"I don't get it." Robbie took a box of whole-wheat crackers from the pantry, poured some into a bowl, and set it on the table. She uncovered one of the dishes—cream cheese dip—and placed it near the crackers.

Robbie pushed the crackers and dip toward Brian, who snatched a cracker, scooped up a dollop of the dip, and stuffed it in his mouth. He asked, still chewing, "What time did you say Vanessa's boyfriend was coming by?"

Robbie glanced at the clock on the stove. "He said he'd be over around seven. I'm glad you're here. I didn't want to be alone with him." She put a covered dish in the oven. "I hope you like lasagna."

"Oh sure, it's one of my favorites."

"It won't be ready for about an hour. Why don't we go into the living room? We'll be more comfortable."

"Robbie, I was wondering if we could take a gander at Vanessa's bedroom."

"You think there may be something of interest in there?"

"It's possible. Besides, we might find the address of her aunt in Ohio."

She pondered that for a second. "Yeah, you may be right. It's this way." Robbie directed Brian to the hall and escorted him into Vanessa's bedroom, flicking on the light switch.

"This place's been trashed," Brian said. He looked around the room in bewilderment. "What happened?"

"Nothing," Robbie said with a chuckle. "Vanessa wasn't a good housekeeper. Her bedroom's like this all the time."

"Jeez, I thought you said she was a good roommate, that she helped around the house."

"She was—except for here, she was always neat. I figured this was her private space, so I didn't mind it resembling the aftermath of a rock concert."

They surveyed the room. There was an unmade bed in the middle, and the floor was layered with dirty clothes, old magazines, and newspapers. On the cluttered dresser were pictures of two children and a collection of knickknacks.

Robbie held up her hands. "Where do we begin?" she asked. "I feel like I'm doing something wrong."

Brian said, "Let's pack her things as we search the room. That way, it'll be ready when her boyfriend arrives."

Robbie nodded. "Makes sense. I have some boxes in the garage. I'll be right back."

Brian slid out the top drawer of Vanessa's dresser. It contained undergarments and socks, and he dug to the bottom but found nothing more. He pulled open the second drawer. It was full of wool sweaters, and he yanked them out and set them on the bed.

Robbie carried in several stacked packing boxes. "I saved these," she said, "when I moved here last year. I knew they'd come in handy. Have you found anything useful?"

Brian took a stack of jeans from the bottom drawer. "No,

just clothes. Do you know who these children are?" He gestured with his chin at the pictures on the dresser.

Robbie put the boxes on the bed. "I believe they're Vanessa's nephew and niece. She had a brother with two kids. As I understand it, they were all killed in a tragic car accident."

"That's too bad. I wonder if they lived in Ohio."

"I'm not positive. It was somewhere in the Midwest."

"Give me a box, and I'll start packing."

"Here." She passed him one. "I'll rummage through the nightstands."

Brian returned to the dresser and continued packing clothes into the box. Robbie knelt in front of the nightstand on the right side of the bed and tugged open the top drawer.

"Nothing in the dresser but clothing," Brian said and slammed the bottom drawer shut. He drifted over to the doorway of the walk-in closet and turned on the light. Like the bedroom, it was in total disarray. "I need a backhoe to get through this mess."

The closet had two walls of clothes on hangers and one of shelves. He approached the shelves and inspected several containers labeled *taxes*. Inside, he found receipts and tax returns for the last two years. Next to a box labeled *office supplies* were two albums filled with photographs. He picked them up and brought them out to the bed, where he sat on the rumpled sheets. "Do you want to see some pictures?" he asked.

Robbie sat next to him and opened one of the albums. It was full of photographs of children in various poses. "This must be her family," she said, flipping the pages and pointing. "I'd guess this girl here's Vanessa. She was a cute little kid. I bet this is her brother."

"This album has high school pictures," Brian said. "Is this Vanessa?"

Robbie studied the photo he'd gestured at. "It is. She's pretty, don't you agree?"

Brian nodded. "It seems she was a cheerleader."

"It's weird. I know so little about her. She was very private."

Brian turned the pages of the album. "She never talked about her personal life?"

"Only once in a while. She mentioned that her brother was killed in an accident but nothing more. I'm one of her few friends, but it was rare that she confided in me. I just found out her boyfriend was abusing her in the last few days. She's a solitary person and kept to herself. I guess that's what made her a good roommate." Robbie closed the album.

Brian put the albums in a box and headed back to the closet. He pulled dresses and blouses off the racks and laid them on the bed. Robbie removed the clothes from their hangers, folded them, and put them in the boxes. "I hate to wrinkle these," she said, "but I don't know how else I can pack them on such short notice." After the closet was empty, Robbie dug through the nightstand on the left side of the bed. "We need to hurry," she said, noting the time on the clock radio. "The lasagna will be ready in about twenty minutes."

"I'll pack up the bathroom," Brian said and slipped into that, also cluttered, room. He found the sink counter dotted with beauty products. He placed the creams, makeup, and mascara into a box and opened the medicine cabinet. Inside, he found eye drops, bandages, and a clear plastic bag of fine white powder. "Robbie, come see this," he said.

Robbie walked into the bathroom and gawked at what he was holding. She looked at him with wide eyes.

Brian said, "It seems your roommate's indulging in recreational drugs."

She covered her mouth with a hand. "What is it?"

"Unless I'm mistaken, cocaine." He unzipped the bag and cautiously smelled the contents.

Robbie was astonished, her cheeks tinged crimson. "In my

house? I can't believe it. She knows my attitude about drugs. Brian, I'm shocked she'd bring that into my home. Get rid of it."

"I will." He emptied the powder into the toilet and flushed. "This may explain her secretive ways."

"It certainly explains her illegal activities. Do you suppose she was dealing drugs? Maybe her boyfriend's a pusher."

Brian picked up a box. "That doesn't jibe with the thefts from the casino." He started taking everything out of the medicine cabinet.

"Well, the cash could've been used to finance her drug purchases. I wonder if she kept anymore of it in my house."

"Let's keep at it."

They continued their search of Vanessa's room but found no more drugs, nothing to tie her to the thefts, and no information on her aunt. When they finished packing all her belongings into boxes, they set them near the bedroom door. Robbie switched off the light and led Brian back to the kitchen.

BRIAN PUT ANOTHER bite of lasagna in his mouth. "You're a great chef," he said. "This is fantastic. I love the seasonings in your sauce. You could cook for your friend Jonathan at his restaurant."

Robbie sat next to him at the kitchen table. "Thank you. It's my mother's recipe." She poured some more wine in his glass. "I'm a little nervous about Vanessa's boyfriend coming over. All this has been a bit unsettling. My life's always been pretty boring, and I'm not used to having a disappearing roommate and cocaine in my home."

Brian reached over and clasped her hand.

Robbie took a sip of wine. "I'm getting more and more concerned about Vanessa. I wish I had a chance to talk with her before she left the lake. I feel uncomfortable not knowing she's all right."

The doorbell rang. Robbie turned to Brian, her expression

anxious. He smiled at her, and they both rose from the table and crossed the living room to the front entrance. Brian said, "Let's see what answers we can squeeze from this guy." He opened the door, and saw a man standing there, holding two large suitcases.

"Is Robbie Taylor home?" he asked, gazing at Brian with a puzzled expression. "She's expecting me."

Robbie peeked around the door. "Come in," she said. "I'm Robbie Taylor—Vanessa's roommate. I guess it's ex-roommate. This is Brian."

"Hi," he said, wiping his feet on the mat and entering the house.

Robbie shut the door. "The snow's starting to fall hard."

"It is. The roads are getting slick, and I don't own a car that's good in this type of weather. I almost slid into a tree driving up the street." He blew on his hands trying to warm them.

"I'm sorry," Brian said, "I didn't catch your name."

"Uh, Marcus. Marcus Hatrix."

"Can I offer you anything to drink?" Robbie asked. "Coffee, wine, a beer?"

"Coffee with rum in it would be great. You know, to warm up the chill." He rubbed his arms.

"Let me take your jacket," Brian said.

Hatrix took it off, gave it to Brian, and they walked with Robbie to the kitchen.

Robbie pulled a bottle of rum from a cabinet and asked, "So, did you work with Vanessa at the Charleston Resort?"

Hatrix nodded. "Yes."

"What do you do there?" Brian asked.

"Security. On grave."

Robbie poured coffee into a mug and topped it off with the rum. She handed it to Hatrix. "How's Vanessa?" she asked. "Her sudden departure upset me."

Hatrix sipped the rum concoction. "Ah, she's okay. Uh, she told me before she left to tell you she's sorry for leaving without notice, but her cousin's sick."

"Cousin? I thought it was her aunt who was ill."

"Oh, ah, yes. She's a much older cousin. Vanessa thinks of her as an aunt due to the age difference."

Robbie was skeptical, her eyebrows drawn close. "She's not answering her phone."

"She left it here by accident. As I told you yesterday, her aunt doesn't have a home telephone."

"Cousin. You said it was her cousin."

Hatrix took a gulp of the coffee. "Right, her cousin doesn't have a phone."

"How do you know she's okay?"

"Why wouldn't she be?" He swallowed another slug of his drink. "She was fine when I put her on the airport bus yesterday morning."

Brian asked, "She hasn't contacted you since she arrived in Ohio?"

"No, but I'm sure she will soon."

"She could've called you from the airport in Columbus."

Hatrix's voice climbed. "She didn't. What's with the cross examination? I'm sure she's fine. Hey, all I want to do is get her belongings. Where's her room?" He glanced toward the hallway.

"On the left," Robbie said. "We've packed all her personal items."

Hatrix set his mug on the kitchen table. "Why'd you do that?"

"We knew it'd be easier for you."

Hatrix said nothing, but it was apparent by his frown that he was unhappy. He followed Robbie and Brian down the hall and into Vanessa's bedroom.

"This is all hers," Robbie said. She waved to the stack of boxes on the floor.

Hatrix said, "I wish you hadn't gone through her private possessions. Vanessa wouldn't appreciate it." He opened a box and picked through its contents.

"Vanessa and I have been roommates for more than a year. I'm positive she wouldn't mind."

"I disagree."

"Listen, Hatrix," Brian said with a stern inflection, "we were trying to help you out. Robbie has as much right to pack up Vanessa's belongings as you. This is her house, after all."

"Did you happen to see a memory card? Vanessa was worried it'd be lost."

Brian skewed his head to the side. "Memory card? I didn't see any card. Robbie, did you?"

Robbie crossed her arms. "No," she said. "I found an old iPod, but I didn't see any memory cards."

Hatrix opened the boxes one after another. "Are you certain?" he asked. He was troubled, and it showed in his eyes. "Vanessa was adamant I send her the memory card."

"What's on it?"

The look Hatrix offered her was rude. "Pictures I took of the two of us at the beach. She's sentimental and doesn't want them to be lost. She asked me to ensure that the memory card with those pictures is sent to Ohio."

"I'm sorry, but we didn't find it. There are some picture albums."

Hatrix scratched a tattooed elbow. "No they're not that kind of photo. Do you have a DVR?"

Robbie pursed her lips. "No, I own an old DVD player. I'm behind on my technology upgrades."

"How about a computer? Maybe she left it in the card slot."

Robbie was irritated, and the grooves on her forehead ticked up even more. "I have a laptop, but I doubt Vanessa ever used it. We can check, though."

In a brusque manner, he said, "I'd like to."

The three left the bedroom and trekked up to the loft and Robbie's office. Robbie stood by the computer on the desk and inspected the memory card slot. "Nothing here," she said.

"What about those?" Hatrix asked, pointing to a stack of memory cards on a shelf.

Robbie patted her chest with one hand. "They're mine."

"Do you mind if I take a peek?"

She raised a shoulder. "It's a waste of time, but go ahead."

Hatrix picked them up and examined the cards, reading the tiny labels on each one. "Vanessa's memory card isn't here."

"I believe that's what I said."

"I wonder where she put it. You say she never mentioned a memory card?"

"No, she didn't. I'm surprised Vanessa would want any pictures of the two of you. The last time we spoke, she was unhappy with your relationship. She told me it was over."

Hatrix bowed his head. "Oh, she was upset about a little argument we had. It was nothing. We made up the other night."

"That so-called disagreement left a bruise under her right eye."

Flustered, Hatrix licked his lips. "It was a mishap. The situation got out of hand, but the bruise was an accident. I apologized, and she's forgiven me." He wiped sweat off his temples and rubbed it on his pants.

A pregnant silence filled the room as Brian and Robbie gazed at him with uncertainty. "When are you joining Vanessa in Ohio?" Brian asked.

Hatrix stroked a forefinger over his chin and thought for a moment before answering. "Uh, not yet. There are some obligations I need to take care of first. I plan to move back there as soon as I can, though."

Robbie asked, "Why doesn't Vanessa just come back to Tahoe when her cousin's recovered from her illness?"

"She's quite sick. They expect a long period of recovery. Besides, we've been talking about moving back to Ohio for some time now. I'm tired of the mountain snow in the winter and the tourist traffic in the summer. Her cousin's illness just upped our timetable for getting out of here."

Robbie stared at him, her eyes probing. "It's strange Vanessa didn't mention her cousin to me."

"Vanessa's a private person. She keeps her personal matters to herself and shares them with few people." He scanned the loft again. "Is there any other place she might've left the memory card?"

"None I can think of."

"Did she have a safe deposit box?"

Robbie scowled. "How would I know?"

Hatrix's voice was curt. "Did you find a safe deposit key in her things?"

"No, we didn't find any keys," Brian said.

"Perhaps she left the memory card with a friend. Do you know any of them?"

"You're her boyfriend," Robbie said, her tone hot. "Don't you know who they are?"

"Ah, I've never met any of her friends, just like I didn't know you. Vanessa and I spent our time with each other."

Robbie glared at him in disbelief.

"Well, I guess I better lug her stuff to my car. Thanks for your help. I know Vanessa will be in touch with you when she's settled." Hatrix turned away and stormed down the stairs.

They returned to the bedroom, picked up the boxes, and carried them to Hatrix's car. Brian and Robbie helped him pack some of them into the sports car's tiny trunk and put the rest in the rear seat. The snow was coming down at a heavy rate, and they couldn't see too well through the plump flakes. After the boxes were loaded in the vehicle, they ran for the porch, seeking protection from the blizzard.

Hatrix said, "I'm shipping the boxes to Vanessa right away."

Robbie asked, "Do you have an address where I can write her?"

His left eye twitched. "No."

"Then where are you sending everything?"

"To the Greyhound Bus Depot in Columbus."

"I see," she said through clenched teeth, considering his words with ever-growing suspicion.

"Vanessa will call soon. I'm certain of it. I'll retrieve her furniture later in the week, but I have to borrow a truck. I hope that works for you."

"I'll be seeking another roommate and need you to get it as soon as you can. I don't want to store it in my garage."

Hatrix lifted up the collar on his jacket. "I'll come for it by Friday at the latest." He traversed the snow-covered driveway to his sports car. Brian and Robbie watched in silence as he started the vehicle and fishtailed up the street into the white-out.

BRIAN SAT ON a kitchen chair. "What do you think?" he asked.

Robbie poured him a cup of coffee. "Something's not right. I'm uncomfortable with his behavior, and I'm positive he's lying. The bit about the cousin who's an aunt just didn't sound plausible. She doesn't have a phone? No way. And he didn't seem to be in a hurry to join her in Ohio. I don't even think he's her boyfriend."

Brian narrowed his eyes. "Why do you say that?"

"He has tattoos." Robbie filled her own mug with coffee and put the French press on the counter.

"Lots of guys do." He took a sip from the mug.

163

She took a seat next to him. "I know, but Vanessa once told me she hated men with tattoos. She said a man who'd been inked was an immediate turnoff."

"He sure was determined to find the memory card. Did you see his face when he saw we'd already packed Vanessa's room?"

"I agree." Robbie tapped her fingers on her coffee mug. "He works at the Charleston Resort. Can you find out more about him?"

"Yes, I'll go see Gail Franklin in the personnel office tomorrow. One thing's for sure, either he's not her boyfriend or he's been lying to her. Vanessa's boyfriend's supposed to be rich, but security guards at the Charleston don't make much money."

Robbie tipped her head toward the front door. "He drives a nice sports car."

"I can guarantee you he's not making the payments on his salary alone."

"I'm very worried about Vanessa. Meeting Hatrix makes me even more uneasy."

Brian reached for his jacket. "I better get going. I have a big day tomorrow. It's our final budget meeting with the general manager. I have a few items to finish up tonight." He leaned over and kissed her. "Thanks again for dinner. It was delicious. I'll call you tomorrow. Why don't we celebrate my successful budget presentation with dinner at the restaurant at the top of the tram at Heavenly?" He boosted himself up from the chair and put his coat on.

"I haven't dined up there in some time. I love the view."

"It seems like there's a theme to this budding relationship."

Robbie stood. "Oh? And what's that?"

"We eat a lot. Why don't we meet at the Charleston Spa tomorrow morning and work off all the calories before we both gain fifty pounds?"

"Good idea. I am feeling a little piggish." She puffed out her cheeks. "I'll see you there at seven."

The two walked to the door and kissed again. Robbie told him to drive with care, as the snow was continuing to come down at a rapid rate. Brian kissed her one last time, and she lingered in the doorway and watched him drive his truck into the snowy night.

ROBBIE CLOSED THE front door to her house and locked it. It was early, and she thought she'd read for a few hours before turning in for the evening.

She stepped up to the loft and took a book from on top of the desk. She saw her computer and remembered it'd been a while since she'd checked her non-work email account. She sat down, double-clicked the email program, and the various messages popped onto the screen. One was from Vanessa. Startled, she opened the email and felt a chill when she saw the message. She noted the date and time on the email—it'd been sent the day before. She read it several times, then hit the reply button, typed *Call me*, and clicked the send icon.

Robbie located an on-line telephone directory and found Brian's home number. She dialed and let the phone ring until the answering machine engaged, then hung up without leaving a message. She wished she knew his mobile number—she'd written it down but it was at her office at work. She swore at herself for not opening her email sooner.

Robbie glanced at her watch. Brian lived ten minutes away, but with the snowstorm, she figured it'd take at least twice that long for him to get home.

She paced the floor, stopped in front of the computer, and read the message again. It said nothing about Marcus Hatrix or a sick aunt, cousin, or anyone else. The email mentioned memory cards and called them her life insurance policy. "That's what Hatrix wanted," she said out loud.

Robbie trotted down the stairs and over to the armoire. On it was an envelope with her name written on the front in a familiar flowery cursive. Inside was enough money for a month's rent and a moving company. After about fifteen minutes, she dialed Brian's number again. Still no answer. She gazed out the window and saw that the snow was falling at a steady speed—almost a foot had accumulated since the storm began.

Robbie returned to Vanessa's bedroom and pulled open the drawers in the dresser and nightstands. She ducked her head under the bed. Finding nothing, she circled back to the loft. She sat in a chair, picked up a book, and tried to read a few pages. She couldn't concentrate. Her eyes roamed across the words, but nothing registered. All she could think about was Vanessa.

Lifting the phone, Robbie dialed Brian's number once more. This time, he answered. "Brian," she said, gasping, "I was worried about you. What took you so long to get home?"

"Have you looked out your windows?" he asked with a squawk. "The roads are a disaster. There's an accident on the highway by Round Hill, and traffic's backed up for miles."

"Well, I'm glad you made it home safe!" She paused, the information from the email burning in her brain. "Brian, the main reason I was trying to contact you is I received an email from Vanessa." Robbie read the message, punctuating it with editorial comments. "She says nothing about a sick cousin or hooking back up with her boyfriend. She left me an envelope with money to pay for a moving company so there's no reason for her boyfriend to come here and pick up her furniture."

"Then what's he doing with her possessions?"

"Don't you see? The video memory cards. Vanessa says in her email that they're her insurance policy. That's what Hatrix wanted. There are no pictures of the two of them on the beach. Whatever's on those cards is her protection, and he wants them."

"Hatrix didn't mention more than one memory card."

"I know, but her email's specific. It says two. Maybe he only knows about one."

"But we didn't find any."

"I'll dig around some more as soon as I hang up."

"Hunt for keys as well. Hatrix asked about a safe deposit box. She could've hidden a key somewhere."

Robbie ended the call and surveyed the loft, wondering where she should begin her search. She rummaged from room to room throughout the house, but when, after two hours, she hadn't found any memory cards, keys, or anything else, she realized it wasn't going to be easy to solve this mystery.

SEVENTEEN

IT WAS DARK when Brian steered his truck into the parking lot of the Charleston Resort. The storm had subsided, but it had left almost two feet of snow on the ground. Anticipating a slow trip to the casino, he'd started before sunup. In four-wheel drive, he'd had no trouble at all, and it didn't take as long as he'd expected.

Entering the spa, Brian was surprised to find Robbie already dressed in her workout clothes and doing exercises. He changed and joined her on the floor mats. He stretched out his legs. "I'm amazed you got here before me," he said.

Robbie touched her toes with her fingertips. "I'm an early riser. Besides, I couldn't sleep, so I thought I might as well get up and do something constructive."

"How long have you been here?"

She bounced her fingers off her toes. "Oh, I arrived around six."

"I didn't sleep well myself. I had too much on my mind. You didn't call back last night. I assume you didn't find the memory cards?"

Robbie shook her head. "I found nothing."

"Where does that leave us?"

"Maybe Vanessa took them with her to Ohio. But her email said she left the cards as an insurance policy. I'm stumped."

"So am I." Brian tried to make contact with his own toes but was unsuccessful.

"Are you ready for some stair climbing?" Robbie pointed to the machines across the room.

"I am."

They cruised over to the devices and hopped aboard. "Twenty minutes," she said and programmed her machine.

Brian did the same, and they climbed the mechanical stairs, both building up a sweat in minutes. "I was thinking," he said, interrupting the monotony of the workout, "about the memory cards."

Robbie's breathing was labored. "What about them?"

"If Vanessa didn't keep the cards at your house, how about here at the Charleston?"

Tiny beads of perspiration ran down her temples. "Where?"

"In her locker. Most of the employees have one in the locker room by the cafeteria. She could've left them there."

Robbie grasped a small towel from the handrail of the stair climber and wiped her face. "Can you get into her locker?"

"It shouldn't be too difficult. My friend in the Human Resources Department ought to be able to help. I was going to speak with her about Marcus Hatrix anyway."

She held the towel to her chin. "Do you suppose he knows you work here?"

Brian swabbed his chin with an arm. "He didn't act like it. He works graveyard, and it's rare I'm around that late."

"If Hatrix finds out you're employed here, it could be a problem. He may become suspicious. If he believes we have the memory cards and discovers you're a director at the resort, who knows what he might do."

"We don't know what's on the memory cards."

Robbie hung her towel back on the handrail. "He really wants them. It must be something incriminating."

"Let's hope it explains what's happening here."

Robbie checked the console on her machine. "When we get off these things, how about a game of racquetball?"

Brian's squinted at her. "Racquetball? I'm more the baseball type."

Robbie waved her hand at the empty room. "Not this morning. It's just you and me in the spa. We can't field a team. It's going to have to be racquetball."

Brian gripped his shirt collar and wiped off trails of sweat from his temples. "I've played the game maybe once or twice in my life."

"Good. Let's play for money. What's your excuse when you lose?" She grinned, her white teeth glimmering.

Brian laughed. "I haven't decided yet."

After twenty minutes on the stair climbers, Brian followed Robbie to the front desk of the spa. They checked out rackets and whisked over to the courts. They played for about forty minutes, each winning a game.

"Are you up for another one?" Robbie asked, her skin glistening.

Brian was panting hard. "Let's call it a draw for today and play again this weekend."

"You know I'll beat you," Robbie said with another crafty smile.

He spun his racket. "Hey, I won one game. You didn't kick my butt as bad as you thought you would. Next time, though, I'm picking the sport."

"That's fair, but we need to break our tie. I'll reserve a racquetball court for Saturday morning."

"I better go to work. Don't forget dinner tonight at the top of the tram."

"I'm looking forward to it."

"I'll call you later this afternoon. If all goes well with the budget presentation, I should be able to leave work by five." Brian leaned over and kissed her. "I need a shower." He grimaced.

"I like the musky smell of sweaty men."

He winked. "I'll remember that."

AFTER A STEAM and a shower, Brian dressed and wandered through the Charleston's casino on the way to his office. The place was deserted. The storm would be good for the ski resorts, but until the roads were cleared, business at the casinos would be slow. The weather forecasters in San Francisco had warned travelers to stay away from the mountains, and judging by the small number of gamblers in the casino, they were heeding that advice.

A mature woman sat in an desolate section of the casino floor, pressing the spin button on a penny slot machine and staring at the spinning reels. The sound the machine made echoed down the aisle of vacant slots.

Brian always dreaded the impact of winter storms on the resort. He knew everyone would be turning to the Marketing Department for promotions to combat the weather.

Montgomery always became agitated when it was this dead. He wouldn't be in a frame of mind to spend any money. Brian was frustrated by his bad luck and knew his budget presentation needed to be outstanding.

Walking into his outer office, he found Beatrice at her desk, one ear attached to the telephone receiver. "Oh, no," she said. "I hope it doesn't happen. He's such a nice man. Brian won't like that at all."

Her words caught Brian's attention, and he propped himself on the corner of her desk, waiting for the conversation to end. She hung up and looked at him. "That was my friend Connie," Beatrice said. "She's in the dealer's lounge. Says Keith Wallace is

171

telling everyone Jack Mancini's being fired soon and there'll be new management in the casino."

Brian pushed his lips against each other. "Oh, I don't believe that's true."

"He's told several of the dealers." She adjusted her purple dress. "Most of them are upset. Wallace isn't popular. They say he's a dictator."

"He's bragging. Trying to build himself up. Jack's a great casino administrator, and Wallace's attempting to undermine his reputation and promote his own."

Beatrice handed him a stack of manila envelopes. "You're right, but his plan's working. Connie told me many of the dealers believe that Jack's history, and a few of them are already sucking up to Wallace. A lot of power plays are occurring. Some of the dealers trying to get promoted see Wallace as their ticket to advancement."

"That's human nature. It's sure to make Jack's life even more difficult than it already is, though."

Beatrice picked up some slips of paper. "You have a few messages. Rick Anderson called. He needs you to phone him as soon as possible."

"Oh jeez, I have a bad feeling about that. With the snow storm we can't afford anything going wrong."

"He didn't say what he wanted, but told me to tell you it's important."

Brian hustled into his office and got Anderson on the phone.

"There's a problem," Anderson said in a solemn voice.

Brian massaged his temples. "Don't tell me. I'm on edge as it is."

"The final cuts of the commercials are stuck in Sacramento."

"What? What do you mean? Why the hell are they down there?"

"We sent them to a graphics house in Sacramento for final

polishing. The snowstorm's closed the highway, and our courier's waiting for the road to open."

"Can't they email them up?"

"The file's too large."

Brian could feel his heart pounding. "Goddamn it, what are we going to do? Our presentation—"

Anderson broke in. "It'll be okay. The storm's over, and they should be able to clear the roads soon. We have time, but of course we won't be able to see the commercials at our eleven o'clock meeting."

Brian moaned. "I can't believe it. Without those spots, there's no chance of having the budget approved. It was our lone hope."

"You're underestimating how good your presentation is. Remember, a week ago the winners' TV commercials didn't exist. You have an excellent story, with or without the new advertisements. Don't be concerned, though—we'll get the spots here in time."

Brian's tone was an octave higher than normal. "You don't understand how the bad weather affects Montgomery. When the roads are closed, this place loses hundreds of thousands of dollars every day. I'm asking for millions."

"Brian, it'll be fine. I'm bringing the entire staff for the meeting. Even if the commercials don't make it to the lake in time, we'll be prepared to put on a good show. We have the rough cuts and sketches of the commercials. We'll be able to convince Mr. Montgomery to fund your budget."

Brian banged his fist on the desk. "You have to be right."

"I've seen you give presentations before—you're very convincing. The one you gave to the convention authority last month was fantastic. We'll be at there at eleven to go over our plan of attack."

Brian turned his head and sighed out a discouraged rush of air. "Okay, Rick. I'll see you then." He hung up the phone and rolled back in his chair, then closed his eyes and tried to clear his mind, taking a hearty breath. After a few minutes, he felt himself begin to calm down and realized the team could make a great presentation with or without the new television commercials.

Brian swiveled his chair around and looked out the window. The sun was shining, the snow shimmering on the trees. The mountains were draped in white and the lake was sapphire.

He could see cars creeping up and down the road in front of the casinos. Snowplows were working their way along the highway. *Not to worry,* he thought—everything's going to be fine.

EIGHTEEN

A LOUD KNOCK summoned Marcus Hatrix off the sofa, and he opened the front door to find his boss standing there. "What brings you here?" he asked, gesturing for him to come in.

"I'm worried about Vanessa's recording. Did you find it?"

"No, but her roommate had already boxed up all of her clothes and such, so I couldn't poke around. I found no memory cards in what was packed. I asked, and her roommate said she didn't know anything about it."

The man took off his jacket. "I'm sure Vanessa was lying about the whole damn thing. How could she make a video of you in the count room without being seen? If her roommate didn't know about the memory card, it's reasonable to assume it doesn't exist."

Hatrix flopped down on a recliner. "I think you're right, but I'm making another visit to her house. I want to search the place without her roommate there. I have a key—I took it out of Vanessa's purse."

The man sat on the sofa after clearing away some porn magazines and betting sheets. "Not a bad idea. I'm sure she was bluffing, but I agree that one more look around won't hurt."

"I'll hunt for a key as well. It occurred to me she may have hidden the memory card in a safe deposit box."

"Maybe, but be cautious. We don't want the roommate to catch you in the house."

"Just so you know, last night, the roommate, Robbie, gave me the third degree. She asked a lot of questions. I did a good job, though—I'm pretty sure she doesn't suspect anything's wrong. You don't need to worry."

The man's face was stiff. "I have no choice."

Hatrix ran both hands through his thick hair. "Boss, I was wondering, how long do you suppose it'll be before our operation's back in action?"

"When we find a replacement for Vanessa. It won't be easy."

"I'll start trying to line up someone who can take her place. I'd say I know a dozen people who'd do the job."

The man raised an open hand. "Slow down, damn it. We need to be careful. We can't rush into this. We have to look for someone who fits into our plan and has the perfect temperament. I don't want one of your old girlfriends."

Hatrix threw his head back. "Ah, you don't have enough faith in me."

"No, it's not that. I must be extra cautious. There's a lot at stake here."

"I have to get this going very soon. I'm running out of cash fast."

The man's eyebrows fluttered up. "You're low on money? What the hell have you been doing with all of it?"

"My luck's been lousy. I'm sure it'll turn around, but until then, I'm having debt issues."

"You've saved nothing?"

Hatrix smiled, his expression somewhat sheepish. "The sports book keeps calling me. One of these days I'll hit the big one. A perfect parlay card."

"What a way to spend your life. Don't you realize that, in the long run, the house always wins?"

"I know. I just enjoy the excitement of the wager. I can't help it. I don't suppose you'd lend me a little until the thefts resume?"

The man lowered his voice. "I'm not a bank."

"Please, I promise I'll repay you. Besides, I've done some dirty jobs. You owe me."

"I'm not obliged to give you a damn thing."

"What I mean is, I took care of Vanessa's body. I retrieved her stuff. I take the risks at the casino. Without the extra cash coming in from the resort, I need some help."

The man stared at Hatrix with a cold eye. "I'll call the Payroll Department and arrange for a paycheck advance."

Hatrix held his hands out. "But I was hoping for more money than that."

"It's not my problem. You have to stay away from the sports book."

Pissed, Hatrix jammed his fists together. "We have to find someone to take Vanessa's surveillance job. I can't wait to go back into the count room. It's a shame—all that money sitting there, waiting for us."

The man examined his manicured nails. "I'm having some financial difficulties of my own. Damn boat's costing me a fortune. It's been in the red since the day I bought it, and it doesn't appear there's an easy fix."

Hatrix jabbed a thumb at his chest. "I'm going to search for Vanessa's replacement. I promise I won't get us some airhead who'll screw everything up."

The man's look was dark. "Be careful."

"It shouldn't be difficult."

"You must be suspicious of everyone. I don't want you talking with anyone I haven't met first. Do you understand me?"

Hatrix shrugged. "Sure, boss."

"I mean it. There's too much at stake for you to go telling one of your bimbo girlfriends about our scheme."

"I hear you. I have as much at risk in this as you. I can't go back to prison. You've never been there, but I'm sure you can imagine it's not a nice place. It's even worse here in Nevada. The penitentiary in Ely's brutal."

"I bet it is. Okay, enough chat. I better to get back to the office. Call me if you find the video card at Vanessa's place. I could be concerned over nothing, but it won't hurt to check it out further."

"What do you want me to do with her clothes? Her cosmetics?" Hatrix gestured to a door at the back of the room. "It's all in my garage."

The man slanted his head to the left. "I see you have a fireplace. You could start a nice little blaze with the right kindling."

"Oh, yeah. I still have to pick up her furniture. I won't be able to arrange for a truck until Friday."

"Do what's necessary to get this over with." The man stood, put on his coat, and exited the house.

Hatrix turned to the hockey game on the television. The score was San Jose three, Montreal one. He swore at the TV. He was about to lose another bet.

AFTER READING ALL his email, Brian decided he'd pay another visit to Gail Franklin in the personnel office. He needed to keep his mind off the snowstorm and the wayward television commercials. It would be a good distraction to find out more about Marcus Hatrix and take a look at Vanessa Daine's locker. Arriving at the Human Resources Department, he asked for Gail and was escorted to her cubicle.

"Back so soon?" she asked, tapping a pen on her chin.

Brian smiled. "I have a couple more favors to ask of you."

"Sure, anything, Brian. You know that."

"It's about Vanessa Daine."

"Have you spoken with her yet?"

"No, and I take it she hasn't contacted you either."

Gail took a sip of a soda. "Her final paycheck's still awaiting processing. We can't do a thing until we talk with her."

"I want to take a peek at her locker." Brian had no intention of explaining that he was searching for memory cards. "I thought it might give us some clues how to reach her."

"Sounds like a stretch."

"True, but we're now concerned for her safety. She sent an email to my friend that suggested she may be in some sort of trouble."

"Gee, I hope she's all right."

"And that leads me to the second favor. Her boyfriend works here. I was wondering if I could see his personnel file."

"What's his name?"

"Marcus Hatrix. I'm guessing it's spelled, H-A-T-R-I-X. He's a security guard."

Gail typed his name into the computer on her desk. "Hatrix, yes, he's been employed here for two years on the graveyard shift. Let me get his file." She sprang out of her chair and went over to the cabinets along the back wall of the room, opened the drawer marked "H", and lifted out a manila file folder. "He's a mean-looking fellow," she said as she walked back to her desk.

"You have his picture?" Brian asked.

"Yes, we keep photographs of all our employees." Gail handed him the folder.

Brian nodded, remembering his picture was taken when he was hired. He peered at the photo. It was the man who'd come to Robbie's house the night before. "Would you help me through this?" He gave the file back to her. "I'd like to know the basics of his employment."

Gail opened the folder and leafed through the papers. "Well, let's see, as I said, he's worked in security for the last two years. Before that, he did a stint in the Navy, was a bouncer at a nightclub in Oakland, and had a job with a collection agency."

"He seems the bouncer type."

"That's strange. There's no security clearance paperwork." She flipped through the pages, searching for the documentation. "We require a background check on all employees who work as security guards. Nothing major—a police check to make certain they've never committed a crime and a credit report. I don't see anything in this file."

"Is that unusual?"

"Oh, yes. We don't want to hire someone with a criminal record. Not with the amount of money that's in the casino. You wouldn't believe how many felons try to gain employment anyway."

Brian's eyes narrowed. "Then how'd Hatrix get a job if he didn't have a security clearance?"

"I'm not sure. Perhaps someone in upper management recommended him. I can't imagine it'd happen any other way. Maybe Elliot Thomas. It's not unusual that we'd employ someone at the suggestion of higher ups. Half the blackjack dealers are hired based on Jack Mancini's referrals."

"You say he could've been recommended by Elliot Thomas?"

"That's possible and would explain the missing security clearance documents."

"Is there anything else of interest in the file?"

Gail fingered through the pages. "No. He's an average employee—no write-ups, no commendations. He comes to work, does his job, and goes home. Have you asked him about Vanessa Daine's whereabouts?"

"Yes, I spoke with him last night. He said she was in Ohio."

Her brow furrowed. "Don't you believe him?"

"Something about his story doesn't ring true, and I'm not certain I can explain why."

"I wish I was more help."

"No, you've been a great. Thank you. Can we take a look in Vanessa's locker now?"

Gail returned to the computer and typed in Vanessa's name. "She has two lockers—one in the basement and another by the casino cashier."

"The one by the cage is for her purse. It would've only been used when she was working. It's not a place to store personal items for any length of time."

"Her locker in the basement's number one-forty-eight. The key's up front."

Brian accompanied her to the counter near the Human Resources entrance.

"I need the master key to the lockers," Gail said to the receptionist. "It's for a term."

"Is it that easy to get into someone's locker?" Brian asked.

"Yes, we tell every employee their lockers are subject to search without notice. We hope it keeps them free of contraband. We don't want narcotics and such kept in any of the lockers." The receptionist gave Gail a key.

"Does it occur often?" Brian asked.

"As you may be aware," Gail said, "there's a great deal of drug use here at the lake."

He thought of the cocaine they'd found in Vanessa's bathroom. Brian and Gail left the personnel office and trudged down the three floors to the locker room. Row after row of beige lockers filled the area. Gail scanned the room. "Let's see," she said, "one-forty-eight. It's over there." She strode over to a locker in one corner and unlocked the door. The locker was empty.

They stared at the vacant space. "She must've cleaned it out before she quit," Gail said, stating the obvious.

"No clues here," Brian said. "Oh well. Let me know if you hear from her. Anything. Phone calls. Email. Please keep me informed."

"I will. I'm worried too. It's unusual for an employee to quit and not pick up their last paycheck. Something must be wrong."

NINETEEN

BRIAN, ALICE MACKAY, and the representatives from the advertising agency spent several hours going over the final plans for the budget meeting. The television commercials hadn't made it up the mountain, and everyone was tense.

At one o'clock, they headed down the hall to the executive conference room to set up the displays and ready the room for Montgomery. Brian continued to be angry about the missing television spots, while Rick Anderson assured him that, with or without them, the presentation would be fantastic.

"Haven't the roads been cleared yet?" Brian asked again, in what for him was an uncharacteristic whine.

"There was an avalanche by Placerville," Anderson said. "They're clearing the highway as fast as possible. We still have a chance."

Alice looked at Brian. "Quit your bellyaching," she said. "You're getting on my nerves."

With time running out, Brian resigned himself to the fact that he'd be giving the presentation without the new advertisements. He knew worrying would do him no good.

At one-thirty, Tom Montgomery swaggered into the room, followed by Elliot Thomas. In the last few weeks, Thomas seemed to be Montgomery's shadow. The two men moved to the front of the conference table, and each pulled up a seat. The dreaded accountants sat with stoic faces next to them. Brian stood and introduced the people in the room. Montgomery was cordial yet distant. Thomas nodded but didn't speak.

After the introductions, Brian turned to Montgomery and explained the aspects of the marketing budget for the upcoming year. His palms were moist, and he tried to forget that his advancement in the Wyman Corporation rested on a successful presentation.

With the help of the advertising agency, he showed colorful PowerPoint slides of the promotions they planned to conduct, direct mail they would be sending, and the big name entertainment they wanted to book into the showroom.

As the meeting progressed, Montgomery sat in silence, staring at the walls or doodling on a scrap of paper. Brian knew the meeting wasn't going well. He wasn't impressing the general manager at all. Montgomery wasn't asking any questions, and that was a bad sign.

Anderson sensed the same thing and knew it was time to liven up the proceedings. He whispered in his assistant's ear, and the woman walked to the back of the room. Anderson signaled to Brian that they were ready for the next portion of the presentation.

Brian stepped over to the wall and switched off the lights. An awkward silence filled the darkened room.

Montgomery coughed and asked, "What's happening?"

Brian didn't answer, praying the show would begin. After another uncomfortable moment, music played, and a strobe light flashed. A curtain in the back of the room opened, and four showgirls in full-feathered regalia pranced out. Spotlights beamed on them.

Montgomery's head jerked back, and even Thomas sat up

straight in his chair. The tall women strutted around the area, each carrying a placard with different aspects of the budget.

As the showgirls paraded to the corners of the room, a man and woman burst out from behind the curtain. The two broke into a chorus as specifics of the financial impacts of the budget were revealed. A tiny smile crept over Montgomery's lips as the singers warbled on about the virtues of the marketing plan.

Brian relaxed when he saw Montgomery's reaction. He was watching the entertainment and running the budget summation through his mind when he felt a tap on his shoulder. Standing behind him was a smirking Rick Anderson, holding the video cards of the new television commercials. A huge grin enveloped Brian's face.

Anderson wiped his forehead and mouthed, "Whew."

The singers and showgirls concluded their performance, and the lights in the room came back on. "Any questions, Mr. Montgomery?" Brian asked.

"This has been amusing," the general manager said. "I appreciate your creativity, but I'm not convinced I want to spend that much money next year."

The robotic accountants were bobbing their heads in agreement.

Brian was alarmed but maintained his composure. "Yes, sir," he said, "but we've saved the best for last. We have a commercial presentation that'll tie all these marketing plans together and ensure that next year, we do banner business."

Montgomery's expression reflected considerable doubt. "Why do I find that hard to believe?" he asked.

Brian pointed to Anderson, who pressed the play button on a DVR, and the first of the two television commercials played on the large screens. It was soon apparent that Montgomery enjoyed the video. "I'm surprised," he said, "but I liked that. You know, it adds a touch of class to show me paying the money to the winners."

"We thought so too, sir," Anderson said. "You have a commanding presence in front of the camera."

Alice rolled her eyes at Brian.

Anderson played the second spot and received another favorable appraisal from Montgomery. The accountants had no desire to argue with the general manager and sat in silence.

Brian said, "The commercials would set us apart from the competition."

"He's right," Alice said. "Mr. Montgomery, if you remember, most of our competitors have eliminated their television advertising. They're relying almost one hundred percent on direct mail and print. Our videos on both social media and TV will run without competition."

Anderson folded his arms and said, "The beauty of these spots is the flexibility they offer. We can add new winners' videos every time you get one."

"Do you have more video available?" Montgomery asked. "How about the young lady who won the hundred-thousand-dollar keno ticket two months ago? She gave me a sloppy kiss when I handed her the money."

Brian said, "We can obtain that video from the surveillance library. Any video kept by the Surveillance Department can be edited into the commercials."

"Find the one of the keno winner. Boy, she was beautiful." He rubbed his hands together. "Elliot, do you remember her? She was a knockout."

Thomas grunted in the affirmative.

"I can find that video," Brian said.

"If we acquire the footage right away," Anderson said, "we can edit it into the commercials in a jiffy."

"Do it," Montgomery said.

Brian said, peering at Thomas, "May I get into the surveillance room this afternoon?"

Thomas scowled at him, then looked at the general manager. "Mr. Montgomery," he said, "I don't want outsiders in the surveillance areas. We have a lot of ongoing investigations, and I don't like it when my people are interrupted. We store many sensitive videos there."

Brian stared at Elliot Thomas. They stored sensitive videos. Vanessa Daine's videos. Her memory cards. That was where they must be.

"Shepard, you're just going to have to do without them," Thomas said with clear displeasure in his voice. "My people are too busy to track down your cards, and I don't like having distractions in my Surveillance Department."

Brian eyed him with a feeling of urgency. He had to get into the surveillance room and search for Vanessa's recordings. He said, "I'll be in and out in less than half an hour. I won't disturb your people. I've been there before and know how to read the memory card catalogs. I can retrieve the video in minutes."

"Oh, why not, Elliot?" Montgomery said. "What can it hurt?"

Thomas's face was tight. "I'd advise against it," he said.

"No, let Shepard find the keno video. Arrange for him to get into the surveillance room this afternoon."

Thomas glared at Brian and shook his head.

"Excellent," Anderson said. "Brian, like I said, if you'll get the video to me, we'll create a new version of the spot right away."

"I insist on seeing it," Montgomery said. "Shepard, your budget's more expensive than I expected, but the way those winners' commercials tie in with the promotions and the entertainment lineup is great. I'm impressed. I'll need to assess the entire property's budget, but I think I can approve most of what you've requested. I may have to find something to cut in another department."

Brian's smile was victorious. "Thank you, sir," he said. "This program should ensure a strong year."

"It better. I wish you had a marketing plan to overcome last night's snowstorm."

"I'm working on it."

"The storm aside, this company's having a cash flow crisis due to the low pit hold percentage. We can't seem to win a table games bet in the casino. Until we do, I'm really counting on you to drive large volumes of customers into this resort."

"This marketing plan will do that, sir. I expect the hold problem will be resolved soon as well."

Montgomery gazed at him with an antagonistic eye. "Your colleague, Mr. Mancini, better see to it."

"I'm confident he will."

"He's running out of time."

With that comment, it was clear the meeting was over. The general manager stood up and marched out of the room. Before Elliot Thomas departed, Brian made an appointment to meet him at the cashier's cage, Thomas again expressing his opposition. He knew, however, that he couldn't overrule Tom Montgomery.

BRIAN RETURNED TO his office, picked up the telephone, and dialed Robbie's mobile number. "I had an idea," he said when she answered.

"Brian," she said, "how was your budget presentation?"

"It went well. We had a few stressful moments waiting for the TV commercials to arrive here from Sacramento—the storm closed the highway—but Montgomery liked it. He said he'd approve my budget. It was during the meeting that I realized where Vanessa probably stored the memory cards she describes in her email. The video library in the Surveillance Department. It's an area where they keep all the surveillance videos—the memory cards are logged there and held for future use. I'm sure Vanessa's cards are there."

"Can you get to them?"

"That's the beautiful part. I'm going to the Surveillance Department this afternoon to obtain a video for one of my commercials, and while I'm there, I can look for Vanessa's recordings. I'm not yet certain how to find the memory cards without raising suspicion, but I'll come up with something."

"I'm sure they have thousands of memory cards. How will you know where to begin?"

"There are separate logs for the cards they store a short time and the ones they keep for an indefinite period. I plan on focusing on the long-term logs."

"It still sounds tedious."

"It will be, but I'll just search for memory cards cataloged by Vanessa. What's her full name? In the video logs, the person who catalogs the memory cards puts their initials next to the card number. Do you know her middle name?"

"Gee, Brian, I don't know...I remember she didn't like it. Hold on, I know it'll come to me. Myrna, Mona, I can't recall the exact name, but her initials are VMD."

"Great, that'll be a big help. I'm returning to the Surveillance Department today at four. I'll stay as long as I can, or until I track down Vanessa's memory cards. I hope it's the latter."

"Should we cancel our dinner plans?"

"At Heavenly, yes, but I must see you. If I locate the memory cards, I'll want to review them with Jack as well."

"Why don't I phone Jack and Hailey and invite them over to my house for dinner? Nothing fancy—I'll order a pizza."

Brian was almost panting. "I can't wait to be with you," he said, surprised once again by his own fervor.

"Be careful in the surveillance room. We don't know who's behind the thefts. Whoever it is, they won't appreciate your presence."

TWENTY

BUSINESS IN THE Charleston's casino was still slow when Brian set out for the cashier's cage. The roads to Lake Tahoe were now open, but it was apparent that traffic was light and few customers were making the journey up the mountain.

The old lady he'd seen earlier in the day was at her slot machine, staring with determination at the spinning reels. Almost seven hours had gone by since he'd last watched her at the machine. He wondered if she'd been playing the same one all that time.

Approaching the security booth near the casino cashier, Brian glanced at the guard but didn't recognize the man. He waited for more than twenty minutes, agitated, but there was no sign of Elliot Thomas.

Brian paced, then, with great annoyance, caught the attention of the security guard and asked if he'd call Thomas's office. The officer seemed put out by his request, but after Brian identified himself, he picked up the telephone. Brian could hear him wend through a series of secretaries. He turned to Brian and cupped a hand over the mouthpiece. "I'm sorry, Mr. Shepard," he said, "but Mr. Thomas isn't in his office. His secretary says he's off-property. Do you want to leave a message?"

"Let me speak with her," Brian said and reached for the phone. He introduced himself and asked about Thomas's whereabouts.

The secretary said, "I'm sorry, but Mr. Thomas has an appointment out of the building." Her tone could best be described as cranky. "I don't know when he'll return."

"Gee, that puts me in a bind. I need get into the surveillance room. Mr. Montgomery directed that I obtain a video recording of a big keno winner."

"Mr. Montgomery?"

He could hear her skepticism. "We're using the video in an advertisement."

"Oh, dear. I don't know how to contact Mr. Thomas. He's not answering his mobile phone."

"Perhaps Derrick Stagg could help me." Brian knew he'd be cooperative.

The woman paused. "Yes, that might work. I'll see if I can locate him. Hold on." He waited for a few minutes, until the secretary came back on the line. "One moment, please, for Mr. Stagg."

A few seconds later, Brian heard Stagg's voice and he explained his reason for returning to the Surveillance Department. Stagg said there'd be no problem and that he would meet him at the security booth in five minutes.

Brian was pleased he could return to the video storage library without the presence of Elliot Thomas. His hassle getting into the surveillance room would be worth it, knowing Thomas wouldn't be lurking over his shoulder. It'd be difficult enough finding Vanessa's memory cards as it was and, without a doubt, impossible if he had to contend with an unhappy observer.

ONCE STAGG ARRIVED at the security booth, he led Brian through the tangle of hallways, doors, and the elevator to the Surveillance Department. Entering the main room, Brian was again fascinated by the wall of video monitors and the silent people who sat in front of them. He still found it difficult to believe anyone could steal money from the count room under the eyes of so many security personnel.

Brian and Stagg walked past the row of video monitor workstations and over to the storage library. Stagg said, "I have a meeting with the Gaming Control Board in five minutes. Can you find the video without my assistance?"

"I suppose so," Brian said, hiding his glee at his continued good fortune. First no Thomas and now no Stagg. He was going to be left alone to hunt for the memory cards. Lady Luck hadn't given him a break earlier in the morning but was smiling on him now. "Would you give me a quick refresher course?"

Stagg turned to the bookshelf. "The video you're seeking is in the long-term logs. You'll need to look here, in one of these catalogs." He pulled a binder from the shelf and passed it to Brian. "The memory cards are cataloged by date and subject. If you run into a problem, ask one of the surveillance people for Alex Jameson. He'll give you a hand."

"I should be okay."

"Don't forget to log out the memory cards you take. We have to account for all the videos borrowed from the library. Elliot would explode if you took one without logging it out."

Brian chuckled. "I will. I'm pretty sure I'm not a favorite of Elliot's. I won't do anything to make him angry at me."

"That's wise."

After Stagg left Brian alone in the video library, he surveyed the area, trying to familiarize himself with the layout. He was surrounded on three sides by shelves containing tray after tray of memory cards, each one marked with a number.

Brian decided he'd better find the video of the keno winner first. Once he had that recording, he'd have the luxury of locating Vanessa's memory cards with no fear of running out of time.

Brian flipped open the logbook and scanned the page of entries. The keno winner video had been recorded in August. He sifted through each of the keno listings during that month and found one with the title: *$100,000 Keno*. He wrote down the number and searched for the memory card on the shelves. The catalog system was simple and straightforward, and it took him no time at all to find the correct one.

Sitting in front of a monitor, Brian inserted the memory card in a DVR, pressed the play button, and watched as pictures of the casino played back at him. He wanted to make sure this was the right video. He'd have a damn hard time explaining to Montgomery if it turned out he had the wrong one. He pushed the fast-forward button and saw the place come alive in quick motion.

Within minutes, Brian observed a keno board with eight blinking numbers. He tapped the play button, and the video returned to a normal speed. *Those must be the winning keno numbers,* he thought. The camera panned back to reveal a voluptuous brunette in her twenties hopping up and down and hugging everyone in sight.

Brian stared at the video as the woman was surrounded by well-wishers and personnel from the Keno Department. It showed the woman filling out paperwork—he guessed it was tax forms—as men in dark suits circled her. One of them was Tom Montgomery.

The general manager ushered the young lady over to the keno counter and spoke with her for a brief period. Sarah Calder, the cashier and credit manager, handed a stack of hundred-dollar bills to Montgomery. He tore the strap off the money and counted out the currency into the woman's trembling palms.

Brian could see the flash of a camera and remembered he'd sent the casino photographer to take pictures of the event. As Montgomery doled out the money, the woman shook with excitement. After all the bills were in her hands, she grabbed him by the neck and gave him a kiss on the lips. He leered and grinned so wide his cheeks must have hurt.

Brian hit the stop button on the DVR and removed the memory card. He logged it out in a file folder and laid it on the table. It was now time to locate the missing videos recorded by Vanessa Daine.

Brian opened a long-term logbook and looked for Vanessa's initials: VMD. He checked every page in the first log but didn't see any entries with her initials. He put the book away and studied the catalogs. Extracting another one from the shelf, he again leafed through the listings. The dates in this log were more than a year old. He wanted something more recent.

Brian worked through the logbooks until he found one with entries posted the preceding day and some almost two years old. He turned the pages, identifying twelve listings with the initials VMD.

He wasn't sure where to begin but thought he should focus on the most recent entries. Then again, he wasn't certain when Vanessa had recorded the videos. The first cataloged memory card was dated October 20th, and he jotted the library code number on a Post-it note and stepped over to the shelves. Finding the card, he inserted it in the DVR and pressed the play button. Images of the casino emerged on the monitor. Brian hit the fast-forward button and saw the video speed by but could perceive nothing of interest. It took about five minutes for the video to end, and he returned the memory card to the tray on the shelf.

Brian reviewed the log and searched for the next entry with Vanessa's initials. Pulling out the card, he stuck it in the DVR and concentrated on the video. Once more, nothing seemed to be of significance. He watched the video on each memory card in the same sequence they were cataloged. He noticed most of the videos focused on individual people but didn't see what value these recordings would have to Vanessa. His eyes were becoming tired from scrutinizing each of the videos, and he rubbed them. Shaking his head, he pored through two more logbooks and examined Vanessa's entries but found nothing unusual.

Frustrated, Brian grabbed another binder—this one titled *Special Projects*—and slogged his way down the ones with VMD next to the posted subject. He was concerned to see that there were many but viewed each one with resolve, worried about the time. He'd been in the storage library well over an hour, and it'd be difficult to explain should Stagg return. He had four more videos to check out in this catalog, so hastily he pulled another memory card from the shelf and pushed it in the DVR. Again, nothing unusual. Brian feared that maybe Vanessa hadn't kept the memory cards in the library after all. Perhaps he'd guessed wrong. Even if she had, there were many more catalogs and too many videos for him to peruse today. He was ready to give up. The task was too daunting.

Just a few more, Brian thought, and took another memory card from the library shelf and popped it in the DVR. Once more, he could see nothing of any relevance in the video. He shoved the second to last card from that catalog in the DVR and poked the play button. Like all the others, the monitor jumped to life, but in seconds, he could tell something was different. He wasn't seeing pictures of the casino. No, it was the soft count room. Brian felt his pulse accelerate. He inspected the logbook and the topic posted for the memory card. It was titled *Thomas*. He pressed the fast-forward button and watched the count room on the screen until a figure materialized in the picture. He pushed the stop button, moved the video backwards, and tapped play.

Brian saw a big man wearing a hood and carrying a bag

enter the soft count room. The guy placed the bag on the table and walked over to one of the cabinets along the back wall. He took a ring of keys from his pocket and unlocked the metal mesh door.

Brian wished he could recognize the man, but the hood concealed his face. After opening the cabinet door, the guy latched on-to the first drop box on the top shelf and yanked it out of the cabinet. He set it on the table and, with another key, opened it. Brian could see the box was brimming with currency. The man took hundred-dollar bills from inside and put them in his bag. Brian was mesmerized by what he was seeing and realized he was holding his breath in disbelief.

Once he'd removed the money from the box, the hooded man locked it up, returned it to the cabinet, and retrieved another one. He again laid the box on the table and fished out the hundreds.

Brian couldn't believe what he was seeing, but it explained the low hold. This was a theft on a grand scale. He stabbed the fast-forward button and watched the thief repeat the larcenous process over and over again as the images flew across the monitor.

As the video neared the end, he saw the man lock up the drop box cabinet, take the bag from the table, and exit the room. The picture on the screen faded to snow soon after. Brian hit the stop button and ejected the memory card from the DVR. He was tucking it inside his jacket pocket when he heard a voice he dreaded shout out across the surveillance room.

"Shepard," Elliot Thomas said, his tone enraged. "What the hell are you doing in here?"

Brian turned to him, holding his left arm against the memory card that wasn't yet inside his pocket. "Oh, hey, Elliot." He was trying his damnedest to act nonchalant. "I'm here to get the keno video Montgomery wanted." He stood.

"How long does it take?" Thomas barged toward Brian. "Stagg told me he let you in here over an hour ago."

Brian could feel perspiration streaming down his armpits. "I couldn't find the video. I guess I didn't understand the catalog system as well as I thought, but I just found it." He picked up the keno winner memory card from the table and waved it in Thomas's face, hoping Thomas wouldn't notice he couldn't lift his left arm which was still squeezing Vanessa's card to his side.

Thomas looked at the logbook on the table. "No wonder you couldn't locate the video. This catalog has nothing to do with casino winners. This log's for special projects and it's confidential. How much did you see?"

"I saw the first page. All it shows are catalog entries, for god's sake. It didn't have any keno listings during August of this year, so I moved on to the next book. Here, let me put it back on the shelf." Brian grabbed the catalog and reached up to place it in the library. As he lifted the binder, the memory card under his arm began to slip. He pushed the binder onto the shelf and whirled around, catching the small card with his elbow.

Thomas shot him a quizzical frown and inclined his head to the side.

Brian was sweating, his shirt soaked, and the perspiration was causing the memory card to slide even more. He was certain any second it'd tumble to the floor. "I better be going," he said. "I must take this video to the advertising agency. Montgomery wants the television commercial pronto."

Thomas was suspicious, his eyes narrowing. "What's wrong with you?"

"Not a thing." Brian's heart was pounding so loud, he was convinced Thomas could hear it. "It sure is hot in here, though. You should call the engineering office and have them check the ventilation."

"I don't like this." Thomas's cheeks were red with rage. "Montgomery was wrong to allow you in here. From now on, if you require a video, my people will find it. I don't like you snooping around my department."

"F-Fine. In the future I'll do just that. I needed this video immediately to appease Montgomery. Next time I'll call you." Desperate, Brian clutched the memory card between his elbow and side.

"It was my intention to retrieve the keno winner video *for* you."

"I'm sorry, but I had to have the recording today. You were supposed to meet me at four."

Spittle shot out of Thomas's mouth as he spoke. "I had an emergency meeting in Carson City. I never expected you'd come here without my permission."

"I had Montgomery's authorization. Derrick Stagg was obliging and brought me here."

"I'll take care of Stagg."

Brian shook a finger at him. "Don't blame Derrick, goddamn it. He was accommodating my request."

Thomas glowered at him. "It's my department, and I'm the one who makes demands of my people."

"What's done is done. The next time I need a video, I'll call you and only you."

Thomas continued to eye him with extreme displeasure, his nostrils flared.

Brian tried to relax, but the precarious position of the memory card made it impossible.

"It's time for you to leave," Thomas said and stomped out of the video library.

Brian took the opportunity to seize the memory card and slip it in the pocket of his jacket. For the first time in minutes, he was able to breathe. He now wanted out of there as fast as possible.

Brian trailed Thomas through the surveillance room and to the elevator lobby. He glanced down at his jacket, irrationally afraid the memory card in his pocket was visible through the fabric. He slouched so the jacket hung away from his body.

The elevator arrived, and the two men boarded the car and stood in silence. At the first floor, Brian exited the elevator. Thomas didn't follow. "You know your way to the casino," he said.

Brian said, "Thank you again for all your assistance..." The doors closed before he could finish his sentence. "...asshole."

BRIAN RETURNED TO his office, took Vanessa's memory card from his jacket pocket, and placed it in his briefcase. He was elated he had the video but wouldn't be at ease as long as he was still at the Charleston.

He picked up the phone and dialed Robbie's number. He couldn't wait to tell her what he'd found. She answered and said, "Brian, my home's been broken into."

Alarmed, he asked, "What happened?"

"The house was ransacked. Jack and Hailey are here with me now. I called them, and they came right over. We searched the place, but whoever was inside's long gone."

"Is anything missing?"

"Not that I can tell. There's a good mess, though. It's going to take me some time to make a complete inventory, but I don't think anything's gone. He had a key. No windows were broken, and I know the doors were all locked when I left. I'm sure the prowler was Marcus Hatrix trying to find Vanessa's memory cards."

"I don't like the thought of it, but it's a reasonable guess."

"I should've known he'd want a better look around my house. Remember how upset he was when he saw we'd packed up her possessions?"

"Well, it was a waste of his time. I found one of Vanessa's memory cards here."

"You did? Fantastic."

"It was in the surveillance video storage library. I didn't get a chance to locate the second card, but it doesn't matter. The one I have's incredible and explains what's been occurring. I'm leaving the Charleston now, and I'll be at your place in fifteen minutes."

NOT WANTING TO take any risks, Brian slipped out of his office through the side door and took the back stairs to the first floor. By the time he left the Charleston the road had been cleared and driving was not a problem. After checking the rearview mirror, and surveying the traffic around him, he felt secure that he had removed the video from the casino without being discovered.

Brian considered stopping by the liquor store and picking up a bottle of wine, but after eyeing his briefcase, he thought better of it.

He pulled up to Robbie's house and was greeted at the door by Jack. "It sounds like you've had an interesting day. Robbie says you found one of Vanessa's videos."

Brian took off his jacket and tossed it on the sofa. "Is she okay?"

"Yeah, she's fine. A little unnerved that someone rifled through her place, but she's dealing with it. Tell me about the recording."

"Let me see Robbie first." Brian hurried through the intruder's mess in the living room. He found Robbie in the kitchen and embraced her. He didn't want to let go of her, but once assured she was all right, he opened his briefcase and took out the memory card.

"What's on it?" Hailey asked.

Brian said, "An explanation for the low hold at the Charleston. Let's take a peek." He led them to the loft and

Robbie's computer. Brian switched it on and inserted the memory card in the machine, then clicked the play icon, and the four watched as the video rolled.

"Look at him," Jack said, pointing. "Goddamn it, do you see that, Hailey? I can't believe it. He's just stuffing hundred-dollar bills into the bag."

Brian said with sarcasm, "And you wondered why the casino has a low hold percentage. You have a partner getting the first count."

Robbie asked, "How can this be taking place without everyone finding out? Where's the security?"

"That's a good question," Jack said. "Any thoughts, Brian?"

"I'm not certain," he said, shaking his head. "I've been up in the surveillance room several times now, and I don't see how the entire department could be in on this. Even on the graveyard shift."

"Perhaps Vanessa was alone in the surveillance room when these thefts were happening."

"No, Jack. There are always a handful of people observing the monitors. It'd be difficult to get so many accomplices."

"We're talking about a lot of money."

"What about Vanessa?" Robbie asked.

"She was involved up to her eyeballs," Brian said. "We know now for sure."

Her expression was grim. "It's been three days, and I haven't heard from her yet. I'm so concerned."

"Hatrix said she's in Ohio."

"I think he's the man in the video."

"You can't see his face," Hailey said.

"I know. But see, Brian, the guy in the video's a large dude, like Hatrix." Robbie motioned to the computer. "They have the same build."

Brian concentrated on the screen. "Yeah, I agree," he said.

"What are we going to do now? Call the sheriff?"

"We have a recording of a major casino theft. We need to contact Cory—he can get things rolling with the Gaming Control Board."

"Yes, but we must piece this together better," Jack said. "We have some unanswered questions, such as how'd the fellow in the video obtain the keys to the drop boxes?"

"Listen to this," Brian said. He pounded a fist into his open hand. "Elliot Thomas is the Director of Surveillance and Security, right? Well, his name was used to catalog Vanessa's digital recording. All the memory cards in the storage library are logged in books, and this one was cataloged under the title, *Thomas.* Elliot Thomas is behind all of this—I'm certain of it. It all adds up. The memory card was filed under his name, he's in charge of the Surveillance Department, and the extra keys to the drop boxes, cabinets, and the soft count room were delivered to the security office. If you ask me, I'd say he's the mastermind behind the thefts. You should've seen how he reacted to my being in the surveillance room. He almost caught me with Vanessa's video. I know he wondered why I had a guilty look. He told me he didn't want me in the surveillance rooms anymore. We now know why."

"This is unbelievable," Robbie said. "I wonder how Vanessa became involved in this. We'll never know how all this happened if we don't contact her. She has the answers to our questions."

Brian gestured to Jack. "We need to talk with Cory as soon as possible. We can show him the video and get his advice on how to proceed."

Jack said, "Let's meet Cory at your cabin tomorrow at noon. That'll give me time to speak with Ben Genetti and find out what he has to say about the fifth set of high security keys."

Robbie asked, "Mind if I join you at your meeting? I'd like to know what Cory recommends we do about Vanessa."

"Sure," Brian said. He smiled at her. "I'm positive he'll appreciate your insight."

"Hey, where's the pizza?" Jack asked. "I'm famished."

Robbie said, "Yes, we have to celebrate Brian's success with his budget presentation."

"It went well?"

"It did," Brian said. "Montgomery loved the television commercials. If he hadn't, I wouldn't have found Vanessa's video. He requested I use a recording of a specific keno winner in one of the spots and gave me permission to go up to the surveillance room to retrieve the video. That gave me the opportunity to search for Vanessa's at the same time. I can't emphasize enough how unhappy Elliot Thomas was about that." He turned to Jack, his face serious. "The problem is, Thomas and his buddy, Keith Wallace, have convinced Montgomery you're responsible for the low hold percentage. They say it's poor management."

Jack's eyes flashed. "Just my luck. Damn it."

The four friends made their way down the stairs to the kitchen, where Robbie pulled a bubbling pizza out of the oven.

"Mmm, smells good," Hailey said. "What can I do to help?"

"Would you select a bottle of wine from the rack?" Robbie asked, gesturing to the wine rack next to the refrigerator. "There's a nice cabernet on top."

Hailey struggled to reach the bottle.

"Here, let me get it for you," Brian said. He took the wine from the rack and handed it to her.

"My, aren't you gallant?" Hailey said with a sparkle in her eyes.

"I am. Always have been."

"I don't know about that, but I've noticed a change in you. You do seem to be much more pleasant."

"I wonder why that is?" Jack asked. He fixed his gaze on Robbie and grinned.

TWENTY-ONE

ONCE AGAIN, BRIAN woke up before his alarm went off. That was starting to annoy him, but he had so much on his mind, he couldn't sleep more than a couple of restless hours. He thought of Robbie and smiled. He enjoyed being with her but was somewhat afraid of the feelings he was having. He couldn't stop thinking about her. Jack had said he could tell he was smitten. To Brian's surprise, he knew it was more than that.

Brian dragged himself out of bed and endured the drudgery of a shower and shave. He prepared himself a quick breakfast of cereal and a banana, then took off for the Charleston Resort.

Crossing into his outer office, he of course found Beatrice on the telephone. She was deep in conversation, whispering to the party on the other end of the line. Seeing him, she made a hasty end to the call and hung up the phone.

"What was that all about?" Brian asked.

She had a sly smirk on her face. "Nothing much. Just girl talk."

He studied her with twisted lips. "Spill it, Beatrice. I know you. Something's up. What gives?"

She leaned closer to him, the thrill of hot gossip glowing in her eyes. "Well, last night, there was a dinner party in the South

Shore convention room. It was a bunch of social mucky mucks from the Tahoe basin. You know, all the lakefront homeowners. A fancy affair with lots of gowns and jewelry. Every luxury car at the lake was parked in the garage. I hear the food was fabulous. Lobster, crab, and the most tender prime rib—"

Brian cut her off, as always wishing she'd get to the point. "And?"

"Mr. Montgomery and his wife were there. They were arguing and made quite a loud ruckus."

"Hmm. Do you know what were they bickering about?"

Beatrice was almost out of breath, she was so excited. "It seems Mr. Montgomery was talking with this pretty redhead. I hear he has a thing for attractive women. Mrs. Montgomery didn't like it one bit. They had words, and she left in a huff. She ordered her limousine driver to take her home, and he was last seen leaving with the redhead. The whole convention staff's abuzz."

"Such a soap opera." Brian was feeling a little guilty for becoming involved in Beatrice's passion. "Enough of this. I'm behind on my paperwork because of the budget presentation, and I need to work. My inbox is overflowing."

"I hate to say this, Brian, but your day won't be starting out well."

His left eyebrow rose as she said that. "Yeah, why not?"

"Skip Sullivan. Your problem child."

"What now?"

"He missed the late show last night."

Brian bristled. "He what?"

"He said he was ill, but I was told he was so drunk he couldn't stand up, let alone perform."

"Jesus, I'm tired of his antics. Why didn't anyone call me?"

Beatrice shrugged. "I'm sure there was nothing you could do. Sullivan was out of it. He couldn't see straight. I hear the customers in the showroom were upset and the maître d' had to give them all rain checks."

"Damn it, that'll cost us a bundle. I'm phoning his agent and renegotiating his contract. Sullivan has another week here, and we can't afford to have him canceling shows."

"There's more bad news, Brian. The entertainment reporter from KTVN wants to speak with you. He's looking for the inside scoop on Sullivan. I told him Skip was ill, but I'm not certain he believed me."

"I guess I better give him a call. You're right—this is going to be a lousy morning."

"I'm still not done ruining it. Elliot Thomas was just here, fuming about what he thinks is lost revenue in the casino. He was furious with Skip Sullivan and is blaming you for booking, and I quote, 'a drunken idiot.' He didn't have anything nice to say about you or Sullivan. I defended you the best I could."

"Where's Thomas now?"

She aimed her chin toward the hallway. "He went to Mr. Montgomery's office. He said he'd get hold of you later."

"I can't wait," Brian said with a sardonic lilt." He muttered to himself while walking into his office. It was bad enough Thomas was after Jack, but now he was talking with the general manager about the temperamental entertainers Brian was booking into the showroom. Didn't Thomas realize most celebrities were high-strung?

Brian forced himself to push those thoughts aside and spent the rest of the morning trying to catch up on paperwork and projects he'd put on hold. Rick Anderson stopped by the office to pick up the video of the keno winner and promised it would be edited into the commercials without delay.

Brian contacted Skip Sullivan's agent in Los Angeles, and they had a long discussion about the antics of the popular comedian. The agent promised to have a word with his client and said he would take care of the problem. Brian was less than comforted by his assurances, but there was nothing more he could do.

He phoned Tom Galloway at KTVN and told the reporter Sullivan was fine and just hadn't felt well the previous night. He neglected to tell him the reason. The reporter sounded suspicious but didn't press the issue. Galloway asked for an interview with the comedian, and Brian advised him to contact Sullivan's agent.

Brian departed his office at eleven o'clock. He wanted to take a spin around the casino before going to the Port of Subs for sandwiches. Business in the casino had improved from the previous day. The roads had been cleared of snow, and the skiers were arriving. Groups of pretty women in sweaters were standing in the lobby of the hotel as hunky men in parkas tried to attract their attention. Now that sufficient snow had fallen, he thought it was time to get his own skis out of storage and ready for the slopes.

Meandering through the casino, Brian looked up at the domed plastic bubble concealing a surveillance camera. He wondered if he was being observed. An uncomfortable feeling came over him, and he decided it was time to leave the Charleston Casino Resort.

BRIAN HAD BEEN home just a few minutes when Jack, Robbie, and Cory arrived. He'd spread the sandwiches and lunch fixings on the kitchen table, and they each took something to eat.

"Enough of the suspense," Cory said with a mouthful of a turkey bacon club. "Jack says you know what's behind the low hold problem at the Charleston. Tell me everything."

Brian said, "We have a recording we need you to see." He took the memory card from his briefcase and put it in the laptop computer on the counter. "I retrieved this video from the surveillance library at the casino."

Brian clicked the play icon, sat down, and the hooded man appeared on the screen.

Cory viewed the action, transfixed. "This is unbelievable," he said. "How'd you acquire this?"

"It's a long story," Jack said.

"Tell me every detail."

Brian, Robbie, and Jack told Cory all they knew, starting with Vanessa Daine and ending with Brian taking the memory card from the surveillance room the previous evening.

"There's more," Jack said. "I met with Ben Genetti this morning." He turned to face Cory. "Genetti's the security guard who took four sets of the drop box, cabinet, and soft count room keys to the vault after they were delivered by the locksmith from Reno."

"What did he say?" Brian asked. He inched forward in his chair in anticipation.

"He admits he took the keys to the vault but says he didn't sign for them when they were shipped by the locksmith. I bet you can guess who did take possession of the keys when they were delivered."

"Marcus Hatrix," Robbie said.

Jack pointed at her. "Right you are."

"What else did Genetti say?" Brian asked, staring at Jack.

"He told me Hatrix received the keys from the locksmith and asked him if he'd take them to the vault. Genetti agreed and followed all the proper procedures. He insists he was given four sets of each key. It's clear Hatrix kept the fifth one for himself."

Cory said, "It bothers me that the memory card in the surveillance library was cataloged under the name *Thomas.* If Elliot Thomas is involved, this goes deeper than I'd have ever imagined."

"We don't have any proof other than the recording and the log."

"The video's substantial evidence, but it would be a mistake to go to Montgomery and accuse Elliot Thomas of theft until we have something more concrete."

"Then what do we do?" Brian asked.

"Let me speak with my boss, William Cavanaugh, chairman of the Gaming Control Board. This is serious. The state of Nevada works hard to maintain a clean gaming industry, and I'm positive Cavanaugh will want to determine what's going on ASAP."

"What do we do about Vanessa?" Robbie asked. "I haven't heard from her in days. And Hatrix wants to pick up her furniture tomorrow night after I get off work. Should we call the sheriff?"

Cory gave her a reassuring smile. "Let me take care of that. I have some good connections with law enforcement around here. In the meantime, I insist that all of you be careful. It's obvious a lot of money's been stolen from the Charleston and I'm confident the thieves, whoever they are, will do whatever's necessary to protect themselves."

"What about Hatrix?" Brian asked.

"I'll talk with Chairman Cavanaugh this afternoon and see what direction he wants us to take."

"We need him to make a decisive move," Jack said. "The heat's on me at the casino."

Cory nodded. "I appreciate your circumstances. I'm certain Chairman Cavanaugh will act on this as fast as possible. I'll call you after I've spoken with him."

"Make sure he knows the position we're in."

Brian plucked the memory card from the laptop and handed it to Cory. "Take good care of this," he said.

Cory took it and put an arm around Brian's shoulders. "I'll have copies made as soon as I return to the office."

After lunch, they escorted Cory to his car and watched him drive away. "Now we wait and see," Brian said.

"It's difficult when you're in the dark," Jack said, closing his eyes for a second. "I hope I'm not fired before the lights come on."

"That won't happen."

They all left Brian's cabin and returned to their respective jobs, where they each attempted to concentrate on work, but it was impossible.

DRESSED IN LEVI'S, a white shirt, and a tweed sport jacket, Brian hopped into his truck and headed for what he hoped would be a romantic evening with Robbie.

Before leaving his cabin, he'd received a call from Cory Wyatt. The chairman of the Gaming Control Board wanted to meet with them right away and Cory was arranging a get-together for the following morning.

Brian agreed to join Cory and the chairman at their offices in Carson City. Cory had already contacted Jack, who'd said he'd attend, but he'd been unable to reach Robbie. Brian told him he was having dinner with her that evening and would let her know about the meeting.

"Tell her it's essential she be there," Cory said, an inflection in his voice that made it clear it wasn't a request but a demand.

Driving through the trees toward Robbie's house, Brian thought about the events of the past week and how much his life had changed in such a short period of time. It was all happening so fast. The pressures of his job were mounting, there were the thefts at the casino, and there was Robbie.

Robbie…just thinking about her made his heart rate pick up. He'd never met someone like her before.

Brian's iPhone rang, and he dug in his pocket for it. He looked at the screen. It was Rachael Banks. The phone kept ringing. He'd met her in a bar a few weeks ago, and she'd been hot and into him. He remembered she was a good kisser. They'd exchanged telephone numbers. The phone continued to ring. He let it go to voicemail.

BRIAN GAZED OUT the window and across the basin. The aerial tram at Heavenly Lake Tahoe climbed up the mountain above the lake to an elevation of 8,250 feet above sea level. Heavenly was one of the largest ski resorts in the country—straddling two states, it had thirty chair lifts and some of the best skiing found anywhere. From almost every slope, there was a breathtaking view of Lake Tahoe and the surrounding mountains.

It was getting dark, and Brian could see the lights on the other side of the lake. A storm was looming and black clouds were billowing over the summits of the Sierras. He delighted in the ascent while Robbie showed some apprehension as the car glided above the treetops. She was pretty in a pair of white slacks and a blue blouse. Her long hair flowed over her shoulders, and he could smell the gentle fragrance of lilacs.

"Don't you like heights?" Brian asked. He peered down at the jagged rocks below.

Robbie fidgeted with a silver bracelet. "Heights I don't mind. It's trams I don't like. When I was a child, I heard about a tram falling off its cable at Squaw Valley. I know it was a long time ago, but it made me always fear these contraptions."

Brian turned away from the window. "I try not to reflect on tragedies like that."

At the top of the mountain, the two entered the restaurant and ordered dinner. Brian selected a nice Sonoma County Fume Blanc, and the two of them relaxed and enjoyed each other's company. Brian relayed the request from Cory about the meeting with the chairman of the Gaming Control Board. Without hesitation, Robbie said she'd be there, and they decided not to bring up the subject again. For the rest of the night, they laughed and told stories. Most of all, Brian realized this relationship was becoming something extraordinary.

That night, they made love for the first time. It seemed the most natural thing in the world and Brian had never enjoyed himself more. He hoped she did too.

When their lovemaking was over, they lay in each other's arms in silence. Brian thought about how different it was to make love with someone he cared about. Not that he'd been some stud who'd had hundreds of one-night stands. He wasn't like that. Well, maybe a little, but this was special. He tried to pinpoint the difference, but couldn't be sure. He was positive, though, that he'd never felt this way before.

TWENTY-TWO

BRIAN, ROBBIE AND Jack sat in the large paneled office in front of a huge mahogany desk. On the other side was William Cavanaugh, a big man in his late fifties. He had jet-black hair and a rugged complexion and appeared every bit the cattle baron he'd been prior to his appointment to the chairmanship of the Nevada Gaming Control Board.

To Cavanaugh's left were Cory and a woman who'd been introduced as Teri Porter, an investigative agent. Porter was a young black woman wearing a stylish red-and-brown dress. To Cavanaugh's right were two men in dark suits who'd been identified as special agents.

Brian was anxious. He wondered if Robbie and Jack felt the same way, but their demeanor showed nothing.

Chairman Cavanaugh said, "I want to thank you for coming down here on short notice." He had a calm but deliberate voice. "I've been briefed by Agent Wyatt and have reviewed the recording you provided. This is ominous, and I must tell you I was disturbed when I saw it."

The three of them sat in silence and stared at the chairman.

Cavanaugh's bushy eyebrows accented his grave face. He said, "I'm going to tell you something that maybe I shouldn't, but it's necessary. I need your assurances what I'm about to say and the plan we're proposing will be kept in the strictest confidence."

One by one, Brian, Robbie, and Jack pledged discretion to the chairman.

Satisfied, Cavanaugh said, gazing at Jack and Brian, "I've had conversations with people in the industry, and both of you have developed fine reputations. You have impeccable backgrounds. And you, Miss Taylor, have quite a good standing as well. My friends in construction in Douglas County speak highly of you and your work. I say this because I understand how difficult this has been for all of you. Through no fault of your own, you've become involved in a serious matter."

Brian asked, "What are you planning to do to solve this?"

Cavanaugh looked at him. "I'll get to that in a bit. First, I must tell you I've always been uncomfortable with some of the management at the Charleston Lake Tahoe."

Brian was surprised by this and glanced over at Jack, who was just as perplexed and raised an eyebrow.

Cavanaugh said, "When Elliot Thomas came before the Gaming Control Board requesting a work card, I had my doubts. Thomas's background wasn't perfect. Prior to working at the Charleston, he was employed by a trucking company. At the time, we suspected it might've been controlled by the mob."

Jack asked in disbelief, "Why did you give him a work card?"

"Ah, Mr. Mancini. Jack…may I call you Jack?"

He nodded. "Please do."

"Politics is a strange animal. No doubt you know Sal Wyman, the owner of the Charleston chain of resorts, and the clout he has in this state? Wyman asked the governor to approve Thomas's work card application."

"That doesn't seem right," Brian said.

"Why would he do that?" Jack asked.

"Well," Cavanaugh said, hesitating, "let me explain. You see, Sal Wyman was fraternity brothers at USC with Elliot Thomas's father. The senior Thomas asked Wyman to give his son a job at the Charleston Lake Tahoe, so Sal secured employment for him and put some pressure on the governor to grant the work card request. The governor did so, hoping to please Sal—after all, he was a significant contributor to his campaign."

The room fell quiet for a moment as they each stared at the chairman with an incredulous expression.

Cavanaugh waved a finger. "I know what you're thinking," he said, "and I must put a stop to your conjecture right now. If I'd had any proof at the time that Thomas was unsuitable for a work card, I wouldn't have allowed him to get one. No matter what the governor wanted. I'm sorry to say it now seems that granting it was a major mistake."

Brian said, "I believe Marcus Hatrix was hired at the Charleston based on a reference from Elliot Thomas. He was employed without a security check."

Cavanaugh crossed his arms. "It doesn't surprise me."

"So what are you going to do?"

"Let me spell out a few things," Cory said, "if you don't mind, Mr. Chairman."

Cavanaugh gestured to him. "Go ahead, son," he said.

"All we have as evidence is the disappearance of Vanessa Daine and a video recording—logged under the name Thomas— of an unknown person taking money out of the soft count room. The rest's speculation."

Brian asked, "If all the evidence is circumstantial, what are you doing to find out what's occurring?"

Cavanaugh glanced first at Robbie, then at Teri Porter, who up until then had been silent. "Teri," he said, "would you detail what we have in mind?"

215

"Yes, sir, Mr. Chairman," she said. Porter turned to Brian, Jack, and Robbie. "We've devised a plan we're confident will produce the evidence required. Proof implicating everyone who's involved in this crime."

Brian asked, "And how do you intend to do that?"

"With your help. All of you."

"I'll do anything I can," Jack said.

"We appreciate that. Both you and Brian should keep as low a profile as possible. Go about your work quietly."

Brian shrugged. "Sounds easy enough," he said.

"It is. The difficult part will be for Robbie."

Surprised, Robbie wrinkled up her nose. "Me?" she said. "What would I do?"

The chairman stroked his chin with a forefinger. "Miss Taylor...Robbie," he said, "you're our wildcard. You'll be the integral part of our ploy. We need you to infiltrate the theft ring at the Charleston Resort."

Robbie was bewildered by his words, her eyes questioning. "How can I do that?"

Porter said, "You're the only one who's able to make contact with Marcus Hatrix and be credible. He knows you were Vanessa Daine's roommate, but he doesn't know how much you know about her and the thefts at the Charleston. We want you to call Hatrix, tell him you know what's been going down and want a share of the easy money. We'd like you to arrange to take Vanessa's place in the Surveillance Department and find out how they're getting the money out of the soft count room without being detected."

"Robbie," Cory said, "tell Hatrix you have Vanessa's video recording—the memory card—and know what's been happening. Explain to him you've lost your job, and without Vanessa as a roommate, you'll be evicted from your home if you don't come up with some quick cash."

"You make it sound so simple," Robbie said. "What if Hatrix denies it all or something worse?"

"Robbie's right," Brian said, ire in his tone. "This is crazy. We can't risk her safety. I'm amazed you're asking her to do this. Why don't you have one of your agents go undercover?"

"There's no convincing way we can do that," Cory said. "How would we interject one of our agents into this without raising suspicion?"

"It's too dangerous for Robbie."

Gesturing to the two large men in dark suits Chairman Cavanaugh said, "I promise you, Robbie, your welfare's our first concern. My agents will make a priority of that. We'll have you wired during all your conversations with Hatrix and have our agents nearby at all times."

"I don't know," Robbie said. "First of all, I'm not positive I could even do it, plus I have a job. How can I work at the Charleston as well?"

"I'll take care of that. I've spoken to the owner of your construction company. Walter Etcheberry is an old friend of mine and has agreed to let you take some time off."

Robbie's voice inched up. "It's not that easy. I can't just leave. I have many projects in the works. We break ground on a new shopping center in Gardnerville next week."

Cory said, "Our problem is we see a very narrow window of opportunity. We assume Vanessa's position at the Charleston won't be open long. We need to act now, or we may miss any chance of nailing the criminals. You do want a better understanding of Vanessa's disappearance, right?"

"That's not fair," Brian protested, feeling protective of Robbie and irritated with his old friend. "We all hope to find out what's happening, both at the Charleston and with Vanessa, but asking Robbie to risk her life is unreasonable."

"We don't feel she'll be in much jeopardy. Our agents will always be around."

Robbie's eyes met Brian's. "I'm doing it," she said.

He was astounded, and his mouth dropped open. "Are you certain?" he asked. "You don't know what you're getting yourself into. It could be dangerous."

"I'm aware of that, and I dislike the idea of leaving work on such short notice, but I owe it to Vanessa to find out what's going on."

Brian shook his head. "I don't trust Hatrix. He's seen me. What if he figures out I'm in management at the Charleston?"

"That's a risk we hope you're willing to take," Cory said. "We need you to lay low. We know he works the graveyard shift and didn't recognize you when he was at Robbie's place the other night. We intend to keep it that way…for her sake."

Brian set his gaze on Chairman Cavanaugh. "This is much too risky."

"I agree with you," Jack said. "I don't think she should do it."

"I'll be okay," Robbie said, a determined look in her eyes. "The gaming agents will be there to guarantee that. Hatrix is coming over to my house tonight to pick up Vanessa's furniture. I'll talk with him then."

Cavanaugh said, "Please know we're grateful for your cooperation. We're asking a great deal, and had you declined our request, we'd have understood."

"I'm doing it for Vanessa…Jack, Hailey, Brian. My friends are being hurt by this, and I want it to stop."

"You're sure about this?" Brian asked. He took her hand and squeezed it.

Robbie bobbed her head up and down with vigor. "Yes, I am."

"Well then," Cavanaugh said, "what we should do now

is discuss the details of this plan. Robbie, you said Hatrix is coming to your home this evening?"

"Yes, he's collecting the furniture Vanessa left in her bedroom."

"Perfect. Teri, why don't you take these fine people to your office and confer on strategy? I'm afraid I have a flight to Las Vegas and must be on my way. Again, I thank all of you for your assistance. Miss Taylor, you have guts, and I admire that in a woman—in anyone, for that matter. If you need anything, please don't hesitate to call me. This department's here for you—don't ever forget that. We'll back you up."

"Thank you, Mr. Chairman," Robbie said. "I intend to get this over with as soon as feasible."

"With your help, we will." Cavanaugh rose from his seat and said his goodbyes. Brian, Robbie, Jack, and the gaming agents congregated down the hall in another office where they spent the next hour reviewing the fine points of the plan. The agents agreed to meet Robbie at her house at four o'clock that afternoon to position listening devices and set up areas where they could secretly monitor her meeting with Hatrix.

Confident they each knew their part, they followed Cory Wyatt out of the Gaming Control Board offices. "We'll take good care of Robbie," Cory said in a whisper to Brian. "I promise."

"I'll make sure of it," Brian said. His face was cold and hard as granite.

As BRIAN ENTERED his outer office, Beatrice said, "You just had a visitor."

He reminded himself not to take his foul mood out on her. "Oh, and who's that?"

"None other than the great Skip Sullivan himself."

"What did he want this time? More outrageous demands?"

"To apologize."

Brian blew out a sarcastic breath. "Yeah, right."

"No, I'm not kidding. He was sober and rather charming."

"Is this the same Sullivan I know? The drunk we had to almost carry out of my office? The guy who called in sick when he was too wasted to perform?"

"The very one. He spent quite some time with me. Gave me an autographed picture and one for my best friend."

"So now you like him?"

"Yes, I do. I've always enjoyed his television show. Skip explained to me he's been having a lot of personal issues, and they've affected his behavior. He's been fighting with his girlfriend. They made up over the telephone, and she's flying up here to join him."

"And I suppose this means he's not going to cause me anymore trouble?"

"I'm sure he won't, but you still have to fix the problems he created the other night. Mr. Montgomery phoned and wants to speak with you about Sullivan—the message is on your desk."

The lines on Brian's forehead edged higher. "When did he call?"

"First thing this morning. He wanted to know where you were. Brian, I didn't know, so I said you had a meeting with the advertising agency. I wish you'd told me you'd be late. I hate lying."

"I'm sorry, Beatrice. Something came up, and I didn't get around to contacting you." He gave her his best pitiful look.

She folded her arms. "Well, I don't know whether I should accept your apology."

"You forgave Skip Sullivan."

"I received two autographed pictures in exchange."

"I'm certain I can do the same."

"You're not famous, but I guess I'll let you off the hook.

You better not do it again, though. I can make life around here miserable."

Brian laughed. "Don't I know it."

"So where were you?" Beatrice wasn't one to let the unknown remain unasked. She might miss some good gossip.

"I had some errands to run. You know, my redwood deck construction."

"Your deck? It's winter—haven't you noticed? There are two feet of snow on the ground."

Brian wasn't a good liar. He knew he needed to nudge her in another direction. "We better both get back to our jobs." He zipped into his office before she had a chance to respond, sat down in his chair, and tried to work. It was hopeless. His mind kept wandering to thoughts of Robbie—how much he'd enjoyed making love with her the night before, how close he'd felt to her.

Brian was feeling so many emotions he'd never known before. One of those was abject fright. He was afraid that what she was doing for Chairman Cavanaugh was perilous and she'd be harmed. Vanessa Daine had disappeared, fate unknown. He prayed the same wouldn't happen to Robbie.

TWENTY-THREE

AGENT TERI PORTER was with Robbie in her living room. She adjusted the collar on Robbie's blue sweater. "I can't see the microphone," she said. "It's concealed well. Say something so we can test the transmission."

Robbie dipped her head in the vicinity of the hidden microphone. "Testing, one, two, three."

Teri wagged a finger at her. "Don't do that. It doesn't appear normal. You don't need to lean toward the microphone. It's powerful, so speak in a natural way."

"Oh, okay. I'm sorry. I'm a little nervous." She licked her lips.

"You'll do fine. Just be yourself. You know what to say. Stick to the script, and it'll work out like we've planned."

Robbie elevated her shoulders. "I'll do my best."

There was a knock at the front door, and Robbie glanced over at Teri, her face strained and skin pale.

Teri lifted a curtain and peered through the window. ""It's Brian," she said.

Robbie let out a relieved sigh, rushed over to the door, and opened it. "Brian," she said, "come in quick before anyone sees you."

He barreled through the entrance and closed the door, then put his arms around her. "Are you ready?" he asked.

She half-shrugged. "I guess so."

"You can back out."

Robbie shook her head. "No, I'm going through with this."

"You be careful," he said in a whisper. "I don't want the woman I'm falling for—the one I made passionate love—"

"Brian," she said, interrupting him, "be quiet. I'm wearing a microphone. Every word we say is being monitored."

"It is? Well, I don't care who knows about my feelings for you." That was quite a statement for Brian Shepard.

A hint of pink suffused Robbie's cheeks, and she pushed him away.

He smiled at her. "Did you take care of your work?"

"Yes, Walt told the crew I was attending a builder's conference in Atlanta. I rescheduled the appointments on my calendar and assigned the critical jobs to my assistant. I don't like leaving without more time to prepare, but I suppose they can get along without me for a few weeks."

"Hatrix could arrive at any time," Teri said. "I hope he's alone. Our plans will be all screwed up if he brings along help."

"Where do you need me?" Brian asked.

"In the garage with Cory and the other agents."

"Where will you be?" Robbie asked her.

Teri pointed to the front door. "In a van across the street. We have a recording station there as well. As Chairman Cavanaugh promised this morning, we have this place well covered. In addition to your wire, there are microphones hidden throughout the living room, the kitchen, and Vanessa's bedroom. We won't miss a word that's said."

Robbie turned to Brian. "It seems they have everything taken care of. I feel safe."

He stared at her, uncertain.

"Let's go see Cory," Teri said.

Brian and Robbie trailed the gaming agent down the hall, and they stepped into the garage. Inside, they found Cory Wyatt and the same two agents who'd been in Chairman Cavanaugh's office that morning. Cory was wearing jeans and a green flannel shirt, while the other agents sported identical black sweatshirts with GCB printed on the front in white lettering. There was recording equipment on a table in a corner.

"Your microphone's working fine," Cory said. "Your voices are coming in clear." He grinned like the Cheshire Cat. "I guess you two had fun last night." He winked at Brian.

Robbie glared at him. She was in no mood for male machismo.

"Do you have any questions?" Teri asked her.

"No," Robbie said. "I'm ready."

"Remember, you're not a big name in construction any longer. You're an unemployed clerk and must act like one."

"I understand."

"What do you want me to do?" Brian asked.

"Nothing," Cory said. "Stay here with me and listen to what's going on in the house. Grab a set of headphones. If any problems arise, we can get to Robbie in seconds."

"We're well prepared," Teri said. "Robbie, until Hatrix arrives, why don't you go inside and relax—read a novel or watch some television."

"I doubt I can concentrate on a book," she said. "Maybe I'll listen to some music and flip through a few magazines."

One of the gaming agents said, "Make sure you shut the music off when Hatrix arrives. It may interfere with our microphones."

Robbie nodded. Brian kissed her and hugged her tight, and she returned to the house. Teri slipped out of the garage through the side door.

"Now comes the boring part," Cory said. "Waiting. Want to hear a good joke?"

"No," Brian said. He shifted his eyes to the other agents. "Is this going to work?"

Cory poured coffee from a Thermos into a cup. "It depends on how badly they want to replace the Daine woman at the Charleston Resort. That, and how convincing Robbie is."

Brian's expression was stressed, his skin sallow. "I wish there were another way."

"You know there isn't. Robbie's our one chance of getting into the Charleston theft ring. We have no other viable options."

Brian noted the time on his watch. It was five-thirty, and he wondered what time Hatrix would make his appearance. He paced around the garage, imagining all the things that could go wrong with this plan.

"Brian," Cory said after a while, "why don't you take a seat? It could be a long night, and there's no use worrying. Hatrix isn't even here yet."

Brian ignored his friend and continued to walk back and forth.

"I heard from Kristi Chaplin." Cory said, trying to distract him. "She asked about you. Said she hasn't seen you since the reunion."

With total disinterest, Brian asked, "Yeah, what's she up to?"

"She got hitched. Married a banker."

"No kidding. It's about time she snagged someone."

"Like you?"

"I haven't snagged anyone, but I'm doing a hell of a lot better than Kristi Chaplin."

"You do have a way with women. I guess I owe Jack twenty bucks. But you're right, Robbie's special. I'm happy for you."

"She is, and I don't want anything happening to her. I haven't known her long, but she's different from any person I've ever met."

"I realize that. We all do. It would have to be some woman to get you this worked up."

TWO HOURS PASSED without any sign of Marcus Hatrix. "What if he doesn't show?" Brian asked. He was still pacing the floor.

"I don't know," Cory said. "I guess we'll have Robbie reschedule. It's early, though."

"I can't stand this waiting."

"I know. It's always been one of your character flaws. Why can't you calm down?"

"Too much is at stake."

Through the garage door, they heard the roar of a large truck pulling up in front of the house. Cory and Brian glanced at each other, and the two gaming agents in dark sweatshirts checked the volume and settings on the recording devices.

"It's Hatrix," one of the agents said, adjusting his headphones. "Porter says he's alone." They heard the slam of the truck door and, moments later, the peal of the doorbell.

ROBBIE INHALED A heavy breath when she heard the chime and put down her magazine. She padded over to the iPhone dock, turned it off, and took a second to compose herself. Then she caught another full breath and opened the front door. Hatrix was standing there, and to her, he seemed rather ominous.

"Sorry I'm so delayed," he said. "I hope it's not too late for you, but the game went into overtime. I had to see who won. I had a bundle riding on Notre Dame."

Robbie leaned against the door. "It's no problem. Did they win?"

A satisfied grin materialized on his face. "Sure did. It's about time my luck changed."

She gestured with a hand. "Come in."

Hatrix crossed the threshold into the house. His hair was

unkempt, and based on his breath, his teeth could use a good brushing. For that matter, his whole body needed a thorough scrubbing. His offensive odor indicated he hadn't taken a shower in quite some time.

Robbie closed the door and backed away from him. "Can I offer you something to drink?" she asked.

Hatrix's expression wavered. "Ah, I should pick up Vanessa's furniture."

"A beer or two won't hurt. I'll have one too." It was Robbie's aim to get him to relax and trust her. *Alcohol might help things along,* she thought. She told him to make himself comfortable, walked into the kitchen, and retrieved two cold Coors Lights and a couple of glasses. She used that short break to bolster her courage. *Stop trembling,* she told herself as she poured the beer. *You'll give yourself away.*

Carrying the beer into the living room, Robbie found Hatrix sitting on the sofa and handed him one. She sat next to him. "How's Vanessa?" she asked. "I haven't heard from her yet."

He took a sip. "Fine. I talked with her this afternoon. Her cousin isn't doing well. Vanessa said her convalescence will take longer than she'd anticipated."

Robbie knew he was lying and was comforted by that. She'd never be able to pull this off if Hatrix was in contact with Vanessa. Based on Vanessa's email, though, she was sure he wasn't. "Tell her to call me when she has a chance."

"I will, but as I told you before, she doesn't have a phone. She called me from a payphone in a laundromat."

Robbie studied him, contemplating her next words. "I think you said you're employed at the Charleston Resort?"

"Yes, I work in security." He drank a long swallow of beer from his glass.

"Do you enjoy your job?"

Hatrix raised his shoulders. "It's okay. It pays some of the bills."

Robbie showed him a teasing smile. "It sounds to me like you make pretty good money betting on football."

"Oh, I wish."

"Expensive, huh?"

"You don't know the half of it. I've lost my ass. I wish I knew why Lady Luck keeps spurning me."

"How the hell do you afford it?"

He considered her question with an eyebrow cocked. "I have my ways."

"Vanessa does too." Robbie sipped some beer.

"Oh, yeah?"

"She has some expensive habits. Her tastes are a lot more upscale than her wages from the Charleston would cover."

"I wouldn't know." Hatrix slurped more beer. He belched.

"Why not? You're her lover."

"Well, ah, yes, ah, um. I, I guess she does charge up her credit cards."

Robbie dropped her voice to a hush. "Vanessa confided in me often. We became close friends."

He stared at her. "Is that right?"

"Oh yes."

"What did you talk about?"

The corners of her mouth curled up. So far, she was pleased with the way it was going. She could feel herself calming and becoming more confident. "Different topics, you know—fashion, men, money. Most of the time money."

Hatrix enjoyed a long pull of his beer and wiped foam from his lips with a shirtsleeve.

Robbie grinned. "That's what life's all about, isn't it? Money."

He raised his glass in a toast. "Hear, hear. I like you, Robbie— you think the same as me."

"The problem is, without cash, you can't have much of an existence nowadays. I've never believed those people who say it doesn't buy happiness. It would for me."

"Yeah, me too."

Robbie sighed. "I need to find a way to get more. Right now, my world's a mess. I just lost my job, and with Vanessa gone, I won't be able to pay the rent on this place."

"What about your boyfriend? The dude who was here the other night when I picked up Vanessa's clothes. Doesn't he have any money?"

"Ha. Not a cent. I have to loan *him* money half the time."

"That's too bad."

"I want to acquire money Vanessa's way." Robbie eyed him, waiting for his reaction.

"And what's that?" His tone was guarded.

"Don't play dumb with me. I know how she was able to afford the good life."

"Is that so?" A sudden nervous jerking started below Hatrix's left eye.

"Yes, I told you we were close friends. She explained everything to me."

Hatrix's skin tone became ashen, a sheen of sweat on his face. "I don't know what you're talking about."

"Oh, Marcus, don't play games with me."

He wasn't sure how to respond and wet his lips.

Robbie smiled. "I do have to say, you guys have the perfect scam."

He again said nothing, but it was obvious he was taken aback.

"It's brilliant. No doubt you're the brains behind it."

"Behind what?" He hung his head.

"I understand how it works. Vanessa told me what was going on."

Hatrix didn't look at her. "She was sniffing too much blow. The ramblings of a coke addict."

"We're both aware of how Vanessa was able to afford those drugs. She didn't make enough working as a surveillance coordinator at the Charleston to afford cocaine. And, when Vanessa described to me what was happening, she was sober."

He glanced up, and his eyes burned into hers. "You know what we're doing?"

"Yes, all of it. Believe me, there's nothing to worry about. I certainly won't be telling anyone. In fact, I wish I were a part of it. The easy money—the financial freedom."

Hatrix said with righteous anger in his voice, "You have Vanessa's video—the memory card—don't you?"

With exaggerated sarcasm, Robbie said, "You mean the one with the pictures of you and Vanessa on the beach? How romantic."

"You know what I'm talking about."

"You should've seen your face when I said I knew nothing about the video."

"Where is it?"

"In a safe place, I can assure you. Marcus, don't get me wrong. I have no reason to do anything with the video. That was Vanessa's plan—to use it to get out. I have no intention of doing that—the opposite, in fact. I want to join you."

"How much do you know?" Hatrix took his beer and emptied the glass.

"The thefts at the Charleston. Vanessa didn't tell me all the minutiae, but she shared the gist of it. And I saw the recording. You stole cash from the table game drop boxes before the casino had a chance to count the money. It's a perfect inside job."

He bit his lower lip. "Why did she tell you about that? Why would she do that?"

"As you know, she wanted out. Why, I'll never understand.

I guess she didn't have the backbone for it. After you two had that last argument she told me everything. I was surprised to say the least." Robbie could see a myriad of emotions flashing through his expression, from disbelief to suspicion.

"When was the last time you spoke with her?" he asked.

She sipped her beer. "Sunday morning. That's why I was so stunned when you called and informed me she was in Ohio."

"Her cousin." He wobbled his head with a little too much faux drama.

"I need you to know your secret's safe with me. I admire what you've pulled off. But with Vanessa gone, your cash situation is sure to be suffering. I don't suppose you're looking for someone to replace her? If so, I'd be more than happy to oblige." Robbie held her breath, waiting for him to speak.

His gaze lingered. "How do I know you can be trusted? I don't know a thing about you."

"Nor I you. However, we both desire the same things in life, and we can help each other achieve them. At least until Vanessa gets back from Ohio. Even then, I doubt she has any intention of going back to work at the Charleston. We both understand she hates being involved in this kind of thing."

"I don't like this." Hatrix stood.

Robbie's heart pounded faster.

He looked at her with intense eyes. "This isn't some sport. You act as if we're playing a game of cards. This is real, the stakes are high, and you're putting your nose where it doesn't belong."

Robbie tucked her hands behind her back so Hatrix couldn't see them trembling. "I know. I wasn't even sure I should approach you about this, but I'm in an untenable situation. Plus, I imagine you want this scheme up and running again."

"You're right about that." Hatrix returned to the sofa and clasped his hands. "I'm not sure, though. I have to think about this." His mind was racing. He was desperate to be back in business—he was basically out of cash and had a loan to pay off. He wondered if his boss would ever consider Robbie as a replacement for Vanessa.

Robbie stroked her fingers through her hair. "Take your time. I'm not going anywhere. All I can do is search for another job that pays enough for me to scrape by."

"Where did you work?"

"As a clerk in a construction company. With the downturn in building, they had a budget cut, and I was the first one axed."

"The little guy's always getting shafted."

"I hated the job anyway. I was being exploited for paltry wages. But with a roommate, I was able to rent this house. Now, I don't know what to do."

"I need to talk to someone. I'm not the only one involved. Maybe, and I mean maybe, we might have something for you."

Robbie smiled with a satisfaction he would never understand. "That would be great. I can be trusted, believe me. You don't know what this would mean to me."

"You do realize there are some serious risks?"

"Of course I do, but I can't keep living like this."

"What about Vanessa's video? The memory card. Give it to me."

"Marcus, you speak with your associates and tell them about me. If all goes well, I'll be happy to turn over the video."

"And if it doesn't?" His inflection was harsh.

"Oh, I'm…I'm sure it will."

Hatrix deliberated for a minute, thinking hard. "Okay, I'll get back to you. Nothing may come of this, but I like your style and it could pan out. I better haul out Vanessa's furniture now—I have to be at the Charleston by ten. Can you give me a hand? I'll carry all the heavy pieces, but I might require some help with the doors."

"Not a problem." Robbie led him down the hall to Vanessa's bedroom. There wasn't a lot of furniture—a bed, two nightstands, and a dresser. It took them less than half an hour to load it all on the truck. While they worked, Robbie tried to coax information about the thefts from him, but he wasn't too forthcoming.

"There's time for that later," he said. "I'll need to discuss this with my partner."

"When will I hear from you?" she asked. "I'm sort of desperate. My rent will be due soon."

"Maybe the first of next week. One way or the other, I'll be in contact with you. I have your number."

"You better hurry before the phone's disconnected."

"I can relate. Thanks for the help and the beer. I'll be in touch." Hatrix departed.

Robbie closed the door behind him and sat down on the couch. She felt a mixture of emotions—elation at her success—and fear. She trembled again and this time did nothing to hide it.

CORY CLAPPED HIS hands. "Incredible," he said.

"She has a lot of nerve," Brian said. "I'd never be able to do what she just did."

"Robbie was perfect. I know Hatrix believed her—I would too."

The two men left the garage, went down the hall, and entered Robbie's living room where they found her on the sofa, rubbing her temples. She looked drained.

"Was I okay?" Robbie asked. "I guess I was successful. I believe he bought my story, but at times, I wasn't certain. What do you guys think?"

"You were fantastic," Cory said. "Robbie, you couldn't have done any better. You'd make a great undercover agent."

She rolled her eyes. "No thanks."

Teri joined them and also gave Robbie accolades.

Brian sat beside her and held her hand. "You were great," he said. "You were so convincing, it scared me."

"Why's that?" Robbie asked.

"You're not really that greedy, are you? I don't have much money."

She tossed her hair back. "What do you suppose will happen next?"

They both turned to the gaming agents for an answer.

"Of course we hope Hatrix takes the bait," Teri said. "We have to wait for him to contact Robbie."

"Others are involved," Brian said. "At least we've confirmed that."

"Yes," Cory said. "He needed to speak with his partner."

"Elliot Thomas?"

Teri said, "Hatrix is sure not the architect behind this. He seems more the muscle."

"I agree. He doesn't strike me as being too bright. He gets caught up in his own lies—Vanessa's aunt, her cousin, he's lost in his story—and I'm confident he has to convince someone else to take Robbie into the theft ring."

"I'm afraid you're correct, and I'm sure Elliot Thomas, or whoever it is, will be much more difficult to persuade than Marcus Hatrix. But after hearing Robbie's performance tonight, I'm sure she'll do just fine."

Cory said, "Robbie, you could sell bibles at an atheists' convention. You did an exceptional job."

"Thanks," she said and let go of Brian's hand.

Brian tried to pull her closer to him but could immediately tell she wanted some space.

"We need to wrap it up," Teri said. "I expect agents Scott and Gibson have the recording gear packed by now."

"Robbie," Cory said, "this may be disconcerting, but there's a tap on your phone. It's in case Hatrix or one of his gang calls."

She raised her hands and said, "I guess you have to."

Teri asked, "Would you feel more comfortable if we had someone monitor your house?"

"I'll be all right. I should be safe, don't you agree?"

They all stared at each other, and an uncomfortable hush fell over the room.

Brian said, "Why don't I stay here and keep you company?"

Turning to Robbie, Cory said, "If you want us to watch your home, let us know. If not tonight, then tomorrow. Call us any time, and we'll send agents."

"I'll be fine for now," Robbie said. "If circumstances change after Hatrix contacts me, I'll let you know."

"We better get going," Teri said. "I'm taking the audio recordings back to Carson City tonight. I'll phone you tomorrow. Again, thanks for everything, and I hope you realize how grateful we are for what you're doing."

A faint smile formed on Robbie's lips.

Cory asked, "Brian, do you understand how important it is for you to keep a low profile? We don't want Hatrix to discover who you are."

"I know," he said, "but I have a job to do. I've never run into him before, so I don't expect a problem."

"Keep in mind it's for your own protection," Teri said.

Brian nodded, accepting the gravity of the situation. The two gaming agents walked out of Robbie's house, leaving her alone with Brian.

"I'll be okay," she said, trying to convince herself. "I will."

Brian eyed her with care. "As I said earlier, I'll be here to protect you tonight."

"I'm tired and not up for sex."

"Oh, I bet I can change your mind."

Robbie shook her head. "You can sleep on the sofa."

"The sofa? Where's my incentive to look after you?" he said with a teasing smile.

She scrunched her face up. "You need incentive? Fine—maybe we can cuddle."

Brian had never been the cuddling kind, but with Robbie, he was willing to give it a try.

HATRIX WAS AT home with an ear attached to the telephone. "Turn down the damn television," the man on the other end of the line said. "I can't hear you."

Hatrix cut across the room to the remote on the coffee table. The Lakers were up by four. He grinned, lowered the volume, and returned to the call.

"Did you pick up Vanessa's furniture?" the man asked.

"Yeah, boss," Hatrix said. "She didn't have much. My visit had some surprises, though."

The man snarled. "I don't like those."

"It's Vanessa's roommate, Robbie Taylor. She knows what's going on."

A loud groan came through the handset. "Damn it, Vanessa was telling the truth. Goddamn, this Taylor woman must have the recording. This is trouble, I tell you, a big problem."

"Wait, boss, it's not. I'm sure of it."

"But she has the video." His voice was rising.

"Robbie wants in."

A long pause ensued as the man registered this statement. "She knows how we were getting the money?"

"Oh, yes." Hatrix was nodding as if his boss could see him. "She's viewed the video. She understands how we operate. Vanessa told her what was happening."

"Damn. This couldn't be worse. I was afraid something like this would occur."

"You're not listening to me—she wants to join us, and I'm

sure she'd be perfect. She's aware of what's going on and wishes to be in on it. She lost her job and needs the money."

"I should trust some destitute woman I've never met? I don't think so. What've you been smoking?"

"Boss, she'd be ideal. Meet with her and you'll see. We have to resume the thefts, and Robbie would fit perfectly."

"Does she know about me? Who I am?"

"No. I just told her I had a partner."

"A partner?"

"Well, you know what I mean. I didn't mention your name, though."

"Good, keep it that way. What about the memory card?"

Hatrix pursed his lips. "Ah, um, ah, she has it."

He said with vehemence in his tone, "Why didn't you take it?"

Hatrix gritted his teeth. "Yeah, right, like it was that easy. Uh, she said she'd give it to us if we let her in."

"I don't like blackmail."

"It's not that, and she didn't put it quite that way."

"Regardless, I want to talk with her and check her out. If I don't approve of what I see, we have a disaster on our hands."

"I get a good feeling about her. She's bright and seems to be real nice. Hot too."

"Does she suspect anything about Vanessa?"

"Oh, no, she believes Vanessa's in Ohio."

"You say this Robbie's out of a job?"

"Yeah, she was just laid off."

"Where was she employed?"

"She worked for a construction company. They had some budget cutbacks. Didn't Vanessa ever talk about her?"

"No, she said she liked her roommate, but nothing more of consequence. I'm not bringing someone into this without knowing her background. What contractor did she work for?"

"I don't know."

"Okay, I'll do some research and see what information I can find on Robbie Taylor. We have too much at stake, and I don't like the fact she has Vanessa's video. She's holding something over our heads, and I'm not one bit happy about it."

"Wait until you meet her. You'll see."

"Set up a get-together for tomorrow at four o'clock—my place."

"I'm asleep at that time of day. Couldn't we make it earlier?"

"No, I have an early morning conference, then a meeting on the *Sierra Queen* at eleven. A group of investors may be interested in taking the piece of junk off my hands. After that, I'm taking my stockbroker to a late lunch. You say you want to get started stealing from the Charleston again—if so, you can miss a few hours of your beauty sleep."

"You're the boss. Found some buyers for the *Queen*, huh?"

"Maybe. I hope so—the boat's squeezing me dry."

"I'll call Robbie first thing in the morning. If she can make it, we'll see you at four."

"Make sure she's there."

"Yes, sir. Oh, one other thing. I was asked a strange question by one of the security guards at the resort. Ben Genetti. He asked how many sets of keys I received from the locksmith. You know, when they were delivered to the casino last winter. Of course I told him I just got four, the four he took to the vault."

"Why'd he want to know?"

"He said Jack Mancini was asking about the key procedures."

"Goddamn it. Mancini's becoming a problem. It's time I do something." Without a goodbye, the man hung up.

Hatrix grabbed the remote and ratcheted up the volume on the television. The Lakers were now behind by five with three seconds left in the game. Again, he'd picked the wrong team.

TWENTY-FOUR

BRIAN WOKE WITH Robbie asleep next to him and watched her gentle breathing. They had made love the previous night. Their cuddling progressed to sex pretty fast. Brian stroked her hair. She was like a princess, but he knew there was more to her than just beauty. She had a side to her that didn't hesitate to go undercover for the Gaming Control Board. That was the person he wanted to get to know better.

Brian crept out of bed, careful not to wake her from her slumber. He pulled on his pants and walked to the kitchen, where he brewed himself some coffee. For about a half-hour, he sat at the table and sipped the java, reflecting on the events of last evening.

"Is this a private time?" Robbie asked. She was standing behind him, wearing a pretty blue robe. "You seem absorbed in thought."

Brian's smile was weak. "I was, but you're more than welcome to join me."

"A penny for your thoughts."

"The price is more than that."

"Oh, how much?" Robbie sat down next to him.

"Give me a kiss, and you'll be paid up in full."

"I may hold out."

Brian beamed. "So that's how it's going to be. I was thinking about what you're doing. The difficult part's just beginning."

"I know, and I'm not certain I'm up for it."

"You are. I'm positive. It's the unknown dangers that scare me, though. We don't know everyone we're dealing with. Considering how much money's being stolen from the Charleston, the stakes are high. If Marcus Hatrix and his cohorts decide they don't want you in on this, they're not going to let you walk away. You know too much. It's risky."

Robbie winced, her eye twitching. "I've considered that. I have to believe that the Gaming Control agents will keep me safe."

Brian grinned at her. "I enjoyed myself last night."

"I noticed. You're quite the overachiever."

"Did you enjoy yourself?"

Robbie paused and stared at him. "I was a little distracted. There's a lot on my mind."

Brian leaned over and tried to give her a kiss, but she dodged his attempt as the telephone rang. Robbie stood and picked up the phone on the counter. "Hello," she said. "Oh, hi Marcus." She turned toward Brian with a face full of surprise. "Yes, it's good to hear from you. I'm amazed you're calling so soon."

Brian rose from the chair and stepped over to her. He listened with concern as she spoke.

"That's fine," Robbie said. "Where should I meet you? Oh, sure, pick me up anytime. I'll be ready. Thanks, Marcus, I'll see you this afternoon." She put down the phone and stared at Brian. "That was quick. I don't know why, but I expected a longer wait. His partner would like to meet me at four o'clock. Today."

"It doesn't give us much time," Brian said. "We need to call Cory right away."

She hesitated for a moment. "Yes."

"Robbie, are you okay?"

"I am. It just hit me, however—I'm doing this. I wasn't all that bothered, meeting with Hatrix. I'd met him before and wasn't impressed. Last night with him didn't trouble me too much—I was in my own home—but this is different."

"Sit down." Brian led her to a chair. "Robbie, you can always stop this. It's never too late, you know that."

"No, I'll be all right. Give me a minute to collect my thoughts."

"I have to call Cory." Brian picked up the telephone and dialed his friend's number. He reached an answering service and told the operator it was crucial she contact Agent Wyatt immediately. "Tell him it's urgent." He hung up.

"Don't worry," Robbie said. "I want to do this—for Vanessa, if nothing else. I just needed a second to pull myself together."

"Are you sure?" he asked.

"Brian, I'm ready to do this. I need you to back off a little. It's freaking me out."

A few minutes later, the phone rang. It was Cory. Brian explained the situation, and Cory told him he and the other gaming agents would be over as soon as they could. Cory also informed him he'd already spoken with Chairman Cavanaugh, who was pleased with Robbie's success the preceding night. He said, "Tell her the chairman says his prayers are with her."

"So are mine," Brian said and closed his eyes with a feeling of growing dread. "So—are—mine."

AGENTS PORTER AND Wyatt were standing in the living room of Robbie's house, Robbie and Brian sitting on the sofa.

"Any questions?" Teri asked.

"What if they say no to my proposition?" Robbie asked.

"We're optimistic that won't happen, but if it does, you have to convince them you're no threat. You must assure them you have no intention of speaking with the authorities."

"And if they don't believe her?" Brian asked.

"Should you need help, we want you to say you're not feeling well. That'll be our cue you're in danger, and our agents will rescue you as soon as they can. Do that as a last resort—if you think you have no other options. It'll be better if you talk your way out of it, but your safety's our utmost concern. We're relying on your judgment to determine when you need assistance."

Robbie nodded. "I understand," she said.

"Where will your agents be?" Brian asked.

"It depends on where Hatrix takes her," Cory said. "As soon as we know the location, we'll surround the area."

"What if you lose them en route?"

Cory gave him a biting expression. "We won't."

"It's time for us to disappear," Teri said. "Break a leg, Robbie."

A frail smile emerged on her face. "Thanks, Teri," she said.

"Come on, Brian," Cory said. "Why don't you go to your cabin, and we'll call you when Robbie's back?"

Brian glared at him. "No way," he said. "I'm staying with you. I'd go crazy if I went home. I must know what's happening."

"The chairman wouldn't approve," Teri said.

"I don't give a damn. He doesn't have a personal interest in the outcome. I won't take no for an answer. I'm going with you."

Teri threw up her hands and looked with frustration at Cory.

"You should listen to the agents," Robbie said.

"I won't be a problem," Brian said, surprised she was agreeing with them. "I have no intention of causing a scene."

Cory thrust a finger at him and said, "You better not or you'll be jeopardizing Robbie's life."

HATRIX ARRIVED AT Robbie's house at three-thirty. He was wearing jeans and a San Francisco Forty-Niners sweatshirt. It appeared he'd taken a much-needed shower, and Robbie could smell his pungent cologne as she locked her front door and followed him to his car.

"I hope your partner and I hit it off," she said after getting into his vehicle and fastening her seatbelt. Her stomach felt as if it were full of butterflies, but she was also exhilarated in an odd sort of way.

"You will," Hatrix said. He started the sports car and backed out of the driveway.

"What's he like?"

He turned to her. "Intense."

She tipped her head. "In what way?"

"He's intimidating."

"He intimidates you?"

"Robbie, I may have misled you."

She narrowed her eyes. "Oh, in what way?"

"The man you're about to meet is my partner, but the thefts at the Charleston Resort couldn't take place without his approval."

Robbie looked at him, a little confused. "What are you trying to say?"

"He's my boss," Hatrix said, his tone almost sheepish. "We're partners, but the major decisions are his. He has the final word."

"Oh, I see."

"I guarantee you—I'm an integral part of the operation."

"Who is he?"

"I'd prefer he make the introductions. I will tell you this— he's a powerful man."

"That doesn't bother me. Is he some sort of mobster?"

Hatrix burst out in a raspy laugh. "No, I don't think that would be accurate."

"I admit I'm nervous."

"Try to relax." He drove his car along the highway, moving north—away from Round Hill.

"Where are we going?"

"You ask too many questions."

A frown crept across Robbie's face. She was afraid she may have raised some suspicion in him.

"Hang on, and you'll see."

They drove down the highway and through Cave Rock, a tunnel carved into a giant rock formation along the lake's shoreline. After passing through it and traveling a couple more miles, Hatrix steered the car off the highway and drove into an exclusive area of homes called Glenbrook. Not long after the turnoff, he rolled up to the entrance of a private driveway. He pressed a remote control button, and the iron gates in front of them opened.

They moved along the driveway toward the lake. Large snow-covered pine trees and thick vegetation lined the winding road. The car whooshed over a small hill, and the mansion came into view. The immense home featured three turrets with two stories of windows. The Tudor design reminded Robbie of an English manor.

Hatrix drove his car under the porte-cochere. "This is it," he said.

"Wow, it's magnificent," Robbie said. "I didn't even know there was an estate here. It's so secluded."

"I know. It's unbelievable. This place has something like thirty-five rooms. The view of the lake's awesome."

"The money stolen from the Charleston paid for all this?"

"Yes and no. I'll explain later. Let's go in and meet the boss."

Robbie eased out of the car and surveyed the ornate entrance of the mansion. Stained glass framed the giant double doors.

"Don't dawdle," Hatrix said. "I don't like to keep him waiting." They walked up to the entry, and he tapped the doorbell. A dramatic chime echoed from inside. Moments later, the butler, a mature gentleman in a black suit, opened the door and motioned for them to enter.

Robbie peered over her shoulder toward the highway. She hoped the gaming agents weren't far away. She took an anxious breath as Hatrix shepherded her into the house.

TERI LOOKED AT Brian and Cory and snapped her smartphone shut. "We have a location," she said. "It's one of the lakefront mansions in Glenbrook that you can't see from the road. Our agents will be taking positions all around the area."

The three of them were sitting in an unremarkable black Ford cargo van. Cory was behind the wheel of the vehicle, which he'd pulled off the highway and parked behind a stand of trees. Teri was in the passenger seat, and Brian was on a bench seat behind them. Inside the van were various recording devices monitoring Robbie's every word. They were receiving a clear transmission from her hidden microphone.

"Robbie's doing well," Brian said, trying to reassure himself.

"I wonder who owns the estate," Teri said.

"Gibson's checking right now," Cory said. "We should know the owner's name soon."

Brian asked, "Do you think they'll suspect a set up?"

"I doubt it. If they thought anything was wrong, I don't believe the meeting place would be a private residence. They'd have selected a more remote or obscure location if they had any suspicions about Robbie."

"The place's not out in the open. You heard Robbie comment on how secluded it is."

"I'm sure everything's fine. Trust my instincts."

Brian held his tongue and glowered at his friend.

"Wyatt, you have a copy?" a man said from the radio.

"Yes," Cory said, speaking into his microphone. "Gibson, what's up?"

"We know the name of the property owner."

"Go ahead."

"According to the sheriff's department, the title holder of the home is an Abigail Wyman."

"Wyman, thanks. Abigail Wyman. Why does that name sound so damn familiar?"

"Because," Brian said, excited, "Abigail Wyman's the wife of Tom Montgomery, the general manager of the Charleston Casino Resort."

TWENTY-FIVE

THE BUTLER ESCORTED Robbie and Hatrix through the enormous entry hall to the parlor. It was full of dark, impressive antiques, and the walls were covered with paintings—Van Gogh, Monet, Picasso. She assumed they were originals.

"Some digs," Hatrix said.

Her eyes scanned the room. "That's an understatement. The artwork's spectacular."

"The boss is a collector."

"It takes a lot of money to accumulate pieces like these."

"His wife's loaded."

"Why's he involved with the thefts if he's so wealthy?"

"He wants his own money. The missus keeps a tight rein on the finances. He likes the fact that he can use his own cash without her knowing what he's spending it on. I don't blame him."

"Tell me, Marcus. Who is this man? Who's the boss?"

"My, you're inquisitive," a man said behind her.

Robbie spun around to see Tom Montgomery standing in the doorway—the general manager of the Charleston Resort himself. She's seen his picture in the newspaper many times. The sunlight through the stained glass windows created an aura around his body, and as Hatrix had said earlier, he was intimidating.

"Why are you asking so many questions?" he asked.

She held out a hand. "Robbie Taylor. It's a pleasure to meet you."

Montgomery walked over and shook her hand, gazing at her, intrigued. She was wearing a maroon sweater that accentuated her white skin, and he was attracted. "You're not what I'd imagined," he said. "Marcus, you failed to tell me Miss Taylor's so striking."

Hatrix was inclined to protest but thought better of it and kept quiet. He hunched his shoulders.

"You didn't answer my question, Miss Taylor. Why do you ask so many questions?"

Robbie gave him a nervous smile, her lips quivering. "I'm sorry," she said, "I didn't hear your name." It was better if he didn't know that she knew who he was. Not yet anyway.

Montgomery looked at her, his green eyes ablaze, and ignored her inquiry. "Can I mix you a drink?"

"What do you recommend?"

"How about a vodka martini? I already made a pitcher."

"That would be fine." She sat down on the sofa and crossed her legs.

"I'll have a beer," Hatrix said, reminding them he was in the room.

Montgomery said, "Well now, Miss Taylor—"

She said, interrupting, "Robbie, my name's Robbie."

"All right, Robbie." He poured a cocktail and handed it to her. "How is it you know so much about Vanessa's work at the Charleston?"

Robbie took a sip of the martini. "Let's get straight to the point. We both know I'm aware of all your activities at the casino. Your little theft scam. I want to be in on it." She crossed her legs in the opposite direction, feeling his eyes caress her thighs.

Montgomery chuckled. "Little theft scam. Yes, I guess you could call it that. You're quite blunt."

"No, desperate. I don't know what Marcus has told you about my situation, but I'm in a serious financial bind."

"You and half the population of this country. That's not the criteria I'm seeking in another, shall we say, partner." He turned to Hatrix and grinned.

"Monetary difficulties are part of it, but I can guarantee I'm the perfect person for you." Robbie too glanced at Hatrix and smiled. "Survival's not my ultimate goal. With the loss of my job and Vanessa's sudden departure, I have an immediate cash shortage. I can assure you that my circumstances are temporary. A woman with my brains and beauty doesn't worry too long about her next meal. However, I yearn for more. A whole lot more." She stood, strolled to the Van Gogh, and stroked the frame of the painting. "You must be able to identify with that."

Amused, Montgomery chuckled again. "Oh, I do. You aspire to a nice comfortable life. Don't we all?"

"I'm hoping for more than that. I want to live in luxury without the constraints of a regular job. I have a feeling you're just the person to help me achieve that."

CORY LEANED BACK in the driver's seat. "Robbie's a charmer," he said. "She's doing very well."

Brian agreed but felt uncomfortable with what he was hearing. Robbie was conversing with Montgomery with such ease and conviction...It occurred to him the persona she assumed when talking with the Charleston's general manager was a stranger to him. His Robbie, the woman he'd fallen in love with, was not the same woman who was speaking with exuberance about greed and corruption. She'd behaved the same way with Hatrix the previous day. Where was this coming from? Was she acting, or was there a darker side to her, one she'd hidden from him?

"Tom Montgomery," Teri said. "Who would've ever imagined he's a crook? What would make a man of such wealth and power get involved with this crime?"

"More power and wealth," Cory said. "In this case, most of what he has isn't his own. It's his wife's."

"Do you suppose she knows what's going on?" Brian asked.

"Steal from her own daddy?" Teri said. "Never. I've met her. Her concerns in life are social events and charity work. Her father's taken good care of her—she has more money than she could ever spend."

"Have you met Sal Wyman?" Cory asked her.

She looked at him and shook her head. "No, but I hear he's a character."

Cory let out a breath. "That's an understatement. He's a little guy—just over five feet tall—but he's tougher than an angry pit bull. He started with nothing forty years ago and opened a small bar at the far end of the Las Vegas Strip. Back then, he catered to tourists on their way through town. He's a smart businessman and transformed that bar into one of the largest hotel/casinos in the world. Since then, he's developed properties at Lake Tahoe, Atlantic City, San Diego, and owns three riverboat casinos in Mississippi."

"Quite a success story," Brian said. "I've met him once. He spent the weekend skiing at Heavenly, and Jack introduced me to him. He has to be in his late seventies, but still sharp as a tack—a shrewd businessman. In my mind, there's no question Wyman knows nothing of Montgomery's activities. Don't you agree?"

Cory bobbed his head. "I'm certain he'd bust an artery if he knew what was happening. Chairman Cavanaugh's positive Wyman doesn't know about the thefts. One of the reasons we're putting so much effort into this undercover operation is that it's the chairman's intention to clear this up as soon as we can. He wants to protect Wyman's reputation."

Teri said with a jagged smile, "And the governor's biggest campaign contributor."

MONTGOMERY SAT NEXT to Robbie on the sofa. "Tell me about Robbie Taylor," he said.

She sipped her martini. "Not much to say. I'm a native of San Francisco, raised in the Pacific Heights area of the city. I graduated from high school with a bad case of wanderlust and traveled throughout Europe, doing odd jobs at resort hotels. I met a guy and followed him here—to Lake Tahoe. I was your typical ski bum—worked for the ski resorts during the day and partied at night."

Montgomery took a taste of his drink. "Pacific Heights, that's pricey. I take it your family has money?"

"Had it. Daddy lost it all in the Great Recession. He's a contractor. Got caught up in the condo craze."

"And the guy?" He lifted an eyebrow.

Robbie smiled. "Lost track of him ages ago."

"How long have you been in Lake Tahoe?"

"Five years now. The life of a ski bum's great, but when the snow melts, so does the work. I've tried different jobs in the casinos, and my last work was as a clerk for a construction company. All pretty low on the income scale, and it makes it tough to pay the bills. That's how I met Vanessa. I was searching for a roommate to share the rent, and she answered an advertisement I placed online."

"She mentioned you a few times."

Her eyes locked on his. "Have you heard from her?"

He looked away. "There you go again. Let me ask the questions. You'll have your chance later."

When he turned back toward her, Robbie said, "As I told Marcus, I lost my job, and with Vanessa moving out, I'm broke. I don't want to get another low-wage position or have to work for tips."

"What about your new boyfriend?" Hatrix asked, again trying to edge into the conversation. "The one I met the other day."

Robbie patted the sleeve of her sweater. "What about Brian?"

"Tell us something about him."

"Well, if I had to describe the relationship, I'd have to say…I guess you'd call it physical. He's quite attractive."

"Does he know about any of this?" Montgomery asked.

Robbie let out a quick chortle. "No. He's a carpenter I met one night at a bar. He'd never understand how you're stealing from the casino. He's not too bright—just drop-dead handsome. No, he knows nothing about this, and I aim to keep it that way."

BRIAN'S FACE WAS crimson. "She's making me sound like some male bimbo," he said.

Cory laughed. "You're such a stud. Do you know what I mean, or should I speak slower?"

"Funny, ha, ha. She can downplay our relationship without describing me as a fool."

"She's doing fine," Teri said. "Montgomery seems to be believing her story."

Brian combed a hand through his hair. "Now that we know he's involved, can you arrest him for the thefts?"

"No, Brian, we can't. There's no hard evidence a crime's occurred."

Brian raised his voice. "What are you talking about? You have an audio recording of Montgomery and Hatrix chatting about the scam and Vanessa's video. The recording was labeled Thomas. Thomas Montgomery."

Teri gave a nod. "We have Montgomery talking about thefts but nothing to tie him to the video and no proof any money was taken from the casino."

"But the table games low hold percentage, what about that?"

"All casinos have occasional low hold problems," Cory said. "If we arrest Montgomery and Hatrix with what we have so far, they'd be back on the street in an hour. We have to catch them in the act of stealing the money. We have to tie cash from the Charleston's casino to Montgomery, Hatrix, and anyone else who may be involved."

Teri said, "That's why Robbie has to carry on with this charade. We need her to get this theft operation back in business. It's essential we catch them with the currency in their hands."

"You make it sound like it'll be easy," Brian said.

"If Robbie keeps up this performance, it just may be."

MONTGOMERY ASKED, HIS eyes focused on her, "Why should I let you join us?"

Robbie took a nervous sip of her cocktail. "Marcus told me you both want the cash flowing. I can help you right away. I know what's been happening—Vanessa told me most of it. I'm the right person, I assure you. I have the precise mixture of smarts and larceny you need." She winked at him.

There was a large grin on Hatrix's face. "What did I tell you, boss?" he asked. "Robbie would be perfect for us."

Montgomery shot him an icy glare. "I didn't ask for your opinion," he said.

"We have to start this up again." Hatrix sounded unsure if he was crossing a line but willing to persist. "We're both desperate for money. Remember your boat?"

Montgomery set his lips. In an easier tone of voice, he said, "It's unfortunate, but the ship will continue to be a liability for me. When the investors I met with this morning saw the engine room, they told me they wouldn't be interested in buying it as an operating vessel. They offered to purchase it for scrap but were only willing to pay me the cost of hauling it away."

"You own a boat?" Robbie asked. "What kind?" She put her empty martini glass on the end table to her right.

"The *Sierra Queen*. It's one of the tourist paddle-wheelers at the Ski Run Marina."

"No kidding. I took a ride on that ship last weekend. It's kind of rundown. The public address system's a disaster."

"Tell me something I don't already know."

"It sounds like a good reason to resume the thefts at the casino. With the money, you can fix up your paddleboat. What do you say—can I join you and get the cash coming in?"

Montgomery thought for a bit, then extended a finger toward the door. "Marcus, would you mind leaving us for a few minutes?"

Hatrix looked at Montgomery like a small child who'd been told to go to his room.

"Please, Marcus." His voice was firm. "I want a few words with Robbie. In private."

"Okay," he said. "I understand, boss. Sure. I'll be in the next room if you need me."

Hatrix slunk away, leaving Montgomery and Robbie alone. "Can I pour you another drink?" he asked, holding up his own empty glass.

"Yes," Robbie said. She was still feeling edgy and hoped another cocktail would calm her anxiety. She picked up her glass and passed it to him.

Montgomery stood and moved over to the bar. "What do you think of Marcus Hatrix?"

Robbie shrugged. "Not so bright, but he seems loyal."

A slight smile on his face, he dispensed two fresh cocktails. "Blunt once again. You're right, though, and it's what makes Marcus the perfect person for me. He's smart enough not to do anything foolish, capable of doing the legwork, and follows orders. He's quite competent, I promise you."

"Is there a point to this?"

Montgomery walked back over and gave her the cocktail. "Oh, yes, Robbie, there is. You strike me as an intelligent woman—too sharp, I'm afraid. I don't want a partner who's always one step ahead of me."

Robbie held up an index finger. "You're looking at this the wrong way. I'm bright enough to see the possible dangers and spot potential opportunities as well. Isn't that why you used Vanessa in your plan? She's not a stupid rube like Marcus."

"She had other motivations."

Robbie took a swallow of her martini. "Not unlike me?"

"Let's just say there were other reasons as well."

Robbie grinned. "Oh, you're so funny."

"I beg your pardon?"

"I know what Vanessa's motivations were. She was in love."

"Ah, yes, but what does that have to do with me and her role in our operation?"

"You said it yourself—it was her incentive. She was involved in the thefts at the Charleston as an act of romance."

Montgomery nodded. "Marcus, of course."

Robbie shook her head. "No, you."

CORY PEERED AT Brian in the rearview mirror. "What's she doing?" he asked. "She's going too far."

Brian raised a shoulder. "Robbie's felt all along that Hatrix was lying."

"About what?" Teri asked.

"Ever since Robbie first met Hatrix, she's been positive he's not Vanessa's boyfriend."

"What gives her that impression?" Cory asked.

"I'm not sure if I can explain—Hatrix's tattoos, women's intuition. I don't know. She knew Vanessa and believes something's wrong with Hatrix's story."

Cory gestured at the transmitter. "Why's she telling this to Montgomery? It's not taking her anywhere productive."

"Vanessa. Robbie's concerned about her. She wants to know what happened and why she disappeared."

"That's all well and good," Teri said, "but she could end up blowing this whole undercover operation."

MONTGOMERY'S EYES WIDENED with surprise. He sat next to her. "Excuse me," he said. "I don't know what you're talking about."

Robbie said with confidence, "Vanessa was in love with you."

Montgomery drank a swig of his drink. "Oh, no, you're mistaken. Marcus and Vanessa are involved."

"Are we going to start being dishonest so soon in our relationship?"

"You're guessing."

"Am I wrong?" Robbie swirled her martini and took another sip.

Montgomery stared at her. "Do you have a reason for this speculation?"

Robbie ran a finger along the rim of her glass. "It goes back to my motivation. Unlike Vanessa, my incentives are the same as yours—pure greed. Vanessa wanted different things in life, but I know this—she was very much in love with you. She hated working in the surveillance room at the Charleston but did it for you. That's why she was so upset with your, shall we say, eccentricities."

He asked with a growl in his voice, "What's that supposed to mean?"

"An attractive gentleman such as yourself—I'm certain you could have any woman you desire. I assume temptations arise all the time."

A muscle in Montgomery's jaw stood out in high relief.

"Before Vanessa left for Ohio, she told me you were using her. My guess is there's another woman. Am I correct?"

"I'm afraid I don't see any point to this conversation."

Robbie held up her glass. "With me, there's no baggage. I'd be in it for the money, nothing more. Your personal relationship with Vanessa got in the way of the thefts at the Charleston."

"You're a beautiful woman." He reached over and caressed her arm. "Perhaps you too may be interested in more."

Robbie paused, concentrating on his face. She pushed his hand away. "I think not. I do have a boyfriend."

"A physical relationship, I believe you said."

"Yes, and right now, that's all I'm interested in. With him."

Montgomery leered at her. "Leave the door open just a skosh. I have a talent for that type of relationship."

She gave him a crooked grin. "I'm sure you do. You're an intriguing man. Quite an enigma."

"I don't know if I've ever been described that way before." He crossed his arms in satisfaction.

"Take it as a compliment. Well, how about it? Have I passed the test? Am I in?"

His voice became low and serious. "What about the recording?"

"Oh, yes, the video. Vanessa's recording of Marcus in the count room. It's here." Robbie rummaged in her purse, pulled out a memory card, and handed it to him.

Montgomery examined it. "I trust there are no copies." It wasn't a question.

Robbie gave him another clever smile. "Why would I make a duplicate? I've made my motivations clear."

"Yes, you have—it's why I'm asking the question. I'd hate to be the victim of blackmail."

"Blackmail? No, I prefer to be in control of my life. Sure, for a while, I might profit from it, but how long would that last? I can't see a man like you succumbing to blackmail for long. I suspect such a threat on my part would lead to some serious risks to my health."

"You're right," he said spitefully. "I'm not a man who takes threats lying down. Vanessa would vouch for that."

"I know. It explains her abrupt departure to Ohio. Is she okay?"

Montgomery avoided eye contact. "She's well. Her relative's ill."

"Do you have a number for her?"

He glanced up with a piercing gaze. "We were talking about blackmail."

She eyed him, mulling over what she was about to say. "I have no intention of blackmailing you. I've made no copies of the video. I want to join you and be a team player. As I see it, the benefits are far greater working with you than having you as an enemy."

Montgomery rose to his feet, took a couple strides to the bar, and poured himself another drink. He didn't offer her one. He turned, sipped the cocktail, and studied her.

To Robbie, it felt as if he were probing her soul, and she was uncomfortable. She had to break the tension. "What do you have to lose?" she asked.

"Everything," he said. "But you do seem determined."

"I am. I suppose you'll want to verify my background."

Montgomery offered her an arrogant smirk. "You're naïve, young lady. I've already checked you out."

Robbie was feeling lightheaded. "I just approached Marcus about this yesterday. How could you do that so soon?"

"Walter Etcheberry's a longtime acquaintance of mine. His company built this estate ten years ago. I called him at home earlier this morning and asked about you. You didn't think I'd allow you into my house without first finding out more about you, did you?"

A drop of perspiration trickled down the nape of Robbie's neck. What if he'd found out who she really was? What if he was just toying with her?

"Etcheberry said you were a fine employee. A little high-strung, but a decent worker. He's sorry the slowdown in construction projects forced your dismissal."

Robbie could feel her heart rate slow. Walt Etcheberry had plenty of friends, but it was apparent Gaming Control Board Chairman William Cavanaugh had more influence with him than Tom Montgomery. She wondered how many others were aware of her situation. "Then you know I'm being straight with you. I have no ulterior motives. I can do this. You won't regret it—I guarantee it."

"I hope not."

"I'm in?" Robbie asked with a buoyant gleam in her eyes.

"I swear, Miss Taylor, conversing with you is like playing a game of chess. I believe I've been checkmated."

"No, we both win. Now tell me, since we'll be working together, don't you think I should know something about you? You haven't even told me who you are."

"I guess that's fair. My name's Tom Montgomery, and I'm an executive at the Charleston."

She tilted her head to one side. "General manager's the top spot, if I'm not mistaken."

"You know?"

"I'm not as naive as you might believe. I knew someone high in management must be involved in the thefts. I recognized you the instant I saw you. Your picture's in the society pages all the time. You have a very attractive wife, I might add."

Montgomery flipped a hand. "Touché. Enough of this—any more pertinent questions?"

"When do I start?"

"The first thing we must do is get you a job in the surveillance room."

CORY SMILED AND said, "I was skeptical of her tactics, but she pulled it off."

"A home run," Teri said. "Don't you think so, Brian?"

He didn't answer, too deep in thought.

"Brian, did you hear me? Robbie was great."

He blinked, coming out of his trance. "Yes," he said. "She did well. What happens next?"

"We set up the sting," Cory said. "Robbie needs to find out, in detail, how the money's being taken and who else may be implicated."

"How are you going to catch Montgomery?"

"We have to follow the path of stolen money," Teri said, "and hope it leads to him. At the appropriate time, our agents will wager marked currency at the Charleston's gaming tables. We've recorded the serial numbers of thousands of dollars' worth of hundred-dollar bills and stamped them with ink visible under ultra-violet light."

"And your agents will gamble with that money?"

Teri nodded. "Our undercover agents will go to the gaming tables and exchange the marked currency for casino chips. The marked bills will be in the drop boxes, waiting for our loyal henchman, Marcus Hatrix, to pick them out."

"How do you know yours will be taken from the boxes? There are thousands of dollars in each one."

"We'll have to be lucky, but in Vanessa Daine's video, he just took hundred-dollar bills. Our agents will play several hundred dollars on as many tables as possible. If one of those bills turns up in Montgomery's, Hatrix's, or anyone else's possession, we'll have enough evidence to make an arrest."

Brian rammed his fists together. "You can nail Montgomery?"

Cory said, "If we find marked currency in his hands."

"Do you think it'll play out that way?"

"A lot depends on Robbie. She needs to find the money trail and make certain it leads to him."

"We know it does." Brian's voice was rising in anger. "You heard him, and we have the video recording. I don't understand why you aren't arresting Montgomery right now. Why put Robbie at any more risk?"

"Brian," Teri said, "I understand your concern. We all share it, but we've told you before—so far, all the evidence against Montgomery is circumstantial. There's not yet proof that any money's been stolen from the Charleston or that he's enjoying the first count. Until we find the marked currency in his possession, we have no case."

"Hatrix and Taylor are exiting the mansion," a man said on the radio. "Maintain your distance."

The vehicle driven by Marcus Hatrix roared out of the driveway and onto the road, going south toward Stateline. When Hatrix's car had passed their location, Cory's van followed a safe distance behind. "It appears they're going back to Robbie's house," he said.

Brian said, "I don't like that goon, and I hate it when he's alone with her."

"She's not alone," Teri said. "We have agents all around her."

"I abhor Hatrix being near Robbie."

"Get used to it, pal," Cory said. "For the next few weeks, they'll be with each other a lot."

Brian had a sinking feeling in his stomach. He knew Cory was correct, and there was nothing he could do about it.

TWENTY-SIX

AFTER HATRIX DROPPED Robbie off at her home, she stayed outside for a few minutes, breathing in the cool alpine air. She was walking to the front door when the van with Brian and the gaming agents pulled into the driveway. Brian lunged out of the vehicle, rushed over to her, and embraced her. Her body became rigid. "Are you all right?" he asked.

Robbie peered at him but couldn't hold his gaze and turned her head. "It went as planned," she said. "I'd like to go inside and relax." She pushed him away.

Brian was startled by the tension in her voice and raised an eyebrow.

The gaming agents joined them, and they entered the house. Teri said, "Robbie, we need to go over a few details and then we'll leave you alone. I bet this has been exhausting for you."

Robbie closed her eyes for a second. "A little," she said.

Brian took her hand and led her to the sofa. "I'll get you something to drink," he said.

Robbie sat down. "No, I'm not thirsty."

Brian removed his jacket and sat next to her. "How'd you know Montgomery?"

She stared at him for a moment, then looked down. "I did recognize him from the newspaper. He was at a charity fundraiser last month. I don't understand why he's stealing from his own casino."

"It's his father-in-law's resort," Cory said. "He just runs it. I guess he likes sharing in the profits."

Robbie twisted a few strands of hair around her finger. "Brian, I know why you were so nervous about your budget presentation. The man's frightening. I'm still trembling."

"You seemed to hold your own," Brian said. His tone wasn't complimentary, and he regretted it at once. "You did great. I know how scary Montgomery can be. What's your next step?"

"Weren't you listening to our conversation? That reminds me—I need to take this microphone off. It keeps poking me in the side." Robbie lifted her sweater, revealing the microphone wire and small transmitter attached to her shirt. She removed the device and gave it to Teri. "Anyway, if you were paying attention, you know they're getting me a job in the Surveillance Department at the Charleston. The same one Vanessa had."

Brian frowned at her.

"I'm to go to the casino on Monday and meet with Elliot Thomas."

Brian shook his fist. "I knew he was in on this. The way he reacted when I was in the surveillance room made it obvious."

"I don't think so, Brian. I sense it's just Montgomery and Hatrix. No one else."

"What gives you that idea?" Cory asked.

Robbie shrugged. "I don't know. It's a feeling. I have the distinct impression Montgomery wants as few people as possible involved."

"I trust your intuition," Teri said. "You were right about him being Vanessa's lover."

"I was trying to shed some light on her whereabouts. I didn't get far."

"You tried," Brian said. He reached over and stroked her right hand, but she pulled it back. His forehead rutted. Why was she acting so strange toward him?

Cory said, "Your transmission was a little garbled when you discussed some of the particulars after your meeting with Elliot Thomas. Can you clarify that for us?"

Robbie said, "I'll get my paperwork processed at the personnel department after I visit with Mr. Thomas. Following that, I'll meet with Montgomery and Hatrix, and they'll go over the details of the thefts. If all goes well, I'll clock in at eleven that night. The first week, they want me working Monday to Friday. I switch to having Mondays and Tuesdays off, Vanessa's old schedule, the next week. It's hard for me to get my head around the fact that I'll be working the graveyard shift. Ouch."

Teri said, "We'll need to wire you for your meetings with Thomas and Montgomery and, of course, when you're in the Surveillance Department. We'll be here at eight o'clock to prep you and set up the microphone."

Robbie said in a voice laced with sarcasm, "I can't wait."

"Remember," Cory said, "when at the Charleston, you can have no contact with Brian. Now that we know Montgomery's in on this, it's more important than ever. If he sees the two of you together, he'll become suspicious. It could be dangerous."

Robbie nodded. "I intend to keep my distance, that's for sure."

Brian frowned again.

Robbie stood and accompanied the agents to the front door. They thanked her and promised that her undercover work should soon be over.

Robbie closed the door after Cory and Teri had left. "I pray they're right," she said, "and this whole mess will have a quick conclusion. I'm not certain how long I can keep up this act."

Brian chuckled. "I don't believe you. Your performance today was masterful. I wonder if I even know you. Who is this Robbie Taylor with so much larceny in her heart?"

She put on a beleaguered expression. "The girlfriend of a carpenter, or weren't you listening?"

"A carpenter? Where the hell did you come up with that?"

"You specialize in deck construction, as I recall."

"Did you have to make me sound like a dim-witted gigolo?"

"I had to think fast. I was never sure what Montgomery was going to ask next. I blurted out what came to mind."

"Did you mean it?"

"What?"

"Our being together is just physical?"

Robbie's eyes wandered to the ceiling. "You enjoy it too."

"Of course, but you didn't answer my question."

She ambled across the room and glanced out a window at the distant lake. "Brian, we've known each other just a short while."

"And?" He held his breath, not quite certain why she wasn't giving him a direct answer.

"I'm tired, and I want to rest. This has been difficult for me. Vanessa's missing, and I'm worried sick about her. I've had to think and act like a crook, for god's sake. I crave time by myself. No, I'm desperate to be alone. I have to reflect on what's happening."

Brian patted his chest with a hand. "I can appreciate that."

"No, I don't think you do. I've made a mistake letting our relationship move too fast. I'm not ready for the serious one that seems to be developing. Even without everything that's going on, I'm not sure what I need. For now, until this is over and I come to terms with my own feelings, it's best we cool things off.

I can't take all these different emotions. I have to focus on Robbie Taylor, the criminal. Like I told Cory, I need to keep my distance from you."

Brian didn't know how to respond. He leapt up from the sofa, stepped over to her, and put a hand on her shoulder.

She brushed it off.

He said in a distressed voice, "Robbie, we have something special."

"I see us as having a great friendship."

Brian blinked at her, shocked. "Friendship? It's a hell of a lot more than that. Robbie, I've fallen in love with you. I never thought it could happen to me, but it did."

"I'm sorry, but I don't feel the same way. If you think about it, you'll agree. You have a crush. Maybe some lust. The sex was good. We've known each other, what, maybe a week?—two at the most."

He couldn't believe what she was saying. Hours ago, everything had seemed fine to him. How could it change so quickly? The world was spinning in slow motion, and his insides were being torn apart. "There's such a thing as love at first sight."

Robbie grimaced. "Oh, get real. Our first encounter left you with nothing but contempt for me."

Brian felt as if he were drowning in strange new sensations. They were the feelings he'd always avoided before by never falling for anyone. "Robbie..." He again reached out and attempted to hold her.

She twisted away from him. "Please, just go."

Brian was pissed, his jaw tight. He didn't want to leave. This had to be a bad dream. He loved her. He hadn't planned on it, but he did. He'd found someone he hoped to spend the rest of his life with and couldn't accept the look on her face. The one saying she didn't feel the same way. He had no idea what to do. "There must be something I can say to make you change your mind."

Robbie avoided his haunted eyes by lowering her head. "No, there isn't."

"I don't understand why you're doing this."

Her hazel eyes shifted up to his but she didn't say a word.

He grabbed his jacket from the sofa. "If you need me, I'll be at my cabin. I'll call you later tonight."

"It isn't necessary for you to do that. I'm sorry if I've hurt you. I didn't mean to."

Brian fumbled putting on his coat, not finding a sleeve, and marched to the door. He stopped and glared at her, but she turned away. He stumbled to his truck and climbed in, his mind numb. He sat with his head pressed against the steering wheel for a couple of minutes before starting the engine.

Driving up the road, Brian tried to sort out his tattered emotions. It was now clear to him why he'd preferred a life of serial dating to a relationship. He'd always been careful not to open himself up to heartbreak. This was the one time he'd let down his guard, and it had become a complete disaster. Maybe it was karma. How many times had he hurt a woman's feelings and never given it more than a couple moments of thought? If he'd known then how much it hurt, maybe he would've been more thoughtful, less of a jerk.

HIS PSYCHE A wreck, Brian decided against going to his cabin and instead drove to the Charleston. Alone at home, he knew he'd do nothing but brood about Robbie. He'd be better off if he tried to get some work done at the office. Settling in behind his desk, he examined the financial results for the week. Revenues had rebounded from the snowstorm, and as was to be expected with the thefts on temporary hold, the casino was keeping the normal win percentage.

After about an hour of not being able to concentrate on anything, Brian left his office and headed for the casino floor. It was a Saturday night, and the place was jumping. Hordes of gamblers lined the slot machines and sat at the blackjack tables. Slot jackpot bells rang over the crowd.

Despite the hum, Brian didn't feel the usual flow of adrenaline. The casino was full, but he felt empty. He didn't care about gambling and, in fact, wished he were employed in something else. Anywhere but at a casino. The woman he loved had just spurned him and his boss was a thief. He wanted it all out of his mind.

Brian heard his name being called and turned to see Jack waving at him from a blackjack pit. Jack wore a dark suit and seemed every bit the stereotypical casino boss. He strode over to Brian and said, "Let's go to the lounge, where we can talk. I have to know how it went."

Brian nodded, and the two men walked through the casino to the Edgewater Lounge and sat at a secluded cocktail table. A waitress came over and took their drink orders—soda with a twist of lime for Jack and a double vodka on the rocks for Brian.

"You look like hell," Jack said.

Brian tensed his lips. "Thanks, I feel like it."

"What's the matter? Didn't it go as planned?"

Brian wanted to say no, it was all wrong—wrong, damn it, she doesn't love me—but he didn't. "Robbie pulled it off like we planned. You'll never believe this, but Tom Montgomery's behind it all. She met with him at his estate."

Jack's eyes widened. "Montgomery?" He stopped speaking, recognizing he was in a public area and would need to lower his voice. He said in a whisper, "Tell me—I must know everything."

The drinks were delivered, and Brian told Jack all about Robbie's meeting with Montgomery at his lakeshore mansion.

Jack was stunned at the realization that their boss, the well-regarded general manager, was a criminal. "I'm flabbergasted," he said.

"Yeah, it's difficult to understand," Brian said.

"How's Robbie holding up through all this?"

Brian wasn't sure what to say. Jack was one of his closest friends, but he decided that, for now, it was best to keep his feelings to himself. "She had him wrapped around her little fingers. No small achievement, as we both can attest."

"When does the Gaming Control Board expect to arrest him?"

"Not until he's tied to the stolen money." Brian explained the legal situation and the lack of evidence to convict of both Hatrix and Montgomery. "Robbie meets with Elliot Thomas Monday morning. The strategy's for her to start working in the Surveillance Department that evening."

Jack's eyelids drooped. "Thomas. Is he involved also?"

"We don't know. His name hasn't yet come up, but my gut feeling is yes."

"How long do you suppose Robbie will have to work in the Surveillance Department?"

"Until they have enough evidence to make an arrest. This means catching them with some of the stolen money. I'm certain it'll take a few days for her to get her bearings. I know they want to train her as fast as possible. I'd say she'll be there at least two weeks."

"Let's hope it's shorter."

Brian said in a sullen tone, "This has turned into a nightmare for all of us."

"Well, despite all the problems, Keith Wallace being my biggest one, I now have a reason for some optimism. I can see the light at the end of the proverbial tunnel."

"Let's pray it's not an oncoming train."

Jack folded his arms. "Why do you say that?"

Brian rubbed his temples. "Oh, I don't know. I'm sorry,

it's been a long day, and I'm so goddamned tired. Sometimes it's hard to be positive."

"Are you sure that's it?"

"Yes, it's going well. I expect to see that asshole, Montgomery, in handcuffs soon."

Jack finished off his soda. "I better get back over to the pit. I don't want to leave Wallace unattended. At least he hasn't fired anyone today." He pushed up from his chair. "What are your plans for the evening?"

"I'm doing it." Brian rattled the ice in his empty glass.

"Take it easy."

"Don't worry about me. I'm a big boy."

"Make sure you act like one." Jack gave him a warm slap on the back and returned to the gaming floor.

BRIAN STARED OUT across the casino. He envied the mindless tourists playing the penny slot machines. They didn't seem to have a single care.

"Mr. Shepard," a man said.

Brian glanced up to see Skip Sullivan and a gorgeous young blonde.

"May we join you?" Sullivan asked.

Brian rose from his chair and motioned for them to sit. "Please, call me Brian." He held out a hand to the woman.

"This is April Vaurnet," Sullivan said. "The love of my life."

Brian shook her hand. "April, it's nice meeting you." He admired the expensive diamond necklace showcased by her plunging neckline. Her blue dress did little to hide her ample breasts.

As they sat down, Sullivan said to April, "Brian's responsible for booking me here at the Charleston Resort."

"How was your first show?" Brian asked. He took a seat and signaled for a cocktail waitress.

April snuggled up to the entertainer. "He was fabulous," she said. "The audience was in stitches."

Brian smiled, a sliver of teeth showing. "You've sold out every night so far, and I know you'll be doing the same the final week of your gig."

The waitress showed off her skimpy outfit by sashaying up to their table. They ordered drinks. For the first time all day, Brian was starting to relax. The double vodkas were helping.

"I'm still trying to get used to the main room," Sullivan said. "In the past, I've just played in small comedy clubs."

April said with a broad grin, "You're a famous star now."

Sullivan held up an open hand. "The power of television."

"Don't underestimate yourself, honey. Everyone knows you're talented."

"She's right," Brian said. "Skip, you're a gifted and witty comedian, and you're welcome to come back to the Charleston anytime. You're good business for this place."

Sullivan said, "It's generous of you to say so, considering how much trouble I've caused."

"Hey, let's not worry about that. It's history. It's clear you've straightened yourself out now."

The cocktail waitress placed beverages in front of each of them. Brian raised his glass of vodka. "To forgetting the past," he said.

"I'll drink to that," Sullivan said, clicked his glass against Brian's and April's, and took a healthy sip of his drink. "Why don't you come to my second show? I bet you could use a laugh or two. We can go out afterwards and do some bar hopping. It'll be a lot of fun."

Brian didn't hesitate for a second. "Why not? I've nothing better to do."

"Fantastic," April said. "I'll have someone to sit with during Skip's routine. I hate being alone."

Brian, the comedian, and the blonde enjoyed several more cocktails before departing for the theater. Sullivan's performance was hilarious, despite the fact that by the time he strolled on stage, he was rather intoxicated.

After the show, they partied at a late-night dance club where the liquor flowed. It wasn't long before they were all so drunk that not one of them could string a sentence together without slurring. The last thing Brian remembered before passing out around five o'clock in the morning was that he'd forgotten to phone Robbie. He was sure she didn't miss him.

WHEN BRIAN REGAINED consciousness, his head felt like he'd gone ten rounds with the world heavyweight champion, the room was spinning, and his stomach was doing backflips. He tried to go back to sleep but hurt too much. He wanted to get up, but it was too painful.

Brian wondered how he'd gotten home and, despite the agony, dragged himself from the bed and peeked out a window. His truck wasn't in the driveway. *Good, at least he hadn't driven*, he thought, squinting against the sun reflecting off the snow on the ground.

Brian leaned against a wall and tried to keep his balance while the room blurred and he rubbed his eyes. A queasy feeling came over him, and he tore to the bathroom, where he heaved into the toilet. Then he crawled to the corner of the bathroom and stretched out on the cool tile floor. After a while, he forced himself up, weaved back into the bedroom, and grabbed his sweatpants. After putting them on, he looked at his bed and was startled to see April Vaurnet, naked and sound asleep.

Brian put his hands over his face and hoped this was all a bad dream. He staggered through the living room and into the kitchen, where he flipped on the tap. He splashed cold water on his face, filled a glass, and tried to quench his massive thirst. Then he plunked down in a chair and massaged his aching head for a solid and excruciating twenty minutes.

"Good morning," a woman said.

Brian turned to see April standing there, holding a blanket around her nude body. He blinked at her a few times, wishing she'd disappear. Of course she didn't. "I, I, I'm amazed to, to see you here," he said.

"Me too, I guess. I had a good time last night."

Brian was trying to recall the final hours of the previous evening. His memory failed him. "I'm afraid I don't remember much about last night. I must've had too much to drink."

April laughed. "Must've? You did. We all did."

"Where's Skip?"

She adjusted the blanket. "At the resort, I suppose."

"He'll be worried."

"Not if I'm back at the hotel before he wakes up."

"Oh, sure. I'll take you to the Charleston." Brian thought about his truck. "Uh, I seem to have misplaced my Ford."

"You left it at some bar. We took a cab here."

"Oh, yeah. I'm still foggy. I'll get you a taxi."

"Not necessary. I already called one from the phone in the bedroom. It should be here in a few minutes. I better dress."

Brian stared at her, attempting to assess the situation. April smiled at him and sauntered out of the kitchen. He gazed out a window. The cold gray sky hanging over the lake matched his feelings. He put a kettle of water on the stove and closed his eyes, praying the pounding in his head would subside.

Five minutes later, there was the sound of a car horn. Brian pulled himself up from the kitchen chair and trudged into the living room. April was standing there, combing her hair. "That's my cab," she said. "I better hurry. If Skip wakes up before I'm back at the hotel, it's going to get nasty."

Brian wondered what would happen if Sullivan did rouse before she returned. The thought made his queasy stomach feel even worse.

"Thanks for a good time," April said and pecked him on the cheek while he stood there in a stupor. "You're so handsome. Oh, and Brian, let's keep this our little secret." She smiled, her leer lustful.

Brian gave her a slow shake of the head and followed her to the front door, where he rested against the doorjamb and watched her get into the taxi. As the car drove away, the dreaded feeling came over him again, and he ran to the bathroom for a sickening repeat performance.

TWENTY-SEVEN

MONDAY MORNING, THE alarm clock blared and Brian rolled over to turn off the interruption of his slumber. He realized that for the first time in a long time, he'd slept until being awakened by the alarm. He showered, dressed, and drove toward Robbie's place. He wanted to hear her briefing from the Gaming Control Board agents.

Brian hadn't called her on Sunday, not knowing what he should say, but he felt an obligation to support her undercover effort. After all, he was to a great degree responsible for getting her into this situation.

Brian pulled up to Robbie's house a little before eight. Answering the door, she invited him in but didn't look him in the eyes. *It was better that way*, he thought, *as they were still bloodshot from the weekend's festivities.* "Are you nervous?" he asked with as little emotion as possible. It was quite an effort because, despite her rebuff, he knew he was in love with her and couldn't flick his heart on and off like a light switch.

"A little," Robbie said. "What kind of person is Elliot Thomas?" She was all business in her demeanor.

"A jerk. I don't think much of him, and he's not fond of me at all."

"Montgomery called last night. He said my meeting with Mr. Thomas is a formality. He's hiring me as a personal favor to him. He told me Thomas knows nothing about the thefts and to keep my mouth shut."

"I'm surprised. I guess I'm disappointed he won't be arrested along with Montgomery. I was positive he was involved. I had a gut feeling about it."

"Sometimes our feelings are wrong."

His eyes lingered on hers. "Sometimes. Not always."

The Gaming Control agents arrived, reviewed with Robbie the procedures for the day, and attached the hidden microphone under her clothing. They instructed her to speak to the microphone if she was alone and wanted to relay a message. Cory said, "We were able to get taps on all the phones in the surveillance room."

Brian gestured to Robbie. "What's the plan once you've meet with Elliot Thomas?" he asked.

She said, "I go to the personnel office and they process me—tax forms, ID badge, locker, that sort of thing."

"Sure, it's all routine."

"After that, as you know, I meet with Montgomery and Hatrix, and we go over the details of my part in the thefts. I start work at eleven tonight. It's going to be a marathon day."

Brian massaged the knotted muscles in his neck. He too would have a long one. "Where's your meeting?"

"In Montgomery's office."

"Brian, is that near yours?" Cory asked.

He nodded and said, "Yes, just up the hall."

"That could be a problem—Hatrix will be there too. He may see you. You better make yourself scarce at that point."

Brian said with a rude inflection, "I will. I 'm not stupid." He paused a moment, frustrated. "Hatrix won't see me."

The gaming agents explained that they'd set up a command

post in one of the hotel rooms. They'd checked in like any other tourist.

"Is that wise?" Brian asked. "What if the maids see the recording equipment and report it to someone?"

Teri said, "We'll put the do-not-disturb sign on the door and keep our movements in and out to a minimum to alleviate suspicion. We'll get better reception from her microphone if we're in the building."

"I hope you know what the hell you're doing."

"My, aren't you in a good mood," Cory said with a prominent scowl. "We do, Brian. We know damn well."

FOLLOWING THE BRIEFING, Robbie drove to the Charleston Resort for her meeting with Elliot Thomas. When she located his office, the door was open with no receptionist in sight, so she walked right in. Thomas's back was to her. She said in rather bold way, "I'm Robbie Taylor. I have an appointment."

Thomas swiveled his chair around and peered up at her. Like with Montgomery, he couldn't help but admire her beauty, and his eyes glimmered. "Come in, Miss Taylor." He signaled for her to take a seat. "Mr. Montgomery's told me some good things about you, and Tom reserves his praise for only a few people." His smile was unexpected and his pleasant bearing even more so.

Robbie sat down and crossed her legs. "That's kind of him."

"Have you known him long?"

"We've been acquainted for years. I lost my job and asked him if he could help. And, well, here I am. I appreciate what he's doing for me."

Curious, Thomas's eyes narrowed. "Most women as attractive as you would rather run cocktails."

Robbie pointed to her shoes. "I don't like spending eight hours on my feet in high-heels."

"Understandable. What makes you think you'll be a good surveillance coordinator?"

"I have good powers of observation and concentration."

"How about the graveyard shift?"

"Ugh, I'm not looking forward to it at all, but I guess I have to start somewhere. I'm hoping to move to a more desirable shift after I prove my worth."

"Who knows, you may enjoy graveyard."

She touched her necklace in a nervous gesture. "I'm here, ready to give it a try."

"That's what I like to hear. After our chat, you'll go to the personnel office for processing. Tonight, come to the security booth by the cashier and ask for Andy Sanders. He's my graveyard surveillance supervisor. You'll find him easy to work with—he's a nice man. Andy will sign you in and show you around. I'm confident you'll learn your job right away."

"I know I will. I'm a quick study."

"I won't keep you, Miss Taylor. Even though you'll be working for one of my supervisors, I always spend a few minutes with all our new employees. It gives me a chance to get to know them and judge for myself how they'll fit into our operation. Granted, this is an unusual circumstance. When Mr. Montgomery asked me to hire you, I couldn't refuse. After all, he's the boss. However, I have a feeling you'll do fine."

Robbie smiled at him. "I can promise you won't regret hiring me. I understand I used my friendship with Mr. Montgomery to obtain this job, but I'll work twice as hard to prove my value."

"I expect you to do just that. The Human Resources office is down the hall on the left. Tell the receptionist I sent you, and they'll prepare your paperwork without delay."

Robbie stood up from her chair and stepped toward the office door.

"Oh, Miss Taylor," Thomas said, sounding as suave as he

could muster. "If you have any problems, or require anything—anything at all—give me a call."

BRIAN SAT WITH Gaming Agents Wyatt and Porter in a hotel room several floors above. "That prick," he said. "In all the years I've known Elliot Thomas, I've never heard him sound so nice."

"Robbie's an arresting woman," Cory said. "Thomas recognizes her attributes."

Teri shot her colleague a peevish look. "Focus on her intellect," she said.

Cory turned to Brian. "You shouldn't be here. Someone might see you."

"I came up the stairwell," he said. "I'm positive no one did. The one surveillance camera on this floor is by the elevators. As long as Robbie's at risk, I'll be here."

"I agree with Cory," Teri said. "What if someone in your department needs you? It's the middle of the day. It's imperative you go to work and act as normal as possible."

Brian said with a clipped voice, "That's difficult to do when your boss is plotting crimes against your company two doors down the hall. Remember, I have to stay out of sight so Hatrix doesn't see me."

"True, but it'd be better if you were somewhere else."

"You're too wound up," Cory said. "You've got to calm down. It's affecting your judgment and could put Robbie in jeopardy. Go get in a workout."

Brian gazed at him, knowing he was right. He was an emotional car wreck. He wasn't thinking straight, and his nerves were frayed. "Maybe a workout would do me good," he said. "Okay, after Robbie meets with Montgomery, I'll go. I'll have my smartphone—while I'm gone, you have to promise to call me if anything unusual happens." Brian stared at his friend with a morose face. "I feel helpless enough as it is. There's nothing I can do to assist Robbie. Don't leave me in the dark and make matters worse."

Cory put a hand on his shoulder. "You have my word."

"Mine too," Teri said. "Relax, Brian, it'll be fine."

ROBBIE TOOK A seat next to Hatrix in front of Montgomery's desk. "Welcome aboard," Montgomery said. "I expect your paperwork was administered with no problem."

"Everyone was pleasant," she said. "This seems like a nice place to work."

With a wide grin, Hatrix said, "It's great, but your new job pays better than most."

"Let's get down to business," Montgomery said. "Marcus, why don't you give Robbie a rundown of our activities."

"Sure, boss." Hatrix's beady black eyes glinted. "As you know, we take money from the table game drop boxes before it's counted by the casino. No one knows how much money's in each one until the count team arrives later in the morning, so we can take the currency without detection."

"What about security?" Robbie asked. "I hear this resort has guards and cameras everywhere. Is anyone else involved?"

Hatrix shook his head. "There's no one else—that's the beauty of it. It's just you and me. You're right, though, there's a lot of security and cameras all over. That's where you come in."

"Working in the Surveillance Department?"

"Yes," Montgomery said. "You'll have to see the surveillance room for some of this to make sense."

Hatrix said, "He's correct, but I can't talk about this when we're there, so I'll explain as much as possible now. The surveillance room's full of monitors and digital video recorders, DVRs, recording almost every part of the casino, including the soft count room."

Robbie asked, "Are there a lot of people in the surveillance room?"

"Quite a few. The folks there monitor the activities at the Charleston at all times. I'll be able to get into the soft count room without being detected because you switch off a few cameras and put prerecorded video of an unoccupied elevator and count room into two of the DVRs. When you do this, the rest of the surveillance team believes they're seeing live coverage when actually they're viewing prerecorded video. While the videos are playing, I ride down the elevator, go into the count room, and grab the money."

Robbie was astonished and crinkled her eyes. "It's that easy?"

Hatrix's smile exposed his yellowing teeth. "Yep.".

"Ingenious."

"We think so." Still beaming, he crossed his arms.

Montgomery said, "Marcus is over simplifying the ease of this. Timing and good judgment are paramount. The procedures in the surveillance room are tight—Elliot Thomas sees to that."

Robbie asked, "Then how do I put the prerecorded videos into the DVRs without raising suspicion?"

"Special projects. Part of Vanessa's job, and now yours, is to work on special projects. Your official title's *Surveillance Special Projects Coordinator*. It's one of the reasons Elliot Thomas wasn't surprised when I asked him to hire you."

Robbie tipped her head to one side. "I don't understand."

Montgomery took a sip from his coffee mug. "It's a straightforward cover. Your job description includes recording video for special investigations by the general manager. It gives you the perfect opportunity to make frequent changes to the video memory cards without anyone becoming curious about what you're doing."

"How does Marcus get into the soft count room?"

"I have a key," Hatrix said, "but I still have to make it to the count room and that's tricky. After you've put in the prerecorded video of the empty elevator, you need to send the car."

"How do I do that?"

"The control for the elevator's in the surveillance room. You can send the car by pressing a button next to your workstation. It's easy to do without being detected. One other thing—there's a camera in the hallway where I board the elevator and another leading to the soft count room. Both aren't dedicated to a single DVR and must to be shut off."

"Won't it leave a blank video monitors?"

Hatrix uncrossed his arms and scratched his head. "No, there are many more cameras in the Charleston than there are screens. There's a control panel allowing you to select the area you want to view. The cameras in the both hallways can be switched off and other ones turned on in their place."

Robbie nibbled on her lower lip, visualizing the process. "What happens if one of the surveillance workers changes one of the cameras back to a hallway?"

"It won't happen if you're at your workstation. The buttons are close by, and you can guard them. But no one has any interest in the hallways at that time of night. Besides, I'm there just a few seconds—long enough board the elevator and open the door to the soft count room."

Robbie knew her expression was anxious. "How do I know when to do all this?"

"Each night, I'll call you when I'm ready to go. That's when you'll put the prerecorded videos into the DVRs and switch off the hallway cameras."

"I can see some concern on your face," Montgomery said. "Tonight, all you'll be doing is getting accustomed to your surroundings. The surveillance supervisor will give you a tour of the video library and demonstrate how to operate the DVRs.

Marcus will explain where to find the prerecorded memory cards after you've seen the operation."

"Of course, we have to be cautious," Hatrix said. "We mustn't raise any suspicions in the rest of the employees."

Montgomery motioned to Hatrix. "He's right. We'll take it slow and see how soon you're comfortable with your responsibilities. This evening, you'll learn your surveillance job and become acquainted with how the place works. If all goes well, in a week or two, I'll have you put in the prerecorded videos and practice the procedure. I want you to be proficient with your part of this before I risk sending Marcus into the count room."

"I can agree to that," Robbie said. "I'll get up to speed as fast as possible, though. I promise."

"I need you to," Hatrix said. "I lost another bundle on the Cowboys last night. I'm out of cash."

Montgomery threw an unhappy glare at him. He looked back at Robbie and asked, "Any more questions?"

"No," she said. "I'll have some this evening, I'm sure, but until I'm in the surveillance room, not all of this makes sense."

"I advise you to go home and rest. Working graveyard takes some adjustment. Try to sleep so you'll be able to concentrate tonight."

"I don't relish the graveyard shift."

"I've been working grave for years," Hatrix said. "It was tough at first, but you'll adapt. Once you're into the routine, it's painless."

"For the payoff, it'll be worth it. By the way, we haven't talked about how the money's to be divided."

Montgomery said with a wry grin, "I was wondering how long it'd be before you asked that. You'll get twenty-five percent of the take. Marcus' share's the same. I receive a larger portion, as none of this could or would be happening without me."

Robbie smiled. "Seems fair."

Hatrix said, "Even at twenty-five percent, it's a lot of money. You'll be amazed."

"We're limiting our take this time," Montgomery said.

Hatrix's face crumpled with disapproval. "What are you talking about? Why would we do that?"

"We've been too greedy. The low hold percentage has been raising red flags everywhere. We need to modify our thefts so the hold's closer to the norm. If we don't bring the percentages back into line, the Gaming Control Board's going to start a serious investigation. We don't want that."

Hatrix waved his hands around. "They'll never figure out our operation."

"We can't afford to have them poking around more than they already have. It's only a matter of time if we aren't more careful. Our haul will still be substantial."

"But, boss—"

"Not another word. The subject's closed. Enough of this— Robbie has to rest, and I have work to do." He turned to her. "Call me at home tomorrow morning after you're off work and give me an update. Here's my private number." He scribbled his home telephone number on a piece of paper and spun it across the desk. "Good luck. I hope it goes well."

Robbie picked up the paper and stared into Montgomery's still-intimidating eyes. "It will," she said. "I'm sure of it."

TWENTY-EIGHT

BRIAN SLIPPED OUT of the gaming agents' hotel room and down the stairwell. He set off for the spa but thought he should call Beatrice before he started his workout so, finding a house phone, dialed her number. When she answered, he asked, "Any messages?"

"Just one," she said. "Skip Sullivan's agent called."

"I wonder what he wants. Have you heard from our favorite comedian?"

"No, not yet, but it's early. He didn't work last night and is off tonight as well."

"I'll call Skip's agent later. I'm going to be unavailable for a while. If you need me, I can be reached on my mobile."

"Brian, before you hang up..." Beatrice had a palpable melancholy in her voice.

"What is it?"

"You know my friend Loretta, the roulette dealer? She says the word on the casino floor is that Jack Mancini will be fired today."

"Oh, I think that's idle speculation. We've talked about this before. I haven't heard anything."

"Loretta's pretty sure."

"I suspect it's another unfounded rumor. You know this place is one giant gossip mill."

"I hope you're right."

"Me too. Anyway, if you have to get hold of me, just call."

"Where will you be?"

"Playing hooky. Cover for me, okay?"

"I always do, Brian."

"Beatrice, you're the best." He hung up the telephone and wound through the casino toward the spa, looking forward to exercising the demons from his body.

NERVOUS, HATRIX STARED at the man in front of him and licked his lips. "Louie," he said, "this is a surprise. What brings you to this neck of the woods? Grab a beer. There's a game on the flat-screen."

"I don't care to socialize," Louie said. He was a small man—not quite five feet tall—and wore a short-sleeved blue patterned shirt that seemed out of place at that time of year. His pale skin hung on his slight frame. "You better have enough beer for three. I brought company."

Hatrix looked across the front porch and saw a big man in a dark suit propped against the railing. "Who's the ape?"

"Now, that's not a nice way to speak about my friend. You and Henry there have a lot in common. I'm amazed you weren't cellmates."

Hatrix lowered his eyes. "What do you want?"

"Don't play games with me. You know very well why I'm here. You owe me twenty large, and I came to collect."

In a higher-than-usual pitch Hatrix said, "I told you before, you'll be paid. My luck's been going south lately, and my losses have been larger than I expected."

Louie snarled at him. "Not my problem. I want my cash now."

"You'll get it. All of it, I promise. Things are looking up. I should be flush in a couple of weeks."

"Not soon enough, my friend. I have bills too. I need the money, and I insist you pay me today."

"I don't have it—not right this minute. I told you, I swear I'll pay you back the week after next."

"You're not listening to me. I'm not waiting that long."

"Please, Louie."

Louie jabbed a finger onto Hatrix's chest. "Damn you, I want my dough."

Hatrix stared at the loan shark with a pleading expression.

"Oh, Marcus, what am I going to do with you?" He turned and gestured to the sports car parked in the driveway. "You have a nice set of wheels there. Is it paid for?"

Hatrix was silent, dropping his eyes again.

"I'll tell you what—I'll give you two days to sell it and pay me back."

Hatrix groaned. "I can't unload it that fast. Please, I'll pay the loan off in a week or so."

Louie grabbed him by the collar and pulled him close. Although Hatrix towered above him by more than a foot, the menacing look in Louie's eyes was intimidating, and he didn't resist. "Two days, Hatrix," Louie said. "Two days. If I don't have my money by then, I predict your luck will go further south than you can imagine. Henry hasn't hurt anyone in weeks, and he's having withdrawal. Do you understand?"

Hatrix wiped more sweat from his brow. "Sure, okay. Two days. I'll call you."

"Two days, twenty thousand, or I hope your medical insurance is paid up."

Louie spun around and strutted to his car, a black Cadillac SUV. Hatrix stood on the porch and watched with growing distress as the vehicle backed out of his driveway and sped away.

BRIAN PUSHED HIMSELF during his workout and rewarded his efforts with a hot steam sauna. After the steam, he took a cold shower, hoping the contrast between the two would invigorate him. It didn't work. His problems weighed too heavily on his mind.

After dressing, he reached into his jacket pocket and took out his iPhone. The screen showed one missed call from the Mancinis' home telephone. He poked the screen to call back.

Hailey answered the phone after several rings, winded. "Brian, it happened," she said.

"It?" he asked. "What's going on?" He could hear her worry.

"They fired Jack. He's devastated."

Beatrice was correct again, he thought. "When?"

"Jack called me a while ago. He'd cleaned out his office and said he wanted to drive around the lake and clear his mind before coming home. I'm concerned about him. He thought this whole nightmare was almost over. His spirits were higher this morning than they've been in months. This is such a letdown for him."

"I expected we'd catch them before it brought down Jack. It's not the end, however. We'll get the evidence needed, and I know he'll get his job back."

"Oh god, he has to. Until then, I'm worried about his state of mind. He sounded like a zombie when he phoned. No emotion. Oh, Brian..." Hailey sobbed.

Brian's heart sank. "I'll come over to the house. I'll be right there. When Jack gets home, I'll give him a pep talk."

Hailey sniffed. "I'd appreciate it."

"He's one of my best friends, and it's the least I can do. I'm on my way." He hung up, thought for an instant, then dialed the resort. When the operator answered, he asked for 534, the gaming agents' hotel room.

"Wyatt," Cory said.

Without pleasantries, Brian said, "Jack's been fired. I'm on my way to his place right now. I spoke with Hailey, and she's upset."

"You haven't talked with Jack?"

"Not yet. Hailey said he's driving around, trying to cool off. How's Robbie coping after her meeting with Montgomery?"

"She's quite a woman. She's home now and Teri's with her."

"Okay. I'll see you tonight."

"Oh, no. This hotel room's off limits."

"I'm going to be there, and that's final," Brian said in a stubborn tone Cory would recognize. "I'll see you at ten." Brian tapped off the phone and left the Charleston, bound for the Mancinis' home.

PARKING HIS TRUCK in front of the Mancinis' house, Brian saw Jack's Jeep in the driveway and was relieved his friend had arrived home safe. As he jumped out of the Ford, Joker came up to him, barking and wagging his tail. Brian stopped to scratch the dog behind the ears, then walked to the front door. He knocked twice, entered the house, and found Jack and Hailey in the living room. Jack's arms were around his wife, whose eyes were puffy and red from crying.

"I'm sorry, Jack," Brian said.

Jack bowed his head. "You kept telling me this wouldn't happen."

"It's not over. You know that."

"I was a lot more optimistic yesterday."

Brian nodded. "I understand."

Jack's tone was angry. "How could you? You've never been fired before. You're probably glad. You won the career competition. You get a promotion, and I get canned."

Brian was stunned, and his mouth fell open. Jack had never spoken to him like that.

"I'll get us all a soda," Hailey said, trying to lighten the mood. "What would you like, Brian, Coke or Sprite?"

His eyes were locked on Jack's, his jaws clenched. "Coke."

"And you, honey?"

Jack was glaring at Brian, his face red. "Diet."

Hailey hurried out of the room.

"You know that isn't fair," Brian said. "I wouldn't ever be happy you were fired. Yes, we're competitive, but you know as well as I do that, in the end, our friendship comes first."

Jack closed his eyes. "You're right. I apologize. It's not your fault. It's just so goddamned difficult for me to accept that I've been terminated."

"Not because you didn't do one hell of a job. You must know that. You were the scapegoat for one of the biggest casino crimes in the state's history. You asked too many questions, and they couldn't allow it. Montgomery's putting in his own people—managers who won't rock the boat. Ones who'd never call the Gaming Control Board. You're the best in the industry—everyone understands that. Your being fired has nothing to do with your ability or the job you've done."

Hailey carried two sodas into the room. "Brian's right," she said. She pushed up on her toes and gave Jack a kiss on the cheek, then handed him the Diet Coke. "You can find employment anywhere. Once word leaks out you're available, the phone will ring off the hook."

Brian took the Coke from Hailey. "No question about that, but I'm positive that when this whole mess is over, Chairman Cavanaugh will get you back your job at the Charleston. You know he has clout with Sal Wyman."

Jack said, "When Wyman finds out about the thefts, he may eliminate all of Montgomery's management team. That includes you, Brian. I doubt he'll let any of us stay."

"Honey, don't be so pessimistic," Hailey said. "You two are the reason the thefts have been uncovered. Of course they'll want you back."

"Listen to her," Brian said, although he took what Jack said to heart. Maybe Sal Wyman would clean house and terminate all of Montgomery's executives. He too might soon know what it was like to be unemployed.

"Tell me what's going on with Robbie," Jack said.

Brian cracked open his Coke. "She starts working in the surveillance room tonight."

Hailey said, "I don't know how she has the guts to do this. She must be terrified."

"She's stronger than you'd expect." Brian described the meeting Robbie had with Montgomery and Hatrix, and how the gaming agents hoped to catch them with the stolen cash.

"It sounds like a decent plan," Jack said.

"This is astonishing," Hailey said. "I can't believe they've been taking the money right under everyone's noses."

Brian said, "We wouldn't know about any of this if it weren't for Robbie's roommate, Vanessa."

Jack took a gulp of his Diet Coke. "Has Robbie heard from her?" he asked.

"No, not a word. She's disappeared completely."

"Did Montgomery say anything about her whereabouts?"

"He maintains she left Lake Tahoe for Ohio. Robbie's tried to find out more, but so far, no luck. As you might guess, she has to be careful not to ask too many questions or they might get suspicious."

"It doesn't look good for Vanessa. Do you suppose she could be dead?"

"Don't say that," Hailey said. "Think positive."

"I pray you're right," Brian said. "For Robbie's sake, if nothing else."

"I'm so happy you and Robbie are dating." Hailey grinned. "I knew you two were perfect for each other."

"Well, you were wrong."

"Robbie told me you're fun to be around. Jack said—"

He interrupted, a bite in his voice. "You misunderstood. Robbie and I are just friends. I respect what she's doing for Vanessa, Jack, all of us. That's all. Leave it at that."

"Okay. I'm sorry. I didn't mean to meddle."

Brian was about to say something sarcastic but thought better of it. "What do you have to drink around here that's stronger than soda?"

"Hey, buddy," Jack said, "you're here to cheer me up, remember?"

"Yeah, and who's doing that for me?"

BRIAN POKED HIS head through the open doorway of the office. "Excuse me, Mr. Montgomery," he said. "May I have a few words with you?"

The general manager looked up from his papers and motioned for Brian to pull up a chair. "Care for a drink?" he asked. He stood and crossed to the bar at the side of the room.

"No, thank you, sir. I've already had a few cocktails."

Montgomery poured himself a scotch on the rocks. "How are the television commercials going?"

Brian grabbed a seat. "We should have the new version ready soon."

Montgomery returned to his desk and sat down in the overstuffed leather chair. It seemed almost like a throne, and made Brian feel small.

"You wanted to talk, Shepard," Montgomery said. "What can I do for you?"

Brian squirmed. His knowledge of the thefts and Montgomery's involvement in them made him livid. He was there to defend

Jack and speak on his behalf but knew he had to hide his feelings. "Well, sir, I'm concerned about the dismissal of Jack Mancini. He's a good man and one of the most talented gaming executives in the industry. I wish you'd reconsider his termination."

"Mancini's a close friend of yours, isn't he?" Montgomery seized a cigar from the wooden box on the desk.

"Yes sir, but that has nothing to do with it. Jack knows as much about how to run a casino as anyone in the state. His firing's a great loss to the Charleston."

"I don't share your opinion." Montgomery lit the cigar. Smoke wafted across the desk and into Brian's face. "The problems in the casino weren't being corrected by Mancini. The table games hold percentages he's been maintaining are unacceptable."

Brian felt great contempt. With care, he said, "I believe the hold problems were caused by circumstances out of Jack's control."

"Oh, and what's that?"

"Bad luck. I've noticed that in the last week, the hold's right on. Casinos have bad runs. We are in the gambling business, after all. It appears it's changing for the better."

"No thanks to Jack Mancini. Keith Wallace is the one who's straightened out the games department. Wallace runs a tight operation. Mancini was too lax with the dealers. They were stealing from him. Once Wallace put in some stricter rules, the win percentages fell right into place."

"But Mr. Montgomery, the morale in the casino's never been lower. Wallace is an unpopular man, and some of our best dealers have quit."

"I bet they were the ones stealing from us. Wallace's cleaning house. It should've been done months ago."

Brian thought for a second, wondering if he should temper his words. He was too irate not to say something, though. "I don't agree. Our customers, some of our best players, can no longer find many of their favorite dealers. It's causing a lot of problems for my casino hosts."

"You're not in a position to disagree on this. I suggest you pay more attention to your own department and leave the management of the casino to those who know what they're doing."

"Like Jack Mancini."

Montgomery's expression stiffened. "Elliot Thomas is correct. You're spending more time in other departments than you are your own. You've been nosing around in places you don't belong. Why the sudden interest in the mechanics of the casino?"

"As I told Thomas, the more I know, the better I can promote the Charleston."

"Well, I disapprove. From now on, I want you to worry about the Marketing Department and nothing more. Is that clear?"

"Do I have a choice?" Brian regretted his tone the instant the words came out of his mouth. Until Montgomery was behind bars, he was in no position to tempt fate.

"No, you don't. Now get the hell out of my office before you make me angrier than I already am."

Brian knew the conversation was over. He'd built up so much hatred for the man in front of him that any further discussion would just dig him deeper. "Thank you for your time," he muttered.

Montgomery blew a smoke ring into the air and pointed to the door. "Leave, Mr. Shepard. Now."

TWENTY-NINE

ROBBIE STOOD AT the security booth outside the cashier's cage. It was ten minutes to eleven when she asked the guard in the booth for Andy Sanders. "I'm here for my first night on the job," she said.

"Welcome to the slave camp," he said and picked up a telephone.

Robbie gave him a puzzled look and watched him dial. Five minutes later, Sanders, the graveyard surveillance supervisor, approached the booth. Sanders was an older man, in his late seventies. He had thin gray hair and walked with a limp. After introducing himself, he said without conviction, "I'm sure you'll enjoy working here."

Robbie cupped a hand over her mouth and said in a whisper, "I'm glad to hear you say that. The security guard in the booth isn't very nice. He called this place a slave camp."

Sanders glowered at the guard. Also in a whisper, he said, "Ignore him, Miss Taylor—this is his last night. He's been a problem for months. This time, there's enough in his file to fire him and make it stick."

Robbie glanced at the security guard and then at Sanders. "I'm excited about my first night of work."

"Sign in, and I'll show you around." He handed her the access log.

Robbie scribbled her signature and the time on the log. She gave it to the security guard, and they were buzzed into the hallway.

Sanders said, "You'll need to leave your purse in one of these lockers." He pointed to a cabinet in the alcove to her right. "I'll get you a key." He headed over to the counter past the alcove and attracted the attention of one of the vault cashiers. "Marcia, this is Robbie Taylor," he said. "She'll be working for me. Would you issue her a key for one of the purse lockers?"

Marcia stared at Robbie, her eyes judging her. "You must sign for your key," she said, her voice cool.

"You sure do sign your name often," Robbie said.

"Get used to it, sweetie. Around here, you sign your life away." Marcia held up a key. "This locker's yours as long as you're employed here. You log the key in and out every night, but you'll always use the same one."

Robbie filled out the log, stepped around the corner to the alcove, and unlocked the small door on compartment seven. She put her purse inside, locked the door, and moved out of the alcove, following Sanders through the maze of hallways and doors to the elevator. He picked up the phone, identified himself, and the doors opened. They boarded the car and took the short ride up one floor.

Once in the main surveillance room, Robbie was impressed by the video monitors filling one wall. She surveyed the area, trying to match her surroundings with the descriptions she'd heard from Montgomery and Hatrix and looking for the memory card storage library. She was disoriented—it would take her a while to be comfortable with the layout of the area.

"Folks," Sanders said to the people sitting in front of the monitors, "I want to introduce Robbie Taylor. She'll start working here tonight. She's taking Vanessa's position. Robbie, this is Wanda Wiggins, Roger Kleinfield, and Larry Beasley."

Robbie waved. "Hi," she said.

Wanda and Roger mumbled an unenthusiastic welcome and returned to concentrating on the screens in front of them. Larry gave her a lustful grin. Sanders led Robbie to a chair. "This is your workstation," he said. "Your new home away from home."

Robbie smiled, a bit self-conscious. "Seems nice."

"As you can see, we have a lot of video monitors. Each day, I'll assign you certain sections of the casino to focus on. I'll rotate these areas of responsibility depending on the action in the casino, the problems we're investigating, and your various special projects for Mr. Montgomery. Tonight, I want you to observe the others. They'll show you the procedures and teach you what to look for on the screens. Later in the week, I'll have you work in the training academy, learning the casino games."

Robbie inspected the monitors with wide eyes. "This is impressive. Could you give me more specifics on how this place operates? What are you looking for on the screens?"

Sanders sighed, and with little passion, gave her a tour and explanation of the surveillance activities. He was less than talkative, and she asked one question after another, trying to understand the workings of the department. "I have some paperwork to complete," he said finally. It was obvious he'd rather be doing something else. "Why don't you go to your workstation and watch Wanda, Roger, and Larry? You need to get a feel for the job. Scrutinize what they do and ask as many questions as you like."

Robbie knew she wouldn't be receiving much more information from Sanders, so she retreated to her workstation, where she sat down and scanned the wall of video monitors. She could see most of the casino in them. She noticed a row of levers to her right, similar to control sticks on a video game, and cranked one of them to the left. A video screen above her panned over.

"Don't touch that," the woman next to her said. "I have that camera recording a suspected card counter."

Robbie pulled back her hand. "I'm sorry. I didn't realize. You're Wanda, right?"

Wanda had gray hair and a wrinkled face and was wearing a white sweatshirt and green stretch pants. She grabbed the lever and returned the screen to its original position. "Another one with no previous experience," she said to the men to her right. "Just what I need—to spend more time babysitting one of Montgomery's pets."

Robbie didn't understand the woman's hostility. "I beg your pardon?"

"It's not your fault, darling, but I'm tired of working with young women like you, who have no experience in a surveillance room. As if I don't have enough to do. God knows, they don't pay me more to train the new people. The worst part is, girls like you get the plum jobs, like Special Projects. I guess I don't have the looks to be given that assignment."

"Pay no attention to her," Roger said. "She's jealous."

Robbie turned to the gaunt man, who was sitting next to Wanda. "I promise I'll do a good job," she said. "Sure, I don't have any previous surveillance experience, but I'm a hard worker and I'm confident I'll learn fast. I can assure you, I'm not Mr. Montgomery's pet. I don't know him well at all."

"You must've made a good first impression," Wanda said, making a nasty face.

"Give the kid a break," the rotund man at the far end of the room said. "Vanessa worked out fine. I'm confident Robbie will too."

"Larry," Wanda said, agitated, "Vanessa wasn't that great.

Her so-called special projects always took precedence over the real work we do."

The heavy man said, "Robbie, why don't you bring your chair over here? I'll give you a thorough lesson on casino surveillance."

Robbie stood and rolled her chair to the man's workstation. His apparent friendliness had a lecherous quality, making her somewhat uncomfortable.

As the hours passed, Larry explained to Robbie how to do her job. Every once in a while, he placed his hand a little too close to her thigh but withdrew it when she gave him a sharp glare. Larry pointed to a woman on one of the video screens. "Wow," he said. "Do you see the hooters on her?"

Robbie was trying her best to ignore his lascivious comments. "Tell me about Special Projects?"

"Special Projects?" He shrugged. "Busywork, I think, but I suppose you'll be required to do it. Follow me." He heaved himself up from his chair, hiked his pants over his big belly, and walked to the video storage area.

Robbie shadowed him.

A tad out of breath, Larry said, "You'll need to get a clean memory card to record each day's special project. We keep the blank cards here." He gestured to a shelf containing memory cards wrapped in cellophane. "These are the logs." He extracted a binder from the shelf. "Every memory card in the video library's catalogued in these books and stored for easy reference and retrieval."

Robbie picked up one of the logbooks and leafed through the pages, remembering Brian's description of them and how he'd found Vanessa's recording.

"Depending on your task, you'll catalog the memory cards in the short- or long-term special project logs. For the most part, your videos are in the short-term books."

Robbie asked, "Does Mr. Montgomery get a special projects video every day?"

"Yes. If nothing exciting's going on, you can send him video of generic casino shots. I doubt he even reviews the recordings, but I guess he wants us to think he evaluates our work."

"The DVRs, are they standard, like the ones you can buy at an electronics store, or are they different?"

"They operate the same way but have some special software. They're the latest technology, and if you want to find certain portions of a video you can do so in seconds. Of course, it's all digital. For the most part, they work similar to the ones you can purchase at any online retailer. Boy, do I have some great videos at home. Pretty steamy." He leered at her.

Robbie frowned at him with tight lips. "Thank you, Larry. You've been helpful. If you don't mind, I'm going back to my workstation. I appreciate that you've been so patient with me."

He grinned at her with puffy cheeks. "You haven't asked the most important question."

Her eyes were quizzical, eyebrows pulling together. "Oh, and what's that?"

"When's break time? The break room to the right of the elevator is reserved for the surveillance employees. You're allowed two fifteen-minute breaks and an hour for lunch. We're not permitted to eat in the cafeteria with the other resort employees for confidentiality reasons. Most of us purchase a sandwich from the vending machine and eat it in the break room."

"I think I'll spend my lunch reading a magazine. Until I'm accustomed to working graveyard, I won't be able to eat anything at four o'clock in the morning. My internal clock believes I should be sleeping, not eating a ham sandwich."

Larry chuckled. "You'll get used to it. Why don't you take fifteen minutes now?"

"The break room's by the elevator?"

"Yes, the door's to the right. You can't miss it."

Robbie exited the surveillance room and ambled into the well-lit lobby. The elevator was straight ahead, and to its right was a single unmarked door. She opened it to find an unoccupied room about fifteen feet square. The white walls were bare. There were two vending machines on one wall and a brown sofa, a chair, and a television on the opposite side. The TV was on, tuned to a twenty-four hour news channel.

Afraid she'd doze off if she got too comfortable, Robbie opted for the chair instead of the couch. When she sat down, the wire from her hidden microphone poked her in the side, and she remembered she could speak to the gaming agents. "Robbie Taylor here," she said. "I hope you can hear me. As you can tell, it's going well. I know the basics of the job. The people here are strange, though. I guess that's what happens when you work nights in a dark room full of video monitors."

"Talking to yourself?" a man asked from behind her.

Startled, Robbie flinched and jerked her head around to see Marcus Hatrix standing there in his security guard uniform. Her heart raced while she tried to gain her composure. "Marcus," she said. "My god, you scared me. I didn't hear you come in."

He laced his fingers and cracked his knuckles. "Sorry. I called the surveillance room, and they told me you were on a break. How's your first night of work going?"

"Okay. The surveillance room's pretty much as you described it, but I have a lot of questions."

Hatrix stuck his head back out of the break room door, looked each direction quickly, then shut it firmly. "Shoot." He went over to sit on the sofa.

"Which DVRs do I use for the prerecorded videos?"

"The bank closest to the video storage library. The first DVR on the bottom shelf is for the elevator—it's number fifteen. The one next to it is for the soft count room. Number sixteen. You can tell by matching the numbers to the corresponding video monitors."

"Where are the memory cards with the prerecorded videos?"

"In the storage library. Each memory card has a number. Three-three-three's the card number for the soft count room and three-three-four's the elevator."

"What time do you go into the count room?"

Hatrix patted on his watch. "Every night at two-thirty. The swing shift drop boxes come in at two, so all the money's in the cabinets. I'll phone you before I go in. After I call, switch off the hall camera so no one sees me board the elevator, then put the video of the empty elevator in the DVR on the bottom shelf. It's easy—you take out the memory card in the machine and replace it with the prerecorded card. Then you press the play button. Look over to the screen to make sure the video's running as it should be. If it is, do the same with the memory card for the unoccupied soft count room. When you get back to your workstation, switch off the camera in the hallway to the soft count room."

Robbie scratched her forearm. "How long are you in the count room?"

"I go down during my lunch break, so no one questions my whereabouts. I'm there forty-five minutes, sometimes up to an hour. After I'm finished in the soft count room, I'll lock everything up and go back to the alcove by the outer vault and put the leather bag holding the cash in your purse locker. I'll call you when it's all clear, and you can remove the memory cards from the DVRs."

"You place the money in my locker?"

"Yep. Give me your key, and I'll have a copy made before you get off shift."

She reached into her pocket, retrieved the key, and gave it to him. "Why do you leave the money in my purse locker?"

"It's easier that way. I tuck the money bag in the back of my pants. With this security blazer on, the bulge is unnoticeable. But I don't want to carry it around while working—that would be awkward. It would also be suspicious if I took it to my car in the middle of my shift while wearing the uniform. So I put it in your locker. As you know, the purse locker alcove isn't visible to the vault cashiers, so they can't see what I'm doing."

"Yes, but won't a camera record you placing the bag in my locker?"

"You're right. I forgot to tell you about that, didn't I? You'll need to switch that camera off as well."

"Is the bag heavy?"

Hatrix shook his head. "Not at all. That's because I just take hundred-dollar bills. Even with tens of thousands of dollars, it's light. It's also very thin. Start carrying an oversized purse, so you can stuff the money bag in it. No one will wonder why you're leaving with the purse you bring to work each day."

Robbie blinked at him and thought about that. "What do I do with the money after I get off work?"

"I'll meet you at my car, and the two of us will take the Ben Franklins to Mr. Montgomery. It's simple, don't you think?"

"It sounds like it, but I'm a little worried. What if something goes wrong?"

Hatrix waved his hand. "Believe me, nothing will. We've done this a hundred times. You can do it as well as Vanessa."

"I hope I can live up to your expectations."

"Relax, Robbie. Where's your bravado? Think of all the dough. What you need to do after your break's over is find the prerecorded video and practice with the DVRs."

Robbie made a face. "I thought we weren't doing that until after I was more comfortable with the way the Surveillance Department operates?"

"It won't hurt to practice tonight. The sooner you get this down, the faster the cash will start rolling in."

"I guess you're right." She peeked at her watch. "Okay, Marcus, my fifteen minutes are almost up. I better go back to the surveillance room."

"I'll call you later to see how you're doing. And before you go off-shift, I'll give you back your locker key."

Robbie rose out of her chair and accompanied him to the lobby. "The memory cards are catalogued under special projects three-three-three and three-three-four?"

"Yes."

She nodded. "I'll see you in a while."

Robbie returned to her workstation in the surveillance room, where her new colleagues didn't acknowledge her presence. She looked up at the wall of video screens in front of her and made a mental note of the monitors showing the elevator and the unoccupied soft count room. Robbie turned to face the others. "I'm going to familiarize myself with the video storage library," she said. Receiving no response, she took their silence as tacit approval and walked from her workstation to the video storage area.

Robbie stood there, working out the system used to store the memory cards. They were each labeled with a number, and Special Projects 333 and 334 were in the middle of the library. She reached up to the right shelf and pulled out the two memory cards, one after the other. She examined them—they appeared to be the common store-bought variety.

Robbie laid one of the memory cards on the table and, with the other, crossed over to the bank of DVRs. She checked to see what Wanda and Roger were doing. They were concentrating on the video monitors in front of them. Larry was on the phone talking to the cashier's cage.

Remembering that the first DVR on the bottom shelf was

the one for the elevator, she pressed the stop button and ejected the memory card from the machine. Again, she turned toward her co-workers. They seemed oblivious to her actions. She took the video card from the library, inserted it in the slot in the DVR, and pushed the play button.

The machine hummed as it opened the file. Robbie glanced at the elevator video screen. To her horror, instead of an empty elevator, she saw an unoccupied soft count room. She'd placed the wrong memory card in the unit. Panicked, she jabbed the stop button on the DVR and gazed at the monitor. The picture of the vacant elevator had reappeared, but Larry was staring at her.

"Is everything all right?" he asked.

"Oh, oh, sure," she said. "I'm just inspecting the machines."

He shook a finger at her. "Be careful. You might erase a memory card by mistake. Do you need any help?"

"No thanks, Larry. I'm fine."

"Okay. Holler if you want my assistance." He winked and resumed viewing the bank of video screens.

Wanda was eyeing her with disapproval, shaking her head.

Robbie crossed the room to the video storage library, picked up the other memory card from the table, and went back to the DVRs. She popped the card in the slot in the first machine, tapped the play button, and turned to the monitor. It showed an empty elevator. Relieved, she released a heavy sigh.

With the first memory card now in position, Robbie hit the stop button on the second DVR and ejected its card. She stuck the prerecorded one in the machine and pressed the play button, watching the screen flash from live action of the unoccupied soft count room to the recording. For some strange reason, her colleagues continued to pay no attention to her.

Satisfied she now knew the procedures, she reversed her steps and put all the memory cards back in their proper locations.

With the last one back in the video library, she sank into the seat in front of her workstation.

"Just like Vanessa," Wanda said, making a sour face with pursed, craggy lips.

Robbie gave her a sideways glance. "I don't understand."

"Vanessa was always playing around in the video storage library. It appears you'll be doing the same."

"Special Projects," Robbie said, her voice firm. "It's part of my job."

Wanda scowled, her eyes bulging.

"Did you know Vanessa Daine well?" Robbie was hoping to find out more about her sudden departure.

"No, but it was rare that we spoke to each other. She thought she was better than us."

"I hear she sort of vanished."

"Quit without warning," Larry said. "I had a feeling she was leaving, though."

Robbie peered at him. "Oh, how come?"

"I don't know. It was the way she said goodbye on her last night of work. There was finality in her tone. It's difficult for me to describe, but at the time, I thought her behavior was odd."

Wanda said, "I knew she'd be quitting sooner or later. Her boyfriend slapped her around, and last week, she was trying to hide a beauty of a bruise. I could tell, though. My first husband tried to do the same to me—use me as a punching bag. You can't hide that kind of thing from me. I know the signs."

"It's too bad," Robbie said. "But a good reason to run off."

"That's what I think. It's difficult, I know, but leaving slime like Vanessa's boyfriend is the only way out. You have to move away."

"I agree."

Wanda and Larry nodded, concurring, then returned to concentrating on their work. Robbie, too, became absorbed by the video monitors and was startled when the telephone next to her rang. Her co-workers ignored the ringing, so she picked up the receiver. "Hello?" she said.

"Robbie, it's Marcus."

"Hey," she said in a whisper, cognizant the others could hear her.

"Did you find the prerecorded video?"

"I did. I had a few problems, but nothing big." She tried to muffle the conversation and directed her face away from the others. "I'm good with the memory cards, but not the rest."

"The buttons to turn off the cameras are in front of you. Push the first two green ones on the left."

Robbie studied the console and spotted the row of green buttons. She did as Hatrix instructed and pressed the first two. The pictures of the two hallways disappeared from the monitors and were replaced by images of the hotel registration desk and valet parking. "How about the other one?" she asked.

"It's the row of red buttons," Hatrix said. "Flick the first one on the left."

She leaned over and tapped it, and the locker alcove video was replaced by a shot of the Edgewater Lounge. "Okay, I've got it all down now. I can do my part."

"That's music to my ears." Hatrix was delighted—the tone of his voice made that clear. "I knew you'd figure it out. I can almost see the money now. It won't be fast enough, though."

"I feel much more confident now that I've had a chance to walk through it."

"Good. Mr. Montgomery wants you to call him when you're off work."

"I know. I will as soon as I'm home."

"I have your locker key. I'll meet you by the purse alcove when your shift ends."

Robbie heard the click as Hatrix hung up the phone, and she

held the handset a few moments before also hanging up. Wanda shot her another derisive glower, but Robbie ignored her and stared at the monitors in front of her. She saw the various tables on the screens—blackjack, roulette, and craps and realized that now, the biggest game of chance at the Charleston Casino Resort was her own.⊚

TERI, CORY, AND Brian were seated in chairs around the recording equipment. Robbie had ended her shift and departed the casino. "I better leave for Robbie's house," Teri said. "I need to debrief her while all this is fresh in her mind."

"Quite a set-up," Cory said. "Too bad Robbie wasn't in a position to better explain her actions. When Hatrix surprised her in the break room, she became shy about describing what was going on."

"She still did well," Brian said. "You'd be leery too if you were in the same situation."

"Don't get me wrong, I just expected she'd be able to tell us more."

Brian rolled his eyes.

Teri said, "She'll fill in all the details at the debriefing."

Cory motioned to Brian. "You must be tired. Why don't you go home and sleep for a little while."

Brian rubbed his face and said, "I'm fine. I took a quick nap when Robbie was on her second break."

Teri held up an admonishing finger. "That's not enough," she said. "You need more rest than that. Go home and relax."

"I have a job to do, remember? Director of Marketing. I'm supposed to keep up appearances and put in a normal workday."

"He's right," Cory said, "and if he hadn't spent the night here, it wouldn't be an issue."

"I've told you both before."—Brian's volume was creeping up—"I'm committed to this until it's finished and Robbie's safe."

"You still have to sleep," Teri said. "At least go to your office, close the door, and catch some shuteye."

Brian massaged a kink in his neck and rotated his head. "I'll rest after work. I plan on taking an early out. I know I have to be alert when Robbie starts her shift tonight."

"This evening should be pretty dull," Cory said, stroking the two days' worth of stubble on his chin. "Montgomery doesn't want the thefts to begin until he's confident Robbie knows her way around the surveillance room."

"Cory's correct," Teri said. "I don't expect much to happen. Until they begin taking the money, we're in for some long, boring nights."

Brian asked, "When do you think Montgomery will give them the green light?"

Cory said, "I suppose it depends on his comfort level."

Brian kneaded his temples. "He's a cautious man. It could be weeks. I shudder at the thought of Robbie going through this for any length of time."

"Let's hope we don't have to wait long," Teri said. "Montgomery needs money for the *Sierra Queen*. It may motivate him to give the go-ahead sooner than you expect. If not, we can look forward to weeks of the pleasant patter of the surveillance room."

With sarcasm, Brian said, "They're a nice bunch of people. What an odd group. I can tell Robbie doesn't like them."

Teri clasped her shoulders with both arms. "Who would? I pray this ends before creepy Larry does anything. It was her first night of work, and she could already file a sexual harassment suit against that moron."

"I hate that she has to work in such an environment."

"She can handle herself better than most," Cory said. "You have some woman there."

"She's not my woman." Brian's inflection was severe.

Cory tipped his head back in surprise. "Sure, Brian, whatever you say. Jesus, don't chew my head off."

"Stay focused on getting the evidence required to arrest Montgomery. Right now, nothing else is any of your goddamn business."

THIRTY

BEATRICE WAS ON the telephone again. "He fired her for talking with a customer?" she asked. "I thought that was the idea, to be pleasant to them. Shocking. Oh, I have to go. Mr. S. just walked in. I'll call you later." She hung up and looked at Brian. "There are a lot of messages for you."

Brian reached out, took the stack of slips she handed him, and leafed through them.

Beatrice pointed to the phone. "Skip Sullivan's agent's called three more times. He insists you contact him as soon as possible. He's persistent."

"It's what makes him a good agent. Did he say what he wanted?"

She shook her head. "No, he said you'd know."

"I don't. I guess I better give him a ring. Anything else going on around here?"

"Not much. I know Alice has finalized the agreement on the Perez/Davis boxing match. She convinced the promoter to agree to her terms."

Brian contemplated that with satisfaction. "Hmm. Perez/Davis should be a popular fight with the customers. Is Alice in her office?"

"Yes, she'd like you to stop by."

"Okay, I'll go there now."

Beatrice gestured to his office door. "Call Sullivan's agent first. He's making me crazy."

"I thought you went insane years ago?"

She gave him an acerbic smile. "I love you too."

Brian grinned back at her, one of the first times he'd done that in some time. "Beatrice, the way it's been going around here, we may both end up in a sanitarium."

"Oh, no, Brian, we're the last two rational people at the Charleston Resort."

"You may be right." Brian chuckled and entered his office. He sat down at the desk, read his email, and grabbed the memos and manila envelopes piled high in his inbox. He read through the reports, threw most of them in the wastepaper basket, and routed the rest back to Beatrice for distribution.

His desk cleared, Brian glanced at the stack of phone messages and let out a dejected sigh. He picked up the telephone and dialed a long distance number in Los Angeles, then worked through a cadre of receptionists and secretaries until he was connected to Theodore Goldstein, the agent for Skip Sullivan.

"Goddamn it, Shepard," Goldstein said. "What were you thinking? You know how fragile Skip's state of mind has been. How could you do this to him?"

Brian was rattled, and his pulse skyrocketed. "What are you talking about, Theodore?" He knew it couldn't be good.

"I know guys like you. Another notch in your bedpost. And this time, you can brag to your buddies you scored with the girlfriend of a celebrity. You're a real stud, aren't you?"

"Quit shouting and tell me what has you all riled up."

"Don't deny it. Sullivan's girlfriend spent the night with you. You screwed her. We both know it, so don't try lying to me. I spoke with April, and she admitted it."

Brian said nothing, rubbing his forehead.

"April told me when she returned to the hotel suite, Skip was waiting for her. He flipped out."

An immediate pounding began in Brian's head. He closed his eyes and tried to conjure up an excuse. "Skip misunderstood."

"I know that's not true, goddamn it. I talked with April."

"She told Sullivan?"

"No, but he's not a stupid man. Worse yet, jealousy's his middle name. You're not the first—April's done this to him before."

"I wasn't thinking straight. I had too much to drink. We all did." Brian was trying to keep his temper. It wasn't like he was in this alone—April was responsible too.

"You know how delicate Skip's emotional state is. Was a few moments of carnal pleasure worth it?"

"I'll speak with him," Brian said, trying in vain to come up with something that would reassure the agent. "I can calm him down. I'll make up some story."

Goldstein raised his voice. "We don't know where he is."

Brian imagined him tomato red and continued to massage his temples. "Oh, I'm sure he's nearby."

"No, he's gone. April said he took off and she doesn't know where he went. She's looked for him everywhere. I insisted. She doesn't believe it's a big deal, but I know otherwise."

"Have you called the sheriff?"

"Don't be ridiculous. The media monitors the sheriff's calls. Do you want this on the front page of every newspaper in the country?"

Brian imagined the headlines and shuddered. "What should I do?"

"Find him. I'm tied up today, but I'll catch the first plane from LA to Reno that I can tomorrow. In the meantime, track him down. You're responsible for this, and I expect you to locate Skip and make it copacetic."

"I'll start now."

"Shepard, I book the top celebrity names into the Charleston Resorts nationwide. Sal Wyman and I are old friends. You better make it right with Skip and straighten this out, or I can guarantee you, your job's on the line."

Brian didn't like being threatened but knew he was in no position to argue. "It'll be okay. I'm certain Skip's fine. He's at some bar getting drunk. Calm down."

"You better be correct. If not, you'll pay." The agent hung up the phone, but his shouts continued to ring in Brian's ears.

Brian didn't know where to begin searching for the comedian. Security and Surveillance might, but knowing what Elliot Thomas thought of entertainers, and Skip Sullivan in particular, he was the last person to ask for help.

BRIAN TURNED TO see Alice McKay standing in the doorway of his office.

"You look like crap," she said.

"Thanks," he said, "but you're not the first person to tell me that this week."

"Well, it's true. Is everything all right?"

He released a bitter laugh. "Is everything all right? No, Alice, everything's not all right. I doubt it could be much worse."

Alice's forehead was lined with concern. "What's wrong?"

Brian didn't know where to begin. "I won't burden you with all of it, but I could use your assistance. Skip Sullivan's missing. It's a long story, but the fact is, he's gone, and I have to find him. I talked with his agent a few minutes ago, and he's frantic."

"Damn it, Brian, I know you too well. You're not telling me everything I need to know. What the hell's going on?"

"Let's just say that, due to some stupid mistakes on my part, Skip Sullivan's disappeared. Can we leave it at that?"

"I suppose I don't need to know the details." Alice bared a judgmental face. "Why are you always in trouble?"

"I don't know, but can you help me locate Sullivan?"

"Any ideas where to begin?"

"Our best bet's to start in the casinos and bars around the lake."

"There must be hundreds of bars in this basin."

Brian shrugged and held up a hand. "I don't know where else to search."

"The bars make sense, but the two of us won't be enough. Have you phoned Security?"

"No. I'm trying to keep this quiet, if possible. You know what Elliot Thomas thinks of Sullivan."

"Okay, I'll tell you what—I'll send everyone in the marketing office out to help. We can cover more territory that way. Are you sure he's not in the hotel somewhere?"

"According to his agent, April Vaurnet—Sullivan's girlfriend—has looked everywhere. I'm tracking her down first. She knows him better than anyone and may be able to give me some sort of lead."

Alice squinted. "Why do I get the feeling I should follow you around and make certain you don't get into some predicament?"

"It must be some mother complex."

"If you were my damn kid, I'd put you over my knee and give you ten whacks." She pantomimed a spanking motion.

"It'd do me good."

"What've you done?"

"You don't want to know. Let's find Sullivan."

GAMING AGENT TERI Porter watched as Robbie dialed her home phone and adjusted the headphones allowing her to monitor the conversation. Robbie drummed her fingers on the kitchen counter as she waited for the call to go through. When it was answered, she said, "Mr. Montgomery, it's Robbie."

"How was your first night?" he asked.

"It went well. I felt comfortable in the surveillance room. I'll learn the job in no time."

"Did you find the prerecorded videos?"

"Yes, I even put them in the DVRs and practiced the procedures. Marcus asked me to do a dry run. I put both prerecorded videos in the machines and ran through the process."

"Don't rush this. It's too risky. Take your time. We have a great deal at stake, and I don't want to be careless. I need you to work in the surveillance room a while and become used to the operation. You must get to know the surveillance people and gain their confidence. It'll make your activities less obvious."

"I agree. I don't want to hurry this either."

"Then take it slow. It's important that you're involved in the day-to-day functions of the Surveillance Department. It's part of your cover. The harder you work and the better job you do, the less suspicion you'll raise."

"I know, and I guarantee they'll think I'm a good employee in no time."

"Okay, I'll talk with you later. You should go to bed."

"I'm exhausted. It'll take me some time to acclimate to the graveyard shift."

"I don't envy you."

Robbie took a weary breath. "I know it'll get easier—it'll just take a while for me to adjust to the crazy hours."

"I'm sure it will. Call me tomorrow. I'd like an update on your progress every morning. It'll help me gauge when to send Hatrix into the count room."

"Again, I want to express my gratitude for allowing me to join you. You won't regret it."

"When the money starts coming in, I'll be the one thanking you. Now rest." Montgomery hung up, and Robbie put down the receiver and looked at Teri.

"Tired?" Teri asked after taking off the headphones.

"Yes," Robbie said. "I wasn't lying to Montgomery. I'm super fatigued. I tried to take a nap yesterday, but I was too keyed up."

"You've been through a lot, and I won't keep you much longer."

Robbie smiled at her with appreciation.

Teri scanned the notes on the electronic tablet she was holding. "Now, is there anything about the surveillance room you haven't already told me?"

"No, I don't believe so. I explained the library set up for the prerecorded cards, didn't I?"

Teri nodded. "I follow the process."

"It's about all I can remember. My brain's muddled. Maybe after I sleep, I'll think of something more."

"I could use some rest myself."

"Yeah, I bet both you and Cory are beat."

"Yes, but nothing compared to Brian."

Robbie tucked a wisp of hair behind one ear. "How so?"

"We were able to take naps yesterday afternoon, but Brian worked all day and stayed with us all night. He must be ready to drop."

A frown crept over Robbie's face. "He was with you last night? In the hotel room?"

"He listened to every word you said during the shift."

Annoyed, Robbie compressed her lips. "Why's he doing this? He's carrying this too far."

"You must know the man's very much in love with you. He lamely tries to pretend otherwise, but he cares about you."

Robbie turned away and stared out the window and across

the waters of Lake Tahoe. She leaned her head back and closed her eyes. "Damn."

"You know he's one of the good ones. He's more than just attractive."

Robbie faced her. "That's difficult for me to judge—the good ones, I mean. I don't want to be hurt again."

Teri put a hand on her shoulder and made intense eye contact. "Again?"

"A few years ago, I was engaged to a so-called great guy. I caught him with another woman three weeks before our wedding."

"Brian's not him."

"Hailey Mancini told me he's been quite the ladies' man."

"That wouldn't surprise me—he's so handsome and has such a fun personality. The first time I saw him, I was weak-kneed. But I think you've enchanted him like no other. I've never been near a man so concerned about someone as he is about you. Cory says he's known Brian a long time and hasn't ever seen him this way. He's fallen for you big time."

"I have feelings for him too. Strong ones. They scared me, and I panicked. I had to slow it down."

"Well, this is none of my business. Get some sleep, Robbie. You have another long night ahead of you."

"Thanks, Teri. You've been a great help, and I value your support. I couldn't do this without you."

Teri left the house, and Robbie sat on the sofa. It was nice to be alone, with no one scrutinizing her every word and action. Now if she could just quiet the conflicting thoughts in her mind, she might be able to get some rest.

BRIAN TOOK THE elevator up to the penthouse floor of the Charleston Resort. He walked down the hallway, past the elegant paintings adorning the walls leading to Skip Sullivan's suite. He knocked several times before April Vaurnet opened the door. "Brian, what a nice surprise," she said and flashed him a thousand-watt smile.

He stepped into the suite. "Have you heard from Skip?"

"No, but he's done this before, and I'm sure he'll show up sooner or later."

"Theodore Goldstein's freaking out. He seems to believe this is a serious matter."

April swished a wrist at him. "Teddy's a tight-ass. I told him not to worry, but he won't listen."

"Goldstein may be correct. Before you arrived at Lake Tahoe, Skip was a wreck. You know, April, he cares for you, and the other night was unfortunate."

"It was?" April honked in laughter. "Didn't you have a good time? I know I did. You're an exceptional lover." She opened her robe, revealing her large, milk-white breasts.

Brian looked away. "I don't remember much about the other night. I had way too much alcohol."

"If you perform that well drunk, I can imagine what you're like sober." She grinned at him with a lustful eye. "The hot tub's in the other room. Care to join me?"

"No, thank you," Brian said, trying to ignore that the attractive blonde was coming on to him. "I'm in enough trouble around here, and I don't need to make it any worse."

"Oh, why not? It'll be fun."

"It would, you're one gorgeous woman, but we must find Skip."

April's lower lip popped out in a pout. "He's sulking somewhere. In a bar. That's what he does when he wants me to feel sorry for him and beg forgiveness."

"Don't you care for him?"

She shook hair off her shoulders. "Sure I do. I love him, but he's so temperamental. I'm tired of his childish behavior."

"Immature or not, I have to locate him. Skip has shows tonight and Goldstein's coming to the lake tomorrow. If we don't find and talk some sense into him, there'll be fireworks. He's already canceled one show, and if anyone discovers I'm responsible for his disappearance this time, I may lose my job."

"Well then, we'll track him down. Point me to the nearest cocktail lounge, and I can guarantee you he'll be there."

"Goldstein told me you already tried to find him in the bars at the Charleston?"

"Well, I did. Teddy insisted I look all around the place. He's not here. He's sure to be at Harrah's or one of the other casinos."

"We have to start searching now."

"I can't interest you in the hot tub?"

Exasperated, Brian raised his voice. "Stop with the temptation. I'm weak when it comes to sex, and if I'm not careful, I'll succumb to your charms. It's going to get me fired."

"Let me dress, and I'll help you. You're blowing this way out of proportion, though. He does this all the time."

"Humor me, April."

She smiled at him and sauntered into the bedroom to change.

BRIAN AND APRIL began their hunt for Skip Sullivan by visiting the cocktail lounges at the neighboring hotels and casinos. Before departing the Charleston, he'd called Alice to be sure they weren't duplicating her efforts. Alice and her staff were looking for the comedian in the smaller bars around South Lake Tahoe, then going to the west shore and Tahoe City. Brian and April planned to canvass the casinos at Stateline, then over at Incline Village.

Leading April through the Stateline mega-resorts, Brian had difficulty keeping her focused on the task at hand. She was always stopping to try her luck at the slot machines.

"I love these devices," April said. She dropped three coins

into a vintage machine and pulled the handle. The reels spun and three bars lined up. Bells rang and coins dropped into the metal tray. "Wow, Brian, I won."

"April," he said, "we don't have time for this. We need to locate Skip. I'm starting to get worried."

"How much did I win?"

"I don't know." With an angry expression, he handed her a plastic coin bucket. "Cash out at the change booth."

"Fine." She scooped the money from the slot machine tray into the bucket. "I'm glad they don't have these in Hollywood. I'd spend every minute playing the slots."

Brian was growing more aggravated, and it was clear in his tone. "You don't possess much self-control, do you?"

"I do whatever feels good. Free love, let it all hang out—I'm like a child of the nineteen-sixties. I envy the people who lived in that era. People are so serious nowadays."

"Times have changed."

"Not for me, if I can help it."

"I can relate—we're more similar than I'd like to admit—but this is important. Follow me."

Brian dragged April through every cocktail lounge and bar in the Stateline casinos. Each establishment seemed to have dim lighting and, at this time of the morning, sparse crowds. After walking out of the last resort without spotting the comedian, April shook her head. "I'm surprised," she said. "I was positive we'd find him by now. As I told you, he's done this many times."

Brian said, "I think you're underestimating how much Skip loves you."

She clicked her tongue a few times. "I know, but we had a big argument before his engagement at the Charleston. I told him I didn't want his constant control, his jealousy."

"If he's that way, why do you cheat on him?"

April put a hand on her hip. "I've told you, I do what feels good. It's the way I am. I'm a free spirit, and Skip needs to recognize that. I can't be caged like some animal. Skip should appreciate my desires in life."

"And you his. I'm learning that myself."

"I know, but drugs and alcohol make him so irrational. He wanders in and out of sobriety. Sometimes he's straight as can be—a real health nut—and others a lunatic. He has a split personality."

"I don't suppose the drug episodes correspond with your infidelities?"

April stared at him. For the first time, her face showed some real concern. "Maybe you're right. We better find him."

THIRTY-ONE

THE USED CAR salesman crossed his arms. "That's my last offer," he said. "Not a penny more."

Hatrix's voice rose. "You're kidding me. This car's worth more than twice that. It's just a year old. It's loaded and in cherry condition. It doesn't even have ten thousand miles on it yet."

"If I were seeking a new automobile, I'd go to the dealer and buy one. Take it or leave it."

"That's robbery. Look at that interior—not a spot."

"I'm sorry, sir, but the car's not worth it. You know as well as I do that the minute you drove it off the lot, it lost a ton of its value. If you think you can do better, go to another dealer."

Hatrix glared at the man. "I already did. I even went to a pawn shop."

"You can always try Craigslist or eBay. You never know, some sucker might pay your asking price."

"I don't have the time. I need the money now. What pisses me off is I don't want to sell the car. I'm in a short-term cash crunch, and in a week or so, I'll have enough to buy five new ones."

The salesman looked at him with faux empathy. "I wish I could help you. Is it a deal or not?"

Hatrix eyed him with distain. "No deal. I'll find another way."

"Suit yourself—I'm open until eight if you change your mind."

"I won't." Hatrix jumped into his sports car and drove away, wheels screeching.

BRIAN DROPPED SKIP Sullivan's girlfriend off at the hotel suite and returned to his office. Alice had left a message that she too had been unsuccessful in locating the comedian but she and her staff would continue to search.

By that time, Brian was exhausted and told Beatrice he was going home. Driving up the highway, he saw the street leading to Robbie's house, and before he knew it, he was heading in her direction. His subconscious was sure he could change her mind about their relationship.

Brian rang the doorbell, and after a short wait, Robbie answered the door. She was surprised to see him, somewhat uncomfortable in his presence, but waved him in.

"I wasn't sure if I'd wake you," he said. A roaring fire in the hearth warmed the room, and he could smell the aroma of fresh-brewed coffee.

"No, I've been up for a while now," Robbie said. "I got about six hours sleep, and I feel much better. Yesterday was a long one. Can I get you a cup of coffee?"

Brian took off his suit jacket and sat down on the sofa. "No, thanks. I don't want the caffeine. I need to get some sleep."

"Teri told me you spent the night at the Charleston in the GCB hotel room."

"Yes. I'm monitoring what's going on."

"It isn't necessary for you to do that. The agents have everything under control."

He gazed at her with sad eyes.

"Brian, let them do their job. You could be in their way."

His jaw clenched. "Did Teri say that?"

"No."

"Then I guess you don't need to worry about it. It's not your problem. I have friends who've been hurt by this goddamn ordeal, and until it's over, I'll be around. Did you hear Jack was fired?"

"Yes, Teri told me. I called Hailey and talked with her earlier this afternoon. She's holding up well, considering the situation. I feel sorry for Jack."

"I know. It shouldn't have happened."

Robbie nodded. "For damn sure."

"How are you doing?"

"Fine." Her bearing and tone were cold.

"Could you elaborate?"

"What more do you want? You were with Teri and Cory and know it went as we planned."

"I wasn't asking about your work in the surveillance room. I want to know how you're dealing with the pressure. It was a personal question."

"My way of coping with this is to keep it from getting personal. I don't know a better way to manage the situation." She bowed her head.

"Why are you shutting me out? I don't understand."

Robbie swept a few strands of hair out of her eyes. "This is my problem, not yours."

"Yeah, right. What about *my* feelings?"

"I'm sorry. I know I've hurt you, but like it or not, I'm involved in this much deeper than you. My emotions are on edge, and a relationship's too much for me to handle right now."

"That's what a relationship's for—to be there for each other." He paused, staring at her with what he very much feared was a clear look of displeasure. He was so tired, he couldn't think anymore. "I won't keep you any longer. I stopped by because I'm concerned about your welfare."

"I know that and appreciate it."

The doorbell rang, and their eyes swung to the front door. "What now?" Robbie said. She crossed the room and peeked through the peephole. Marcus Hatrix was standing there, grinning. "It's Hatrix."

"Oh, great," Brian said. "Should I stay or leave?"

"Whatever he wants, he won't say it in front of you."

"True."

Robbie opened the door and welcomed Hatrix into her home. "Marcus," she said, "you remember Brian?"

Hatrix looked over to him. "Sure," he said. "How's it going?"

"Pretty good," Brian said. "It's nice seeing you again." He turned to Robbie. "I better take off. Tonight's my poker night. The boys expect me to bring the beer, and I need to get to the store. I'll call you later."

Robbie smiled. "Thanks for the afternoon delight," she said.

Brian knew is face appeared pinched. He understood her response was in character—something Hatrix would expect her to say—but it would have seemed more appropriate from someone like April Vaurnet. "Anytime, babe. See you later." He gave her a quick kiss, grabbed his jacket, and left.

"Best-dressed construction worker I've ever seen," Hatrix said after Brian was gone, referring to his suit and tie.

Robbie was unfazed by his observation. "He cleans up nice, doesn't he? He had a court appearance this afternoon. Speeding. He thought he might sway the judge if he wore a suit and pretended to be a businessman."

"Did it work?"

"Sort of. The judge cut the fine in half. Why the visit?"

Robbie wasn't interested in idle conversation. She had to know why he was there. The sooner she did, the quicker she could get him to leave.

"I thought we'd have a little discussion."

"About what?"

"It went okay last night, didn't it?"

"I think so."

"I don't suppose there's anything cold and frosty to drink? I could sure use a beer."

She tilted her head to one side. "Let's go into the kitchen." Robbie led him out of the living room, handed him a beer from the refrigerator, and took out a bottle of Coca Cola for herself. "Is there a specific topic you'd like to chat about?"

Hatrix twisted open the beer and took a slug. "There is." His eyes roved around the room. "This is a nice house. I love the floor plan and the way it's decorated. Man, what a view. How much is the rent?"

"Too high. Marcus, you wanted to talk to me about something. Get to the point. What's on your mind?"

"I need to speak to you about money."

Robbie arched an eyebrow. "One of my favorite subjects. What about it?"

"Well, we're both in a financial bind. You have rent on this place due, and I have a loan to pay off."

"It's why I joined you and Mr. Montgomery—to end my cash problems. In a few weeks, I'm expecting all my financial worries to be over." She took a bottle opener from a drawer and flipped the cap off her Coke.

"What are you doing until then? How will you pay the rent? Your expenses?"

Robbie gave a shallow shrug. "I'll stall my landlord. I'm sure I can persuade him not to evict me until we start pulling in the money."

"Why wait? We can start the money flowing now. I intend to go into the soft count room tonight."

She was taken aback, her expression showing surprise. "Tonight? Oh, I'm not comfortable with doing it this soon."

"Sure you are. You saw how simple this is. You ran the videos last night with no problem."

"You know Montgomery would have a stroke. He told me he'd give me the go-ahead when he felt I was ready."

"He doesn't understand. We both know you can do the job now."

"I still think we should wait for his approval. He doesn't know me well, and if I piss him off, I'll be in trouble."

Hatrix's voice grew louder. "I can't wait."

Robbie put her Coke on the counter. "Marcus, chill out. What's the hurry? We're both after some cash, but let's not be foolish and jeopardize the whole thing."

Hatrix was visibly stressed, his forehead rough with deep wrinkles. "You're not appreciating my bind. I must get some money now. There's a loan shark on my ass. If I don't come up with twenty thousand by tomorrow, I could end up fish food, just like Vanes—" He stopped. A silence hung in the air. "Um, um, van...van...the poor people on the Titanic."

Robbie stared at him, shocked. She knew how he was going to finish the sentence: *Just like Vanessa.*

"I need the cash, and I'm entering the soft count room tonight." Hatrix clearly hoped that if he said it fast enough, she'd move on.

Robbie was dazed. She wanted to confront him about Vanessa, but knew she couldn't. "Let's consult with Montgomery first."

Hatrix's expression was defiant. "No. He'll say no. But once he sees that we were able to start the thefts without any issues, he'll be okay. He needs the money almost as bad as we do."

"I'm not sure..."

"Robbie, I'm going into the soft count room with or without your help. If you don't cover me and I'm caught, this whole goddamn operation will come to an end."

Robbie gestured at the telephone. "I'll call Mr. Montgomery."

"No, you won't. With his permission or not, I'm doing this. There are no other options. If you tell Montgomery, it'll make him angry and he might try to stop us. I can't afford that. I have to get enough dough to pay off Louie."

Agitated, Robbie wrung her hands. "You're not giving me much of a choice."

"I'm not, but it'll go fine. Focus on the bright side—by this time tomorrow, you'll be able to splurge on a new bobble."

"With cash obtained the easy way." Her mind was troubled by the words.

"How about a toast?" Hatrix lifted his beer. "To many nights of fruitful harvest."

Robbie picked up her Coke and pressed it against his bottle. "Cheers."

BRIAN SAW HATRIX leave Robbie's house and came out from behind a pine tree. He'd observed their conversation through a window where he could reassure himself she wasn't in any danger. He was approaching the front door when Teri and Cory drove up. Brian told them about Hatrix's visit. "I stayed outside until he left," he said. "Just in case."

"I wonder what he wanted," Cory said.

"I was about to find out when you pulled up." He rang the doorbell.

When Robbie answered the door, she was close to hysterical. "She's dead," she said. "Vanessa's dead, and believe it or not, we're going to start stealing from the count room beginning tonight."

"Calm down, Robbie," Teri said. "What are you talking about?"

Robbie was trembling. "Vanessa—she's dead. They killed her."

"Did Hatrix tell you that?"

"It slipped out. He tried to cover, but I know what he meant. Vanessa's been murdered."

"Slow up," Cory said, gently patting the air. "Tell us what happened."

Robbie sat in a reclining chair, and Brian stared at her, alarmed. "Hatrix came by," she said. "Brian was here." She glanced at him for confirmation. "Hatrix insists the thefts begin tonight. He owes a loan shark some money and has to pay it back by tomorrow. When he was telling me this, he screwed up. He started to say that if he didn't pay back the money, he would, and I quote, *be fish food just like Vanessa*. He cut himself off before he finished her name and tried to gloss it over, but I know what he meant. Vanessa's dead."

"The thefts start this evening?" Teri asked, focusing on entirely the wrong point, as far as Brian was concerned.

"Yes. Hatrix is going to the soft count room tonight."

"What about Montgomery?" Cory asked.

"Hatrix' isn't telling him. He's doing it without permission. He's stealing from the soft count room this evening, and if I don't cooperate, our whole undercover setup's finished."

"And it should be," Brian said. "This is way out of control. Vanessa's dead, and you could end up the same way. It's much too dangerous. Let's end this now. We may not have enough evidence to convict Montgomery, but it's not worth your life to get it."

Robbie shook her fist. "No. If we quit now, they'll get away with Vanessa's murder, and I can't allow that. I insist on continuing."

"Bringing Vanessa's killers to justice is commendable, but it's not worth dying for."

"My mind's made up." Robbie's face was full of resolve, and it was obvious that no one would be able to convince her otherwise. "I want to go to the surveillance room tonight and do my job. If I don't, we'll never convict Montgomery and Hatrix of Vanessa's murder. Until we have more evidence, I won't stop."

"I don't know," Cory said. "I'm not certain Chairman Cavanaugh would approve of us carrying on. They're not just crooks anymore."

"He wants a guilty verdict on Montgomery," Robbie said, "and you know it. There's been a degree of danger in this all along. I was willing to take the risk before, and I'm prepared to do so now. It should be my decision."

The two gaming agents looked at each other and then over at Brian.

Brian eyed her with apprehension. "You're sure?" he asked.

Robbie folded her arms and said, "I'm positive."

"In that case," Cory said, "we have work to do. I need to send agents to the Charleston to start playing the table games with the marked bills."

"We've already missed two shifts," Teri said.

Cory checked his watch.

"Is that a problem?" Brian asked.

"It's almost five o'clock," Teri said. "The drop boxes for the graveyard shift—and within the hour, the day shift—will have been pulled from the tables and put into the soft count room. That means we'll only have marked bills in the swing shift drop boxes."

Brian rubbed his chin. "Will your plan still work?"

"Probably, but there's a greater chance Hatrix won't take the marked bills. If we had money in the drop boxes of all three shifts our odds would be better."

"There's nothing we can do about it," Cory said. "One shift's better than nothing."

"What if we wait until tomorrow?" Teri asked. "Why risk everything on one shift tonight? Tomorrow night we can have the marked bills in all three shifts."

"No," Brian said forcefully. "They're killers. We can't keep Robbie in this situation any longer. It's too dangerous."

"I think we should do it tonight," Robbie said. "I want this over."

Cory stared at her for a moment. "Okay," he said. "I have some calls to make. A lot of arrangements have to be made."

The gaming agents and Robbie began discussing the plans for the evening. Cory and Teri made numerous phone calls to their offices, and within what seemed like minutes, more agents arrived. The house became a sea of activity centered on Robbie. Brian watched and listened but knew he could do little more than be in the way.

BRIAN RETURNED TO the Charleston Resort with the hope that Skip Sullivan was in his suite preparing for the evening performances. Leaning back in his office chair, he called April Vaurnet and was disappointed to hear Skip hadn't shown up. She promised him again to call the minute she heard from the comedian.

Brian hung up the phone and wandered down the hall to Alice MacKay's office. Peering into the room, he saw her working at her laptop. He gestured to the computer and said, "You won't find Sullivan in there."

She grinned at him. "You're right. His damn ego's too large to fit in this tiny machine."

"No luck?"

Alice shook her head. "None, and we've looked everywhere. I haven't been in so many bars since my college days. Two of my coordinators are still out searching. I take it you've had the same result."

Brian ran both hands through his hair. "I suppose I get the

unenviable task of telling the showroom staff that tonight's performances will be canceled."

"How would you like to work at the ticket window? They have to explain to hundreds of irate customers who made a special trip to see Skip Sullivan that the show's canceled."

"The maître d' is still angry with me about Sullivan's no-show last week. He acts like it's my fault."

Alice gave him a critical eye. "This time it is."

Brian flushed pink with embarrassment. "I expect both Elliot Thomas and Keith Wallace will be giving me their thoughts on Sullivan."

"Oh, you can count on that."

"Do you want to inform the showroom for me?" He looked at her, hopeful.

"Oh, no, you slippery bastard—this is why they pay you the big bucks."

"You're not supposed to speak to your boss like that."

Alice closed her laptop. "Fire me. I could use the time off."

"If you didn't cover my ass as often as you do, I'd be tempted."

"This mess is your problem. You handle it."

"I guess I have no choice."

Alice pointed. "The box office is that way."

Brian sighed and shuffled off to the showroom.

THIRTY-TWO

AFTER BEING BUZZED into the wide hallway, Robbie walked over to the vault cashier and asked for the key to her locker. The cashier pushed the log across the counter and reached over to retrieve the key, then turned to Robbie and said, "Funny, someone's already checked out your key."

Robbie felt an eye twitch. "What? I thought we always kept the same locker."

"You do. It's a mistake." The cashier pulled the key log to her and ran a finger down the entries. "Here it is—one of the new girls in the cage was given your key by mistake. It's no problem, however—I'll give you a different locker."

"No," Robbie said with potency. Hatrix had made a copy of her key the previous night—she needed to have the same one.

The cashier took a step back at Robbie's vehemence. "It's no big deal—the lockers are all the same. I'll assign you another one."

Robbie had to think fast. "You don't understand. I left a paperback book I'm reading in my locker. I must have the same one so I can get it back."

The woman nodded slowly. "Oh, all right. Let me go find the new girl, and we'll look for it. Give me a minute."

Irritated, Robbie stood there waiting. The microphone wire strapped to her chest was already poking her, and she tried to adjust it without drawing attention, aware that cameras were capturing her every move.

The vault cashier came back to the counter. "Jessica's on her way out," she said. "She doesn't remember seeing a book."

Robbie could feel her face tighten. "It's just a paperback."

A couple of minutes later, Jessica strolled through the doorway and over to Robbie. The young blond woman introduced herself and apologized for the mix up. "I didn't realize they gave me the wrong locker. This is my first night."

"It's just my second," Robbie said.

They moved around the corner to the alcove, and Jessica unlocked the small door on compartment seven and looked inside. "See," she said. "There's no paperback book in here."

Robbie tried to act confused. "I guess I was mistaken. Perhaps I left it in my car."

"Gee, I hope so."

They strode out of the alcove and up to the counter. "Did you get your book?" the vault cashier asked.

Robbie's cheeks heated. "It wasn't there," she said.

The vault cashier gave her a contemptuous look. "It seems I chased down Jessica for nothing." She gestured to Jessica. "Go back to work, kid—I'm sorry for the interruption."

Robbie said, her tone matter-of-fact, "Since Jessica came all the way out here, we might as well switch lockers."

"What for? They're identical."

"I know this sounds crazy, but seven's my lucky number. I'd like to keep locker seven." It was a ridiculous rationale, and she knew it sounded like one.

The vault cashier put her hands on her hips. "Oh, now I've heard everything. Seven's your lucky number? Isn't that precious."

Robbie said, turning to the new cashier, "Please, Jessica, do you mind?"

Jessica shrugged. "No, I guess not," she said.

"Thanks." Robbie smiled at the vault cashier. "Well then, it's settled. Would you please give her another locker?"

One corner of the cashier's lips lowered, but she complied. Robbie thanked Jessica again and put her purse in locker seven, then worked through the web of doors and hallways and up the elevator to the Surveillance Department, entering the dark surveillance room and hurrying to her workstation.

"You're late," Wanda said.

Robbie sat down. "I'm sorry. They had a mix-up in the vault."

Wanda shook a bent arthritic finger. "I saw you and I called down to see what was going on. I won't embarrass you in front of the others, but a lucky number? How childish."

Robbie waved a condescending hand. "Whatever." She inspected the video monitors showing the busy casino.

Sanders, the supervisor, said to her from across the room, "Beasley called in sick, and the action in the pit is heavy. We've got our work cut out for us tonight."

"It means no special projects," Wanda said, gloating. "There's too much to do for you to be away from your workstation."

"She's right. With the casino play this strong and Beasley out, you won't have time for a special projects video."

Special Projects were the only way she could cover Hatrix without arousing suspicion. Robbie said, "I thought I was supposed to make a video for Mr. Montgomery every night."

"Yes, you are, but these are unusual circumstances. If it slows, you may have a chance to make one later in the shift. Otherwise, I'll explain the situation to Montgomery. I need you to keep tabs on Gerald Yamamoto. He's on BJ ten, pit two." He signaled to a monitor. "He's up a hundred thousand dollars."

Robbie was astounded, her jaw dropping. "I can't imagine anyone winning a hundred thousand dollars playing blackjack."

"Yamamoto's one of our better customers. He lost over a million dollars here last year. He owns an import-export company in San Francisco."

"If he's such a big gambler, shouldn't someone with more experience be watching his play? This is only my second night—I don't know what I'm doing."

"Believe it or not, we have three other players in the house tonight who are wagering more than Yamamoto. It's their first visit to the Charleston, and we're keeping an eye on them. One may be counting cards. Anyway, Yamamoto's a known entity, and there are no games with him. Even with your inexperience, he's easy to observe."

Skeptical, Robbie's said, "If you say so."

"Ensure the dealers don't make any mistakes. It's the most common problem when we get high-limit action—they become nervous and errors occur. Do you remember the dealing procedures we reviewed last night?"

"I think so. When I have questions, I won't be afraid to ask."

Sanders pointed to a monitor showing a row of blackjack tables. "If you see anything out of the ordinary, call the pit. Likewise, they'll contact you if they have an issue or want you to focus on something specific."

Robbie spent the next several hours observing Gerald Yamamoto bet large sums of money on the blackjack tables. He'd stare, engrossed, at his cards before deciding whether to hit or stand. It seemed an eternity before he'd make up his mind, but with the amount he was wagering, she guessed it was his right. Yamamoto's luck had changed from when she first came on shift. He'd now lost enough that he was taking credit from the casino cashier, signing for hefty markers every few minutes.

Robbie's telephone rang often—most of the time, it was calls from the pit, and in each instance, she wished it was Hatrix. She had to tell him there would be no special projects tonight.

Time crawled. Despite the vast sums of money being gambled in front of her, she had difficulty concentrating. The job was tedious, and the wait for Hatrix to call felt like an eternity. At about two-twenty, her phone rang and this time, it was him. "It's show-time, Robbie," he said.

"Marcus, we can't," she said, trying to speak in a quiet voice. Wanda glared at her so hard she resembled a Shar-Pei. "We're short-handed, and the casino's busy. They told me I couldn't work on my special projects."

Hatrix said in a shout, "You have to. We must start now. I told you, I'm going into the soft count room tonight. I have no choice. I need the money."

"What do you want me to do?" Even whispering, Robbie's tone was sharp. She tilted her head away from Wanda. "Sanders said there'd be no special projects until the business in the casino slows."

"You've got to do something. What about breaks? They're required to give you one. Tell them you have to go to the restroom."

"I'll see what I can do. Where can I reach you? If I can get away, I'll call you."

"Robbie, make this work. I'm at extension three-three-seven-five. Please don't let me down."

Robbie hung up and glanced over to Sanders. He was jotting something in a logbook. Timid, her voice weak, she said, "Excuse me, Andy."

Sanders lifted his eyes from the log. "Yes?"

She cleared her throat. "I was wondering if, instead of taking my break, I could work on a special projects video."

"We're too busy for that," Wanda said. "I thought we made that clear at the beginning of the shift."

Robbie looked at her with contempt, then back at Sanders. "I'd like to do it on my first fifteen minute break. We still get them, don't we?"

Mocking, Wanda said, "Yes, we get breaks. Why waste them on special projects busy work?"

"I'm new here, and I don't want Mr. Montgomery to think I'm not doing my job."

"Don't worry about that," Sanders said. "I'll explain our situation to him."

"Yes, but I can do a special projects video on my break. Please, I'd feel much better..."

He raised an open hand. "It's your personal time. If you insist, go ahead, but remember it's not necessary."

Robbie smiled and brushed hair over her shoulder. "Thanks, Andy—I believe it's important for me to do this."

"Okay. Roger's on his lunch break now. When he comes back, you can take your first fifteen."

It was an hour before Roger returned from his lunch. The wait seemed forever as Robbie watched the clock tick by. With Roger at his workstation, Sanders told her to take a break. She said she would but needed to make a phone call first. Sanders nodded. Wanda harrumphed.

Robbie picked up the telephone and dialed 3375. Hatrix answered on the first ring. "I was afraid you weren't going to call," he said. He was anxious—she could hear the tension in his voice.

She said in a whisper, "I had to wait for my first break, but I can start now."

Relief filled his voice. "Oh, baby, I knew you could do it. I'm on my way in. I have to hurry, though. I should've gone into the soft count room over an hour ago."

Robbie checked the time on her watch. It was three-thirty. "Are you sure there's enough time? The count team supervisor arrives at five. You told me she often gets there early to make certain the paperwork's ready."

"If I move fast. I'll call you when I'm out." Hatrix hung up.

Robbie put down the receiver and rushed to the video storage library, extracted memory cards 333 and 334 from the shelves, and sidled up to the row of DVRs. She pressed the stop button on the first one on the bottom shelf and ejected the memory card from the machine, placed 334 in the slot, and slapped the play button. She surveyed the monitor and saw the unoccupied elevator. A hint of a smile touched her lips.

Robbie stepped to the next DVR on the shelf and hit the stop button, hearing the machine moan. She pushed the eject button on the DVR. Nothing happened. She tapped the eject button again with the same result. Her heart quickened. She jabbed the stop button and the eject button. Once more, nothing.

Robbie poked the record button, and the machine hummed. She engaged the stop button again. The DVR gurgled to a halt. She pressed eject. Zero movement.

Panic exploded through her chest and made her light-headed. Hatrix would be on his way to the soft count room any minute. She slid a finger along the memory card slot and tried to see what might be jamming it. She felt nothing unusual. She again pushed the eject button with fury.

"I'm having trouble with the DVR," she said in a low voice to the hidden microphone. "The memory card's stuck."

"Problem?" Sanders asked from behind her.

Robbie jerked around. "Oh, you startled me."

"I'm sorry. Is the DVR giving you trouble?"

"Yes, it is." Her hands were shaking, and she clasped them together to mitigate the movement.

"Let me see what I can do. What are you recording?"

"Y-Y-Yamamoto. I thought Mr. Montgomery would be interested in seeing some of his play."

Larry pointed to the machine. "Not on that DVR."

Her pulse was pounding. "Why not?"

"It's for the soft count room. See the monitor number? If you want to record Yamamoto, you'll need to use this one." Sanders gestured to another unit two shelves over. "Number seventy-two."

"Oh, no, then I've made a terrible mistake. I've already taken the memory card that was in the DVR out." Lying was becoming easier. "My card's jammed in the machine. I need to remove my memory card and put the original back in." She hoped Sanders would believe what she was saying and put on an amiable expression.

Sanders examined the device. "This machine's a little temperamental. It happens every once in a while, but I know how to unjam it." He stuck a pen in a corner of the card slot and at the same time, hit the eject button. The memory card popped out of the DVR. "Voila," he said.

"Thank you," Robbie said, more grateful than he'd ever know.

"Give me the soft count card, and I'll put it back in the machine."

Robbie handed him memory card 333. He inserted it into the DVR and pressed the record button. "There you go," he said. "Yamamoto's DVRs over there."

She smiled with true appreciation. "Thanks, Andy."

"Anytime." Sanders limped to his workstation.

Robbie pushed the stop button on the soft count DVR and tapped play. The prerecorded video of the unoccupied room filled the monitor. She returned to her workstation and switched off the cameras in the two hallways, then exhaled a relieved puff of air. She'd done it. Hatrix was now free to pillage the soft count room in secrecy.

THE RECORDING EQUIPMENT was stacked on a table in the hotel

room, and Brian, Cory, and Teri sat there staring at it, mesmerized by the conversations in the surveillance room.

"It's working like we hoped," Cory said. "If all goes well, this will be our last night here."

Brian's face was rigid. "There's a lot that still needs to happen right. You have to admit that Robbie's had some problems."

"Yes, but she has the prerecorded videos in place, and Hatrix is on his way to the soft count room. All he has to do now is take some of the marked bills."

Teri said, "Our agents wagered almost thirty-thousand dollars in marked currency."

Cory snickered. "The tax payers' dollars at work."

"Chairman Cavanaugh ordered our agents to play more than we'd planned in the beginning because we didn't have the opportunity to gamble on the grave or day shifts. The extra money should ensure Hatrix steals some of the marked bills."

Brian whistled. "Thirty-thousand dollars."

Cory said, "You don't understand how bad Cavanaugh wants to nail Montgomery. He went straight to the governor for approval."

"All we can do now is wait," Teri said. "Hatrix will call her when he's out of the soft count room."

Brian yawned in agreement.

"Why don't you take a quick nap?" Cory said, gazing at him. "It's going to be quiet for a while. Get in a few Z's."

Brian rubbed his eyes with the heels of his hands. "I'm okay," he said.

"At least lie on the bed and relax," Teri said. "I promise if something significant happens, we'll let you know."

Brian was beyond tired and decided maybe they were right. "I could use some rest." He hurled himself down on the bed. He soon realized that, despite his exhaustion, he was too uptight to doze. That, and he knew if he did sleep, all his dreams would be about Robbie, Montgomery, Skip, and April. The last thing he wanted was a continuation of his real-life nightmare.

HATRIX DARTED INTO the soft count room, placed the leather bag on the table, and approached the drop box cabinet. He unlocked the metal mesh door on the one marked *Graveyard,* pulled the first box off the shelf, and laid it on the table. Fumbling with the key for the box, he inserted it into the lock and opened the door. The box was packed with currency. He ran his fingers through the uncounted money with a gleam in his eye.

As he'd done many times before, Hatrix snatched hundred-dollar bills from the metal boxes. He knew Montgomery insisted, going forward, that they be more conservative, with less taken, but he didn't care. The theft operation had been on hold for over a week—ever since Vanessa was murdered. No one would notice if he was a little greedy tonight.

Hatrix placed the hundreds in the thin bag. One by one, he extracted the drop boxes from the shelves and removed three or four hundred-dollar bills from each. The graveyard boxes were teeming with cash. Given the extra money, he was grabbing a lot.

Finished with the graveyard drop boxes, Hatrix glanced at his watch. It was four in the morning. He was running late. He edged over to the cabinet containing the day shift boxes. As he had with the graveyard, he lugged them from the shelves and, in an almost mechanical way, harvested the lucrative contents. After stealing from the last one, he paused and took a look at his haul. His efforts had been productive. Obviously, business at the Charleston must've been good, as the drop was significant.

Hatrix noted the time again—it was now four twenty-five. He was running way behind. The count team supervisor would be arriving in thirty-five minutes, and he hadn't even opened the swing shift cabinet door.

Hatrix stared at his watch a final time and decided it wasn't worth the risk. He'd skip the swing shift boxes. He had enough money to pay off Louie, place a bet on the Bengals-Ravens game, and split the balance with Robbie. Of course, he wouldn't tell her he took much more than his fair share.

THE PHONE AT Robbie's work station rang and she reached for the handset. "Hello?"

"It's me," Hatrix said. "Send the elevator."

Robbie asked in a whisper, "You're finished?"

"Yeah, I didn't get to the swing shift drop boxes, but I have enough money to satisfy both our needs."

Robbie could feel the panic again rising up in her body. The marked currency played by the gaming agents was in the swing shift boxes. A guilty verdict could never be achieved if the marked bills weren't found by law enforcement in the possession of Hatrix and Montgomery. She had to persuade him to take money from those boxes as well. "Enough for whom?" she asked.

"What are you talking about?" Hatrix asked. His tone made it clear he was rattled by her query.

"Did you get the twenty grand you need to pay off the loan shark?"

"Ah, yes, I had to."

Robbie whispered as low as she could be and still be heard. "Let's see then—if my calculations are correct, you must've stolen about eighty-thousand dollars. Forty thousand for Mr. Montgomery and twenty thousand for each of us."

Hatrix kept quiet.

She turned her head away from her co-workers. "As I recall, Montgomery wanted you to limit the amount of cash you reaped each night. Eighty-thousand dollars is a lot. What would he say?"

Again, Hatrix remained mute.

"You're not telling me the truth. I bet you have enough to pay your loan and not much more. What'll Mr. Montgomery's response be when I tell him that?"

More awkward silence. He'd been caught and wasn't smart enough to formulate a plausible explanation.

Robbie cupped a hand around the receiver. "Marcus, I'll keep your secret, but I deserve some extra money."

"How much?" It came out as a murmur.

"Oh, I'd say ten-thousand dollars would satisfy me."

He raised his voice to a yell. "Ten thousand? I don't have it. Not after I deduct my loan money."

With quiet vigor, she said, "You haven't taken any money from the swing shift drop boxes."

"No, I didn't, but I'm running out of time. The count team supervisor arrives here in less than thirty minutes."

"Then I suggest you get busy. The swing shift drop's always the largest. If you hurry, you can collect the ten thousand with ease."

"But—"

"Stop squawking and go to work. If you start now, you'll be out of there with time to spare. I'll leave the elevator doors open, so you can make a hasty exit."

"Okay, okay, I'll call you when I'm done." Hatrix clicked off.

Robbie put down the receiver and massaged her temples. The pressure was getting to her.

TERI LOOKED AT Brian and Cory as they listened to Robbie. "She sure knows how to manipulate Hatrix," she said.

"It's a good thing," Cory said.

"Hatrix doesn't have much time," Brian said with another yawn.

"We just need to catch them with one of the marked bills,

and the charges will stick. For Hatrix to not steal at least one of the thirty-thousand dollars our agents wagered, our luck would have to be horrible."

Brian blew out a frustrated sigh. "My luck hasn't been the best of late. What's your plan after the money's out of the Charleston?"

"There's a team of agents surrounding Montgomery's home. When Robbie takes the cash to his estate, we'll make the arrests."

Teri said, "And then it's over, and you can resume your life."

Brian closed his eyes. *What kind of life would that be,* he wondered.

ROBBIE SCANNED THE wall of video screens and held the phone receiver close to her mouth. "I saw you enter the casino," she said.

"I got out of there just in time," Hatrix said. "The count team supervisor was waiting to enter the elevator as I was leaving. Another five minutes, and I'd have been busted."

"Do you have my ten thousand?"

"Yes. I put the money bag in your purse locker. Get the prerecorded videos out of the DVRs and back to the library before anyone notices something's wrong."

"I will. What about Montgomery? What do we tell him?"

"I was thinking about that—let's keep our activities tonight a little secret. Why rile him up? It'll be our bonus for taking the risk."

Montgomery wouldn't end up behind bars that way. "No, Marcus, I don't want to do that. We're partners, and even though you went into the count room without his permission, I'm not cheating him out of everything. Don't even try to argue. I won't debate this." She held her breath, frantic he'd refuse this feeble demand.

"Oh, jeez, if you insist. I'm meeting Montgomery at his mansion after I get off work at seven. He expects me to give him an update on your progress. If I can muster the courage, I'll tell him I was in the count room and took some money. I might as well get the screaming over with. After that, I'll come back to the Charleston and pick you up at valet parking when you get off-shift. We can go to his place together."

"Okay, I'll see you at eight." Robbie hung up, and her eyes moved to the video monitors. She leaned over and switched on the hallway and alcove cameras.

"That's odd," Wanda said. "I didn't see the count team supervisor go down the elevator. She called and asked me to send it, but I didn't see her."

"Maybe she isn't in the elevator yet," Sanders said.

Wanda pointed to a monitor. "No, she's in the hallway leading to the soft count room."

"I saw her in the elevator," Robbie said, hoping to stop the conversation before anyone suggested checking the recordings. She had to remove the prerecorded videos from the DVRs immediately before they noticed any other discrepancies.

Wanda turned to her. "You did?"

Robbie motioned to the video screens. "Yeah, I saw a middle-aged woman in a white jump suit. You must've missed it."

Wanda pursed her lips. "I can't believe I didn't see her."

"No harm, Wanda," Sanders said. "We've had a busy night. It's easy to miss a few things."

Wanda started to protest but stopped, knowing there was no point in arguing. She resumed observing the monitors.

The count team supervisor was now in the count room, but the screen showed that the area was deserted. So far, no one had noticed. "Andy," Robbie said, "I need to finish up my special projects video. Do you mind if I take another break?"

Indignant, Wanda waved a crooked finger at her. "Oh, no," she said. "I always take my lunch at this time. I'm diabetic and need my medicine."

"It'll just take me a minute."

"No," Sanders said firmly. "Wanda's right, she has to have her break. I don't want her sick. You can complete your special projects video when she's back."

Wanda smiled at Robbie with a self-righteous expression and paraded out the doorway. Robbie looked at the soft count room monitor and over to the DVRs. Her mind was racing when the ringing phone interrupted her thoughts. She picked up the handset. "Hello?"

A woman with a deep southern drawl said, "Hi, this is Cheryl from the count team. I need some more drop forms from the vault. Would you send the elevator?"

"Sure." Robbie's voice quivered. "It's on its way." Her heart fluttered. She was going to be caught if the prerecorded videos weren't removed soon. Robbie pressed the elevator button and glanced at the monitor. Of course it showed an empty car. Moments later, the count team supervisor could be seen marching down the hallway toward the vault.

Sanders asked, "Robbie, did you send the elevator for the count team supervisor?"

She eyed him with a worried look. "Is there a problem?"

Sanders rubbed his neck. "I must be as tired as Wanda. I didn't see her in the elevator."

Robbie said, as casually as possible, "She entered it seconds after she called."

Sanders was somewhat befuddled but shrugged and studied the video screens in front of him.

For the next forty-five minutes, Robbie stared with great trepidation at the monitor showing the vacant soft count room. The strong pit action was keeping the others focused on the new high rollers, and they hadn't noticed. Yet. Robbie checked the video screen above her and saw that Gerald Yamamoto wasn't at his blackjack table. She panned the camera around but couldn't locate him anywhere. She reached for the phone and dialed the pit. "Where's Yamamoto?" she asked the supervisor.

"On the way to his suite," the man said. "He was bushed and wanted some sleep. He's wiped out for this trip."

"You beat him pretty good."

"Thank god. We can use the revenue. This'll keep Keith Wallace off my ass. Thanks for your help tonight."

"All I did was observe."

"No, you brought us luck. The minute you came on shift, Yamamoto started to lose."

"You're much too superstitious to work in a casino."

The supervisor laughed, and they both hung up. Yamamoto was gone, and this might be the opportunity she needed. "Andy?"

"Yes, Robbie?" Sanders said, peering at her over the top of his reading glasses.

"Yamamoto's turned in for the night, and business in the casino's slowed quite a bit. Is it okay if I work on my special projects video? It'll just take me a few minutes. I can complete it before Wanda returns from her break."

Sanders thought for an instant and nodded. "Go ahead. It might be best if you finish before she gets back. Wanda has an irrational attitude about special projects. Don't take it to heart, though—it's not you."

Robbie smiled. "I won't. I'll hurry." She scooted to the DVRs, stopped both the drives, ejected the prerecorded memory cards, and replaced them with the ones she'd taken out earlier. Then she reviewed the monitors to make sure everything was as it should be. She put cards 333 and 334 into the video library and dashed back to her workstation as Wanda crossed the room, gave her another malicious sneer, and sat down. Robbie said a silent prayer. She'd done it, and a surge of relief came over her. "You can all relax," she said in a whisper to the hidden microphone. "Mission accomplished."

Wanda gawked at her, curious.

Robbie grinned wider than she ever had in her life.

THIRTY-THREE

CORY SMILED AND slapped his hands together. "I wish we had some champagne."

"Don't you think your celebration's premature?" Brian asked. He had to agree, though—despite all the problems, Robbie had done the job.

"It's all downhill from here. When Robbie and Hatrix give the money to Montgomery, we'll be on them like a suntan."

"How are you ensuring her safety?"

"The FBI's been notified," Teri said. "Cavanaugh phoned the Feds last night. They know how to handle these situations. Robbie's wellbeing is their number one priority."

"Relax, Brian," Cory said. "She persevered through this without being detected. The difficult part's over."

The musical ringtone of Brian's smartphone blared. He pulled it from his jacket saying, "Who would be calling me at this hour of the morning?" He looked at the device but didn't recognize the number. He slid a finger across the screen to answer. "Hello?" he said, tentative.

The deep voice of a man boomed, "Mr. Shepard, it's Deputy Fletcher with the Douglas County Sheriff's Department. I'm sorry to bother you so early. The hotel operator at the Charleston gave me your number."

"What can I do for you?" Bewildered, Brian held his breath, waiting for the deputy to continue.

"I'm afraid I have some bad news. The body of comedian Skip Sullivan was found about an hour ago at Nevada Beach. It appears he died of an accidental drug overdose. At least, we believe it was an accident."

Brian closed his eyes. "Are you sure it's Sullivan?"

"Positive. I'd say he's one of the most famous faces in the country. Pity. My wife and I have never missed his show. It's one of the funniest programs on television. Just in case, though, his girlfriend, April Vaurnet, is on her way to the morgue to identify the body."

Hearing April's name, Brian felt a rush of guilt envelop him. Was he in any way responsible for Sullivan's overdose?

Fletcher said, "The reason I'm calling is I have to complete my paperwork, and I was wondering if you'd come by the station and make a statement. I intend to get this over with before the media finds out what's happened. As soon as they do, it'll be a circus down here. I plan to accomplish what I can before they begin to interfere."

"Why do you want my statement?" Brian asked.

"Sullivan was the headliner in the Charleston's main showroom, and you canceled last night's performances. I need to compile as much information as possible about his activities prior to his death. He was a major entertainment figure, and I want to make certain I cover all the bases."

Thinking of Robbie, Brian said, "Could this wait?"

"Please, it won't take more than a couple minutes. I'd appreciate your cooperation."

"Oh, okay." Brian looked at his watch. It was almost seven, and it'd be more than an hour before Robbie finished her shift in the surveillance room. If he hurried, he could give his statement to the sheriff and make it back to the

Charleston before she was off work. "I'll be there in ten minutes."

BRIAN SAT IN an uncomfortable metal chair in the cluttered sheriff's office. Telephones were ringing and officers scurrying around the room. "Would you like a cup of coffee?" Deputy Fletcher asked. In his sixties with a bald head, he stepped over to the coffee maker on the counter next to his desk.

"Please," Brian said.

"Cream or sugar?"

"No, black's fine."

Fletcher poured two cups of coffee and handed one to Brian. "It's a terrible tragedy," he said. "I understand it happens a lot to celebrities, though. I suppose they can't cope with the pressures of fame." He sat in the chair behind his desk.

Brian sipped the coffee. "Did April Vaurnet identify the body?"

"Yes, no question it's Sullivan. The poor girl's broken up. Such a sweet woman—I feel bad for her."

"Where's she now?"

Fletcher pointed over his shoulder. "In one of the back rooms. She's devastated, but one of our female deputies is trying to interrogate her."

Brian's eyebrows floated up. "Interrogate?"

"Oh, I guess that's the wrong word. We just want to get her account of Sullivan's actions prior to his death."

Brian wondered if he'd come up in the conversation. He knew that even if April didn't mention his name, Skip's agent would. "I see."

"Tell me, Mr. Shepard, what do you know about Mr. Sullivan's final hours?"

Brian took another drink of coffee. "Not much. I received a call yesterday morning from his agent."

The deputy perused his notes. "That would be Theodore Goldstein?"

"Correct. Goldstein was upset. It seems Sullivan and April—Miss Vaurnet—had an argument, and he took off. That's why Goldstein called me from Los Angles. He wanted me to find him."

Fletcher's eyes narrowed. "Isn't that unusual? You're not a detective."

"I hired Sullivan, so Goldstein asked for my assistance."

"Why didn't you inform the sheriff's department?"

"Goldstein insisted I not do that. He was afraid the media would get wind of the story. You know how the tabloids would react."

"So you searched for Sullivan?" The deputy was writing something in a notebook.

"Yes, April and I—well, my whole staff and I, plus April—looked for him. We visited almost every cocktail lounge at the lake."

"Sullivan was partial to the bars?"

Brian sipped the coffee and placed the cup on the corner of Fletcher's desk. "Sullivan had a substance abuse problem, and we thought a bar would be the most logical place to find him."

"How well do you know Miss Vaurnet?"

Brian squirmed in the chair. "I met her last Saturday. I had a few drinks with her and Sullivan. We went out after his show at the Charleston. She's a nice woman."

"Did she tell you about her quarrel with Sullivan?"

Brian knew he was going to color the truth. He wet his lips. "No, not all of it. She said he'd disappeared before and not to worry."

"And did you believe her?"

"Yes and no. His erratic behavior didn't surprise me at all. Sullivan canceled a show last week because he was too intoxicated to perform. It was Theodore Goldstein who was most concerned and made me consider perhaps there was a real problem."

"So you and Miss Vaurnet started hunting for Sullivan?"

"My entire staff did."

"I guess you had no luck."

"We wouldn't be here if we had."

The deputy was jotting down additional notes. "Then what did you do?"

Brian shrugged. "Well, there was nothing more I could do. When we didn't find him, I went to the theater and canceled his shows for the evening."

The deputy continued writing. "That I know."

Brian was puzzled by Fletcher's words and gave the man a funny look.

"My wife, Stella, and I had tickets for last night's dinner performance. We were disappointed when the show was canceled. Stella will be even more upset when she hears Sullivan's dead. She thought he was a talented man."

"He was. Do you have any further questions, Deputy?"

Fletcher examined his papers. "You never heard from Sullivan after his agent called you, concerned?"

"No, neither did April, as far as I know."

"Okay, I guess that's all for now. I'd be grateful if you'd contact us if you think of anything else that may be helpful."

"Of course."

"Thank you for coming in. I know it's early, and I appreciate your cooperation." The deputy's smile was uneven.

"I wish we'd met under better circumstances. Again, call if you need something."

"I will, I can assure you."

Brian gazed at Deputy Fletcher with an uneasy feeling. The man was staring back at him with piercing eyes. "I better get moving," Brian said. "With Sullivan's death, I have a lot of work to do back at the Charleston."

"Yes, I'm sure you do," Fletcher said. "Thank you again."

Brian stood up from the chair and walked down the hallway toward the parking lot, stopping at a vending machine and purchasing a cup of coffee. He needed all the caffeine he could consume. With the coffee in hand, he reached the exit, pushed open the heavy metal door, and was blinded by the camera lights of the news media.

"That's the marketing guy from the Charleston Resort," a man said.

More reporters shouted. "Shepard." "Brian." "Mr. Shepard." He raised a hand, trying to block the lights of the photographers.

"What can you tell us about Skip Sullivan?" Tom Galloway, the entertainment reporter at KTVN asked, a cameraman at his shoulder. He pushed a microphone in Brian's face.

"Is Sullivan dead?" a woman from the *Tahoe Daily Tribune* asked.

Brian was caught off guard by their questions but knew he had to say something. He tried to put some words together in his head. "If you'll all calm down," he said. "I'll make a short statement."

The reporters quieted, but the intensity of the television lights and the click of cameras continued to barrage him.

Brian cleared his throat and said, "The sheriff's department's informed me that television personality Skip Sullivan has died. The owners and management of the Charleston Casino Resort would like to extend our sympathies to the family and friends of Mr. Sullivan and express our sorrow at his passing. The world's lost a gifted and talented man, and he will be missed by all."

There was a pause after Brian finished speaking, then the reporters lobbed torrents of questions. "Mr. Shepard, what was the cause of death?" almost every reporter asked at once.

Brian jabbed a thumb toward the doors behind him. "I'd prefer those inquiries be answered by the sheriff's department."

"Was it a suicide?"

"Are drugs involved?"

"Was he murdered?"

"Please," Brian said with a pleading voice. "Again, those questions should be asked of the sheriff."

An attractive woman reporter, one Brian had once dated, asked, "How's April Vaurnet?"

"I haven't talked with Miss Vaurnet, but I've been told she's distraught."

"Was she involved?"

"No. I'm sorry, but I have nothing more to say at this time."

The questions kept coming, but Brian waved a hand, indicating he was finished speaking. He jogged to his truck, followed by the reporters, and refused to make any additional comments. He dove into his vehicle, started the ignition, and drove away, almost running over a cameraman in the process.

BRIAN RETURNED TO the Charleston Resort, the reporters still on his mind. His goal of keeping a low profile had been shattered. He wondered how long it'd be before Hatrix saw him on television. He was certain his interview would be on CNN within the hour. He hoped Hatrix didn't see the news until after the arrests were made, or if he did, that he was too stupid to make any connections. He cursed Skip Sullivan for dying and blamed himself for being a catalyst.

Brian knocked on the hotel room door, and Teri opened it. He was quick to slip into the room. "How's Robbie doing?" he asked.

"She gets off work in fifteen minutes," Teri said. "It's been uneventful."

"We may have a problem." The dark circles under his eyes were deeper than ever.

"What's wrong?" Cory asked, hearing the strain in Brian's voice.

"Like I told you earlier, Skip Sullivan's dead. Overdose. I drove over to speak with Deputy Fletcher and told him what I knew about his last hours. As I was leaving the sheriff's office, I was confronted by reporters from KTVN, KCRA, several radio stations, and the local papers. I made a statement. I couldn't help it—they caught me by surprise. I had to say something."

"Oh, no," Teri said.

"That's for sure. If Hatrix sees me on TV, Robbie's cover will be blown."

Cory said, "With luck, he won't have a chance to watch television. There's no choice but to proceed anyway. Robbie goes to Montgomery's house right after work. The minute she meets with him, the FBI will burst in and make the arrests."

Teri said, "I'm confident this will be over in a couple of hours."

Cory picked up his keys from a table. "I'm going to the parking lot to get the van ready. Join me as soon as Robbie's out of the surveillance room, and we'll follow her and Hatrix to Montgomery's mansion."

Teri motioned to the telephone. "I'll call Cavanaugh and tell him we'll be on our way soon."

Cory exited the hotel room, leaving Brian and Teri alone.

"Are we making it through this?" he asked the agent. The stress was becoming too much for him, and he wiped his temples with his shirtsleeve.

"I think so, Brian," Teri said. "Even with the problems we've had, we're moving in a positive direction. Once Robbie meets with Montgomery, it's over. You, Robbie, and Jack can return to your normal lives."

"I wonder if that's possible." He breathed out a heavy sigh.

"Have faith. Nothing's better than a happy ending."

"Right now, I can't even imagine what that is."

HATRIX SAT IN the parlor of Tom Montgomery's immense home. Montgomery was wearing a dark-purple robe and had been reading the morning paper when Hatrix arrived. The local news was on the television, but the sound was off.

"Please, boss, I know you're mad at me," Hatrix said, "but it was flawless. I ducked in and out of the soft count room with no concerns at all. Robbie did a great job."

Montgomery loomed over him, shaking his fist. "I can't believe you risked our operation. Greed's interfering with your judgment."

"My judgment's fine. I knew after Robbie's first night of work that she was ready. She's a smart woman."

Montgomery bent over in Hatrix's face, their noses just inches apart. "It wasn't your call. I make all the decisions around here, and you know it. This is my set up. Without me, you'd be a common street thug trying to hustle your next meal."

The whites of Hatrix's eyes were prominent. He knew this was a serious matter, and it was risky to ever cross Tom Montgomery. "I'm sorry, boss—I needed the money."

"Your gambling's becoming a threat to me. You have an addiction, and it's turning into my issue."

Hatrix stooped his head and shoulders forward. "No, sir, it's not a gambling problem. It's a hobby. A diversion. That's all."

Montgomery's features were an angry red. "You risked everything to cover your betting debts."

"But, boss—"

"Shut up. Wait until I get my hands on Robbie Taylor."

"I talked her into it, Mr. Montgomery. It wasn't her fault. I forced her."

Montgomery stabbed a finger at him. "I don't care—I'm scaring the hell out of her. I want her to know who's in charge."

"I gave her no choice. I told her I was going into the soft count room, and if she didn't cover me, we'd all be in trouble."

Montgomery stared at Hatrix with incensed eyes. "Don't you dare do something like this again."

"I won't—believe me. I'm sorry it happened." Hatrix's expression was doleful.

Montgomery clenched his jaw a few times. "I guess I should ask what the take was."

Hatrix was relieved Montgomery had stopped shouting and seemed to be moving on. He nodded. "I did as you requested. I limited the number of hundred-dollar bills I took from each drop box. I snagged about nine grand."

"I'm furious about this, but I'll be glad to have cash coming in again. The electrical system on the *Sierra Queen's* starting to fail. The wires in the galley are all corroded, and we won't be able to take on passengers for about a week. And that's if I can find a new captain. The one I had quit—said the ship was too run-down."

Hatrix grinned. "See. Even though you're mad at me, you need the cash too. I know I was wrong, but the money pipeline's flowing once more."

Montgomery bounced a forefinger over his chin. "Robbie's good?"

"Oh, yeah. She's super intelligent and a fast learner. Tough too."

"Yeah, that's been my impression of her as well."

"Hey, there's her boyfriend." Hatrix pointed at the television. "I wonder what's going on."

Montgomery turned to the large flat-screen and frowned. "What are you talking about?"

"That's Robbie's boyfriend. I met him a couple times at her house."

Montgomery grabbed the remote control from the coffee table and ratcheted up the volume.

The television blared, "The owners and management of the Charleston Casino Resort would like to extend our sympathies to the family and friends of Mr. Sullivan and express our sorrow at his passing. The world's lost a gifted and talented man, and he will be missed by all."

"What's he doing on television?" Hatrix asked.

Montgomery snapped his fingers at him. "Quiet."

They watched the rest of Brian's interview in silence. When it ended, Montgomery said, "She said her boyfriend was a construction worker."

"It's what she told me," Hatrix said. "Why's he on TV?"

"That man is Brian Shepard."

"Yeah, so?"

"Shepard's the Marketing Director at the Charleston."

Hatrix's dark eyes flared. "He's not a carpenter?"

"Damn, she lied to us." Montgomery threw the television remote at the floor, where it broke into pieces. "Damn it."

Hatrix's held up both hands. "It's no big deal. So she didn't want us to know about her boyfriend."

"You don't get it—that's Brian Shepard."

"So?"

"You idiot. Shepard's been asking a lot of questions at the casino. He spent time in the surveillance room. He and his friend, Jack Mancini, have been making inquiries about the low hold percentage problem at the Charleston. This is bad, very bad."

"I'm sorry, boss. I don't understand."

"Shepard and Taylor. This can't be a coincidence." Montgomery thought for a minute, his finger on his lips. "When you pick up Robbie at the Charleston, don't bring her here."

"Okay, where do you want us to go?"

"The *Sierra Queen*."

Hatrix's tipped his head to the side. "Why the boat?"

Montgomery gave Hatrix a harsh glare. "I'm going to take care of two problems at once."

THIRTY-FOUR

ROBBIE GLANCED AT the surveillance camera as the elevator descended and thought about her actions the previous night. She wondered if *she* was now being watched. When the doors parted, she walked down the hallway toward the purse lockers. Arriving at the cabinet, she unlocked the small door of compartment seven. Inside, just like Hatrix had promised, was a thin leather bag. Curious, she nudged the zipper open and saw the bag was stuffed full of money. She zipped it back up tight, stuffed it in her oversized purse, and draped the strap over a shoulder.

After turning in the locker key, Robbie stopped at the security booth, signed out, and set out through the lavish resort. Opening the door at the side of the casino, she could feel the cool air on her face. She gazed at the mountains and saw that another storm was brewing west of Lake Tahoe, dark clouds amassing on the horizon.

Robbie only had to wait a few minutes before Hatrix drove up in his sports car. She opened the passenger door, lowered herself into the vehicle, and smiled at him. "We did it," she said. There was a thrill in her voice. "Marcus, we did it."

Hatrix stared at her but didn't utter a word. He hit the accelerator and sped through the parking lot.

THE GAMING AGENTS and Brian were in the same black Ford van they'd used days earlier. Cory was driving it a few hundred feet behind Hatrix's car. "Here we go," he said. They trailed Hatrix's sports car through the Charleston Resort's parking lot. "She's coming in clear."

Hatrix's vehicle pulled into the intersection. "He's turning left," Brian said.

Cory's forehead creased with sudden alarm. "This isn't good."

"Where's Hatrix taking her?" Teri asked, as if expecting one of them to know the answer.

They followed Hatrix's car over the state line into California and away from the casino district. Hatrix drove about half a mile down the highway, into a supermarket parking lot, and idled in a remote section.

Cory steered the van over to the side of the road. They listened.

"I want my money," Hatrix said.

"Sure, Marcus," Robbie said. "I guess we do need to divvy up the cash before we go to Mr. Montgomery's estate. Twenty-thousand dollars for you and ten for me, right?"

Brian and the gaming agents couldn't understand Hatrix's garbled reply over the radio transmitter.

It took Robbie and Hatrix twenty minutes to total up the money and divide their shares. "You're quiet," Robbie said after they finished counting.

Hatrix's voice was flat when he said, "Not much to say."

"Why not? You're twenty thousand richer."

"Remember my loan? I don't get to keep it."

"Oh, yeah. Well, there's always tomorrow."

Hatrix's non-response was worrisome, and Brian looked over at Teri with troubled eyes.

Hatrix's car zoomed away again, and Cory started to turn the van around and drive toward Montgomery's home.

"Hold on, Cory," Brian said. "They still aren't traveling north."

Cory slowed the van to a halt and waited. Hatrix's sports car cruised out of the parking lot and down the highway...to the southwest. They quieted to listen for Robbie and Hatrix over the radio.

"Where are we going?" Robbie asked. "Mr. Montgomery lives in Glenbrook."

"We're not going there," Hatrix said.

"Why not?"

Hatrix didn't answer.

"Marcus, what's the story? I thought we were supposed to meet Mr. Montgomery at his mansion."

Teri said, "You don't suppose Hatrix is double-crossing Montgomery and taking off?"

"Why?" Cory asked.

"They have thirty-nine thousand dollars."

"That doesn't make sense," Brian said. "He thinks he has a money factory at the Charleston."

They stopped speaking when they heard Hatrix's voice on the transmitter. "Mr. Montgomery will be meeting us at the *Sierra Queen*."

"His boat," Robbie said. "Why there?"

"He didn't say."

"You're scaring me. Is everything all right?"

"All I know is Montgomery wants to see us at his paddleboat."

"What are we going to do?" Brian asked. "The FBI agents are at Montgomery's house."

Teri picked up her smartphone and dialed. "I'll get them to the marina," she said.

"What's Montgomery up to? Hatrix sounds strange."

"I know," Cory said. "He isn't his usual glib self."

"Oh, god." Brian put his hands over his face. "I can't believe this is happening. We're so close."

"Relax, Brian. This'll work out."

"You've been telling me that for days now. I'm damn tired of it."

"The FBI's on the way," Teri said. She folded her phone shut with a snap.

"Do they have a boat? If not, I hope they can walk on water."

HATRIX DROVE HIS car to the dock, where Robbie saw Tom Montgomery standing on the deck of the *Sierra Queen*. The sight of him gave her goosebumps. She climbed out of the vehicle, hoisted the strap of her purse over a shoulder, and ambled toward the boat. Trudging up the gangplank, she had the urge to turn and run but talked herself into continuing. She could never avenge Vanessa's death if she quit now. When she reached Montgomery, she asked, "Why are we meeting here?"

He studied her features, then gestured to the entrance of the ship. "It's cold out here. Let's go inside."

Robbie turned to the door, heaved it open, and entered the vessel. Montgomery stayed outside and had a short discussion with Hatrix. Then they both came into the lounge, and Hatrix headed for the wheel room to pilot the paddleboat out of the marina. The inside temperature was comfortable, as the engine was running. Robbie rubbed her arms, trying to warm up. She surveyed the area and remembered how rundown the boat was on her cruise with Brian. "You should paint this thing," she said. "No wonder your business is lousy."

Again, Montgomery didn't reply to her comment and instead strolled over to the bar and poured himself a glass of scotch. "Tell me about Robbie Taylor," he said.

She let out a nervous laugh. "I thought we had this conversation last weekend."

His face was dark, his lips thin. "Indulge me."

"Okay, Mr. Montgomery, I'll play your game. Robbie Taylor

was an unemployed woman who didn't have a dime to her name. Now, thanks to her new partners, she's on her way to a life of wealth and luxury." She pulled the money bag from her purse, walked over, and handed it to him.

"Enlighten me about your boyfriend."

Robbie asked, surprise in her voice, "Why on earth would you want to know about him?"

Montgomery glared at her. "I just do."

She stared at him, feeling a shortness of breath. "What's going on?"

"I'd like to know about your boyfriend. What's his name?"

Robbie knew something was very wrong. She felt cold again despite the heaters. "Uh, Brian."

"He's a construction worker?"

She glanced down. "A carpenter."

"Where's he working?"

Robbie looked up. "Why do you care? What does he have to do with anything?"

Montgomery took a slow saunter to a window and gazed out over the lake. He waited a moment, then said with a sickening smile, "I was wondering why your boyfriend, the carpenter, moonlights at the Charleston Casino Resort as my Director of Marketing."

"OH, SWEET JESUS," Brian said, horrified.

Cory flung his head back. "Oh, god."

Teri reached for her mobile phone and dialed. She spoke with the FBI, who assured her they were on their way and would be at the marina within minutes.

Cory pointed to the *Sierra Queen*. "The ship's leaving the dock," he said.

Brian slid open the door and leapt out of the van.

"Where are you going?" Teri asked.

"I'm not waiting around here for the authorities," he said. "Robbie's in real danger now. I'm getting a boat."

"Brian, what good will that do?" Cory asked.

"I can rescue Robbie."

"How?" Teri asked, but it was too late. Brian was running toward the boat shop.

"I'll go after him," Cory said. "Stay here and keep tabs on Robbie. The FBI will be here soon. Call the Coast Guard."

Teri agreed with a bob of her head, and Cory took off after his frantic friend.

A CHILL RAN up Robbie's spine. "Mr. Montgomery," she said, "you're mistaken."

"I'm afraid not, Miss Taylor," he said. "We saw Brian Shepard on television this morning. Marcus is certain Shepard, the Marketing Director at the Charleston, is your lover. How do you explain that?"

Robbie hesitated, trying to compose her thoughts. She could feel the *Sierra Queen* begin to move. "Marcus is incorrect. This guy must just look like my boyfriend. My Brian's a construction worker. A carpenter."

His green eyes bored into hers. "What's his last name?"

"C-C-Cooper. B-Brian Cooper."

"Well then, it shouldn't be difficult to find your Mr. Cooper."

Robbie shuddered when Montgomery drew a smartphone from his jacket.

"Where does he live?" he asked.

"South Lake Tahoe," she said in a mumble.

Montgomery dialed Information. "Yes, Operator, I'm interested in the number of a Brian Cooper in South Lake Tahoe."

Robbie watched him in disbelief, her eyes wide.

"Thank you, Operator." He tapped on the phone and ended the call. "No listing, Miss Taylor."

She said in a soft voice, "His number's unlisted."

"Well, of course it is. Why am I not surprised? What's the number?"

Robbie didn't know what to say. Anything she said would be revealed as a lie. "I don't remember."

Montgomery waved his mobile phone. "You don't remember? You don't recall your boyfriend's telephone number?"

"He always calls me."

"Oh, come now." His teeth pulled back in a snarl. "It doesn't matter anyway. I did some checking on Brian Shepard. All I had to do to find out about his personal life was ask his secretary. She had a book's worth of information. Do you know what she told me?"

Robbie's tongue was paralyzed.

"Shepard's an attractive man, popular with the secretarial pool. His personal life's often the subject of discussion among the secretaries. Want to guess what his secretary, Beatrice, told me about him?"

Still silent, Robbie was more terrified than ever.

"He's been dating someone named Robbie. An unusual name for a woman and quite a coincidence, don't you think?"

Robbie knew there was nothing she could say to dispute his accusation. "What are you going to do?" she asked.

BRIAN RAN TO the boat shop and flew to the front counter. A long-haired kid in his late teens sat behind it reading a comic book.

"I need a boat," Brian said.

The kid had a vapid appearance. "Sorry, dude. No rentals today."

Brian looked indignantly at him. "Why not?"

"There's a small craft warning on the lake. A storm's gusting in, and the Coast Guard says no boat rentals. Come back when the weather's better."

"Listen, dude," Brian said, emphasizing the word dude. "I don't give a damn about any small craft warning. I demand a boat, and I want it now. It's an emergency."

"No can do, dude. I'd lose my job if I rented you one."

Brian's anger was growing, his cheeks turning red. "I don't care about your stupid little job. Get me a goddamn boat."

The kid shrugged. "Sorry, dude."

Brian came around the counter and grabbed the stunned young man by the shirt collar, pushing him against the wall. "Give me a key to one of the boats."

"Okay." The kid's eyes were as big as saucers. "They're on the board." He pointed to a row of keys hanging on hooks.

Cory entered the shop as Brian was releasing the young man. "Brian," Cory said, "what the hell are you doing?"

"This dude accosted me," the kid said.

"Come on," Brian said, barreling past Cory. "We have to get to Robbie."

"You're crazy," Cory said.

"You're right about that," the young man said. "I'm calling the cops."

Brian thrust a finger toward him. "You do that," he said. "And tell them to hurry."

THE OLD PADDLEBOAT rattled as it chugged across Lake Tahoe. Montgomery looked at Robbie and asked, "Who else besides Shepard knows about us?"

"Just Brian," Robbie said, thinking frantically, trying to concoct a believable story. "We were going to split the money."

Montgomery finished off the whiskey and put the glass down. "I don't believe you. What about Mancini?"

"Jack? He doesn't know about any of this. None of it."

"Then explain why both Shepard and Mancini have been nosing around the Charleston."

Robbie bit her lower lip. "Jack was concerned about the table games hold in the casino and keeping his job. But not Brian. He knew what was happening. Remember, Vanessa explained it to me, and I told Brian."

Montgomery considered that for a second. He crossed his arms. "Why was Shepard in my office begging me to rehire Mancini?"

"They're old friends. Known each other since grade school."

Montgomery flipped a hand in the air. "Nice story, but I'm afraid your credibility is zero."

"You must believe me, it's true. Brian and I were planning to share the money. We know a good thing when we see it."

"Shepard doesn't strike me as the type of person who'd condone embezzlement, let alone participate."

She said, jeering at him, "Neither do you."

Montgomery stared hard at her, his eyes cold and dispassionate. "You're a pretty woman…and a pretty good liar too."

Robbie eyed him—trying to determine how bad the situation was. She wondered if she should let him know about the hidden microphone. *Not yet*, she thought. *Let's play this out a little longer.*

Hatrix thundered down the stairs and into the lounge. "I've got this baby on auto-pilot," he said. "We're headed for the center of the lake."

Montgomery turned to him and motioned to Robbie. "Restrain her and take her to the engine room. I'll join you in five minutes."

"Yes, boss," Hatrix said and walked up to Robbie. He shoved her against a wall and began tying her hands behind her back with a rope.

Montgomery gave her one last derisive glance and left the lounge.

"Marcus, don't do this," Robbie said. "How can you let this happen?" The tight rope was hurting her wrists.

"You didn't tell us the truth, Robbie," Hatrix said. "Who knows what else you've lied about. I'm sorry, but it has to be this way."

Robbie looked at him over her shoulder. "Was it necessary to kill Vanessa?"

"She threatened to expose us. Montgomery had no choice."

Strands of hair were in her face. "But I won't. I promise."

"Montgomery doesn't believe you." He paused, glaring at her with fury. "And I don't either." He yanked hard on the rope one last time before tying it.

"Ouch. That hurts."

"Like I care."

Hatrix jerked her away from the wall and pushed her toward the door to the engine room. The stairs were steep, the lighting dim, and the heat from the motor stifling. Hatrix guided her around the large diesel engine to the back of the room, sat her in a heavy metal chair, and tied her feet to its base.

Robbie trembled, not know what was going to happen. "What about Brian?" she asked. "He'll come for me. He knows I'm with you."

"Guaranteed, he'll never find you."

"He'll contact the sheriff."

"Not if we get to him first."

"Let me go. I promise I'll disappear and you won't hear from me again."

Hatrix chuckled maliciously. "You know, honey, that's the same thing Vanessa said before her death."

"What are you going to do with me?"

"Montgomery's solving two problems at once—you and this tub of a boat. I'd say in about twenty-five minutes, there'll be an explosion on Lake Tahoe rivaling any of its famous fireworks."

Robbie reeled in horror, her mouth hanging open. "Oh, god, please, Marcus, no."

"Shut up."

"The authorities know I'm on the *Sierra Queen*."

"Yeah, and I'm the next President of the United States."

"It's true." Tears streamed down her cheeks. "Pull up the back of my sweater. There's a hidden microphone and transmitter."

Hatrix yanked on her sweater. "That's not a transmitter. It's an iPod. How dumb do you think I am?"

Robbie couldn't believe he really was that stupid. "It's not an iPod. It's a recording device."

"Even if it were, and it's not, it would have no range out on the lake. Even less so down here. We're ten feet below the surface."

"Do you want to risk it?"

Hatrix stared into her frightened eyes and hesitated for an instant, giving her hope. Then…"It's over, Robbie," he said. "No use wasting your breath." Hatrix lumbered to the front of the engine room. Robbie sat there, bound and praying for her life.

THIRTY-FIVE

THE CLAMOR OF the diesel motor was loud, and Montgomery had to shout. "Are you sure it's enough dynamite?" he asked.

"It is," Hatrix said, strapping the explosives to the engine. "There's enough here to send this tin can to the bottom in less than five minutes."

"You're positive? It's imperative the *Sierra Queen* goes to the lake floor. Lake Tahoe's sixteen hundred feet deep out here, and if she's on the bottom, the insurance company will never be able to prove fraud."

"I almost have enough explosives to sink a ship twice this size."

"I guess you know what you're doing."

Hatrix was annoyed he had to defend his knowledge of bomb-making. "I worked with this kind of stuff when I was in the Navy. I may not know much about a lot of things, but this I do."

Montgomery nodded. "Okay. I believe you."

"What are you going to tell the insurance company? How will you explain the explosion?"

"I'll tell them we just repaired a gas leak in the fuel line. We were doing a service run when the explosion occurred. I'll say the repairs must've been defective."

"I'd buy it." Hatrix lifted a timer from his jacket pocket and fastened it to the engine.

"How much time do we have?"

"Twenty minutes." Hatrix set the timer on the bomb. The clock attached to the explosives began ticking off the seconds. "It should give us enough time to board the cabin cruiser tied alongside the *Sierra Queen* and motor far enough away to be clear of the blast."

"It should be fun to watch the explosion."

Hatrix's voice was hoarse. "It's too bad we have to leave Robbie on board," he said, looking toward the other end of the engine room. The laboring diesel was in the way and he couldn't see her.

The man smirked. "We have no choice."

"She showed me an iPod under her sweater and tried to convince me it was a wire and transmitter and that we were being recorded."

"She's a desperate woman. You're sure it was an iPod?"

"No question—she can't fool me."

"You better be right."

"I was hoping I could score with her."

Montgomery cast an eye at his wristwatch. "You'll have to settle for porn."

Hatrix frowned.

Montgomery aimed a finger at the stairs. "We have to get out of here."

ROBBIE TUGGED AT the ropes to no avail. They were knotted tight and cutting off her circulation. The heat from the engine was making it difficult for her to breathe. "Help me, Brian," she said, assuming the microphone was able to transmit over the waters even from down here. "They're blowing up the *Sierra Queen* and me with it. I don't have much time left."

The engine of the ship hummed, and she could hear the paddle's rhythmic slap against the water outside. She listened for Montgomery and Hatrix but could no longer detect any voices. All she heard was the diesel engine and the slap, slap, slap of the paddles rotating around and around. Robbie imagined the bomb on the other end of the room making a similar cadenced sound: tick, tick, tick.

Robbie no longer had feeling in her hands, and the numbness was creeping up both arms. "Oh, Brian, Teri, Cory, please save me." She knew it was futile, though. They couldn't help her now. The bomb would go off soon. She hoped she didn't feel any pain and prayed the blast would kill her instantly.

She thought about her widowed father and worried that he wouldn't have anyone to take care of him. Her mother flashed into her mind. "Help me, Mama."

Robbie remembered the dog she'd had as a child, her senior prom, and her graduation from college. She laughed morbidly. It was said that, prior to dying, your life passed before your eyes. She now knew that was true. Her mind was in overdrive, and everything and everyone she had ever loved was on it.

Robbie shifted her weight trying to get blood to her extremities. Her blouse was soaked with sweat. Tears ran down her cheeks. She still had so much in life she wanted to experience. Across the room, the clock on the bomb registered fifteen minutes. The sticks of dynamite wrapped with black wires waited for the timer to tick off the last few minutes.

BRIAN STRUGGLED TO keep the small boat from capsizing. The wind was howling, and the waves grew larger every minute. He could see the *Sierra Queen* in the distance and wrenched hard on the throttle, trying to milk more horsepower from the engine.

"The water's too rough," Cory said over the roar of the motor. "Go back. The Coast Guard will rescue Robbie."

Brian ignored him, concentrating on the paddleboat in front of them.

Cory said even louder, "It's not worth the risk."

Brian pulled harder on the throttle. "It is to me."

"What are we going to do when we reach the *Sierra Queen*? Montgomery isn't going to invite us on board for coffee."

"I want him to know the authorities are on-to him. You have the power to make an arrest. He won't harm Robbie, or us, if he knows the FBI's on their way."

Cory pounded a fist on his chest. "You're out of your mind. I'm unarmed. He won't listen to me." A sizable wave smashed into the side of the boat, and they struggled to keep their seats in the craft. "You need to slow down," Cory said. "You'll cut through the water much better at a slower speed. If you don't, we'll be swimming to the *Sierra Queen*."

Brian knew Cory was right. At this speed, in these turbulent waters, the boat could flip. Nevertheless, they wouldn't catch the paddleboat if he slowed. It was a risk he'd have to take.

"Brian, did you hear me?" Cory asked over the growl of the engine and the thundering waves. "Slow down."

Brian's expression was stubborn. "We're gaining on them."

THEY WERE NEARLY to the *Sierra Queen* when Brian put the boat into idle. "I wish I had a pair of binoculars," he said. It was snowing, and the visibility was bad.

"What's wrong?" Cory asked.

"I'm not sure." Brian pointed at the paddleboat. "Look at the left side of the ship."

Cory shielded his eyes from the blustering snow and peered toward the vessel. "A sports cruiser's tied alongside."

"Someone's boarding it."

Cory squinted. "I see at least two people getting into the cruiser."

"Can you see Robbie?"

"I can't make out their faces. It's snowing too hard."

"Why are they leaving the *Sierra Queen*?"

"Maybe she's having mechanical difficulty."

"You don't leave a large ship for a smaller one in this kind of weather."

"The paddlewheel's no longer moving."

Brian and Cory heard the motor of the sports cruiser buzzing through the water, heading for Zephyr Cove.

"What should we do?" Cory asked.

Brian shoved the throttle forward. "Board the *Sierra Queen*."

BRIAN WAS HAVING trouble keeping the boat close enough to the paddle-wheeler for Cory to tether their boat. "Loop the rope around the rail already," he said with frustration.

Cory wiped the snow from his eyes. "I'm trying. My hands are so cold, I can't grip it very well."

"Let me help." Brian's own hands were so frigid and stiff, it was difficult for him to hold on to the steering wheel. He turned the wheel of the boat toward the *Sierra Queen* and scuttled over to help his friend. The two of them fumbled, and twice, Brian had to return to the controls and steer it into a better angle. After a few more minutes of struggle, they succeeded in threading the rope through the railing of the *Sierra Queen* and tying the boats together.

They climbed over the railing and onto the deck. "Where to now?" Cory asked.

Brian gestured to his left. "This way." He hustled down the slippery deck, scrambled to a door, and attempted to open it, but it was locked. They both tried to see through the window, the combination of snow and condensation making it difficult.

Cory said, "There's a door on the other side of the deck. Let's give it a try." The two men bolted around the deck and skidded to a stop in front of the entry. Brian wrenched the handle, and the door popped open. The main lounge was deserted and they crossed to the other side.

"The upper deck," Brian said. He took off up the stairs. They bounded to the top and gazed around the empty area. This space, too, had an eerie feeling. The rumble of the ship's engine was vexing. They moved to the front of the paddleboat and found that it was also vacant.

"No one's on board," Cory said. He peeked into the desolate wheel room. "They've abandoned it."

"Why? It doesn't make any sense."

"I don't know." Cory's forehead was lined, his lips pressed firmly.

"You check the galley—I'll see what's below decks." Brian descended the stairs to the main lounge. He walked over to the bar and picked up the single glass on the counter. A hint of scotch was in the bottom. Seeing the access door to the engine room at the rear of the lounge, he put down the glass and made a bee-line for it. Pulling it open, he could hear the reverberation of the diesel engine. The stairs were steep, and he was careful with his footing while descending. The noise of the diesel became more ominous when he entered the engine room. The smell of fuel was strong, and the heat intense. The lighting was minimal, and he was tentative while inching his way around the massive motor.

Brian spotted the bomb, and his heart beat faster as he watched the seconds flying by. The timer indicated there were less than six minutes before the explosives would detonate.

"Cory," Brian called out, as loud as he could. He realized he couldn't be heard above the blare of the engine and sprinted to the stairway, then stopped. He turned to listen. He glanced at the bomb. Five minutes. He'd thought he heard something above the din of the motor. Brian maneuvered around the engine and saw her.

Robbie's eyes were shut. "Help me," she said. "Please save me, Brian." She was repeating it over and over again.

"Robbie," Brian said, feeling a mixture of relief and panic. He ran to her. "Robbie." He grasped the ropes binding her hands. The humidity in the room had swelled them, and they were too tight to loosen.

"Brian." She wasn't sure if she was hallucinating or he was real. "T-The bomb. They have a bomb on the boat."

"I saw it." Frantic, he scoped out the area for something to cut the ropes.

"Brian, are you down here?" Cory yelled from the stairway.

"Around the engine," he shouted. "I need your help." He picked up a screwdriver from a shelf on the wall and tried to lever it between the swollen ropes.

"Where are you?"

"Back of the room. Robbie's here too."

Cory rounded the motor. "Oh, thank god. Robbie, are you okay?"

She stared back at him, disoriented, and half-nodded.

"Give me a hand, Cory," Brian said. "I can't get the ropes untied."

"I have a knife," he said, retrieved it from a pocket and tossing it to Brian.

"We have to hurry. Montgomery's planted a bomb. It's on the other side of the engine."

Cory loped around the motor to take a look at the explosive device. He said in horror, "Brian, it'll go off in less than two minutes."

"I know." He was cutting the ropes from Robbie's feet. "Can you defuse it?"

"No, there isn't enough time."

Brian sawed through the last rope, and they stumbled for the stairway. Robbie's hands and legs were numb, and she had difficulty managing the stairs.

The bomb ticked off the seconds as they crashed through the lounge and onto the deck. The blowing snow was blinding, and Robbie fell on the icy surface. Brian helped her up, but tumbled himself trying to support her body.

"We'll never get to the boat in time," Cory said, terror in his voice.

The clock on the bomb ran off the inevitable five, four, three, two, and one.

Brian, Robbie, and Cory were jumping over the railing of the *Sierra Queen* when the bomb exploded, the blast catapulting them farther out into the frigid waters of Lake Tahoe. A huge ball of fire shot into the air, and debris rained down on the water, smoke pouring from the wounded vessel. The falling snow and rushing water of the lake turned to hot steam. There was a second explosion when the fuel tank ignited. Another massive fireball roared across the water.

The paddleboat groaned, her metal twisting and water charging into the opening in her hull. The bow of the ship rose off the surface as water filled her once-empty cavities. Within minutes, the *Sierra Queen* had sunk below the surface, leaving behind giant swells of spinning water and floating chunks of burning debris.

Brian clung to a piece of the wooden paddlewheel as angry waves splashed over him. "Robbie," he yelled. She was about twenty feet from him, struggling to keep her head above water. A wave picked her up and slammed her down. She plunged under the surface and didn't come back up.

Brian let go of the paddlewheel and swam to where he'd last seen her. The thirty-nine-degree water sapped his strength, and blood from a cut above his eye blurred his vision. "Robbie." He dipped beneath the surface and spotted her flailing below the waves. He kicked his way to the top, took a deep breath, and dove back underneath the water, where he was able to grab her by the arm and pull her to the surface. Emerging above the waves, she choked and coughed, fighting for air.

Brian fought to keep her head above the surface while he treaded water. His strength was diminishing, but he kicked and paddled his way toward a large piece of floating wreckage. The waves pounded them, and he thrashed about for air. He grasped a drifting beam and clung to it as best he could. The piercing cold was causing his arms to lose their feeling, and he was afraid he'd be unable to keep his grip on Robbie.

Brian looked around, hoping to see the small boat he and Cory had tied to the paddleboat. Maybe the blast hadn't destroyed it. It was nowhere in sight. Even if it hadn't sunk, the wind would've blown it far away by now. Without it, Brian knew they would soon perish.

Brian thought of Cory and wondered if he survived the blast. He scanned the water for his friend and saw nothing but the dark waves. He held Robbie close as she battled for every breath, tears of despair streaming down his face.

A HORN BLARED not far away, bringing Brian out of his daze. He blinked icy water out of his eyes. A Coast Guard rescue boat loomed not twenty yards from where they bobbed in the water. A searchlight atop the craft shone out across the lake, flakes of snow dancing in the beam of light. Brian cried out, a pitiful attempt, but didn't have the strength for anything more. He clung to Robbie, his hold ever weaker, and they rolled through the water as the cold waves hit them. He shouted once more as the searchlight swept by. The boat sped on, the crew not seeing them. "Here, please," Brian called weakly. "We're here." The searchlight swiveled around and passed across them again. The light swooped over them a few more times, and then it stopped. It was blinding, but Brian didn't care.

Two Coast Guards-men in wetsuits dove into the lake and

swam to them. They arrived just in time, as Brian could no longer hold both Robbie and the floating piece of debris. As the men in wetsuits took her from him, he informed them Cory Wyatt was somewhere out in the water.

The Coast Guard boat pulled up alongside them, and Brian seized the life preserver thrown his way while the men in wetsuits attended to Robbie. He looked up at the bow and knew he lacked the strength to climb up the side. He clung to the life preserver, floating up and down in the waves and hoping the sailors would assist him.

"Give me your hand," a man called down from the boat.

Brian could see several sailors on the deck, one was reaching out for him. He tried to raise his arms, but his muscles wouldn't move. He felt one of the men in wetsuits grab him from behind and thread the life preserver over his shoulders. The sailors aboard the boat tugged on the rope, hoisting him out of the icy lake. His arms burned when he was plucked out of the water and onto the deck. The wind and snow howled in his face, and the sailors rushed to him with blankets.

"Where is she?" Brian asked, trying to see through the raging snowstorm.

"She's coming on board now," one of the sailors said.

Brian watched as the men lifted Robbie onto the deck and draped blankets around her. He tried to stand up to see her better, but his legs were weak, and he fell in the attempt.

"We have to get you inside," a sailor shouted to be heard over the wailing wind.

"Is she going to make it?" Brian's voice was anguished.

"It's too soon to tell."

The sailors carried them both into the boat's cabin. The air was warm, and Brian basked in the sensation. A sailor handed him some dry clothes, wool slippers, and a thick jacket. After drying off, he put them on and almost wept at the burn of feeling starting to return to his hands and feet. Given a cup of hot coffee, he sipped it, savoring the warmth. "Any sign of Cory?" he asked a sailor, coughing.

His eyes sorrowful, the man looked away. "We'll keep searching. We won't give up. There are other Coast Guard boats in the area."

Brian hung his head and said a short prayer. He knew the odds were against it, but he couldn't give up on his friend. He staggered over to Robbie. Several medics were concentrating their efforts on her. "How is she?" Brian asked one of the men.

The man adjusted the blankets around her shoulders. "We have to get her to a hospital as fast as possible. Her body temperature's much too low."

Overwrought, Brian's breath caught a sob, his eyes watering. "Will she be okay?"

"We have to raise her temperature." The medic turned to him. "How are you doing? Let me see that cut above your eye."

"I'm warming up, but all the feeling in my toes isn't back yet."

The medic cleaned Brian's wound. "The cut's superficial," he said. "You won't even require stitches. Let me examine your feet." He probed Brian's toes. They were painful to the touch, and Brian yelped.

The medic said, "It may hurt, but it's a good sign. It means you have circulation to your toes. You're lucky—you should be in the same condition as the young woman here."

Brian explained what she'd been through. He stroked her hair back. "Please take good care of her," he said. "This is a special lady. I need her in my life."

THE COAST GUARD rescue boat docked at the Ski Run Marina, and the medics rolled Robbie's stretcher to an ambulance. It took off with lights flashing and siren blaring. Despite their protests, Brian refused further medical attention. Jack Mancini arrived and chastised him for not getting checked out at the hospital but knew he was stubborn and the effort futile. Teri was shaken when told they'd been unable to find Cory. Brian was trying to console her when a man in a dark suit approached and identified himself as Mike Gillespie, an agent with the Federal Bureau of Investigation. He explained they had an all-points bulletin out for Montgomery and Hatrix. "As we speak, agents are at both of their homes and the Charleston Resort."

"Do you have enough evidence to convict?" Jack asked.

Gillespie nodded. "The district attorney believes so. If they're in possession of the marked bills, we can charge them with grand theft. And of course, there's the insurance fraud, the kidnapping and attempted murder of Robbie Taylor, and the killing of Vanessa Daine."

"You're forgetting about Cory Wyatt," Teri said.

Brian put an arm around her. "I'm sorry," he said.

Tears trickled down her cheeks.

Brian had to turn away, knowing he too was on the verge of a breakdown. "I'm going to the hospital to be with Robbie," he said. "Jack, will you give me a ride?"

"Sure," he said. "I'm parked over there." He pointed to his Jeep.

Brian looked at the FBI agent. "I'd appreciate it if you'd keep us posted on your progress. I can be contacted at the hospital. I'll be home after that."

"We'll be in touch," the agent said.

Brian put a hand on Teri's arm. "Would you like to come with us?"

She wiped tears from her eyes and said, "No, Brian, you go ahead. You need to care for Robbie. I want to stay here while they search for Cory."

He hugged her. "I'll be praying for him."

Brian and Jack left Teri Porter on the dock as she stared with dread across the dark, violent lake.

THIRTY-SIX

BRIAN EASED INTO the hospital room to find Robbie asleep. The doctors had told him that, despite her ordeal, she was responding well to treatment and they expected a full recovery. As a precaution, though, they wanted to keep her overnight for observation.

Brian crept up to the bed and sat on a corner, picked up her right hand, and caressed it. He could sense the love he had for her pass between them with his touch. After a while, her eyes fluttered open, and she smiled at him. "Hi there," she said.

Brian said in a quiet voice, "How are you feeling?"

"Better. I'll be okay soon enough." She rubbed the raw, scraped wrist, avoiding the tubes taped carefully to undamaged skin. "It seems like a dream...everything that's occurred."

"It's more of a nightmare—in particular when I think about Cory—but I agree it's difficult to believe any of this happened."

Robbie squeezed his hand. "No word on him?"

Brian closed his eyes for a second. "It doesn't look good."

"I'm sorry. I know how close you two are."

"I just can't accept it."

"Have they arrested Montgomery yet?"

"No. FBI agents are at his mansion and the Charleston, and they have an APB out for both him and Hatrix."

"It's only a matter of time."

"Montgomery doesn't know the sheriff's after him. And as far as he's concerned, you're dead. I'm sure he'll show up at his estate soon. He expects the sheriff to come by and tell him the *Sierra Queen's* exploded, and he'll be ready to feign astonishment and call his insurance company."

"I'd love to see his face when they slap on the handcuffs. I'd give anything to be there."

Brian tightened his grip on her hand. "I'm just glad it's over. We can get back to our lives. Ones we've put on hold."

Robbie peered deep into his eyes, concerned. "Brian, you need some rest. You must be exhausted."

"That's not the right description. More like the walking dead. I'd love to go home, step out onto my deck, and soak in a nice relaxing hot tub."

A feeble grin shone on her face. "You don't own a hot tub."

"True, but that's okay, since there's no deck either."

Robbie laughed and patted his hand.

"I'm going to go home and sleep a couple of hours. I might take a hot bath too. I'm still chilled from our dip in the lake. I'll come back to see you later tonight."

"I'll be here."

Beaming, Brian leaned over and kissed her on a cheek.

"Thank you," she said in a raspy whisper.

"I'll see you in a little while." He slipped out of the hospital room.

Robbie closed her eyes and, for the first time in days, dreamed in peace.

JACK DROPPED BRIAN off in the Charleston Resort's parking lot.

About six inches of snow had fallen, and he had to scrape it off the truck windows before he could head for home.

Driving up the highway on the way to his cabin, he couldn't stop thinking about Robbie. She'd seemed to indicate they could now resume their relationship, or had he read her wrong? Maybe she was just expressing gratitude for saving her life.

His emotions had been on such a wild ride with her. Was he willing to take that journey again? His logical self told him "no" and that he should be wary. He remembered the way he'd felt when Robbie told him she didn't love him and asked himself why he'd risk that kind of pain again. He wouldn't have to worry about it if he resumed his life as Lake Tahoe's resident Lothario. But there was an emptiness to that way of living. He hadn't understood that until he met Robbie.

Parking the truck in his the driveway, he let out a prolonged scream, realizing that he would have to endure the possibility of being hurt once more. He had never met a woman like Robbie Taylor before and doubted he ever would again. He had to follow his heart.

He entered his cabin and took a relieved breath. It felt so good to be home. He walked to the big picture window, stared at Lake Tahoe, and watched the sun gliding over the horizon, a final orange glimmer of light sparkling on the water. He noticed yet another storm was approaching the lake from the north.

Brian thought of Cory with deep sadness. Jack told him as they were leaving the hospital that Cory's body had been found. He could hardly believe it and his heart ached. He remembered a night back in college when they were set to go on a double date and Cory's stood him up. Brian, his date, and Cory ended up at a drive-in movie, with Cory sitting in the backseat, bitching about his dismal love life. Brian smiled at the recollection. He had so many wonderful memories of Cory, Jack, and Hailey. He felt a lump in his throat, and a tear seeped from the corner of his eye. He wiped it away, but another soon followed.

Brian crossed the room to a cabinet and took out a bottle of whiskey. He picked up a glass from a nearby shelf and poured himself a healthy amount of the liquor. He wandered back to the window and took a sip. Then looked up and froze, his spine tingling like fire. In the window, he could see Tom Montgomery standing behind him.

"I wouldn't mind a drink myself," Montgomery said, gesturing to Brian's whiskey.

Brian's heart jumped into his throat. He put down the glass and turned around. "How the hell did you get in here?"

Montgomery sniggered. "Does it matter?"

"What do you want?"

"I'd like you to tell me about Robbie Taylor."

"What about her?" Brian was trying to remain calm, but was well past panic.

"At least you don't deny knowing her."

Brian shrugged. "Why should I?"

"Let's cut the crap. I know about your arrangement with Miss Taylor. It sounds to me as if you'd be enjoying the better end of the deal. You realize not only half the money but the opportunity to sleep with that gorgeous woman."

Brian wasn't sure what to say. He could play along or deny it all. Would it be wise to confront Montgomery about the *Sierra Queen* and the attempted murder of Robbie? Should he tell him she was alive? One thing he knew for certain, Montgomery was there for one reason—to silence him.

"I'm surprised, Shepard," Montgomery said. "I had you pegged as a party boy. Never thought you were the criminal type. Then again, for a woman like Robbie Taylor, I'd do the same."

Brian held up his hands. "All right, Mr. Montgomery, you

caught me. So what? You'll have your percentage, and I'll get mine. We can all live happy, wealthy lives."

"Ah, but there's a problem. I don't trust you or Robbie, and I don't do business with people I'm not comfortable with."

"No, you can have complete confidence in us. You have a good thing going, and we want a piece of it. Can you blame us?"

Montgomery glared at him, his eyes hostile. "Robbie lied to me...and you are too."

"You're wrong."

Montgomery shook his head. "I don't think so."

Brian thought a moment, then said, "It doesn't matter what you believe. The FBI's searching for you right now." He took a breath, waiting for the reaction.

Montgomery was amused, his lips upturned. "What do you take me for, Shepard, a fool?"

"It's true. The Nevada Gaming Control Board, the FBI, the sheriff, they all know you've been stealing from Charleston. You see, Robbie was wearing a hidden microphone the entire time she was at your home, at the Charleston, and today when you tried to kill her aboard the *Sierra Queen*."

Montgomery's face went taut. "What are you talking about?"

"Chairman Cavanaugh of the Gaming Control Board set up the sting. The GCB's been monitoring Robbie for the last week. It's all been recorded, and I imagine you'll be spending a long, long time behind bars. Unless you receive the death penalty. You murdered Vanessa Daine, and today, a Gaming Control Board agent was killed in the blast aboard the *Sierra Queen*. It's all been documented, and of course, there's the testimony from Robbie herself."

Montgomery gaped at Brian with a mixture of rage and surprise.

Brian pointed at him and smiled. "You assumed she was

dead, didn't you? I hate to disappoint you, but Robbie's very much alive."

"She can't be." Incredulity strained his voice.

Brian crossed his arms and rubbed them. "She was suffering from a bad case of hypothermia, but is recovering and more than willing to be a witness against you at your trial. Oh, and to ensure she gets to testify, there's a guard outside her hospital room."

"You're lying. That can't be true."

"Phone the hospital—she's there. At Barton."

Montgomery reached in his jacket and pulled out a mobile telephone. He called Information for the number for Barton Memorial Hospital, then called the hospital and cringed when the operator told him she was in room 138. He hung up and glowered at Brian.

Brian said with a snarl, "It's over, Montgomery. Why don't you call the authorities and save us all a lot of trouble? There's nowhere you can hide."

"Hatrix," Montgomery said.

Marcus Hatrix stepped into view.

A shiver ran up Brian's backbone. "I should've known you wouldn't come alone," he said.

Montgomery gestured to Hatrix. "Have you been listening?"

"Yes, boss," Hatrix said. "What are we going to do?"

"Keep a close watch on Shepard. I need to think."

Hatrix's eyes tore into Brian's.

Montgomery paced the floor, stopping every few minutes and scowling at Brian.

"Give yourselves up," Brian said. "You have nowhere left to go." It was a taunt he wasn't sure he should be making.

"Shut up," Montgomery said. "I'm tired of you. Not another goddamn word, or I'll have Hatrix shut you up. Hatrix, restrain him with something. He's making me nervous."

"Is that necessary?" Brian asked, now sure he should've kept quiet. "I won't speak again, I promise." He sat down on the sofa.

"I'm not going back to prison," Hatrix said.

Montgomery said with a spray of saliva, "This wouldn't have happened if we hadn't hurried to replace Vanessa."

"But, boss, you checked Robbie out and agreed she was the perfect person for us."

Montgomery punched a clenched fist into his hand. "No, we rushed into this, and now we're screwed."

"It's too late to do anything about it now. We've got to run."

"Right now, this cabin's the safest place for us. Neither of us can go home. The authorities will be waiting. We can't risk it."

"What are we going to do?"

"I have to make some phone calls and see if I can sneak us out of the country."

"Where will we go?"

"I don't know yet. I need to cash in a few favors."

Montgomery pulled out his smartphone and made several calls. Hatrix fidgeted, while watching with obvious worry as his boss worked on their escape.

Brian's home telephone rang, and before the answering machine had a chance to engage, Hatrix ripped it from the wall and flung it across the room, where it shattered into fragments. "Hey," Brian protested. He received nasty looks from both men in return. The phone in the master bedroom continued to ring. Hatrix marched down the hall and into that room, and the ring stopped with a crash.

When Montgomery hung up his iPhone for the last time, he turned to Hatrix. "It's all set," he said. "We have to get to King's Beach. From there, I've made arrangements for a chartered jet from Truckee to Brazil."

Brian broke his pledge to keep silent. "You'll never make it to King's Beach," he said. "The FBI has the roads blocked. They know you'll try to leave Lake Tahoe."

Montgomery frowned at him. "I told you to shut up."

"He's right," Hatrix said. "How are we getting to King's Beach?"

"The sports cruiser."

"We can't go out on the lake tonight," Hatrix said in a stressed and graveled voice. "It's starting to snow again. I had a hard enough time keeping the boat afloat this morning. It's too small with just one undersized inboard. There's no way we can go out on Tahoe at night in this weather. The clouds are covering the moon. It's pitch black."

"Got a better idea? We can hug the shoreline. It'll take us some time, but I see no other option."

"I guess we have to. It'll be difficult, though—there are a lot of rocks that'll be almost impossible to see in the dark."

"It's the best way to reach King's Beach."

Hatrix motioned to Brian. "What about Shepard?"

Montgomery face filled with malice, giving it the dull expression of a shark. "Take care of him. I'll be in the car."

Hatrix's face paled. "You want me to kill him?"

"You told me you've always dreamed of being a gangster. Prove it by becoming a hit man." He sneered at Brian and stomped out of the cabin.

BRIAN SPRANG UP from the sofa and stared at Hatrix. Their eyes locked as Hatrix pulled a revolver from inside his jacket. The hair on Brian's neck stood at attention, and his eyes widened. "Marcus, don't do this," he said.

Hatrix aimed the gun at him.

"You're not a murderer." Brian knew he had only seconds to talk Hatrix out of shooting him. "I don't think you're that sort of guy. You didn't kill Vanessa, I know you didn't want to blow up Robbie on the *Sierra Queen,* and I bet you have no real desire to take me out."

Hatrix continued to point the gun at Brian. His hand shook as his finger wrapped around the trigger, sweat forming on his upper lip. He lowered the gun a tad.

"There's a big difference between theft and homicide," Brian said. "You're leaving the country for Brazil. I can't stop you. You don't need to snuff my life out to escape."

Hatrix reached out, extending the gun toward Brian's chest.

"Marcus, don't." He clenched his eyes shut in anticipation of the end.

The gun fired with a loud blast.

Brian opened his eyes to see a cloud of dust swirling in the air. He glanced up and saw a bullet hole in the ceiling of his cabin. Hatrix was gone.

Brian felt dizzy with relief. He slapped his hands to his chest and took a breath for the first time in what felt like minutes. "Jesus," he said. "Thank you. Thank you. Oh my god, I can't believe it. He didn't do it. He couldn't do it. He didn't have the guts." Brian relaxed a bit, but his hands were still shaking, his pulse throbbing. "Thank you." He once again gaped at the bullet hole in the ceiling. Weak-kneed, he hobbled over to the couch and sat down, resting there for about five minutes as he tried to catch his breath.

Brian gazed around the cabin, still panting. His life may have been spared, but now he had to contact the authorities. The disabled phone was strewn across the floor in pieces, the bedroom phone was in the same state from the sound of that crash, and his iPhone had been rendered worthless when he jumped in the lake that morning. Brian would have to leave his cabin to get the sheriff.

As he picked up his keys from the coffee table, he heard a noise at the front door and saw the doorknob turn. Fear overtook him again. He'd been wrong. Hatrix had the nerve to kill him after all and was returning to finish the job. The door opened a crack, and a gun barrel poked through the gap. Brian's body tensed at the sight. He was paralyzed with fright and couldn't move.

The door swung open a little more, and Jack's face peeked through.

"Jack!" Brian said. "Thank god. Oh, oh, oh, thank god." He was close to tears.

Jack lowered the gun. "Goddamn, are you all right?"

Brian put his hands on his head. "I thought I was until you showed up. You scared the crap out of me. My heart feels like it's going to explode."

Jack held up his left hand. "I didn't know what to expect when I opened the door. I heard a shot and saw a man run out of the cabin and get into Montgomery's car—that gold Mercedes he always brags about. I was afraid I wouldn't find you alive."

Brian was still gasping for air. He bent over and put his hands on his knees. "I shouldn't be. Thankfully, our friend Marcus Hatrix doesn't have the stomach for murder. How'd you know to come over?"

"Robbie called me. She was worried when you didn't show up at the hospital. I phoned here a few times but kept getting a busy signal and became concerned as well."

"Hatrix was irritated when my telephone rang. That's why there was a busy signal." Brian pointed to the pieces on the floor.

"I thought I better stop by and see if you were okay. What were they doing here?"

"T-They were here," Brian said, choking on the words, "to shut me up. I should've known that, until they were in jail, I'd be in danger. I told them the cops are after them. You wouldn't believe the expression on Montgomery's face. He looked like someone had shoved a Buick up his butt. Cold-hearted sucker, though—he coolly made plans to evade the authorities, then ordered Hatrix to kill me. I'm lucky Hatrix has a conscience, it saved my life. I'll take a hole in the ceiling over one in the ground any day."

"The cops will catch them soon. There's nowhere to hide."

"They plan to flee to Brazil."

Jack threw up his hands. "You're kidding, right? They'll never make it out of the Tahoe basin. Every road's blocked."

"They're going to King's Beach. Montgomery chartered a plane in Truckee."

"They won't get there."

"They're taking a boat—the sports cruiser they used to abandon the *Sierra Queen* this morning."

"They're venturing out on the lake in this weather? At night? The waves must be five feet high, and the wind's ferocious."

Brian was starting to breathe slower. "They intend to creep along the shoreline."

"We have to call the sheriff and stop them."

"We can do that, but I was thinking..." Brian gave Jack a devious bounce of his eyebrows. "Do you recall back in college, the prank we pulled on the Sigma Nu fraternity?"

"Prank? We burned down their homecoming float. We were drunk. We were almost suspended from school."

"That's right. Do you remember how we set their float on fire?"

"We threw a Molotov cocktail over the fence. What does it have to do with Montgomery?"

"They'll be hugging the shoreline in their cabin cruiser. You know the shore of Tahoe as well as I do. When the boat goes past the point, north of Cave Rock, it'll pass between the cliff and those large rocks. You know where I mean."

"Yes, we fish around there all the time."

"It's the one clear passage unless they go far out into the lake. They won't do that in this weather. Not at night."

"Yeah, I suppose that's a reasonable assumption."

Brian gave him a mischievous grin. "I have some gasoline in my storage shed. Let's make a Molotov cocktail. When the boat passes between the cliff and the boulders, we'll light the fuse and throw it aboard. They'll scurry like rats to get off."

Incredulous, Jack narrowed his eyes. "Do you think it'll work?"

Brian rubbed his hands together. "It's worth a try. After what those men have done to us, we have to do something." He and Jack exchanged a look, both knowing it wasn't really about justice. It was revenge. It was about Cory, Robbie, Vanessa and everyone who'd suffered due to Montgomery's greed.

"Can we make it to the point before Montgomery?"

Brian took a fleeting look at his watch. "If we hurry. The roads aren't too bad. We could be there in fifteen minutes. The cliff is less than fifty feet from the highway."

"What about the cops?"

"Call them—they can scoop our bad boys out of the water."

Jack eyed Brian with a serious expression. "Do you remember whose idea it was to torch the Sigma Nu homecoming float?"

Brian's tone was grim. "Yeah, Cory."

THIRTY-SEVEN

JACK AND BRIAN worked their way down the hillside, plodding through deep snow and headed for the cliff that towered thirty feet above the water. "Be careful," Jack said.

"We better pick up the pace," Brian said. "Montgomery's boat will be coming by soon, if we haven't already missed it."

"I don't hear anything yet."

"We still need to hurry. We have to climb to the rim of the cliff and find a good position." He shined the beam of his flashlight toward the drop-off in front of them.

Jack tugged his knit hat down around his ears. "Boy, it's cold out here."

Brian lifted the collar of his jacket. "We can maneuver around these rocks easier if we go this way." He led Jack to the left side of a boulder, toward the icy ledge. "Watch your step—it's slippery."

Jack dug his boots into the snow and inched around the ridge. The snow was deeper than they'd expected. Brian had to get on his hands and knees to navigate around the next outcropping of rock. Following behind, Jack lost his footing and slid about four feet down the side of a boulder. "Are you all right?" Brian asked, pointing his flashlight at his friend.

Jack uttered a few profanities but assured him he was fine, gripped one of Brian's hands, and pulled himself back up.

"Do you hear that?" Brian asked. "It's a boat."

"Do you think it's them?" Jack asked.

Brian wiped snow from his face. "Who else would be desperate enough to be on the water in this weather?"

"We need to move faster." Jack worked his way around another rock. "We can't miss them."

Brian gestured to his right. "There's a notch in the cliff up ahead. I've seen kids dive off it in the summer—it'll be a good vantage point."

"Those kids must be crazy." Jack surveyed the ledge. "It's a long drop to the water."

"And we're not out of our minds?"

Jack laughed at the irony. The two men hugged the ridge of the cliff until they came to the notch. They shoveled the deep snow with their gloved hands, clearing an area where they could work. Then they peered over the side, listening to the sound of the approaching cruiser. Jack was excited, his voice rising. "Here they come," he said. "Get the torch ready."

Brian took the Molotov cocktail out of his knapsack. It was crude, an empty liquor bottle filled with gasoline and stuffed with an old rag, but it would suffice. He watched with elation as the boat, its spotlight focused forward, roared near their perch and was all ready to ignite the rag when the engine of the sports cruiser got quieter.

Jack squinted. "What's going on?" he asked.

"I don't know," Brian said. "They must not be able to see the passage between the cliff and the boulders."

The boat did a half circle and maneuvered to the west.

Brian was alarmed, his heart beating rapidly. "They're trying to go around the point," he said.

"The waves are too rough," Jack said. "They'll never make it."

"If they do, our plan's ruined."

They strained their eyes, trying to see the small craft in the dark, stormy waters. The engine sputtered as waves battered the sports cruiser. A large one crashed over the bow, sending water into the cabin. The motor buzzed in vain as the rushing torrent pushed the boat toward the shore.

Brian stretched out a finger. "Look," he said, "they're turning around."

Jack brushed snow off his jacket. "They had to. That last wave just about swamped them."

The sports cruiser veered close to the shore below Brian and Jack's perch. Brian lit the fuse of the Molotov cocktail.

"This one's for Cory," Brian said and threw the flaming brew over the ledge at the cruiser. His skill as a baseball pitcher in college guided the blazing bottle to the center of the deck. With a crash, flames enveloped the outside seating and spread to the helm. Thick black smoke billowed into the air.

In an instant, the engine halted, and Montgomery and Hatrix climbed on-to the railing above the burning deck. They were shouting as the flames rose higher. It was hard to make out, but they appeared to be arguing. Brian and Jack couldn't contain their laughter as they watched the two frantic fugitives jump into the frigid waters of Lake Tahoe.

Brian picked up his knapsack. "Let's go," he said. "I want to be on the shore when they come out of the drink."

Jack was right behind him as they wound their way away from the cliff, skiing on their boot heels down the slope toward the snow-covered beach. The sound of sirens could be heard in the distance.

When they arrived at the water's edge, Brian shined his flashlight across the water. Snow glistened in the light while he looked for Montgomery and Hatrix. After a minute, he could see both men flailing in the water, trying to swim through the rough waves. The cabin cruiser continued to burn, and the bigger the flames became the more brightly the shoreline was illuminated.

Brian leaned against a boulder and lifted the gun from his knapsack. Jack did the same, and the two of them stood in silence watching Montgomery and Hatrix crawl out of the frigid lake. Montgomery was dragging his briefcase, and there was little question the stolen money inside would be soaking wet. Brian fixed his gun on him and walked over to the man. "Nice night for a swim," he said with scorn.

Wet and shivering, Montgomery looked rather pitiful. The strong, distinguished man Brian had come to despise was now small and withered. Jack hustled over to him, pushed him into the snow, and patted him down, searching for a gun. He took the briefcase and handed it to Brian.

Montgomery attempted to stand, but slipped and fell. He tried to get up again. "Don't move," Brian said, pointing the gun at his head.

"I'm so cold," Montgomery said. His lips were blue.

"Isn't that too bad. You didn't give a damn about my life, and I don't give one about yours. I hope you freeze to death."

"Brian," Jack said, focusing on Hatrix who was propped against a snow-covered rock and trying to catch his breath, coughing out of control. Jack grabbed him by the collar and shoved him to the snowy ground. Hatrix was too weak to resist. Jack removed a revolver from the sopping wet man's belt and pitched it into a snow bank. The sirens stopped above them, and they could hear the shouts of the lawmen charging down the hillside.

Brian kicked snow at Montgomery and said, "Letting you go to a nice warm jail cell's too good for you." He raised his gun and aimed it at the man.

"He's not worth it, Brian," Jack said.

Brian glared at Montgomery, hating him. His gun was still pointed at the man's chest, and his finger twitched on the trigger, emotions warring within him. One of his best friends was dead, and the woman he loved had barely escaped the same fate. Montgomery stared at Brian, his face frozen with fear. Brian charged forward, his arm outstretched. He cocked the gun.

"Shepard," a man shouted.

Brian recognized the voice of Mike Gillespie, the FBI agent.

"Don't be a fool," Gillespie said.

Brian hesitated, then lowered his gun as the FBI agents surrounded Montgomery and Hatrix, handcuffing them both. Jack walked over to Brian and put an arm around his shoulders. "It's over, my friend," he said. "It's over at last."

Brian reached around and hugged him. "I'm tired, Jack. Take me home."

They hiked to the highway, where Agent Gillespie intercepted them. He said, "I don't know what you two cowboys thought you were doing out here, but I suppose it worked."

Brian watched as Montgomery was led away by the FBI agents. He turned to Gillespie and said, "Good thing you arrived when you did."

BRIAN AND ROBBIE were sitting in the living room of his cabin enjoying the sunset, Lake Tahoe shimmering in front of them.

"Montgomery's trial will begin next spring," Brian said. "I talked with Agent Gillespie, and he expects a quick verdict on all counts."

They were both silent for a while.

Robbie clasped one of his hands. "I'm so sorry about Cory," she said. "I know you're hurting."

Brian was silent for a time, trying to master his grief. Then he said, "I miss him very much. I keep expecting him to barge through the doorway any second, ready to tell me another joke."

She stroked his hand. "When my mother died, I felt the same way."

"I spoke with his mom and dad yesterday—they were my surrogate parents during college. They're devastated. I promised them I'd visit soon."

"They'll appreciate it, I know. How's his wife doing?"

Brian sighed. "About as well as can be expected. Like me, she's in denial. Hailey and Jack have been a great help to her."

"They're good people."

"Jack was offered the assistant general manager's job at Harrah's."

"He's not returning to the Charleston Resort?"

"I don't know. Sal Wyman begged him to come back. He promised him a promotion and a substantial raise in pay, but I'm not certain what he's going to do. He'll make the right decision— he always does. He deserves the best."

"Is Mr. Wyman giving you a promotion as well?"

"Let's just say he's showing his gratitude by not firing me."

That confused Robbie, and her forehead wrinkled.

Brian bowed his head. "It's related to the Skip Sullivan incident. I'd rather not get into it."

She nodded, silently accepting that. "What's the next step for you?"

"I'm hoping to sort out everything at the Charleston and start over. There are some projects I need to finish. Number one's editing a new general manager into my television commercials." He chuckled.

Robbie smiled at him. "I wasn't referring to your job. It was a personal inquiry."

Brian gazed deep into her eyes. "I want a fresh beginning

there as well. How about it, Robbie? Would you...?" He held his breath.

She squeezed his hand. "You know, Brian, you have such a wonderful view. You just need a deck. And I'm pretty handy with a hammer."

About the Author

Steve Trounday has been a senior marketing executive at many of northern Nevada's most prominent casino resorts. He is writing a series of mystery/thrillers set in the fascinating world of casino gambling, each with intrigue and a little romance. For more information on Steve's books go to his website at stevetrounday.com.

Made in the USA
Monee, IL
26 October 2020